When Stars Collide

ALSO BY SUSAN ELIZABETH PHILLIPS

Dance Away with Me

First Star I See Tonight

Heroes Are My Weakness

The Great Escape

Call Me Irresistible

What I Did for Love

Glitter Baby

Natural Born Charmer

Match Me If You Can

Ain't She Sweet?

Breathing Room

This Heart of Mine

Just Imagine

First Lady

Lady Be Good

Dream a Little Dream

Nobody's Baby but Mine

Kiss an Angel

Heaven, Texas

It Had to Be You

When Stars Collide

A Chicago Stars Novel

Susan Elizabeth Phillips

HARPER LARGE PRINT
An Imprint of HarperCollins*Publishers*

HarperCollins books may be purchased for educational, business, or sales promotional use. For information, please e-mail the Special Markets Department at SPsales@harpercollins.com.

FIRST HARPER LARGE PRINT EDITION

ISBN: 978-0-06-309009-5

Library of Congress Cataloging-in-Publication Data is available upon request.

21 22 23 24 25 LSC 10 9 8 7 6 5 4 3 2 1

For teachers everywhere who
continue to show up for their students.
We owe you our gratitude.

You can't wear a crown with your head down.

—Beyoncé

When Stars Collide

1

Olivia Shore gazed out through the darkened window of the limousine toward the private jet parked on the tarmac. This was what her life had come to. Flying around the country with a brainless, overpaid jock and too many bad memories—all to hawk a luxury watch.

It was going to be the longest four weeks of her life.

Thaddeus Walker Bowman Owens leaned closer to the jet's window and peered out at the limousine that had stopped by the plane. Exactly thirty-eight minutes late. A driver emerged and pulled a suitcase from the back, then another, then a third. A garment bag appeared next, followed by a fourth suitcase. He drew his head away from the window. "What in the hell have I got myself into?"

Cooper Graham peered around him to see what he was looking at, and then gave Thad's tailor-made virgin wool pants and cashmere silk sweater a semi-smirk. "Looks like you might have a little competition for the best dressed list."

Thad scowled at the man who was both his best friend and a perpetual thorn under his skin. "I like good clothes."

"Half the time, you look like a damn peacock."

Thad shot a meaningful look at Coop's jeans and hoodie. "Only in comparison to you." He crossed his legs, resting one of his feet, clad in an Italian dress boot with a glove-soft interior, on the opposite knee. "Still, it was nice of you to come see me off."

"The least I could do."

Thad leaned into the leather seat. "You were afraid I wouldn't show up, weren't you?"

"It might have crossed my mind."

"Tell me how you did it."

"How I did what?"

"How you managed to convince Marchand Watches—excuse me, Marchand *Timepieces*—that having me as a brand ambassador was just as good as having the legendary Cooper Graham."

"You're not exactly a nobody," Graham said mildly.

"Damn straight. And I've got the Heisman to prove it. The one trophy even you don't have stowed away on your shelves."

Graham grinned and clapped him on the shoulder. "Your lack of personal jealousy is what I most admire about you."

"Since Marchand is the official watch of the Stars, and they couldn't have you, they wanted Clint Garrett, didn't they?"

"His name might have been mentioned."

Thad gave a snort of disgust. Clint Garrett was the brilliantly talented, egotistical young asshole quarterback the Chicago Stars had signed last year to replace the void they hadn't been able to fill when Coop had retired. The same Clint Garrett who Thad was supposed to make a better player and—oh, yeah—substitute for if the idiot kid got injured.

When Thad had come out of college sixteen years ago holding that Heisman, he'd seen himself as another Coop Graham or Tom Brady, not as a guy who'd end up spending most of his NFL career as a backup for the starting quarterbacks on four different pro teams. But that's the way things had turned out. He was recognized as a brilliant strategist, an inspiring leader, but there was that almost trivial weakness in his peripheral vision that stood between him and greatness. Always a bridesmaid, never a bride.

A stir at the front of the plane drew their attention to The Diva who had finally graced them with her presence. She wore a belted tan trench coat over black pants, along with royal-blue stilettos that added five inches to her already impressive height. A few trails of dark hair emerged from the sides of a printed scarf wrapped around her head like in old photos Thad had seen of Jackie Kennedy. Along with the scarf, the pair of big-ass sunglasses perched on her long nose made her look like a jet-setter right out of the 1960s or maybe an Italian movie star. She tossed down a designer tote bag big enough to hold a golden retriever and took a seat near the front without acknowledging either of the men.

As the faint scent of luxury perfume, high culture, and undiluted arrogance wafted its way to the back of the plane, Coop unfurled from the seat. "Time for me to get out of here."

"Lucky bastard," Thad muttered.

Coop knew Thad well enough to know that The Diva wasn't entirely responsible for Thad's bad mood. "You're what that kid needs," he said. "Clint Garrett has the talent to go all the way, but not without the old man getting him there."

Thad was thirty-six. Only in football years was that old.

Coop headed for the front of the plane. He stopped as he approached The Diva and nodded. "Ms. Shore."

She inclined her head, barely acknowledging the man who'd been one of the greatest quarterbacks in the NFL. Thad had the God-given right to throw all the shade he wanted at Coop, but that highbrow opera singer didn't.

Graham tossed Thad an amused glance and left the plane, a rat fleeing a sinking ship. Thad doubted Coop had thought twice about turning down Marchand's lucrative offer to serve as brand ambassador for their new Victory780 men's watch. The ex-quarterback didn't like being away from his family, and he definitely didn't need the money. As for Clint Garrett . . . Young Clint was too busy chasing women and driving fast cars to waste his time representing a prestige company like Marchand, official watch of both the Chicago Stars and the Chicago Municipal Opera.

Despite what he'd said to Coop, Thad wasn't entirely surprised Marchand Timepieces had come after him to promote their Victory780 watch. They needed a Stars player, and Thad gave good interviews. Also, that old Heisman had garnered him plenty of publicity over the years. Still, anybody with eyeballs knew it wasn't

Thad's throwing arm or glib rejoinders that had sealed the deal with Marchand. It was his pretty face.

"You're even better looking than The Boo." Coop had tweaked him the first time they'd met, referring to the great Stars quarterback Dean Robillard.

Thad's looks were a curse.

One of his favorite ex-girlfriends had told him: *"You've got Liam Hemsworth's nose, Michael B. Jordan's cheekbones, and Zac Efron's hair. As for those green eyes . . . Taylor Swift for sure. It's like all the good-looking celebs in the world threw up on your face."*

He missed Lindy, but she'd gotten fed up with his noncommittal crap. After she'd broken up with him, he'd sent her a new laptop so she'd know there were no hard feelings.

Over the years, he'd done everything he could to roughen up his appearance. He'd grown a beard a couple of times, but then people started telling him he looked like the dude in *Fifty Shades*. He'd tried a porn-star mustache only to have women say he looked distinguished. He'd even gone for irony and sported one of those asinine man buns for a while. Unfortunately, it looked good on him.

In high school, everybody got pimples but him. He'd never needed braces or gone through an awkward phase. He hadn't broken his nose or gotten one of the chin scars every other player in the League had. His hair wasn't thinning. He didn't have a paunch.

He blamed his parents.

But the one positive thing about his looks, along with his lean, six-foot-three body, was the extra cash it earned him. And he did like making money. Over the years, he'd lent his face to a men's cologne, his butt to designer underwear, and his hair to some overpriced grooming products he'd never bothered to use. And now this.

Four weeks on the road to promote Marchand's new Victory780. Some photo shoots and interviews, along with a guest appearance at their big Chicago Municipal Opera gala as a finale. No sweat. Except for one snag. He wasn't Marchand's only brand ambassador. While he was promoting the Victory780, opera superstar Olivia Shore would be touting their ladies' watch, the Cavatina3.

"Bonjour! Bonjour!" Henri Marchand appeared at the front of the plane, arms outstretched, his French accent oozing from him like Nutella from a warm crêpe. The long brown hair slicked back from his face fell over the top of his collar. Even without a beret perched on top of his head, he brought the air of the Continent with him. He was thin, maybe five nine, with a narrow face

and sharp features. His impeccably tailored, charcoal wool suit had the European cut brawnier American-born men couldn't pull off, although Thad had a similar striped neck scarf he sometimes wore in the European way because—why not?

Marchand advanced on The Diva. "Olivia, *ma chérie.*"

She extended her hand. He kissed it like she was fricking Queen Victoria, even though Thad happened to know she'd grown up in Pittsburgh, the only child of two deceased music teachers. Thad had done his homework.

Henri gazed toward the back of the plane, once again extending his arms. "And Thaddeus, *mon ami*!"

Thad gave him a bro-wave and contemplated stealing the name of his tailor.

"We will have such an adventure together." More arm waving. "First stop, Phoenix, where you, *madame*, sang a breathtaking Dulcinée in *Don Quichotte.* And you, my friend Thad, threw a seventy-yard touchdown pass against the Arizona Cardinals. Glory days, yes? And the glory still shines brightly."

For The Diva, maybe, but not for Thad.

Henri turned to the young woman who'd followed him on board. "This, *mes amis*, is my assistant Paisley Rhodes." Was it Thad's imagination or did Henri's overly bright smile dim?

Paisley looked ready to head across campus for her Psych 101 class: a long swath of straight blond hair, too-perfect nose, slim figure dressed in a short skirt, blouse with a French tuck, and ankle boots. She also looked bored, as if stepping on a private jet took major effort.

"Paisley will be assisting us throughout our tour. If you need anything—anything at all—please let her know."

Thad half expected a "whatev" to come out of her mouth because Paisley couldn't have looked less interested in assisting anyone. He suspected a favor had been called in to get her hired.

The girl's eyes settled on him, and he saw her first flicker of interest. Ignoring The Diva, she headed back to take the seat right next to him. "I'm Paisley."

He nodded.

"My dad is, like, this huge football fan."

Thad made his standard response. "Glad to hear it."

As the plane took off, she proceeded to tell him her abbreviated—but not abbreviated enough—life story. Recent graduate of a Southern California college with a degree in communications. Just broke up with her boyfriend. She was an old soul in a young body—her assessment, not his. Her life goal: to become a personal assistant to a big—any big—celebrity. And—wait for it—her grandfather was a good friend of Lucien Marchand, which explained how she got the job.

She examined the watch on her wrist, one of Marchand's basic models. "I never wear a watch." She tapped her phone. "I mean, what's the point, right? But they're, like, making me wear a Marchand for the tour."

"Bastards," he said, with an absolutely straight face.

"I know. But my grampy says I have to start somewhere."

"Good ol' grampy."

"I guess."

To her credit, she left him alone in favor of her phone after the plane took off. He tilted back in his seat, closed his eyes, and indulged in his favorite fantasy, one where Clint Garrett threw three interceptions, broke his tibia, and was out for the season, leaving Thad to pick up the pieces. Clint, the poor bastard, ended up stuck on the bench watching Thad lead the Stars to the Super Bowl.

Henri Marchand's silky French accent disturbed his fantasy. "I trust you've had time to read through the materials I sent about the Victory780."

Thad reluctantly opened his eyes. He had a good memory, and he had no trouble recalling the details about the watch he'd been hired to promote. Henri Marchand, however, wasn't taking any chances.

"We've been developing the Victory780 for over ten years." He settled on the next seat. "It's a state-of-the-art chronograph watch, but it still reflects our classic Marchand heritage."

"And a twelve-thousand-dollar price tag," Thad noted.

"Prestige and precision have their price."

As Marchand began expanding on the integrated self-winding movement and larger mainspring of the 780, Thad studied the watch he now wore on his wrist. He had to admit it was great looking, with a heavy steel bracelet, platinum case, and black ceramic bezel. The watch had a sapphire crystal, metallic blue dial, and three steel-rimmed sub-dials he could use to time his runs or to see how long Clint Garrett could go without saying "dude."

"Tonight we have dinner with five of our biggest accounts," Marchand said. "In the morning, you'll be doing radio interviews—sports stations and morning talk—while Madame Shore visits the classical music station."

Giving The Diva plenty of time to relax her precious vocal cords while Thad ran his ass off.

"Newspaper interviews after that. Some important bloggers. A public event in Scottsdale with photos."

Thad had done product promotion before, and he knew exactly how these things worked. His name and

Shore's name opened the door for more interviews than Marchand could book on the brand's name alone. Thad would be asked about his career, the state of pro football, and every current controversy in the NFL. In the process of answering, he'd be expected to talk about the watch.

Marchand finally excused himself and returned to The Diva's side. Paisley reappeared and once again settled in the seat across from him. Thad noticed she hadn't yet approached The Diva. Only him.

"Henri told me to give you this. It's your updated itinerary." She handed over a black folder embellished with the Marchand logo.

Thad was familiar with the schedule. For most of the next month, he and the Disagreeable Diva were being well paid to travel around the country promoting the brand. Eventually, they'd end up back where they started, in Chicago. While Thad took a two-week break, The Diva would be in rehearsals for the Chicago Municipal Opera's production of *Aida*. On the Sunday night after the premiere, Marchand Timepieces was sponsoring a charity gala in conjunction with the Muni. After that, Thad's obligations were over.

"I put my number on the first page," Paisley said. "Text me any time. *Any* time."

"I'll do that." He responded curtly—right on the border of rude—but he needed to nip this in the bud before it went any further. He had enough difficulties ahead of him dealing with The Diva, and he didn't want any complications from Henri's assistant. Besides, he hadn't been into twenty-one-year-olds since he was twenty-two.

She tossed her long hair. "I mean it. I want you to know you can count on me."

"Got it." He slipped his headset back on. She finally took the hint and left him alone. He dozed off to Chet Baker.

The Diva sat in the opposite corner of the limo, sunglasses still on, cheek resting against the window. So far, the only communication she'd shared with Thad was a look of active hostility when they'd gotten off the plane. Paisley's thumbs raced over her phone, more likely texting a friend than doing any work. Henri was also on his cell, engaged in an energetic conversation. Since Thad only spoke some menu French, he couldn't decipher the topic. The Diva, however, understood. She opened her eyes and waved a hand.

"C'est impossible, Henri."

The way she said Marchand's name . . . pushing the *Aw-ree* from the back of her throat. When Thad said the name, it took all his energy just to drop the *h* and the *n*. Forget all that back-of-the-throat stuff.

Their subsequent exchange didn't enlighten Thad about exactly what was so *uh-poss-eeee-bluh*, but as they pulled up to the hotel, Aw-ree enlightened him. "We've had a slight change of schedule. We need to move up today's interviews immediately after we check in. An inconvenience, but these things do happen, as I'm sure you understand."

Not even ten minutes later, he and The Diva were being ushered into the hotel's presidential suite, with Henri and Paisley following. In addition to a luxurious living area, the suite had a dining room, kitchen, grand piano, and big French doors that opened onto a sweeping terrace. A large coffee table in the center of the living room held platters of pastries and assorted bottles of wine and mineral water.

"You have a few minutes to freshen up before the reporters arrive," Henri said. "Paisley will bring them in."

Paisley looked petulant, as if escorting reporters wasn't part of her job description. Henri didn't seem to notice. Or maybe he did and was pretending not to.

The Diva disappeared into the bathroom. As Henri double-checked the refreshments that had been laid out for the reporters, Thad wandered onto the tiled terrace to take in the view of Camelback Mountain. If only he were doing this promotion with a female rock star instead of a stuck-up opera singer. The next four weeks stretched in front of him like an endless road headed exactly nowhere.

In the bathroom, the stuck-up opera singer leaned against the closed door, squeezed her eyes shut, and tried to make herself breathe. It was more than she could bear. Being forced to travel with an animal like Thad Owens was the final calamity in the disaster of these past few weeks. No matter what, she couldn't let him see any weakness in her, any vulnerability he believed he could exploit.

If she'd known what was going to happen, she wouldn't have even considered signing this contract with Marchand. She'd never backed out of a contract in her life, but she couldn't imagine how she'd endure this next month. Smiling. Talking. Being congenial. And making sure she was never alone with him.

Her phone vibrated in her pocket. She took off her sunglasses and glanced at the screen. It was Rachel checking up on her. Rachel, her dear, steady friend who understood in a way no one else could. Olivia slipped the phone unanswered back in her pocket. She was jittery, unfocused, too raw to talk to Rachel now.

She unwrapped her scarf. Her hair was a mess. She didn't care. Instead of straightening it, she sat on the lid of the toilet seat and closed her eyes. Donizetti's "Pour mon âme" had been playing in her head all day. The aria from *La fille du régiment*, with its nine high C's, was a showpiece for the world's best tenors. Adam hadn't been one of them, yet that hadn't stopped her former fiancé from trying to perform it.

She blinked her eyes hard. The Cavatina3 on her wrist came into focus. A yellow-gold and stainless-steel bracelet, an ivory dial with diamond chips by the numerals. Cavatina. A simple melody without a second part or a repeat. In music, a cavatina was straightforward and uncomplicated, unlike either the luxurious Cavatina3 watch or her own very complicated life.

She gazed at the white envelope that had been in her apartment mailbox that morning. It was addressed to her in the same neat, block-printed letters as the first note she'd received two days earlier. She forced herself to open it. Her hands were shaking.

Only five words. *You did this to me.*

Swallowing a sob, she ripped it into tiny pieces and flushed it down the toilet.

Paisley ushered in two of the newspaper reporters and disappeared into the corner with her phone. Ironically, the music critic was big and beefy; the sports reporter small and wiry. The editor of the lifestyle section arrived soon after, a middle-aged woman with short hair slicked to her skull and multiple ear piercings.

Thad had yet to meet a member of the press who didn't appreciate free food. Each of the men polished off a couple of cannoli along with a half dozen lemon cookies while the lifestyle editor sipped a glass of chardonnay and nibbled a few almonds. Thad exchanged small talk with all of them, hiding his irritation that The Diva was still sealed up in the bathroom. Just as he got ready to pound on the door and ask her if she'd fallen in, she deigned to join them.

She'd set aside her trench coat, along with the scarf and sunglasses, and she advanced toward the reporters, stilettos clicking, studiously ignoring him. Her sweep of dark hair coiled in one of those loose bun things, which—along with her royal-blue stilettos—brought her height to someplace in the vicinity of his. Her figure was formidable: broad shoulders, long neck, straight spine, and trim waist, all of it accompanied by skyscraper legs. She was neither skinny nor plump. More . . . He searched for the right word, but all he could come up with was "daunting."

Along with her stilettos and black slacks, the open throat of her white blouse showed off a gold rope necklace with a pigeon egg–sized stone that appeared to be a giant ruby. She wore multiple rings, a couple of bracelets, and the Cavatina3. He liked his women small and cuddly. This one looked like a tigress who'd raided an Hermès store.

The men rose as she approached. Henri performed the introductions. She extended her hand and gazed down her long nose at them, her lips curved in a regal smile. "Gentlemen." She acknowledged the lifestyle editor with a handshake and gracious smile before she folded herself into the chair across from Thad, ankles crossed off to the side, broomstick up her ass.

He deliberately slouched into his chair and stretched out his own legs, making himself comfortable. The classical music critic led off, but instead of addressing The Diva, he turned to Thad. "Are you an opera fan?"

"Haven't had much exposure," he said.

The sports writer picked up on that. "What about you, Ms. Shore? Do you ever go to football games?"

"Last year I saw New Madrid play Manchester United."

Thad could barely disguise a snort.

The sports writer exchanged an amused look with him before turning back to her. "Those are European soccer teams, Ms. Shore, not American football."

She adopted a *girls will be girls* look that Thad didn't buy for a second. "Of course. How silly of me."

There wasn't anything silly about this woman, from the throaty resonance of her voice to her figure, and something told him she knew damn well they were soccer teams. Or maybe not. For the first time, she'd spiked his curiosity.

"So you've never seen Thad Owens play?"

"No." She gazed directly at Thad for the first time, eyes as cold as a January night. "Have you ever heard me sing?"

"I haven't had the pleasure," he said with his best drawl. "But my thirty-seventh is coming up, and I'd sure welcome a round of 'Happy Birthday' to mark the occasion."

The lifestyle editor laughed, but The Diva didn't crack a smile. "Duly noted."

The classical music critic launched into some questions about a concert The Diva had given last year in Phoenix and a follow-up about European opera houses. The sports writer asked Thad about his fitness regimen and his thoughts on the Cardinals' prospects for next season.

Paisley had returned to her cell phone coma. Marchand offered more wine. "We're honored to have two people as accomplished as Madame Shore and Mr. Owens as our new Marchand ambassadors. Both of them are style setters."

The lifestyle editor took in Thad's gray slacks and quarter-zip raspberry cashmere sweater. "What's your fashion philosophy, Mr. Owens?"

"Quality and comfort," he said.

"A lot of men wouldn't be brave enough to wear that color."

"I like color," he said, "but I'm not into trends, and the only jewelry I wear is a great watch."

She cocked her head. "Maybe a wedding ring someday?"

He smiled. "I wouldn't wish me on anybody. I'm too unreliable. Now when it comes to reliability"—he extended his wrist, earning his paycheck—"this is what I count on. I've worn Marchand watches for years. That's why I was attracted to their invitation. They've outdone themselves with the Victory780."

Henri beamed. The lifestyle editor turned to The Diva. "What about you, Ms. Shore? How would you describe your fashion philosophy?"

"Quality and *dis*comfort." She surprised him by slipping off her stilettos.

The style editor's gaze traveled from Thad's raspberry sweater to The Diva's black-and-white ensemble. "You seem to prefer neutral colors."

"I believe in elegance." She glanced at Thad with open contempt. What the hell was wrong with her? "Bright pink is best kept on the stage," she said. "I'm only speaking for myself, of course."

His sweater wasn't fucking *pink*. It was *raspberry*!

"I'm very selective," she went on, her attention returning to the lifestyle editor. "That's why the Cavatina3 is the perfect watch for me." She took it off and handed it to the reporter to examine more closely. "My schedule is demanding. I need a watch I can rely on, but also one that complements my wardrobe and my lifestyle."

Commercial over.

They answered a few more questions. Where was Madame Shore living? How did Mr. Owens fill his time during the off-season?

"I needed a break from Manhattan," The Diva replied, "and since I like Chicago, and it's in the middle of the country, I rented an apartment there a few months ago. It makes domestic travel easier."

Thad was deliberately vague. "I work out and look after everything I'm too busy to take care of during the season."

Paisley missed her first cue to escort the reporters back to the lobby but finally got the message. After they'd disappeared, Marchand announced Olivia's and Thad's luggage had been delivered to the bedrooms that adjoined opposite sides of the suite. Henri gestured around the living and dining areas, along with the small kitchen. "As you can see, this is quite convenient for interviews and tomorrow's photo shoot. The chef will be making tonight's clients' dinner in the private kitchen."

The Diva's head shot up, and her dramatic eyebrows drew together. "Henri, may I speak with you?"

"But of course." The two of them moved toward the door into the hallway.

Thad was pissed. She obviously didn't like the idea of them sharing the suite. Fine. She could move to another room because no way was he giving up that big terrace. Ever since he was a kid, he'd been more comfortable outside than inside, and being cooped up in hotel rooms for too long, no matter how big they were, made him jumpy. He wasn't going anywhere.

Olivia had only taken a few steps before she realized she'd made a mistake. The doors had sturdy locks, and if she insisted on moving to another room, Thad Owens would realize she was afraid of him.

She touched Henri's arm. "Never mind, Henri. We can talk later. Nothing important."

As she picked up the stilettos she'd abandoned, Thad moved behind her. "Just so you know . . . ," he said. "I don't like nighttime visitors."

She sucked in her breath, gave him her fiercest arctic glare, and sealed herself in her room.

Thad heard the lock click behind her. She'd looked at him with so much disdain he'd half expected her to say something operatic like, *To the gallows, you swine!*

Henri beamed. "What a woman! She is magnificent! *La Belle Tornade.*"

"Let me guess. 'The beautiful turnip.'"

Henri laughed. "*Non, non.* She is called 'the Beautiful Tornado' for the power of her voice."

Thad didn't buy the "beautiful" part, not with those dark slabs of eyebrow and that long nose. As for "tornado" . . . "Ice storm" seemed more like it.

Thad made some phone calls and worked out in the hotel's fitness center before he came back to the suite and showered. Through the closed bedroom door, he heard the sound of The Diva singing musical scales. He listened as the notes rose and fell, the vowel sounds subtly changing, from *ees* to *ewws*, then some *mahs*. It was mesmerizing. No doubt about it. The lady could sing. As her tone switched from light to dark, he got goose bumps. How could anybody hit those notes?

With dinnertime approaching, the smells coming from the private kitchen promised a good meal. He changed into a purple T-shirt and a black metallic Dolce & Gabbana blazer with a printed lavender pocket square. It was a little over the top, even for him, but he had a point to make.

He heard Henri's voice in the living room, and as he stepped out, the guests began to arrive. They were all buyers, one from a local jewelry chain, a couple from department stores, and a few independent jewelers.

The Diva emerged in a floor-length black velvet gown. Her breasts caught his attention first. They weren't big, but full enough to push above the gown's neckline. She hadn't cluttered up the view with any necklaces, only a pair of earrings. Her skin was naturally pale, but against all that black velvet, it seemed even paler. She wore the Cavatina3 on one wrist and a variety of rings on her long fingers. She'd tidied up her afternoon hair with a formal twist that was a little old-fashioned, but he had to admit it suited her. She had presence; he'd give her that.

She did her normal grand-entrance thing—arm extended, distant smile, regal stride—and she was right back on his nerves again. He wanted to rumple her up. Knock her off her pedestal. Smear that bright red lipstick. Pull out the pins holding her hair together. Shuck off her clothes and stick her in a pair of ratty jeans and an old Stars sweatshirt.

But as good as his imagination was, he couldn't imagine her like that.

He hated formal dinner parties almost as much as he hated pass interceptions, but he talked to everyone. He was surprised how good The Diva was at it. She asked about their jobs, their families, and willingly looked at photos of their kids. Unlike him, her interest seemed genuine.

The meal began. Thad wasn't much of a drinker, so he cut himself off after two glasses of wine, but The Diva seemed to have an iron stomach. Two glasses, three, then four. One more glass as everyone left, and the two of them headed to their separate bedrooms.

His had high ceilings and a single door that led onto the terrace. He went naked into the bathroom to brush his teeth. As usual, he avoided his reflection. No need to depress himself. But despite its size, the bedroom felt stuffy and confining. He pulled on a pair of jeans and opened the door that led to the terrace.

Tempered-glass fencing offered unobstructed views of the city lights, while the potted trees and flower beds gave the illusion of a park, with strategically placed seating areas for comfort. The chilly night air felt good on his skin.

He thought about the day. About what lay ahead. About training camp only four months away and how much playing time he would or wouldn't get. As he moved around a potted tree to get a better view of the skyline, he thought about his future and a career that had fallen short of his dreams.

Wine wasn't good for her voice. Wine, caffeine, dry air, drafts, trauma—none of it good for her voice, which was why she seldom had more than a single glass of wine. Yet here she was, not just a little drunk, but drunk-drunk. Unsteady on her feet, unsteady in her head. She'd been on edge for days, nerves shredded, ready to detonate. Now, a dangerous, alcohol-fueled energy made her want to gather her gown around her knees, climb up on the terrace rail, and use it as a balance beam just to see if she could do it. She wasn't suicidal. She left that for others. Instead, she wanted a challenge. Better yet, a target. Something to conquer. She wanted to be a superhero, a protector of the weak, a drunken crusader fighting for justice. Instead, she was battling a ghost.

Something moved behind her. Too close. *Him.*

She wheeled around and attacked.

2

Women had thrown themselves at him before, but he wasn't used to getting an elbow to his gut when they did it. She'd caught him unaware, and he gave a woof of pain. At the same time, he automatically reached out to defend himself.

That made it worse.

All he'd wanted was a little fresh air, and now here he was, in a fight to the death with a black velvet–clad termagant.

He grabbed for her arms. "Stop it! Calm down!"

At his age, he should have known better than to ever tell a woman to calm down, and she kicked him hard in the shins. Unfortunately for her, she was barefoot, and she gave her own yelp of pain.

"What the hell's wrong with you!" He trapped her arms and pulled her hard against him. She was tall and strong, but he was stronger. She cried out and went after him again.

He wanted to kill her, but he also didn't want to hurt her. He kicked her legs out from under her.

He had just enough of the gentleman left to take the brunt of the impact as they dropped to the hard tile floor. He hit his damned elbow along with his hip but managed to pin her down by rolling on top of her and grabbing her wrists.

The perfectly composed performer had vanished. She was furious. *"You bastard!"* She spit out the words. "You evil *bastard*!"

When it came to name-calling, she didn't offer much variety, but damn, she was strong. He could barely keep her contained as she fought against his grip on her wrists.

"Stop it right now, or I'm going to . . . I'm going to smack you!" He would never hit a woman in a million years, but she was out of control, and maybe the threat would calm her down.

It didn't. Jaw set, teeth bared, she threw it all right back at him. "Go ahead, you bastard! You just try it!"

For all their drama, opera singers didn't seem to have much creativity about how to cuss someone out. He tried a different approach, loosening his grip on her ever so slightly, but not letting her go. "Take a breath. Just breathe."

"Vermin!"

At least she was expanding her vocabulary. Her hair had come loose and half her breast popped out of her gown, right down to the top of her nipple. He drew his eyes away. "You've had too much to drink, lady, and you need to take some deep breaths."

She stopped struggling, but he wasn't taking chances. He eased some of his weight off her. "That's it. Keep breathing. You're fine." *Crazy as a loon, but fine.*

"Let me up!"

"Give me your word that you won't take another swing at me."

"You deserve it!"

"A debate for another day." She didn't look quite so insane, so he took a risk and rolled off her carefully, alert for a knee to his groin. "Don't throw up on me, okay?"

She struggled to her feet, hair hanging in a crazy tangle, her voice throaty with dramatic menace. "Don't you ever speak to me again!"

"You've got it."

She scrambled awkwardly across the terrace and through the single door that led into her bedroom. The lock clicked hard behind her.

Olivia yanked the draperies shut over the door, weirdly proud of herself. *Bastard! Bastard! Bastard!* She'd never forget the way her friend Alyssa had looked the night Thad Owens had attacked her. Now, the big shot football player had gotten some of his own back.

She steadied herself on the edge of the bureau and managed to get her gown off. She, Olivia Shore, had a new career as a crusader for women. Tonight, she'd dispensed justice, a small blow for rightness in the face of all the disarray around her.

Out of nowhere, her stomach rebelled. She rushed to the bathroom, crouched over the bowl, and lost her dinner, along with the bottle of wine she'd unwisely consumed.

Afterward, she hung out on the tiled floor. Her shoulder stung where she'd scraped it. She set a warm washcloth against it, no longer feeling quite so proud of herself. She was drunk, and she'd acted crazy, and she could not do this. Not when she had so many other problems. And especially not when she had a contract she couldn't break and four more weeks on the road with that piece of vermin.

She crawled into the bedroom, stripped off her underwear, and eventually located her pajamas. Her nighttime routine was highly disciplined. No matter how late or how tired she was, she performed it without fail. Humidifiers running. Makeup remover followed by a foam cleanser, toner, moisturizer, eye cream, and her precious retinol. She brushed and flossed, sometimes used whitening strips on her teeth. Then a few yoga poses to help her unwind. But tonight, she did none of that. With a dirty face, dirty teeth, dirty spirit, and the image of Thad Owens's smug face looming over her, she crawled into bed.

Thad was up early the next morning to shoot the breeze with the local sports radio jocks. Fortunately, The Diva had another assignment, because she was the last person he wanted to see. Paisley, a little worse for wear from whatever she'd done the night before, which almost definitely didn't include work, accompanied him. Much to Henri's displeasure, Paisley had shown up in a pair of ripped jeans, an animal print top, and bright red ankle boots. Not exactly Marchand's image.

She took a seat next to Thad on the couch in the radio station's green room, although there were two other chairs available, and thumbed her phone. "Have you seen the Marchand social feeds? I mean, so basic. Like, who cares? You should tell Henri to let me take over their social media."

She shoved her phone at him, and he looked at the photos she'd taken at last night's dinner: his profile caught against candlelight, his hand on his jacket lapel, his jawline, his eyes. Only one of the pictures showed the Victory780. There were no photos of The Diva.

"If you want to convince Henri to use your ideas"—something he highly doubted would ever happen—"remember there are two brand ambassadors on this tour." *One of whom is a raving psychopath.*

"You're more photogenic."

"She's more famous." It nearly choked him to say it. He handed Paisley back her phone.

"My dad says Henri's the one who wants to move Marchand into the twenty-first century, so whatever. I did some research, you know, like, last night before dinner. Those old watch ads that David Beckham did. They're still sexy AF. Do you have any tattoos?"

"Haven't gotten around to it."

"Too bad." She poked a finger through a carefully placed hole in her jeans. "My dad doesn't think I can do this job, but I've got lots of ideas. Like I definitely want to do some of you in the shower. Because the

Victory780 is waterproof and everything. I could— You could oil up so the water beads on your skin. It'll be iconic."

"Not gonna happen."

"But you could wear swim trunks and everything."

"You and your iPhone aren't coming anywhere near my shower but ask Madame Shore. I'm sure she wouldn't mind. She probably even has a tattoo."

Paisley regarded him doubtfully. "She's kind of scary."

"Once you get to know her, I'll bet she's a pussycat." *The kind with claws and deadly teeth.*

He rose as the producer appeared to escort him into the studio. Out of the corner of his eyes, he saw Paisley take a photo of what was surely his butt.

He didn't see The Diva again until that afternoon when they were scheduled to meet back at the hotel to shoot the photos that would accompany the newspaper stories.

She was sipping tea in the suite when he arrived, and she found something fascinating to stare at in the bottom of her teacup. The Diva knew how to look good for photos. She'd pinned up her hair and angled a printed scarf around her shoulders. Her white pencil dress showed off shapely arms and the impressive set of legs that had tried to emasculate him last night.

Henri appeared with the photographers. As they set up the shoot, Henri asked her about her jewelry. Studiously ignoring Thad, she showed him a wide, matte-gold bracelet set with stones. "A replica of an Egyptian cuff from a dear friend. And this is one of my favorite poison rings." She flipped the domed top open, revealing a not-so-secret compartment. "Easy to fill it with poison and tip the contents into an enemy's drink." She darted an honest-to-God warning look at him.

"Or to off yourself," he tossed back.

He had the satisfaction of seeing her wince.

The photographer was ready for them. Henri posed Thad behind The Diva, and then next to her on the couch. She tucked her fingers under her chin, displaying the watch. He kept his wrist visible.

He'd spent a lot of time getting his picture taken, and he was comfortable in front of cameras, but The Diva seemed antsy, shifting around, crossing and recrossing her legs. One of the photographers gestured toward an armchair near the windows. "Let's try a few shots over there."

The Diva settled in the armchair, and Thad took up a position behind her.

Marchand tugged on today's silk neck scarf. "Thaddeus, may I suggest you put your hand on her shoulder?"

All the better to display the Victory780, but Thad had never been more reluctant to touch a woman.

She flinched, a movement so subtle he doubted anyone else noticed. He had no idea what he'd done to make her hate him so much. He was a straight shooter—blunt when he needed to be—but generally diplomatic. He liked most people, and he didn't make a habit of collecting enemies. He respected women and treated them well. This was her problem, not his. Still, he had to admit to a perverse curiosity.

After the photographers left, Henri suggested they all meet for dinner at eight in the hotel's four-star restaurant. Thad had plans to get together with some former teammates, and he declined. The Diva pleaded fatigue and said she'd order room service later. Henri didn't extend the invitation to Paisley.

Thad excused himself to change into workout clothes, but as he reached the second-floor fitness center, he realized he'd forgotten his phone. He liked to listen to music on the treadmill, and he went back to retrieve it.

The living room's double French doors were open, and she stood on the terrace by the rail. He hesitated. *To hell with it.* He was sick of her crap, and this was his chance to talk to her privately.

He walked over to the open doors but didn't step out. "I'm behind you, and I'd appreciate it if you didn't attack me again."

She whirled around. She'd gotten rid of the big scarf and traded her stilettos for a pair of flats, but she still looked plenty put together in her white dress. Did she even own a pair of jeans?

"Do you need something?" She addressed him as if he were a servant who'd interrupted her.

She was so condescending his teeth started to itch. "I thought you might have something you wanted to tell me."

"I can't imagine what that would be."

"Something on the order of, 'I'm sorry as hell I acted like a lunatic last night, and thank you, Mr. Owens, for not knocking me silly.' Which would have been easy to do."

Her iceberg expression could have sunk a thousand ships. "I have nothing to say to you."

She clearly wasn't worth his time, and he could have walked away. But they were going to be together for a month, and he needed to have it out with her. "You've given me the cold shoulder from the beginning, lady. Do you treat most people like garbage, or am I a special case? I don't give a damn what you think of me, you understand. But I am curious."

Her nostrils flared like an opera heroine about to order a beheading. "Men like you . . . you've got it all. Money. Looks. The public fawning over you. But that's not enough, is it?"

Now he was really steamed. "Here's the difference between you and me. If I have a beef with somebody, I'm upfront about it. I don't hide behind snarky comments."

She drew in a deep breath that expanded her rib cage in a way he'd have found impressive if he weren't so incensed. "You want upfront?" she said. "All right. Does the name Alyssa Jackson mean anything?"

"Can't say as it does."

"What's one more victim, right?"

"'Victim'?" It took a lot to make him lose his temper, but he'd never had anyone regard him with so much contempt. "Exactly what kind of victim?"

She gripped the railing with the hand that held one of her poison rings. "Alyssa and I shared an apartment for a while in the Bronx. It was when you were the Giants' hot new quarterback—the one who didn't last two seasons. But you were the big man in town, and all the women wanted you. Except the ones like Alyssa who didn't." Her lips curled with contempt. "And you don't even remember her name."

He crossed his arms over his chest. "How about you refresh my memory? Exactly what am I supposed to have done to her?"

"I don't know what the legal definition of sexual assault is, but what you did was close enough. I begged her to go to the police, but she refused."

He clenched his teeth against his rising fury. "Now there's a surprise."

"You could have had any woman you wanted, but the easy ones weren't the ones who appealed to you. They weren't the ones who made you feel like a big man."

He couldn't listen to any more, and he turned away only to come to a halt as he reached the door. "You don't know me, lady, and you don't know a damn thing about my character. You also don't know your old friend Alyssa as well as you think, so keep giving me the cold shoulder because we don't have anything more to say to each other."

Thad pounded down the service stairs to the second floor, his sneakers assaulting the stair treads. He'd never needed the gym more.

"Thaddeus Walker Bowman Owens!" He'd been twelve years old, in the car with his mother, and full of himself. They were on their way to his basketball practice when he'd called Mindy Garamagus a slut.

His sweet, mild-tempered mother had pulled to the side of the road and let him have it. A smack right across the face. The first and only time she'd hit him.

"Don't you ever say that about a woman! How does a girl get to be a slut? Ask yourself that. Does she do it all by herself?" Tears had filled his eyes as she'd looked at him as though he were some kind of worm. "The only men who use that word against a woman are weak, men who feel powerless. Don't judge what you don't understand. You have no idea who she is!"

His mother was right. Even then he knew that the only thing wrong with Mindy Garamagus was that she made him feel like the immature twelve-year-old he was.

That night, he'd gotten a similar lecture from his dad. It was long before the word "consent" had become part of the zeitgeist, but the message was loud and clear.

Even without his parents' lectures, he couldn't imagine himself ever taking advantage of a woman. How could sex be fun if you weren't both into it?

He'd once again forgotten his phone, but no way in hell was he going back to get it.

No matter how much money Marchand had offered her, Olivia would never have signed that contract if she'd known she'd be traveling with Owens instead of

Cooper Graham, as she'd originally been told. Graham had a wife, kids, and a squeaky-clean reputation. Traveling with him would have been a nice distraction, something she'd never needed more than she did at this point in her life.

The tension headache that had been lurking for days was back. She exchanged her dress for black yoga pants and a long white top, lay down on the bed, and reached for the headphones she always traveled with. Moments later, she heard the soothing sound of Bill Evans's "Peace Piece."

She tried to relax, but not even the evocative harmonies of the man who'd been one of the world's greatest jazz pianists could soothe her. Something about the unflinching way Owens had looked at her made her uneasy. More than uneasy. *"You don't know me, lady, and you don't know a damn thing about my character."* But she did know his character!

Didn't she?

She couldn't stand the uncertainty. She turned off the music and reached for her phone. Alyssa picked up her call on the second ring.

The two of them had once been close, but now that her former roommate was immersed in motherhood, they'd drifted apart, and it had been at least a year since they'd spoken. "Hey, famous lady!" Alyssa said. "I've missed you. Hunter, get down from there! Jesus . . . That kid . . . Honest to God, Olivia, don't ever have kids. I've been to the emergency room twice with him just this month. Do you have any idea how many things a three-year-old can stick up his nose?"

As Alyssa detailed the exact objects Hunter had stashed in his nasal cavity, Olivia remembered how Alyssa's irreverent humor used to make her laugh.

"So what's up with you?" Alyssa said. "Ready to tackle *Tosca* yet?"

Olivia's mezzo-soprano wasn't well suited for that role, but Alyssa had never had more than a rudimentary grasp of opera. "A temporary gig," Olivia said. "I signed on to promote Marchand watches."

"*Marchand?* Tell me you're giving out free samples."

"Unfortunately not. Also . . ." She gripped the phone tighter. "There are two of us on the road together promoting the brand. I'm traveling with Thad Owens."

"The football player? That's hysterical."

An icicle slithered down Olivia's spine. "'Hysterical'?"

"The soprano and the quarterback. What a combination, right? Is he still hot? That man was gorgeous."

Olivia shot to her feet, dread pooling in her stomach. "Alyssa, I'm talking about Thad Owens. The football player who tried to rape you."

Alyssa laughed. "God, Olivia. You knew that was bogus. Remember? I told you all about it."

"You didn't tell me any such thing!" Olivia exclaimed. "You said he backed you into the bedroom. Pinned you down. You came home crying. And you talked about it for weeks afterward."

"I only cried because Kent walked in on us, and I only talked about it when he was around. Remember how suspicious he was. I can't believe you've forgotten." She pulled the phone away. "Hunter, stop it! Give me that!" She readjusted the phone. "Anyway . . . So I met Thad at a party just when Kent and I were getting serious. Kent went off to shoot pool or something, and Thad and I started talking. One thing led to another, and we were making out. Then Kent walked in on us, and I needed to come up with an excuse quick. I told you all that."

"You didn't tell me anything!" Olivia felt sick. "I tried to get you to go to the police."

"Oh, yeah . . . Now I remember. I was afraid if I told you the truth, you'd tell Kent. You were always the righteous one." Water ran in the background. "Here, Hunter. Have a drink." The water shut off. "Can you believe I walked away from a chance at a relationship with Thad Owens because I didn't want a loser like Kent to dump me?"

Olivia sank back down on the side of the bed and dug her hand into the mattress. "The only loser, Alyssa, is you."

"What are you getting so upset about? It's not like I accused him or anything."

"You did accuse him. To me."

"Did you say something to him?"

"Oh, yes. I said a lot."

"Shit."

"Shit, indeed." In her rush to judgment against Thad Owens, Olivia had forgotten that Alyssa could be both self-centered and manipulative. That was exactly why Rachel had never liked her. Olivia should have trusted her best friend's opinion. She pressed her hand to her stomach. "False accusations have consequences, Alyssa. They make real rape victims afraid to speak out because they don't think anyone will believe them."

"Ease up, okay? Stop being so judgy."

Olivia's voice shook. "Wrong is wrong, and lying like you did is a betrayal of every woman who's been assaulted."

"Jesus, Olivia. You're making too big a deal out of this. You always did think you were better than anybody else."

"Good-bye, Alyssa. And lose my number."

"Hey, you're the one who called me."

"It won't happen again."

Olivia was furious with herself. She hadn't been thinking clearly for days, but that was no excuse for the way she'd attacked him. Some superhero she'd turned out to be. A crusader for justice? How about a dispenser of injustice. She'd known Alyssa wasn't always reliable, and even drunk, she shouldn't have attacked someone without verifying the facts. Adam was already on her conscience, and she didn't need another transgression to add to her list of misdeeds. She had to apologize immediately.

She paced the living room waiting for him to get back from the gym. Eventually, the door opened. She tried to form exactly the right words, but before she could utter a single one, he'd strode past her as if she didn't exist and disappeared into his bedroom.

She started pacing again. This was torturous. She pressed her ear to his door and heard the shower water stop running. She hurried to the closest couch, kicked off her flats, and picked up a magazine.

No one liked to admit when she'd been wrong, but this was a big wrong, and it had to be righted. Once this was over, she could only hope he didn't believe in holding a grudge.

She tugged at the knee of her yoga pants, turned a page of the magazine without having read a word. His door finally opened.

When she'd seen him only as a sexual predator, his off-the-chart good looks had been an insult. But now? He wore a dark blue blazer, faded jeans, a gray T-shirt, and he might be the handsomest man she'd ever met. Thick dark hair, dazzling green eyes set off with dark brows and full lashes, cheekbones that hit the sweet spot between too sharp and too blunt. His top and bottom lips were perfect. If she'd been born with his looks instead of being saddled with her own strong features, she might have had an easier time of it. All that perfection was wasted on a man who threw footballs for a living.

She'd lost precious seconds ruminating over what couldn't be changed, and he was nearly at the door. She jumped up from the couch. "I need to talk to you."

It was as if he hadn't heard her.

"Wait!"

The hotel room door shut behind him. She shot across the room and out into the hallway. "Mr. Owens! Thad! Wait!"

He continued his march to the elevator.

"Thad!"

The doors slid open and he stepped between them. She just made it inside before they closed.

He punched the button for the lobby without a glance in her direction. The elevator began to descend. "Thad, I want to apologize. I—"

The elevator slid to a stop, and an elderly couple got on. They smiled automatically, and then the woman took a closer look at Olivia.

Please, no.

"Olivia Shore! Oh, my goodness! Is it really you? We heard you sing Princess Eboli in *Don Carlos* last year in Boston. You were amazing!"

"Thank you."

Her husband piped in. "'O don fatale.' That high B-flat. Unforgettable!"

"I can't believe we're meeting you in person," the woman gushed. "Are you performing here?"

"No, I'm not."

The elevator stopped at the lobby. Thad strode out ahead of the older couple. Olivia could see they were eager to engage her in a longer conversation. She quickly excused herself and hurried after him.

As the cold marble tiles of the lobby hit her bare feet, she remembered her flats lying next to the couch in the suite. Owens clearly didn't want to talk to her, and she should turn back, but the idea of carrying this weight any longer was worse than the embarrassment of going after him.

He exited through the center front door. Guests turned to look at her as she rushed barefooted across the lobby. Outside, the first taxi in line had its door open, and Owens was speaking to the driver as he got in. She abandoned what was left of her dignity, sprinted toward the car, grabbed the door, threw herself in . . .

And fell right on top of him.

It was like landing on a bag of cement.

The hotel doorman hadn't seen her awkward leap. He closed the car door and gestured for the taxi to move forward to make room for the next car. The cab-driver gazed at them in the rearview mirror with eyes that had seen it all, shrugged, and pulled away.

She scrambled off Thad. As she sprawled onto the seat next to him, he looked at her as if she were a cock-roach, then leaned back and deliberately pulled out his phone. He began scrolling through it as if she weren't there.

She curled her toes against the gritty floor mat. "I'm sorry. I want to apologize. I made a terrible mistake."

"You don't say," he replied with total indifference, his eyes staying on his phone.

Olivia curled her toes deeper into the grit. "I talked to my friend. My former friend. She admitted she'd lied to me about everything. Her boyfriend walked in on the two of you, and— The details don't matter. The point is, I'm sorry."

"Uh-huh." He'd put his phone to his ear and spoke into it. "Hey, Piper. Looks like we're playing phone tag. I got your message, and I should be back in the city by then. Remember to let me know when you decide you're ready to cheat on your husband." He disconnected.

She stared at him.

He turned to her. "You had something to say to me?"

She'd already said it, but he deserved his pound of flesh. "I'm truly sorry, but . . ."

One of those perfect dark eyebrows arched. "But?"

Her temper got the best of her. "What would you have done if you thought you were stuck for the next four weeks with a sexual predator?"

"You have a strange idea of what constitutes an apology."

"I'm sorry," she said again, and then, "No! I'm not sorry. Yes, I am, but— Believing what I did, I had to confront you."

"You might be a great singer, but you're crap at making apologies."

She could only grovel for so long. "I'm a soprano. Sopranos aren't supposed to apologize."

He actually laughed.

"Truce?" she said, hoping for the best even though she knew she didn't deserve it.

"I'll think about it."

The cab turned down a one-way street and pulled up in front of a seedy-looking bar with a neon cactus flickering in the window.

"While you're thinking," she said, "would you mind lending me cab fare to get back to the hotel?"

"I might," he said. "Or . . . I have a better idea. Come in with me. I doubt the guys have ever met an opera singer."

"Go into that awful bar?"

"Not what you're used to, I'm sure, but mingling with the commoners might be good for you."

"Another time."

"Really?" His eyes narrowed. "You think all it takes is a couple of 'I'm sorry's' to make up for character assassination? Words are cheap."

She regarded him steadily. "This is payback, right?"

"Oh, yeah."

"I'm barefoot," she pointed out with a certain degree of desperation.

He regarded her with silky animosity. "I wouldn't have thought of it otherwise. If there's too much broken glass, I'll carry you over it."

"You want revenge this much?"

"Hey, I said I'd carry you, didn't I? But never mind. I know you don't have the guts."

She laughed in his face. A big, theatrical "*ha!*" that came straight from her diaphragm. "You don't think I have the guts? I've been booed at La Scala!"

"They booed you?"

"Sooner or later it happens to everyone who sings there. Callas, Fleming, Pavarotti." She reached for the door handle, stepped out onto the dirty pavement, and turned to gaze down at him. "I gave them the finger and finished the performance."

He didn't move. "I think I might be having second thoughts."

"Afraid to be seen with me?"

"I'm afraid of you in general."

"You're not the first." She marched toward the flickering neon cactus.

3

Decades of fossilized cigarette smoke clung to the bar's walls, and the ancient black and brown floor tiles were a cautionary tale in asbestos abuse. Yellowed rodeo posters were shellacked to the ceiling, brown vinyl stools fronted the bar, and fake Tiffany Michelob lamps hung over the wooden tables.

Olivia considered her yoga pants and her bare feet. "I'm glad I travel with antibiotics."

"I'll bet you the bartender has a bottle of Boone's Farm tucked away somewhere to cheer you up. I know you like your wine."

"Thoughtful."

One of the four oversized men sitting at a back table held up his arm, gesturing toward him. "T-Bo!"

Thad's hand settled in the small of her back, propelling her forward. The men rose, dwarfing the table. Thad glowered at the youngest one sitting at the end. "What's *he* doing here?"

The object of his disdain was maybe in his early twenties, with a big square face, solid jaw, shoulder-length light brown hair, and a manicured beard.

"I don't know. He just showed up." This came from a gorgeously athletic man with a fade—Afro on top and closely shaved sides with a scalp tattoo showing through. He wore a colorfully embroidered men's leather bomber jacket over a bare chest draped with a half dozen necklaces.

"Damn, Ritchie, it's bad enough I have to put up with Garrett during the season," Thad groused. "I don't have to do it now, too."

"You tell him that," the man named Ritchie responded.

Instead of looking at Thad, the target of Thad's abuse was looking at her, which seemed to make Thad recall that he hadn't arrived alone. "This is Olivia Shore. But you should call her Madame. She's a big-deal opera singer doing some research on the life of lowbrow jocks."

He was deliberately trying to embarrass her.

Thad didn't feel one bit bad about embarrassing her. She deserved it. Except she didn't seem all that embarrassed. Instead, she stuck out that damned royal hand as if she expected them to kiss her fingers. *"Enchanté,"* she said, with a French accent so heavy he was afraid she'd choke on it. "And you may call me Olivia."

The idiot child Thad was supposed to help turn into a superstar quarterback gestured to the empty chair next to him. "Come sit by me."

"I'd be delighted."

Hell. Thad tried to remember why he'd thought it was a good idea to bring her along. It was because— Never mind why. She was here now. But instead of being uncomfortable, she looked as though she made a habit of hanging out in dive bars.

Clint pulled out the chair for her. "Since Thad's not doing the introductions, I'm Clint Garrett, starting quarterback for the Chicago Stars. Thad works for me."

"How fortunate for him," she cooed.

"Clint's young and stupid," Thad said. "Ignore him. Now the giant sitting at the other end of the table is Junior Lotulelei. Unlike Clint, he's a real player. Offensive tackle for the 49ers now, but the two of us used to play together on the Broncos. That's in Denver," he added, to needle her. "Liv here doesn't know much about American football. More a soccer fan."

"Olivia," she pointedly corrected him. At the same time, she was regarding Junior curiously, which wasn't surprising since he was three hundred and fifty pounds of solid muscle, and his hair grew so high above his head and so far down his back that it practically lived in another country. "Junior's the best player to ever come out of Pago Pago."

"American Samoa," Junior clarified. "It's the NFL's favorite training ground."

"I had no idea," Olivia said.

Thad continued the introductions. "Ritchie Collins is at the other end of the table." Tonight Ritchie wore a single gold hoop near his scalp tattoo. "Ritchie's the fastest wide receiver the Stars have had since Bobby Tom Denton."

"Ritchie's my go-to guy," Clint said. "Me and him are going to rule the world."

"Not until you learn how to handle pressure in the pocket, little girl." Thad had the satisfaction of seeing Clint wince. "The ugly dude next to him is Bigs Russo." Bigs sometimes got offended if his ugly mug wasn't acknowledged, and Thad didn't see any point in taking chances.

Bigs'd had some new dental work since the last time Thad had seen him, but that hadn't done anything to fix his squashed nose, bald head, and small eyes. "Bigs might look like a broke-down prizefighter," Thad said, "but he's the best defensive lineman in the League."

The other men nodded in agreement, but Olivia seemed concerned that Thad had hurt Bigs's feelings. "I find rugged men incredibly fascinating," she cooed. "So much more interesting than those pretty-boy athletes who model underwear in their spare time."

They all hooted, none louder than Bigs. Thad's resentment eased. He had to hand it to her. The Diva wasn't taking his crap lying down.

"So you two a thing now?" Ritchie asked.

"Oh, no," Olivia replied emphatically. "He detests me. Not entirely without reason. He brought me here to embarrass me."

"That's no way to treat a lady, T-Bo," Junior said.

"She insulted me," Thad explained.

Olivia apparently decided to put it out in the open. "I accused him of something he didn't do. This is his revenge."

"I did notice you aren't wearing shoes," Bigs said.

"She's a nature lover," Thad said. "Half the time she walks around naked, but tonight she settled for bare feet."

"Not true," she said. "But an entertaining story."

"Why'd you do that?" Ritchie asked her. "Accuse him?"

"I was fed some bad information."

Ritchie nodded. "It can happen."

"It wouldn't have if I'd considered my source."

Thad liked the fact that The Diva was being upfront. Maybe she wasn't so bad after all.

The bartender came over to take their drink orders. Thad watched Olivia's gaze switch from her grimy surroundings to his equally grimy apron.

"I'll have iced tea. In a bottle." As soon as the bartender left the table, she offered an explanation. "I'm allergic to *E. coli* bacteria."

They all liked that.

"I'm guessing you gentlemen are obscenely wealthy, so . . ." She made a gesture toward the nicotine-stained walls and mostly dead Christmas tree lights draping a longhorn steer skull. "Why this place?"

"Bigs chose it." Ritchie slid his fingers over the embroidered rose on his leather bomber.

"It's important to keep it real," Bigs said.

Ritchie tilted back in his chair. "This is a whole new world of real."

The Diva didn't seem to mind when the conversation inevitably drifted to football. For someone who made a living commanding center stage, her willingness to step back surprised him. As they tossed around their opinions of sports broadcasters, team owners, and exchanged some general trash talk, she ignored her iced tea and listened patiently.

Clint, not surprisingly, tried to get her to leave with him.

"No shoes," she said.

"I'll buy you a couple pairs of Blahniks on the way."

She laughed.

Thad still didn't get why the kid had shown up in Phoenix, but it said something bad about The Diva's character that she seemed to like the idiot. Still, his opinion of The Diva had changed. He'd made some mistakes in his time, and despite his remarks to the contrary, she'd offered up a damned good apology.

She patted Clint on the shoulder and rose from the table. "If you'll excuse me . . ."

Crossing her legs was no longer an option. As horrifying as the idea of using this particular bathroom was, she really, really had to go. She tiptoed across the floor to the back hallway, letting as little of her bare feet touch the floor as possible. Behind her, she heard Bigs say, "You really shoulda bought her some shoes, T-Bo."

T-Bo. Apparently, that was Thad Owens's jock nickname. If it were up to her, she'd have nicknamed him Butthead.

The women's toilet had a simpering mermaid on the door, while the men's had a dramatic figure of Neptune. Total gender discrimination. She pulled the sleeve of her white top over her hand and turned the doorknob.

It was bad. Really bad. The cracked cement floor was wet in places, with a streamer of sodden toilet paper unfurling toward a semi-clogged drain. And it smelled. She absolutely could not go barefoot into this hellhole.

But if she didn't, she'd wet her pants. And imagine what a laugh Thad Owens would get out of that.

By keeping her feet on the asbestos tiles in the hallway, holding on to the door frame with one hand, and stretching as far as her body would allow, she could just reach the rusting paper towel dispenser with her opposite hand. She pulled off one, two . . . six paper towels. Dividing her stack in half, she slipped three under one foot, three under the other, and proceeded to shuffle inside.

It was inadequate and totally disgusting. When she was done, she scrubbed her hands twice in the cracked porcelain sink and shuffled back across the floor to the door. The paper towels had gotten wet from the filthy floor and begun to shred. She opened the door to see Thad standing in the hallway.

He peered inside. "Now that is nasty."

She shuddered. "I hate you."

"You're not going to say that when you see what I bought off the cook." He dangled a pair of dirty white Crocs in front of her.

She abandoned the ruined paper towels, grabbed the Crocs, and, with another shudder, shoved her feet inside. They were barely long enough for her narrow size tens.

"I'm so not eating here."

"Good call," he said.

When they got back to the table, Bigs was standing in the corner with an ancient karaoke machine.

"And now the real fun begins," Thad said. "A word of advice. Bigs can't sing a note, but don't tell him that."

"For real," Ritchie said with a head shake.

While Bigs was considering his musical options, Clint Garrett tried to get Thad off into a corner so they could talk about "the pocket," whatever that was, but Thad refused to cooperate.

"He hates me," Clint said cheerfully to Olivia when Thad went over to the bar to order another drink. "But he has one of the best football minds in the League, and he's a great coach." When she looked confused, he said,

"The best backup quarterbacks do everything they can to make the starter a better player."

"He doesn't seem to be doing much coaching."

"He will once training camp starts. Then he's all business. Dude'll get me out of bed at six in the morning to watch film. Nobody reads the defense like Thad Owens."

Olivia toyed with her unopened iced tea bottle. "So . . . if you don't mind my asking, if he's so great, why isn't he the starting quarterback instead of you?"

Clint tugged at his beard. "It's complicated. He should have been one of the greats, but he has this thing with his peripheral vision. Nothing that'd be a problem in any other job. Just in this one."

The song choices were as cheesy as the karaoke machine, and "Achy Breaky Heart" began to play. Bigs had the mike, and she winced as he launched into a cruelly off-key version. From there, he tortured Stevie Wonder's "Part-Time Lover." Afterward, he took a break to down his beer and approach Olivia. "T-Bo says you're a big-time opera singer. Let's hear you."

"I'm on vocal rest."

"I heard you doing some kind of singing exercises this morning," Thad said unhelpfully.

"That's different."

Bigs shrugged and took the mike again. His "Build Me Up Buttercup" wasn't quite as bad as "Part-Time Lover," but his rendition of "I Want to Know What Love Is" was so ugly the other customers finally rebelled.

"Shut the hell up!"

"Turn that thing off!"

"Sit down, asshole!"

Thad winced. "And now it begins."

Bigs clenched his ham-hock fists and kept singing, his face flushing red with anger.

Junior looked worried. "If you don't get that mike away from him, T-Bo, he'll end up suspended before the season even starts."

"I'm not singing," Thad responded. "You do it."

"Hell, no."

"Don't look at me," Ritchie said. "I'm worse than he is."

Clint had disappeared, the crowd was getting uglier, and all three men looked at her. "Vocal rest," she repeated.

The three of them rose in unison. Thad took one arm, Ritchie the other, and they lifted her from her chair. While Junior ran interference, they propelled her to the microphone just as the crowd's jeers grew louder and "Friends in Low Places" began to play.

Thad gently extracted the mike from Bigs. "Liv changed her mind. This is her favorite song, and she wants to sing."

"Olivia," she hissed.

To her dismay, Bigs handed over the microphone.

And there she was, *La Belle Tornade*, the toast of the Metropolitan, the jewel of La Scala, the pride of the Royal Opera House standing before a roomful of drunks with a sticky microphone in her hand and a Garth Brooks tune ringing in her ears. She gave it her worst. Perfectly pitched, but quiet. No open, rounded vowels. No soaring high notes or resonant lows. Not even a hint of vibrato. As ordinary as she could make it.

"Take it off!" a bully shouted from the end of the bar as she reached the final chorus.

"Let's see what you got on underneath!" another shouted.

Before she knew it, the entire bar, with the exception of the football players, was shouting, "Take it off! Take it off!"

The temper that had made her give the finger to the odious *loggionisti* at La Scala got the best of her. She whipped off one of the Crocs, threw it at the nearest culprit, and then hurled the other at the initial offender.

Thad appeared from nowhere, grabbed her by the shoulders, and twisted her toward the door. "And now we get out of here."

Apparently, she didn't move fast enough because he swept all five feet ten inches and one hundred and forty pounds of her into his arms and wedged her outside without banging her head on the door.

"Let me go!"

He set her down, pulled her across the one-way street, picked her up again, and carried her into an alley.

"What . . . ?"

"Rats."

She clutched his neck. "No!"

"We'll hang here for a while until things settle down."

She grabbed him tighter. "I hate rodents!" The alley was narrow, with metal fire escapes running up the sides of the brick buildings, and a sentinel of Dumpsters standing guard. "I'm good with bugs, and I had a pet snake when I was a kid, but no rats."

She felt him shudder. "I'm not a big fan of snakes."

"Fine. You handle the rodents and I'll take care of the reptiles."

"Deal."

She held herself stiffly, one hand at his chest, wanting and not wanting to rest her head against his dark blue blazer as she searched the area for vermin. "I'm too heavy."

"I can bench-press three-twenty. You're at least a hundred and fifty pounds under that."

By the time she'd done the math, he was already grinning. She withered him with her frostiest voice. "May we go now?"

"A few more minutes."

He leaned against the brick wall, easily balancing her weight in his arms. She turned her head. Her cheek brushed the soft cotton of his T-shirt. He smelled good. A clean aftershave along with the faintest hint of beer. She gazed at her filthy feet. Something odious was stuck to the top of her instep.

"I have to admit I was a little disappointed in your singing," he said. "You sounded good—don't get me wrong—but you didn't sound much like a first-rate opera singer."

"I told you. I'm resting my voice."

"I guess. But it was kind of a downer after hearing those impressive exercises you do."

She gave him her most noncommittal "hmm" and made another quick scan for rodents.

"Reach in my back pocket," he said, "and pull out my phone so I can call an Uber."

She turned, pressing her breasts against his chest, and reached between their bodies, down across the blade of his hip bone and—very carefully—eased her hand along the slope of what was, not surprisingly, a very firm rear end.

She was now twisted flat against him, cupping his butt while her own butt was hoisted in the air. "I can't—" She felt the bulge of the phone in his pocket. Felt another bulge. Quickly withdrew her hand. "This isn't going to work. "

"It's working for me."

He was provoking her again. She twisted into a semi-upright position without the phone. "We need a new plan." She thought of the rats. "But don't you dare put me down."

He eased her onto the lid of the nearest Dumpster, something he could have done, she realized, from the beginning. "Don't run away."

As if she would.

A few minutes later, he was carrying her from the alley into a waiting Uber.

Neither of them seemed to have much to say as they drove back to the hotel. He stared straight ahead, a half smile on his face. She turned her head out the window and felt a half smile taking over her own face. Despite the dirt, the drunks, the threat of rats. Despite Thad Owens himself. Tonight was the first fun she'd had in weeks.

Her smile faded as she thought of Adam, whose days of having fun were over forever.

The Diva endured the walk across the glittering lobby with her chin raised and her haughtiest expression, daring anyone to mention her filthy bare feet. As they reached the elevator, a desk clerk hurried up to her. "Flowers arrived while you were out, Ms. Shore. We put them in your suite. And you have a message."

She took the envelope he handed her with a gracious nod, but as the elevator rose, she crushed it in her fist.

Thad held the door of their suite open and entered behind her, stepping into the overwhelming smell of too many flowers. Vases stuffed full of a dozen varieties covered the top of the piano.

The Diva sighed. "Rupert again."

"Again? He does this frequently?"

"Flowers, boxes of expensive chocolates, champagne. I've tried to discourage him, but as you can see, it hasn't worked." She extracted a florist card from one of the arrangements, glanced at it, and set it back down.

"Rupert is one of your lovers?"

"One of legions."

"Seriously?"

"No, not seriously! He's at least seventy."

Thad took in the flowers. "Am I the only one who thinks this is creepy?"

"You have to understand opera fans. They feel like a dying breed, and that can make them overzealous when it comes to their favorite singers."

"Are there others like Rupert?"

"He's my most ardent. As for the rest . . . It depends on the production. I've gotten Spanish shawls, cases of good rioja, even a few Iberian hams from the *Carmen* aficionados. And, of course, cigars."

"Why cigars?"

"Carmen works in a cigar factory."

"I know that." He didn't. "So what other weird gifts have your twisted superfans sent?"

"They're passionate, not twisted, and I love every one of them. Silver scissors for *Samson et Dalila*."

"Stay away from my hair."

"Lots of Egyptian jewelry—scarab earrings and bracelets—because I sing Amneris in *Aida*. She's the villain, but she has her reasons—unrequited love and all that. I've even gotten a silver hookah." As an afterthought, she added, "*Aida* is set in Egypt."

"I know that." He did.

"Mozart fans have sent me more cherubs than I can count."

"For?"

"Cherubino. We mezzos are famous for our breeches parts."

"Women playing men?"

"Yes. Cherubino in *Marriage of Figaro.* He's a horndog. Sesto in *La clemenza di Tito.* Hansel in *Hansel and Gretel.* My friend Rachel owns that role."

"Hard to imagine you playing a guy."

"I pride myself."

He smiled. Her passion for her work and loyalty to her fans were unmistakable. Passion was what drew him to people, their enthusiasm for their jobs or their hobbies—whatever gave their life joy and meaning, whether it was making a great marinara sauce, collecting Louisville Sluggers, or singing opera. Nothing bored him more than bored people. Life was too great for that.

She scratched the back of her calf with the toes of one grubby foot. "I'm sure you receive gifts."

"I got a good deal on a Maserati."

"I'll have to mention that to Rupert. Anything else?"

"The occasional loan of a vacation home, plus more liquor than I can drink and too many restaurant meals comped. It's ironic how often people who don't need money get the breaks, while the ones who could use a helping hand come up empty."

She regarded him thoughtfully. "Not exactly the viewpoint of an entitled jock."

He shrugged. "There's a big link between genetics and athletic ability. I got lucky."

She studied him a moment longer than necessary before gazing at her feet. "I need a shower. I'll see you in the morning."

It felt like the end of a good date, and he had a crazy urge to kiss her. An impulse she obviously didn't share because she was already on her way to her bedroom.

He opened the terrace doors and stepped outside. He felt restless, itchy. The Diva was too cavalier about these gifts for his taste. He'd had to deal with a couple of overzealous fans like Rupert, and one of them had turned into a verified stalker. He drummed on the terrace rail, turned back inside, and went to the piano. The note that had come with the flowers lay faceup on top.

La Belle Tornade,
You are my gift from the gods.
Rupert P. Glass

Thad grimaced. The crumpled envelope the desk clerk had given her when they'd gotten back to the hotel lay next to the florist's card. She must have forgotten she'd set it down.

This envelope was postmarked Reno. He wasn't prone to opening other people's mail, but his instincts told him to make an exception.

He pulled out a single sheet of plain white paper printed with block letters.

This is your fault. Choke on it.

The Diva's bedroom door opened. "What are you doing?"

"Opening your mail." He held up the note. "What's this about?"

She glanced at it as she snatched it from him. "The opera world is full of drama. Stay out of my mail."

"This is more than drama," he said.

She lifted her chin, but he noticed her hand was shaking. "It's personal."

"I'll say."

"It doesn't concern you." She turned toward her bedroom.

He cut in front of her. "It does now. If you're involved with crazies, I need to know in case we run into any of them in the next four weeks."

"We won't." That strong jaw of hers set in a stubborn line that told him she wouldn't say more. She ripped the note in two, dropped it in the trash, and headed into her bedroom.

4

Thad returned from his run the next morning to the dazzle of The Diva's vocalizations coming through her closed bedroom door. He found it hard to imagine how any human being could produce such extraordinary sounds. Last night, she'd said she was on vocal rest, but he suspected she'd been trying to dodge karaoke.

In the limo on the way to the airport, it seemed as if the previous night had never happened. He answered his texts while The Diva and Henri chatted away in French. Paisley looked as if she was trying to sleep. As much as he wanted to cross-examine The Diva about that letter she'd received, he restrained himself. For now, he'd keep a watchful eye.

Paisley yawned and pushed her aviators on top of her long sweep of blond hair. "That shirt is dope."

Her eyes looked bloodshot from what he suspected had been another night spent partying. "You could be a model."

"He's been there, done that," The Diva said with the fake smirk she'd adopted to irritate him.

The shirt Paisley had complimented him on was salmon. Salmon, not *pink.* As for The Diva . . . Underneath her Burberry trench coat he caught a glimpse of a boring white sweater and dark slacks. Still, he had to give her props for those big earrings that looked like dangling squares of crumpled gold paper. And she did have a flair for dramatic scarves. Very different from Paisley's jeans and leather jacket.

As they boarded the plane for the Los Angeles leg of their tour, Henri tapped him on the shoulder from behind. "*Bien,* Thad. I have a wonderful surprise for you this morning. I've invited someone to come along with us today."

The dumbass jumped up from his seat. "Surprise!"

The Diva rushed forward. "Clint!"

Henri pounded Thad on the back. "So the two of you can talk about the football, *oui*?"

"Fucking *oui,*" Thad muttered.

Instead of greeting Thad, Garrett concentrated on The Diva. "You clean up pretty good, Livia."

She smiled. "What are you doing here?"

"Henri's a football fan. He invited me to come along today to keep T-Bo entertained." The dumbass finally risked a glance at Thad. "She's got shoes on. So much for keepin' 'em barefoot and pregnant, right?"

Thad lunged forward, only to have The Diva step in his way. "Temper, temper," she cooed.

Clint grinned. Thad had a reputation for keeping his cool, and he could see Clint was proud of having goaded him into losing it. His grin once again reminded Thad that the dumbass wasn't nearly as dumb as he pretended to be. Nobody got to be the starting quarterback for an NFL team by being stupid.

Paisley, in the meantime, stood motionless in the aisle, lips parting, her stunned gaze fixed on Garrett. As Thad settled into his customary seat at the back of the plane, he realized he'd once again settled into second place, but this time, he couldn't be happier.

To Paisley's displeasure, The Diva buckled in next to Clint on the couch, forcing Paisley to take the seat across from him. Thad could almost hear Paisley's mental wheels turning as she tried to figure out how to make her move. She waited until they were in the air. "Okay for me to take a couple of pictures to send my friends?"

"Sure," The Diva said.

Thad smiled to himself. It wouldn't take her long to figure out she was an unwelcome intruder in the lens of Paisley's iPhone.

Sure enough, Paisley talked Garrett into a selfie, but The Diva looked more amused than offended. Garrett got up from the couch. Poor Paisley wasn't used to male rejection, and she couldn't hide her disappointment as he headed back toward Thad. Paisley didn't understand that no woman on the planet could hold the numbskull's attention when his mind was on football.

As Clint sidled in across from him, Thad didn't bother to hide his irritation. Training camp wouldn't start until July, and Garrett knew damn well Thad would give him one hundred percent then, so why did he have to hassle him now? It wasn't like they could run drills on the plane.

A weird moaning sound penetrated the plane. Thad's head came up in time to see Olivia's hand pressed to her mouth. She was staring at the newspaper she must have picked up from the fresh stack in the cabin. She snapped open her seat belt and rushed back to him, the newspaper in her fist. "Look at this!"

He looked.

The photos were on the second page of the Phoenix *Examiner*'s Lifestyle section—one of the formal photos he and The Diva had posed for, along with a paparazzi shot of him carrying The Diva out of the bar last night.

OPERA SINGER AND NFL STAR MAKE SWEET MUSIC

Noted mezzo-soprano Olivia Shore and the Chicago Stars' backup quarterback Thad Owens enjoyed a little PDA last night. The football star and the opera singer have been doing more than promoting a new line of watches for noted French watchmaker Marchand Timepieces. In an earlier interview at their hotel, the cagey couple showed no sign that their relationship was anything other than business, but it looks as if they've crossed into more personal territory.

"This is mortifying!" she exclaimed.

"Mortifying?" He took in the photo. "That's a little overdramatic, don't you think? Wait. I forgot. You're a soprano, so you're allowed to be—"

"We're not a couple!" she cried. "How could they say something like that?"

"I *am* carrying you." He examined the paparazzi photo more closely. As usual, he'd photographed well, but The Diva had been caught at an odd angle so that her very tidy butt looked larger than it was in reality.

She tugged at the silk scarf around her throat as if it were strangling her. "How could this have happened?"

"Bad angle, that's all. Forget about it."

She looked at him without comprehension, and he made a quick U-turn. "I'll admit the whole thing is strange." He thought back to the previous night. No one, including him, had known he and The Diva were going to end up at that bar, so it had to have been a random bystander. And yet . . .

"Is there a problem?" Henri had come back and joined them. Paisley popped up over his shoulder.

Olivia thrust the paper at him. "Look at this!"

"Putain!" Henri choked the ends of his neck scarf. "*Pardon* my profanity, Olivia, Paisley."

Dude was old school for a forty-year-old.

"This is great?" Paisley was an expert at both vocal fry and turning her statements into questions. "Lots of people will see it. Brand recognition and everything."

"Not the sort of brand recognition we aspire to." Henri took a deep breath and shrugged. "Ah, well. These things happen."

"Not to me." Olivia spun on Thad. "This is your fault. I've never had a single paparazzo follow me, not once in my entire career. It's because of you. You and your—your"—her hands flew in his direction—"your face, and your hair, and your body, and those actresses you date . . ."

On and on she went. He let her vent, figuring that, sooner or later, she'd come to her senses, even though she was a soprano.

He figured correctly. She finally ran out of steam and sank into the seat across the aisle from him. "I know this isn't really your fault, but— Nothing like this has ever happened to me."

"I understand," he said with all kinds of sympathy.

Clint snorted.

Olivia turned to Henri, showing a depth of concern Thad didn't feel. He was more upset about having The Diva's name printed before his in the headline.

"I apologize, Henri," she said. "I know this isn't the image you want for Marchand. Nothing like this will ever happen again."

Henri gave one of those Gallic shrugs only a true Frenchman could pull off. "You mustn't distress yourself. Phoenix is behind us, and we have a full day ahead in Los Angeles, yes?"

To his credit, Marchand didn't ask what they had been doing last night. Instead, he gave Paisley a series of instructions about the day's itinerary, but as Paisley retreated, she had eyes only for Garrett.

Olivia eventually moved to her seat at the front and donned the purple headset she pulled from her tote.

Garrett turned his attention back to Thad. "So here's what I've been thinking about, T-Bo. When I was out with that thumb sprain. The Giants game. Third and four. Their D was waiting for the screen, and you shifted to an inside run. How'd you know they were expecting the screen? What tipped you off?"

Thad gave in to the inevitable. "I was reading the linebacker."

"But what did he do? What did you see?"

"Always watch the middle linebacker, you idiot. Now leave me alone so I can kill myself."

Clint reached across the aisle to slap him on the leg. "You know you love me, T-Bo, and we both know why. I'm your last best chance at immortality."

With that, the son of a bitch went off to flirt with Paisley.

More reporters showed up in LA than in Phoenix, and five seconds into the first interview, Thad knew why.

The reporter was young, punk, and tatted. She balanced her notebook on the knee of her black cargo pants and asked her first question. "The two of you come from, like, such different worlds, so how do you, like, explain your attraction?"

Thad could see The Diva getting all ramped up to deny everything, which would only lead to more speculation, so before she could say a word, he cut in. "Aw, we're only friends." He gave the reporter a conspiratorial wink just for the fun of it. What The Diva couldn't see wouldn't hurt her.

Henri rushed forward from his position behind the couch. "Thad and Madame Shore might be from different worlds, but they both appreciate quality."

Thad did his job. He showed off the Victory780, and Olivia roused herself enough to talk about the Cavatina3. Henri expanded his pitch. "At Marchand, we understand that men and women want different things from their timepieces. Men's wardrobes are more conservative, so they tend to like a more ornate watch."

"Present company excepted," Olivia said with a glance at the amoeba print on Thad's dress shirt.

He didn't appreciate her lack of respect for his personal style. Still, he had to admit she looked pretty damn good, even in that black-and-white outfit she'd worn on the plane. Watch on one wrist, bracelets on the other, and her crumpled gold earrings. No other ornamentation, as long as he didn't count her killer gray stilettos.

"The more subtle styling of the Cavatina3," Henri said, "fits perfectly into the life of a successful woman like Madame Shore. It goes from day to night. Office to gym. It's both classic and sporty."

When the reporter tried to turn the interview back to the personal, Olivia stiffened up like a poker. "Thad and I only met two days ago. We barely know each other."

The Diva might be a star in the opera world, but she didn't know crap about dealing with the celebrity press, and that was exactly the wrong thing to say. He smiled. "Some people just hit it off from the start."

"Professionally," The Diva added, as prim as an old lady at a Victorian tea party.

The reporter shifted her notebook to the other knee. "That photo of the two of you looks like you have more than a professional relationship."

The Diva's lips pursed, and he could see she was about to issue another denial, so he jumped in again. "We were having fun, that's for sure. Liv didn't think I could bench press her, but I had my buddy use the timer on my Victory780 to prove her wrong. One minute point four three seconds. I guess I showed her."

The Diva regarded him with so much incredulity she might as well have told the reporter straight out that he was lying.

The reporter laughed. “Okay. I get the message. No more questions.”

Henri accompanied Paisley to show her out, as if he didn’t trust his assistant to do the job alone, leaving Thad with less than a minute before the next reporter appeared. He pulled Olivia off the couch and hauled her through the closest door.

“What . . . ?”

He pressed her against the powder room sink. “Will you relax and stop acting like they found a sex tape.”

“How can I relax? Everybody is going to think we’re—we’re—”

“Lovers? So what? We’re both adults, and as far as I know, neither of us is married. You’re not, are you? Because I don’t mess around with married women.”

“Of course I’m not married!” she sputtered.

“Then we’re good.”

“We’re not good, and we’re not messing around. It looks like we’re—whatever. We only met two days ago.”

“I get it. You don’t want Rupert to think you’re easy.”

“I’m not easy!”

“Tell me about it. Now stop getting so wound up. Relax and smile.” As Thad turned her toward the powder room door, he smiled to himself. It wasn’t like him to give a woman a hard time, but The Diva was such a worthy adversary that he couldn't seem to help himself.

They emerged together, directly in the path of the next reporter.

To his surprise, The Diva pulled on a smile. "You're welcome, Thad." And then, to the reporter, "He wouldn't believe me when I said he had half his lunch stuck in his front teeth. A shame to let a ham sandwich spoil those shiny, white veneers. I'm sure he paid a fortune for them."

His teeth were all his own, but that didn't mean a thing. The Diva had grabbed the ball out of his hands and run it into the end zone.

That night, after the obligatory client dinner, Thad met some of his LA buddies in the hotel's rooftop bar for a late-night drink. He didn't invite The Diva to come along, even though the bar's ivy-covered pavilion and great views were more her style than last night's venue.

He hadn't seen these guys in months, and he should have had a great time, especially since Garrett didn't show up. But after last night, the evening felt anticlimactic, and he was in bed by two.

As Olivia's best friend Rachel Cullen and her husband Dennis settled under a blue umbrella on the hotel restaurant's patio the next day, their hands met, and Olivia regarded them wistfully. "You two are disgusting."

Rachel squeezed her husband's hand. "You're sooo jealous."

"An understatement," Olivia replied. "You found the only man on the planet who was born to marry an opera singer." If Olivia could find his clone, she might be able to have a lasting relationship.

"Best job ever," Dennis said.

Olivia gazed at her friend. "I hate you."

Rachel gave her a smug smile. "Of course you do."

With her silky, ash-blond hair, generous curves, and girl-next-door features, Rachel could have passed for the neighborhood's prettiest soccer mom, while Dennis Cullen's unruly mop of brown hair, big nose, and wiry build made him look more like a musician than his wife, although he made his living working temp jobs in IT.

Olivia and Rachel had met over ten years earlier at the Ryan Opera Center, the prestigious artistic development program at Chicago's Lyric Opera. In the old days of opera rivalries, two mezzos competing for the same roles would never have become such close friends, but at the Lyric, mutual support and collaboration weren't only encouraged but were expected. They'd formed a tight bond, helping and commiserating with each other as they'd worked side by side on the mezzo repertoire. Olivia was the more gifted singer and performer, but instead of being jealous, Rachel had become Olivia's most enthusiastic cheerleader.

As the years had passed, Olivia's career had soared, while Rachel's merely remained respectable, but that hadn't interfered with their friendship. Olivia continued to recommend Rachel for roles. They laughed and cried together. Olivia had been at Rachel's side when her mother had died, and Rachel had held Olivia's hand through Adam's horrible, soul-wrenching funeral, something neither of them would ever forget. As Olivia studied the menu, she pretended not to see her friend's concerned look. Rachel was intuitive, and she knew more was wrong than Olivia was letting on.

Their server appeared. Dennis ordered a chopped Thai salad for Rachel and crab cakes for himself.

"He even orders for you," Olivia said as the server disappeared.

"He knows what I like better than I do."

Olivia had a flashback to Adam, who used to ask Olivia to order for him because he couldn't make up his mind. Being around Dennis could be painful. His dedication to Rachel's career formed a distinct contrast to the resentment Adam had worked so hard to suppress. Dennis was an opera singer's dream husband.

Rachel unwrapped her napkin. "Tell me the story of how you and Dennis met."

"Again?" Olivia said. "I've told you the story a dozen times."

"I never get tired of hearing it."

"She's like a child," Olivia remarked to Dennis. And then to Rachel, "Should I start before or after he hit on me?"

Dennis groaned.

"Before," Rachel chirped.

Olivia settled in. "I'd just started my period, and I had crazy bad cramps—"

"And a sugar craving," Rachel added.

"It's my story," Olivia protested. "Anyway, I decided to soothe myself with a Starbucks Red Velvet Frappuccino."

Rachel, whose sweet tooth continued to plump up her curves, nodded. "Very sensible."

"I'm standing in line and this crazy-looking musician type tries to strike up a conversation."

Rachel poked her husband. "You were totally hitting on her."

Olivia smiled and proceeded with the unnecessary story. "I wasn't in the mood to talk, but he was persistent. And kind of cute."

"And not a singer," Rachel said. "Don't forget the best part."

"A techie, as I learned even before the barista finished making my Frappuccino."

"Which he gallantly paid for."

"And which made me feel obligated to talk to him. The rest is history."

"You're skipping the best part. The part where you gave him my phone number without asking my permission, even though he could have been a serial killer."

"Which he wasn't."

"But I could have been," Dennis said.

Olivia smiled. "I liked him. Unfortunately, I couldn't keep him for myself because I was still under Adam's spell." The table sobered, and Rachel's look of concern returned. Olivia assumed an overly bright smile. "Bottom line. I loved being maid of honor at your wedding last year."

Rachel nodded. "And you sang the most beautiful 'Voi che sapete' anyone has ever heard."

Their food arrived. Rachel was in town auditioning for a role next winter at the LA Opera and they began trading opera gossip—a tenor with too much head voice and a conductor who refused to give Rossini the room to breathe. They talked about the amazing acoustics at Hamburg's Elbphilarmonie and a new biography of Callas.

Olivia envied the pride Dennis took in his wife's accomplishments. Rachel's career always came first, and he arranged his own work around her schedule. Unlike her life with Adam. Only now did Olivia see that Adam had been suffering from depression. He'd had trouble memorizing a new libretto, and his periods of insomnia alternated with nights he'd sleep for twelve or thirteen hours. But instead of getting him to a doctor, she'd broken up with him. And now he was having his revenge.

This is your fault. Choke on it.

Rachel grimaced. "Did you hear that Ricci is singing *Carmen* in Prague? I hate her."

Olivia refocused. "'Hate' is a strong word."

"You've always been nicer than me."

Sophia Ricci was, in fact, a lovely person, although Olivia had gone through a brief period of resenting her because she'd once been Adam's girlfriend. That wasn't, however, the reason for Rachel's complaint. Sophia was a lyric soprano, and whenever a lyric took over one of the few leading roles written for a mezzo, it always stirred up resentment. "Maybe she'll get laryngitis," Olivia said, and then retreated. "I'm being awful. Sophia's an amazing talent, and I wish her well."

"But not super well." Rachel extracted a cashew from her salad. "Just enough so the critics write something like, 'Sophia Ricci's "Habanera," while competent, can't compete with the commanding sensuality of Olivia Shore's exquisite Carmen.'"

Olivia smiled fondly at her generous friend. More than anyone, Olivia understood how much Rachel would love to perform Carmen in a top-tier house like the Muni, but those invitations never came her way.

"I've taken over Rachel's social media," Dennis said. "Exposure is everything. Look at all the mezzos in pop music—Beyoncé, Adele, Gaga. Those women understand how to use social media."

A too-familiar face appeared across the patio. Thad spotted Olivia and headed toward their table. As Olivia performed the introductions, she noticed that Rachel had that half-dazed look so many women seemed to adopt whenever Thad Owens came into their view.

"Please." Rachel gestured toward the empty seat at the table. "We're almost done eating, but feel free to order something."

"I just finished lunch." He looked at Olivia. "A couple of sports reporters."

Olivia felt a stab of guilt knowing he was working harder than she was.

Dennis and Thad exchanged some surface football talk before the conversation turned back to opera. "Lena Hodiak told me she's covering for you in *Aida*," Rachel said. "You'll like her. She sang Gertrude in *Hansel and Gretel* last year in San Diego, and she's lovely."

Thad regarded her questioningly.

"That means Lena is her understudy," Rachel explained. "Covering for Olivia is a thankless job, as Lena'll discover. Olivia never gets sick."

Dennis jumped in. "Tell me about this gig you have with Marchand. How did the two of you snag it?"

"I was at least their third choice," Thad said without a trace of rancor.

"I got a call from my agent last September," Olivia said. "I had an open spot in my schedule, and the money was great. Also, I thought I'd be traveling with Cooper Graham, the Stars' former quarterback."

"Instead, she got lucky," Thad said.

Olivia smiled and glanced at her watch. "I wish we could talk longer, but we have a photo op coming up, and Thad needs time to make sure his hair is perfect."

Thad pushed back his chair. "She's jealous because I photograph better than she does."

Rachel frowned at him, ready to leap to her friend's defense, but Olivia shrugged. "Sad, but true."

Thad laughed. Dennis jumped to his feet and pulled out his cell. "Let me get a couple of photos first for Rachel's social media. I'll tag you both."

Olivia suspected Thad wasn't any more interested in being tagged than she was, but she adored Dennis's enthusiasm. How could she not be envious?

They opened the door of their suite to the sight of Henri engaged in a heated conversation with an elegant woman who appeared to be around his age, perhaps early forties. She had a sleek European look: an all-black pencil dress with multiple strands of pearls at her neck. Her blunt-cut hair fell from a middle part to just below her jaw. Next to her, a cowed Paisley rapidly blinked her eyes, as if she were trying not to cry, making Olivia suspect this woman wasn't as inclined to ignore Paisley's incompetence as Henri. In fairness, while Paisley was spoiled, disorganized, and grossly immature, Olivia had seen the photos on her iPhone, and she had to admit Paisley had a good eye for Thad Owens's ass.

Henri broke off the conversation as soon as he spotted them. "Mariel, look who has joined us. Olivia, Thad, this is my cousin Mariel."

Mariel gave them a very French smile—cordial but restrained—and a businesslike handshake. "Mariel Marchand. It's a pleasure."

She was more handsome than pretty, with a high forehead, aquiline nose, and small eyes enlarged with bold eye makeup.

"Mariel is our chief financial officer," he said. "She's come to check up on us."

Olivia had done enough research to know that Lucien Marchand, the head of the company, was in his seventies and childless. Mariel and Henri, his niece and nephew, were his only blood relatives, and one of them would take over the family firm. It wasn't hard to see that Mariel had the advantage over genial Henri.

"I trust my cousin is not making you work too hard," Mariel replied in an accent less marked than Henri's.

"Only Thad," Olivia said honestly. "I have it easier."

"I heard you at the Opéra Bastille two years ago as Klytaemnestra in *Elektra. Incroyable.*" She turned her attention to Thad without waiting for Olivia to acknowledge the compliment. "You must explain this game you play to me," she said.

"Nothing much to it, really. Run a little, pass a little, keep the ball away from the bad guys."

"How intriguing."

Olivia mentally rolled her eyes and excused herself.

Mariel was with them at their client dinner that night, lending a touch of French elegance to the affair and flattering Thad outrageously. "You have to be so strong to play this game. So agile."

"So brainless," Olivia muttered because . . . how could she resist?

Thad overheard and leaned back in his chair. "Some of us are born to win." He gave Olivia a lazy smile. "Others seem to keep dying on the job."

He had a point. Olivia had lost count of how many times she'd been stabbed to death in *Carmen* or crushed to death as Delilah. In *Dido and Aeneas*, she'd expired from the weight of her grief, and in *Il trovatore*, she'd barely escaped a fiery pyre. None of which took into account the people she'd killed.

Thad didn't seem to know much about opera, so she wasn't sure how he knew about all the bloodthirsty roles she'd sung, but she suspected Google had a hand in it. She'd done some googling of her own and discovered that nearly every article about Thaddeus Walker

Bowman Owens mentioned not only his physical skills and dating life, but the respect his teammates had for him.

She was beginning to understand why, and their four weeks together no longer seemed quite so long.

"You didn't have to come with me, you know?" Olivia said, as they climbed the trail above the Griffith Observatory, not far from where the Uber had dropped them off. It was barely six in the morning, and the air smelled of dew and sage. "If I'd known you were going to be such a grouch, I wouldn't have invited you."

"You didn't invite me, remember? I overheard you last night at dinner talking about hiking up here this morning." Thad yawned. "It wouldn't have been right for me to stay in bed while you're working yourself to death."

"I'm not the only one. Whenever we have any downtime, you're either on the phone or on your computer. What's that about?"

"Video game addiction."

She didn't believe him, although she'd noticed he never left his laptop open. "We're leaving for San Francisco in a couple of hours." She took in the Hollywood sign far above them. "This was the only time I could get any exercise."

"Or you could have stayed in bed."

"Easy for you to say. You've been working out while all I've done is eat."

"And drink," he pointed out unhelpfully.

"That, too. Unfortunately, the era of the obese opera singer is over." She stepped around a pile of horse manure. "In the old days, all you had to do was take center stage and sing. Now you have to look at least a little bit plausible. Unless you're doing the *Ring* cycle. If I had the voice and the endurance to sing Brünnhilde, I could eat whatever I wanted. Let's face it. You can't sing Brünnhilde's battle cry if you're a sylph."

"I'll take your word for it."

She wished she could let loose with a little of Brünnhilde's "Ho-jo-to-ho!" right here on the trail just to see if she could make T-Bo lose his cool, but she didn't have it in her.

They were gaining elevation and moving at a fast enough clip that she needed to watch her footing. She remembered hiking up here with Rachel a few years ago. Whenever the two of them approached a steep ascent, Rachel, who was less fit, would ask Olivia a question requiring such an involved answer that Olivia would end up talking through the entire climb while Rachel conserved her energy. It had taken Olivia forever to catch on to her tricks.

"Enough about me." She beamed at him. "Tell me your life story."

He took the bait as they climbed. "Great childhood. Great parents. Almost great career."

He began walking faster. She fell into his rhythm, at the same time keeping her distance from the drop-off to her left. "I need details."

"Only child. Spoiled rotten. My mom is a retired social worker and my dad's an accountant."

"You, of course, were a star student, quarterback of the high school football team, and homecoming king."

"I got robbed. They gave the crown to Larry Quivers because he'd just broken up with his girlfriend, and everybody felt sorry for him."

"That's the kind of tragedy that builds character."

"For *Larry*."

She laughed. The trail was getting steeper still, the city stretching below them, and again, he'd picked up the pace. "What else?" she said.

"I worked for a landscaping company during the summers. Played for the University of Kentucky and graduated with a degree in finance."

"Impressive."

"I was drafted and signed by the Giants. Also played for the Broncos and the Cowboys before I came to Chicago."

"Why the two middle names? Walker Bowman?"

"Mom wanted her father honored. Dad wanted the honor to go to his grandfather. They drew straws to see which name came first, and Mom won."

They were practically jogging, and she berated herself for that slab of chocolate truffle layer cake she'd had for dessert last night. This was what happened when you hiked with a competitive athlete. A leisurely morning climb turned into an endurance contest. Which she didn't intend to lose.

No question he was the stronger of the two. Her thighs were starting to burn, and she seemed to be getting a blister on her little toe, but he was already breathing harder than she was. Any second now, he'd realize exactly how much breath control a professionally trained opera singer possessed.

"Married? Divorced?" she asked.

"Neither."

"That's because you haven't met anybody as good-looking as you, right?"

"I can't help the way I look, okay?"

He actually sounded testy. Fascinating. She was storing that information away as ammunition for future use when she came to a sudden stop. "Look at that." Out of the corner of her eye, she'd spotted a small hole in the ground underneath some brush. And right in front of that hole . . .

An arm slammed around her chest, pulling her back. She yelped, *"Hey!"*

"That's a tarantula!" he exclaimed.

"I know it's a tarantula." She wiggled free. "It's a beauty."

He shuddered. "It's a tarantula!"

"And it's not hurting a soul. Remember our agreement. I handle the bugs and snakes. You deal with the rodents."

The tarantula scampered back into its hole. Thad pressed her ahead of him on the trail, away from the nest. "Move it!"

"Sissy." She'd begged for a tarantula as a pet, but her staid, conservative parents had refused. They'd been older when she was born, dedicated musicians who'd preferred not having their lives disrupted. Still, they'd loved her, and she missed them. They'd died within a few months of each other.

"I'll bet you didn't know that female tarantulas can live for twenty-five years," she said, "but once the male matures, he only lives for a few months."

"And women think they have it tough."

Her cell rang in her pocket. The number wasn't familiar, probably a junk call, but her thighs needed a break, and she answered. "Hello?"

"*Che gelida manina* . . ." At the sound of the familiar music, the phone slipped from her fingers.

Thad, with his athlete's reflexes, caught it before it hit the ground. He put the phone to his ear and listened. She heard the music coming faintly from the phone. She snatched it away from him, shut it off, and shoved it back in her pocket.

"You want to tell me about that?" he said.

"No." They hadn't reached the summit, but she turned and began heading back down the trail. Then, because she didn't have to make eye contact with him, she said, "It's Rodolfo's love song to Mimì in *La bohème.*"

"And?"

"*Che gelida manina* . . . It means, 'What a cold little hand.'" She shuddered. "I told him not to sing it."

"Who?"

The sun was coming up, and so was the temperature. She fixed her eyes on the observatory in the distance. She didn't have to say anything. She could clam up right now. But he was steady and solid, and she wanted to tell him. "It's a popular audition piece for tenors, but Adam couldn't manage the high C. He had to take it down a half tone—high C becomes a top B-natural. But that only showcases a weakness. I tried to talk him out of auditioning with it, but I couldn't."

"Adam?"

"Adam Wheeler. My former fiancé."

"And this is how the asshole treats you? He calls you up like some lunatic and—"

"You don't understand." She took an unsteady breath. "Adam is dead."

5

Olivia shuddered. "That song . . . It's a voice from the grave."

"Do you want to tell me about it?" Thad phrased it as a request, but it sounded more like a demand.

"It's not a happy story."

"I can handle it." They'd come to a bench on the trail, and he gestured toward it, but she didn't want to sit. She didn't want to look at him. She did, however, want to tell him. She wanted to let down the guard she'd been holding on to so tightly it was choking her and tell this man she barely knew what she'd only been able to hint at with Rachel.

She moved ahead of him so she didn't have to make eye contact. "Adam was a good tenor, but not a great one. He was fine in the more undemanding comprimario parts—secondary roles. He had the will, but not the instrument to handle bigger parts."

"Unlike you."

"Unlike me." She'd also worked harder than Adam, but she worked harder than nearly everyone, and she couldn't fault him for not keeping up. "We had everything in common—music, our dedication to our careers. He'd go into schools and talk to the students about music. He was great with kids. Loved animals. A sweet, sensitive man. And he adored me." She stepped over a rocky trench to a smoother section of the trail. "When he proposed, I accepted."

"Did you love him?"

"He was perfect. How could I not?"

"So you didn't love him."

She hesitated. "I was happy."

"Except when you weren't."

Except when she wasn't. She slowed to keep from slipping on a patch of shale. "I knew it bothered him that I was at a place in my career he couldn't reach." She was ashamed of how often she'd attempted to make herself smaller so she didn't hurt him. She'd turned down a role she should have taken, and when a rehearsal or performance had gone especially well, she downplayed it. But he always knew. He'd grow silent. Occasionally, he'd snap at her for something inconsequential. He'd always apologize and blame his bad mood on lack of sleep or a headache, but Olivia knew the real cause.

They rounded a bend. "I don't like to fail, and I got very good at self-deception. Even though I was growing more and more unhappy, I wouldn't admit to myself that I'd stopped loving him."

"Since none of those rings you like to wear have a diamond in them, I'm assuming you came to your senses."

"Too late." Thinking about it still made her cringe. "A week before the wedding, I called it off. One week! It was the hardest thing I've ever done. The worst thing I've ever done. I waited too long, and I broke his heart."

"Better than condemning him to a bad marriage."

"He didn't see it that way. He was devastated and humiliated." She couldn't dodge this next part, and she finally looked up at him. "He killed himself two and a half months later. Exactly nineteen days ago." Her throat caught. "There was a suicide note. A suicide email, really. Modern life, right? He told me how much he'd loved me and that I'd ruined his life. Then he hit 'send' and shot himself."

Thad winced. "That's tough. Killing yourself is one thing, but blaming it on someone else . . . That's low."

She took in the vista around them without seeing a thing. "He was so sensitive. I knew that, and yet . . . I should have been more careful. I should have broken it off as soon as I knew it wasn't right, but I was too stubborn."

"The phone call you just had . . . The note you got yesterday . . . There's more to this story, isn't there?"

Thad was so much smarter than he looked. "There've been two other notes."

"The one I saw said, 'This is your fault. Choke on it.' Were the others like that?"

"The first one said, 'Don't ever forget what you've done to me.' The morning the tour started, there was another. 'You did this to me.'" A helicopter chopped overhead. "Until now, I thought he'd written the notes before he died and found people to mail them for him. But that phone call . . . It's from a recording he made."

"Obviously, he wasn't the one who made the call."

"Whoever he got to mail the letters must have done it. I don't know. He was never vindictive."

"Until he sent you his suicide email."

"It was wrenching. And these notes . . ."

"Either he planned this before he killed himself, got someone to mail the notes and make that phone call, or you have an enemy on this side of the grave. Do you have any idea who that could be?"

She hesitated, but she was already in this far, and she might as well go the rest of the way. "His sisters were devastated, and they blame me. Growing up, it was only Adam, his mother, and his two sisters. He was the golden child. They all doted on him. Every spare dollar any of them made went toward his voice lessons. After his mother died, it was just his sisters. When I came into the picture, they weren't happy."

"They were jealous of you?"

"It's more that they were protective of him. They wanted him with a woman who'd put his career first. Definitely not one with a big career of her own. If they found out he blew an audition or didn't get a part, they blamed me. They thought I wasn't supporting him in the way I should—that I put my career ahead of his. But I didn't!" She looked up at him, pleading for understanding and hating herself for needing it. "I did everything I could to help him. I recommended him for roles. I turned down some opportunities of my own so I could be with him."

He shook his head at her. "You women. How many men would do something like that?"

"He was special."

"If you say so."

She rubbed her arm and felt the gritty trail dust on her skin. "There was an autopsy, so the funeral was delayed. I don't check my email regularly, and I didn't see it until a week after he died."

"The suicide email?"

"I should never have gone to the funeral. It turned into a scene right out of Puccini. Two sisters mad with grief publicly accusing me of killing him. It was horrible." She blinked her eyes against a sting of tears. "Adam was everything to them."

"That doesn't excuse them for blaming you."

"I think that's what they need to do to work through their grief."

"Very self-sacrificing. I'm traveling with Mother Teresa."

"It's not like that."

"Isn't it? From where I stand, it looks like you're hauling around a truckload of guilt for something you didn't cause."

"But obviously I did cause it. I was a coward. I agreed to marry him, even though in my heart I knew it wasn't right. And then I waited until a week before the ceremony to end it. How's that for cowardly?"

"Not as cowardly as going ahead with it." He drew her gently to a stop. "Promise to tell me if you get any more of these surprises."

"This is my problem. There's no need—"

"Yes, there is. Until this tour is over, whatever happens to you affects me. I want your word that you'll tell me."

She shouldn't have said this much, but there was something about him that invited confidences. She reluctantly agreed.

On the way back, she checked the number on her phone and tried to call. A recorded message said it was no longer in service.

When they returned to the suite, Henri greeted them with the news that there was a weather alert for San Francisco. "I heard from the pilot. We need to leave quickly, or you'll miss your afternoon interviews."

Olivia took a fast shower, grabbed a clean pair of yoga pants, and put on a long white sweater. She'd pull herself together on the plane.

Thad had never seen Olivia without makeup. Even that morning when they'd hiked, she'd had on lipstick and maybe some kind of tinted sunscreen. Now, with a scrubbed face and her hair pulled into a ponytail, she looked younger. Less like a diva and more like a really hot barista working at the counter of a funky coffee shop where none of the mugs matched.

Mariel was already on the plane when they got there. She drew Henri aside for what appeared to be a volatile conversation that indicated a less-than-friendly relationship. Paisley was intimidated by Mariel in a way she wasn't by Henri and spent the trip huddled against the rear bulkhead trying to make herself invisible.

Not long before they landed, Olivia emerged from the plane's bathroom in one of her classic outfits. A charcoal power dress with a crisscrossed purple belt and a couple of her big jewelry pieces. It was stylish, elegant, and expensive. He missed the hot barista.

Mariel sent Paisley off to deal with the luggage and accompanied Henri to Thad and Olivia's live appearance on a noontime news and talk show. Afterward, they taped an interview at one of the local cable stations. The photograph of Thad carrying Olivia came up, and this time Olivia dove right in with the bench-pressing story. The host laughed, the watches were spotlighted, and a good time was had by all.

Except Mariel.

"Olivia should not be so frivolous in her interviews," the Frenchwoman told Thad later that day, as she escorted him to another radio station, while Paisley hid and Henri shepherded Olivia to afternoon tea with a group of fashion bloggers. "There is a certain dignity associated with the Marchand brand."

Mariel's imperious manner was getting under his skin. "It made good television. You're trying to reach younger consumers, and dignity doesn't count for much with them."

Mariel gave one of her Gallic shrugs. She was an imposing woman—no doubt about it—but he was glad to see Henri waiting for him at their San Francisco hotel.

This time, he and The Diva were placed in separate smaller suites, and that night's client dinner took place in the hotel dining room. Thad was growing to heartily dislike these dinners, which lasted forever and required too much small talk. Still, they were part of what he'd signed up for, and he was too well paid to complain.

The Diva, he'd noticed, had been restricting herself to a single glass of wine since their altercation on the terrace. Mariel dominated the conversation with facts and figures about the Marchand brand, and Henri's customary affability seemed ruffled at the edges.

At eleven, when dinner finally ended, Thad headed for the fitness center instead of going to bed. But even after a long workout, he had trouble falling asleep. He kept thinking about the disturbing notes The Diva had been receiving.

He also had the disquieting feeling there was more she wasn't telling him.

After his morning shower, he called her. "Have you eaten breakfast yet?"

"I'm never eating again."

"Problematic."

"Did you see the way I demolished that crème brûlée last night?"

"Not my favorite. Too sweet."

"There is no such thing as too sweet. What's wrong with you? And why are you calling me?"

"I was getting ready to order room service breakfast, and I don't like to eat alone."

"Is that an invitation?"

"It was, but you sound grouchy, so forget it."

"Black coffee for me, and I'll be there in half an hour."

"Wait. I said I was reconsid—"

She'd hung up. He smiled and put in a call to room service—coffee and a couple of poached eggs for him. Coffee and a Belgian waffle for her.

She and the food cart arrived at the same time. She was ready for the morning's photo shoot—a dress that showcased her legs, stilettos, the pigeon's egg ruby necklace. He'd gone for jeans and a multicolored shawl-collar pullover. "You look so comfortable," she said wistfully.

"Another glaring example of gender inequality." He admired the shining swing of her hair, then directed her to the table by the window and pulled the warming covers from their meals.

"You're a sadist," she said, as he set the strawberry-and-whipped-cream-topped waffle in front of her.

"I'll eat whatever you don't want."

"Touch this and you die."

He laughed. He liked Olivia. He liked her smarts and her quirky sense of humor. So what if she was a little high-strung? So was he. He just hid it better.

She picked up her fork. "Did you see the way Mariel kept raising her eyebrows at me last night? All because I was eating my dinner instead of licking it like she did."

"Didn't see that." But he'd heard Mariel tell one of the guests how fortunate it was that Olivia had chosen a career where she didn't have to worry about her weight. Since Olivia's body was as spectacular as her voice, he suspected Mariel was jealous.

"Was your luggage okay?"

It took him a moment to adjust to her change of topic. "What do you mean? Are you missing one of your three hundred and forty-two suitcases?"

"Don't exaggerate. No, nothing's missing, but . . ." She shrugged. "I packed quickly, and things shift around when they're being moved." She waved a dismissive hand. "Forget it."

"You think somebody went through your luggage?"

"I'm probably being paranoid." With more than half her waffle still remaining, Olivia pushed aside her plate.

"Don't let Mariel stop you from enjoying your breakfast," he said.

"I'm full. Contrary to her opinion, I don't make a habit of stuffing myself."

He refilled their coffee cups. "Have you heard from Rupert?"

"No, why?"

"Just wondering if he's come up with anything new to gain your attention."

"What's this thing you've got about Rupert?"

"I had a stalker once. A woman I'd never met who decided we were soul mates."

"Rupert isn't a stalker. He's a fan."

"So was she. She started showing up everywhere I went. Eventually, she got into my apartment. The police were involved. There was a restraining order. It got ugly."

"So what happened?"

"She spent some time in jail and eventually moved out of state."

"Rupert isn't like that."

His own experience, combined with that phone call, the threatening letters, and now the possibility that someone had gone through her luggage made him wary. There was also the mystery of who'd taken the photo of them outside that Phoenix bar four nights ago. Had it been random or something more deliberate?

He cornered Henri later that morning. "Make sure Olivia and I have adjoining suites from now on, will you? And if you could have the staff move me before tonight so I'm next to her, I'd appreciate it."

"Adjoining suites?" Henri didn't seem surprised, but then he was a Frenchman. "Of course."

Thad didn't see any reason to tell Henri this was about security, not sex, even though his own lizard brain kept slithering in exactly that direction.

"They moved me because they had to fumigate my suite," he told Olivia that night as he let himself into the suite next to hers after their last client dinner in San Francisco.

"Fumigate? Against what?"

"Hey, you're the bug expert. Not me."

"There are bugs, and then there are bedbugs. You didn't ask?"

"Naw." The last thing he needed was Olivia talking to the hotel manager about bedbugs. "I think they said something about ants."

"That's odd."

"I don't make the rules. I just follow them."

"When it suits you."

"What do you mean by that?"

"You've got 'rule breaker' written all over that exquisite face of yours. You just hide it behind fake charm." With an operatic sweep, she disappeared into her suite.

He gazed at the door she'd closed between them. He had an instinct for spotting trouble—a free safety shifting his body to the left, a lineman switching the hand he had on the ground. It was part of his job to be alert, and he wanted The Diva nearby. Now all he had to do was come up with a logical reason to keep their connecting door open.

He undressed, brushed his teeth, and pulled on a pair of sweatpants before he rapped on the door between their rooms.

"What do you want?" she said from the other side.

He rapped again.

She finally opened the door. He didn't know exactly what he'd expected her to be wearing, but it was something along the lines of a filmy black negligee with maybe a frilly sleep mask pushed on top of her head. Instead, she wore a Chicago Jazz Festival T-shirt and pajama bottoms printed with dill pickles.

He groaned. "My eyes will never be the same."

She let her own eyes roam over his bare chest, taking her time. "Mine, either."

Her open appreciation of his hard-earned muscles nearly threw him off his game. She smiled, knowing she'd gotten the advantage. "You remind me of an art museum," she said. "Look all you want, but don't touch."

"Some museums are designed for a more sensory experience."

She was tough. She didn't miss a beat. "Been there. Done that. Not doing it again. What's wrong?"

He rubbed his chin. "This is embarrassing."

"All the better."

"I'd appreciate it if you'd keep it to yourself, but . . . Once you're ready to turn out the lights, would you mind leaving the door between us open?"

"Oh, dear . . . Afraid of the dark?"

He thought fast. "More like . . . claustrophobia."

"Claustrophobia?"

"It hits now and then, okay? Forget I asked. I know how you women like to complain about men being afraid to show their vulnerability, but the minute one of us lets you see his sensitive side—"

"It's fine. I'll leave the door open." She regarded him suspiciously. "Maybe you should talk to a therapist."

"You think I haven't?" He improvised. "Bottom line—closed-door phobia is nothing to mess with."

She wasn't stupid, and one of those dark, arched eyebrows shot halfway up her forehead. "This is your first step in trying to seduce me, isn't it?"

He propped his elbow against the doorjamb and gave her a lazy once-over. "Babe, if I wanted to seduce you, you'd be hot and naked by now."

That rattled her. Unfortunately, he'd also gotten hard, so she wasn't the only one rattled.

That night, as he lay in bed in the dark, he heard the jazz strains of Bill Evans's "Peace Piece" drifting through the darkness. The lady knew good jazz.

He escorted The Diva to the hotel lobby the next morning, where Henri delivered the good news that Mariel had left for New York. "Our limo is waiting outside." He glanced at his watch and frowned. "If you'll excuse me, I'll see what's holding Paisley up."

"Probably texting her BFFs," Olivia muttered as they made their way outside.

"You're jealous because she likes me a lot more than she likes you," he retorted.

She grinned. "And she likes Clint more than she likes you, old man."

"I'm gutted."

"Speaking of BFFs . . ." Olivia pulled out her phone and called her friend Rachel. Unfortunately, part of their conversation centered around something called chest voice, which made him want to stare at exactly that part of Liv's anatomy.

Just as they finished, Paisley slid into the limo. The only makeup she had on was left from the night before. She hadn't combed her hair, and she didn't look apologetic. "I overslept."

Henri got in behind her, grim-faced. "So sorry for keeping you both waiting."

"Pas de problème," Olivia said.

Henri and Olivia engaged in a rapid-fire conversation *en français*, which Paisley interrupted. "Ohmygod! You're on Ratchet Up!"

"What is this?" Henri asked.

She lowered her phone. "Ratchet Up. It's this online gossip site everybody reads." She showed them, and there they were. Thad and Olivia. Returning to the hotel yesterday morning from their hike. Olivia's hair was falling out of her ponytail, and Thad had his hand on her shoulder. They looked like a couple.

"This is news?" Henri said. "This is nothing."

Paisley regarded him condescendingly. "People like gossip. I told you that. And Thad and Olivia make a glam couple because they're, like, so different. This is going to get us all kinds of eyeballs."

"Eyeballs?"

"People looking at it," Paisley said impatiently.

Henri remained unconvinced. "I doubt the people who follow that site are interested in buying Marchand watches."

"Are you kidding? All the celebs read Ratchet Up, and this is the kind of stuff we need to post. Or at least feed to the gossip sites."

"No feeding to gossip sites," Olivia said. "I have a professional reputation to think about."

That pissed him off. "What about my reputation? Do you think I want the guys in the locker room thinking I'm dating an *opera singer*?"

He'd made his point, and she had the grace to look embarrassed.

6

To Paisley's delight and Thad's displeasure, Clint Garrett was back on the plane the next day as they left San Francisco for Seattle. "Don't get all worked up." Clint grinned at him. "Livia invited me."

Thad glared at The Diva. "Why?"

He didn't like the evil gleam in her eyes. "Because I like him, but even more, I love seeing how much he irritates you."

Clint shrugged. "That pretty much explains it."

"How long are you going to keep stalking me?" Thad demanded.

"Not much longer. I have some stuff to do next week." Ignoring Paisley's attempt to get his attention, Clint whipped out his computer and pulled up film from the Steelers' loss. "Since you've got some free time . . ."

Fortunately, once they reached Seattle, Clint took off, although Thad knew he'd be back.

They had a formal photo shoot that afternoon, which Henri intended to use as part of a nationwide advertising campaign. Accompanied by a photographer, his assistant, a stylist, and Paisley, they set off for the Seahawks' stadium, where they spent a couple of hours shooting various scenarios. His favorite showed himself and Olivia posed between the goalposts, both of them in evening dress with their watches on display. He wore a tux and leaned leisurely against the goalposts. Olivia, her hair arranged in an elaborate updo and strips of eye black under her eyes, wore a black gown and held the football as if it were a microphone and she was singing into it.

Afterward, they headed north to the Seattle Opera. On a bare stage, they experimented with scenes that referenced *Carmen.* The stylist put Olivia in an elaborate scarlet gown that pushed up her breasts and arranged her hair so it fell over her bare shoulders. The stylist put him in a white shirt that opened to the middle of his chest, tight black pants, and calf-high black leather boots. In their best shot, he lay on his side on the stage floor, head propped on a bent elbow, his other hand showcasing his watch as he balanced a football on end. Olivia loomed over him, her head thrown back, hair flying from a fan just out of camera range, her arm with the Cavatina3 extended. In the background, Henri played a recording of her famous "Habanera" to set the mood.

As the music played and Olivia experimented with various positions, he kept waiting for her to start accompanying herself, but to his disappointment, she didn't. The vocal exercises he heard every morning had become a striptease in his head, and he was increasingly obsessed with the idea of her singing. Just for him.

Henri was rhapsodic about the photos. They were so different from any of Marchand's past campaigns, which were nothing more than well-photographed close-ups of the watch from various angles. "These are going to be extraordinaire! Everyone will be talking about them. This will be our most successful campaign ever."

Thad doubted Mariel Marchand would agree.

It was nearly midnight when they reached the hotel. In his suite, he found a pink satin box on the living room coffee table. He flipped the lid, stared at the contents, and walked over to their connecting door. "Open up."

"Go away," she said from the other side. "I'm too tired to spar with you tonight."

"I sympathize, but open up anyway."

She did, but with a frown. *"What?"* Her lipstick had worn off, and her hair stuck out from all the day's sprays, gels, and pomades. He liked seeing her messy. It made her less formidable. More . . . manageable.

He showed her the satin box. "Just a guess, but I think this was intended for you instead of me."

Inside were four very expensive perfumes: Hermès's 24 Faubourg, Dior's Balade Sauvage, a limited edition of Chanel's N°5, and Tom Ford's Lost Cherry. She picked up the card. "Rupert," she said with a sigh. "And most perfume gives me a headache."

"Exactly the same thing your Rupert does to me. Don't you think this is getting out of hand?"

"Opera aficionados are different from other kinds of fans." She took the box and carried it to her room. "There are going to be some very happy hotel housekeepers tomorrow."

He shook his head and went into his bedroom, but as he began to kick off his shoes, he noticed that the shoulder bag he used as a carry-on was unzipped. The bag held his usual crap: a couple of books, headset, a spare pair of sunglasses, and his laptop. But now, the laptop, which he always kept in a separate compartment, was shoved in between a copy of a Jonathan Franzen novel he'd promised himself he'd read one day, and an account of the D-Day landings he was actually reading. He checked his suitcase and shaving kit. Neither seemed to have been disturbed.

He called the desk. As he suspected from the errant perfume delivery, the hotel had mixed up his and Olivia's suites. Whoever had dug around in his case had assumed it belonged to her.

On their flight to Denver the next day, he mulled over the conversation he'd had with the hotel manager before they'd left. The bellman who'd delivered the perfume box was a longtime employee. The same for the housekeeper who'd serviced their floor. The manager declared them both above suspicion, and Thad didn't argue. Housekeepers and employees with sticky fingers didn't last long. Someone else had been in his room.

The video surveillance footage had proved useless thanks to a party that had been going on in another suite on the floor. Between the grainy video and the number of people coming and going, it was impossible to see anything useful. The manager tactfully suggested Thad might have inadvertently moved the things in his case without remembering he'd done it.

"Possible, I guess," Thad had said. But it wasn't possible. He liked keeping his travel case organized.

Not long before the plane was ready to land, he moved next to The Diva. "Since we don't have to report for duty until Monday, do you have plans for Denver?"

"Sleep in, work out, eat salad."

"Admirable, but I have a better idea. One of my teammates is lending me his house outside Breckenridge. It's beautiful country, and if you want to come along, you can hike instead of being stuck on a hotel treadmill."

"Who's going to be there?"

"Just me."

"And baby boy's afraid to be alone?"

"Now you're making me feel bad." The truth was, he didn't want to be alone with himself right now, and he also didn't want her where he couldn't watch her.

She smiled and then sobered. "What's this really about?"

"Don't make me confess my insecurities all over again."

"You have no insecurities. You're the closest thing there is to a Greek god."

"I'd be flattered if you sounded more impressed."

"You know what they say. Pretty is as pretty does."

He stifled a laugh.

She narrowed her beautiful eyes at him. "Is this about sex—which clearly isn't going to happen—or are you still obsessing over Rupert?"

"Yes. Rupert, those letters, and that phone call. Also, someone got into my carry-on and, I suspect, your luggage. As for sex . . . Why are you so sure it's not going to happen? A good-looking, sensitive guy like myself, and an overwrought opera singer like you . . . Seems possible."

"*Im*possible. I'm too insecure to have an affair with a hot football player like yourself. I do hate the idea of being cooped up in a hotel for the weekend, though. More important, before she left, Mariel booked me into a spa for two nights."

"That doesn't sound bad."

"Except this is a boot camp spa where they get you up at four in the morning for a ten-mile hike, then feed you nothing but radishes and water."

"Mariel is a major pain in the ass."

"It's what happens to women who don't eat."

When Paisley found out what they had planned, she tried to wangle an invitation to join them, but Thad turned her down. "Who even knows if the place has Wi-Fi? It's too big a risk."

Henri wasn't happy about his brand ambassadors slipping away from his watchful gaze, but after Thad reassured him they'd be back in time for their Monday morning commitments, Henri gave in with his customary good grace.

An hour later, Thad and The Diva were driving a rental car west toward Breckenridge.

His teammate's multimillion-dollar, log-and-stone house had four different levels, a curved driveway, and big windows with sweeping mountain views. They unloaded the groceries they'd picked up on the way and changed clothes. When they reconvened in the kitchen, he couldn't help but stare at her. "What's wrong?" she said.

"You're wearing jeans?"

"Who doesn't wear jeans?"

"I don't know. You?"

She laughed. "You're an idiot."

They borrowed heavy jackets and snow boots from the back of a closet and set off on a lower trail, hoping to avoid the deeper snow. Olivia had wrapped a warm scarf around her throat and pulled a headband over her ears. Her ponytail swung across her jacket collar as her breath clouded the air.

After their busy week, he didn't feel the need to talk, and neither did she. He enjoyed listening to the crunch of snow under their boots, the wind ruffling the aspens, and the distant sound of a waterfall. As they reached a set of icy rocks, he held out his hand, but she ignored his help and navigated the rocks with the surefooted grace of an athlete. Taking into account all her dance and movement training, he supposed she was.

As the snow grew too deep to go on, they took their time gazing out over the mountain landscape. He couldn't remember ever being with a woman so comfortable with silence—ironic, considering her profession—and he was the one who eventually broke it. "If you feel like cutting loose with one of your favorite arias, I'd be happy to listen."

She pulled the muffler tighter around her neck. "The air's too cold. We're all insanely protective of our voices."

He'd noticed. She drank lots of water, but never with ice, and kept a humidifier going in her bedroom. She also favored some fairly disgusting herbal teas. One of these days, however, he was determined to make her sing for him. Listening to her on YouTube was fine, but he wanted a private performance.

"I'm making a big salad," she said that evening. "If you want anything else, be nice and don't let me see you eat it."

He'd worked up an appetite on their hike, but after all the heavy food this week, a salad sounded good, especially since he'd sneaked a rotisserie chicken into the shopping cart. Still, he'd lose his macho if he didn't protest. "You're a real downer, you know that?"

"If you'd died as many times as I have onstage, you wouldn't be a big ball of cheer."

"Good point." He opened a bottle of red and poured two glasses. "Tell me about it. What attracted you to opera?"

"My parents were retired music teachers, and I grew up with music in the house." As she gathered the produce they'd bought from the refrigerator, her jeans stretched tight over her butt. It was a great butt. The kind of butt you wanted to squeeze in your hands. The kind of butt—

He'd lost track of their conversation.

". . . listened to jazz, rock, classical, all of it." She straightened, spoiling his view. "I loved making fun of the opera singers. I'd dress up in a funny costume and pretend to sing, exaggerating everything—the gestures, the vibrato, the drama. But when I was around fourteen, I stopped making fun and started trying to imitate the singers in earnest. That's when my formal lessons began. I had some great teachers, and I fell in love with it."

He handed her a glass of wine. "Here's one of many things I don't understand about opera . . . We have a two-week break in Chicago between the end of our regular tour obligations and our final gig, that big gala at the Chicago Municipal Opera. Or at least I have a two-week break. You'll be in rehearsals. Don't big productions like *Aida* take more than two weeks to rehearse?"

"A lot more. But not for an established performer. I've sung Amneris in *Aida* so many times I don't need six weeks of rehearsal. Two weeks is enough for me to adjust to the cast and familiarize myself with any changes in the staging." She gestured toward him with her wineglass. "What about you? What attracted you to football?"

He turned on the faucet and ran the lettuce under cold water. "I always played sports and was good at them, which gave me some serious entitlement issues. It's hard to be humble when you're great at everything."

He'd meant to make her laugh. Instead, she regarded him with something that almost seemed like compassion. "But not as great as Clint Garrett."

No way was he letting her poke around in his psyche. "There's always someone better, right? Even in your case."

"I like competition. It makes me work harder, and not just on my voice. I want to be the best at everything—languages, dance, acting. I'm a classic overachiever."

She sounded almost embarrassed to admit she was ambitious, but there was nothing he admired more than a good work ethic. He started to comment on it only to notice she'd gone still. She held a forgotten tomato in one hand and stared off into space, her lips tense, eyes unhappy. He wondered if she was thinking about her ex-fiancé, the guy who hadn't been able to compete at her level.

"You should never have to apologize for trying to be the best," he said.

She gave him a smile that didn't quite work. "Never."

They ate in the great room, plates on their laps, and watched the stars come out over the mountains. He'd taken a seat not far from her on the couch. Olivia regarded him surreptitiously. He wasn't the kind of man who believed it was sexy to glue his eyes to a woman's breasts or give her one of those smarmy eye-rakes. Instead, he leaned into the couch cushions with his customary lazy grace, an ankle propped on his opposite knee, one arm draped across the back of the couch. She'd known a lot of good-looking men, but despite his wisecracks about his appearance, she'd never once caught him stealing a look at himself in the mirror, and that disconnect intrigued her.

Instead of turning on the television, they talked when they felt like it and listened to jazz. She introduced him to a new vocalist. He introduced her to a saxophonist he'd just discovered. But when he switched the playlist from jazz to her newest album, she protested. "Turn it off. All I hear when I listen are my mistakes."

He'd seen the album's rave reviews, so he doubted there were many mistakes, but he'd watched enough of his own game film to understand. Instead of his successes, all he could see were lost opportunities.

Only as she got ready for bed did things start to turn awkward. He couldn't remember ever spending this much time around such a desirable woman without sleeping with her. Everything about her screamed sex. Her breasts, her butt, that curtain of shiny dark hair. Then there were her smarts and sass. He wanted her. Sex with Olivia Shore had been on his mind ever since that Phoenix dive bar.

He couldn't exactly recall the last time he'd had to make the first move, but something about Olivia Shore made him slip his hands into his pockets instead of around her body. She was so fierce and strong—ready to avenge wrongs and slay selfish lovers with her powerful arias—but he'd also seen her vulnerability.

He had an unsettling thought—a notion that, up until this very second, he could never have imagined entertaining. What if Olivia Shore was out of his league?

Absurd. He was Thad Walker Bowman Owens. No woman had ever been out of his league. He was a star. And Olivia . . . ?

Olivia Shore was a superstar.

With an abrupt good night, he headed upstairs.

After dinner, Olivia had turned on the hot tub on the private balcony outside the master bedroom where she was staying, and now a veil of steam rose from the water into the cold night air. Her muscles ached pleasantly from their hike. A few days ago she'd been sweating in the Phoenix heat, and now she was gazing out on snow. This was one amazing country.

She stripped, opened the door, and wearing only flip-flops, walked carefully across the icy deck and gradually lowered herself into the hot water.

The cold air slapped her face as the heat enveloped her body. She studied the inky, star-laced sky. This would be a perfect moment, if only she could shake off the guilt that refused to ease its grip on her.

The scene at Adam's graveside had been so over the top it belonged onstage. As his sisters, clad in black from head to toe, had laid the last two flowers on his coffin, Colleen, the oldest of the two, advanced on Olivia, her face contorted with grief. *"You killed him."* Her words were little more than a whisper, but they gradually grew louder. "You led him on. Made him believe you had a future when all you cared about was yourself. You might as well have pulled the trigger!"

The onlookers had stared. A few had drawn back. More had inched forward, unwilling to miss a word.

Adam's other sister, Brenda, had rushed to Colleen's side, her face mirroring her sister's grief. Olivia had stood there paralyzed, unable to defend herself against the truth in those words, until Rachel had dragged her away from them to the car. "You can't let this get to you," Rachel had said.

But how could it not?

Olivia jumped as the bedroom's sliding doors opened and Thad stepped out. "I knocked a couple of times, but you didn't seem to hear." He had a towel wrapped around his waist and his feet stuffed into a pair of sneakers. She stared at his bare chest. "Go back to your computer and your mysterious phone calls," she said. "I'm having me time."

"Nobody likes a hot tub hog." He dropped the towel to reveal a pair of navy boxer briefs. "Turn around if you don't want to see these come off."

She definitely did want to see, and if she were a different woman with a different profession, she might let herself enjoy everything this deliciously sexy man had to offer, but her relationship with Adam had caused enough destruction in her life. For all Thad Owens wanted was the world to see him as a good-natured guy who lived for football, she wasn't fooled. Every instinct she possessed told her he wasn't nearly as straightforward as he pretended to be, and the last thing she needed in her life right now was more complexity.

She waited a few seconds for him to settle into the water before she looked. He'd grown some beard stubble since the morning, and the glow from the hot tub lights intensified the green of his eyes, while feathers of steam drifted around his broad shoulders. The rush of heat racing through her body didn't come from the water temperature.

He leaned against the tub's edge. "I was about to get in the shower when I saw you down here."

The possibility that he'd seen her traipse naked across the deck unsettled her, even though she liked her body. She liked the height that gave her presence onstage and the strength that allowed her to endure long performances. Pop stars who relied on microphones could afford to be rail thin, but opera singers' unamplified voices had to carry out into the audience over a full orchestra. While the era of the obese opera singer had ended, a small, malnourished body couldn't cut it, either. Yet those super-thin bodies were probably what Thad Owens feasted on.

The realization that she was thinking about how a professional athlete-playboy would judge her body made her angry with herself. But also curious. "What do you think is most attractive in a woman? Body, brains, or power?"

"All of the above."

"But if you could only have one?"

"Let me point out that you're the person who's reducing women to a single attribute."

She smiled. "I was speaking theoretically."

"Then how about we reverse the questions? What's most attractive to you in a man? Body, brains, or power?"

"Point made."

"I guess we all have certain physical traits we're attracted to."

Thick, dark hair, great chest, perfect profile.

"What really attracts me is a person who has a passion," he said. "Their job, their hobby. Whether it's saving tigers, or making a great barbecue sauce. I like people who want to suck all the juice out of life."

He kept surprising her. She understood exactly what he meant because she felt the same way. "What's your passion?" she asked. "Or is the answer too obvious?"

The way he hesitated made her suspect he was about to make another wisecrack, but he surprised her once again. "Being the best. Just like you said. What else is there?"

She'd watched him with Clint Garrett. She'd seen how much he resented Clint, yet she'd also overheard enough of their conversations to know he was determined to make Clint a better player. She wondered how he'd resolve this conflict inside himself. Or maybe he hadn't.

They fell into quiet, but this silence didn't feel as comfortable as their others had. Maybe it was the dark, the brush of water against her skin. Maybe it was the sight of those muscular shoulders emerging from the water. She imagined herself sliding over to him. Pressing her hands against his chest. His hands coming to her breasts. She imagined— "I'm getting out."

She hadn't brought a towel, only flip-flops. He was better prepared. She reached over the side and grabbed the towel he'd left there. "I'll bring you another one."

"Don't cover up on my account."

"You're not going to seduce me." As soon as the words were out, she wished she hadn't spoken them.

"Hey, you're the one who keeps bringing up sex."

She shot up in the water, gripping the towel around herself. "Liar. You bring it up every time you waltz around in front of me without a shirt."

"I've never once waltzed around—"

"And when you look at me with that face." She climbed out.

"I can't help my—"

"And bat those green eyes."

His voice raised in outrage. "I never batted an eye in my life!"

She stomped across the snowy deck in her flip-flops. "Every time you— You—" She grabbed the bedroom doorknob.

It was locked.

7

Stunned, Olivia spun toward him. "You locked the door!"

He reared up from the bubbles. "What do you mean?"

"The door! You must have pushed the lock when you came out here."

"I didn't do anything to the lock. Let me see."

He rose—his body steaming in the cold night air, a male Aphrodite emerging from an artificial sea.

The veteran of a hundred locker rooms wasn't self-conscious about nudity, and she should have been too focused on the locked door for more than a passing glance, but she wasn't.

He was magnificent, every part of him. Shoulders and chest, narrow hips, lean and powerful legs. And . . . *Wow.*

He moved in front of her and tried the knob. "You're right."

She forced herself to refocus. "Of course I'm right!"

"What kind of idiot would use a lock like this on a balcony door?"

"They're your friends, not mine."

He felt above the door frame. "See if you can find an extra key anyplace out here."

There was no furniture, nowhere to really look, but she poked around anyway. "Nothing. Why didn't we bring our phones? We should have brought Paisley."

"Depressing thought." He abandoned his fruitless search above the door and reached for his boxers. "I don't suppose any of those classes you take taught you how to pick a lock?"

"Lock-picking isn't a requirement for grand opera, but I can order dessert in seven languages."

"Currently useless, but still impressive. We'll find another way in."

"It's freezing!" Like any serious opera singer, she religiously guarded herself against chills with scarves around her throat, herbal teas, and vitamin supplements, yet here she was.

"Get back in the water."

As cold as she was, she couldn't stay in the water while he set out alone trying to rescue them. She was better than that. Shivering, she followed him down the single set of stairs to the frozen ground. The motion-activated security lights came on. She wrapped the wet towel tighter, but it was useless for anything except modesty. "You didn't leave the keys in the car by any chance?" she asked. "Stupid question. None of us who live in Chicago leave keys in our cars."

They moved toward the front of the house. He craned his neck to look up at the windows. Her teeth were chattering so loudly that he heard them. "There's no reason for both of us to be freezing our asses off. Get back in the water."

"And have you take all the credit for rescuing us? No way. Besides, I can tolerate cold better than you."

"I'm a trained athlete. How do you figure that?"

"I have more body fat."

His gaze moved from the second-story windows down to her chest. "In all the right places."

"*Seriously?*" Her towel had indeed slipped, and she jerked it back up. "We're about to die from hypothermia, and you're looking at my breasts?"

"You're the one who brought them up."

If she hadn't been so cold, she would have laughed. Instead, she adopted some fake outrage. "As soon as this tour is over, I'm never speaking to you again."

"Doubtful."

"You're not that irresistible."

"Up for debate."

He was irresistible. To any woman who didn't possess an iron will.

They rounded the corner to the front of the house. Her flip-flops kept sinking into the snow, her toes had gone numb, and they were both covered with goose bumps. "How l-long . . . do you think before we d-die?"

"I don't know. Five minutes?"

"You don't know that!"

"Of course I don't know that! And w-we aren't going to die. The hot tub, remember?" He jiggled the front doorknob, but it, too, was locked.

Her teeth were rattling so hard her jaw hurt. "We . . . c-can't stay in the water f-forever."

His teeth had also begun to chatter. "Henri'll come looking for us when we don't show up."

"We c-can't stay in the hot tub all night."

He gave her a level-eyed look that told her she might be acting like a brainless heroine from a 1950s rom-com instead of a woman who commanded center stage. She pulled herself together. "We're going to . . . b-break a window."

"Now there's an idea." He was already heading for the far side of the house.

"You don't need to be . . . s-s-s-arcastic." Her damp towel had stiffened, beginning to freeze. "Oh, God, I'm cold."

He stopped walking and pulled her into his arms. "Body heat transfer."

Neither of them had much body heat, but it still felt good. Her cold cheek against the side of his cold neck. His arms encircling her. Their thighs pressed together.

She felt a bulge press against her and drew back.

He grinned through his chattering teeth. "I'm not apologizing. It's good to know I still have some decent blood flow."

She wanted to go right back into his arms, but she widened the distance between them.

It had started to snow. One flake. Another. They landed in his hair, on her shoulders. Because of the design of the house, the front and side windows rose too high above the ground for easy access. They headed toward the rear of the house.

She might have a higher proportion of body fat, but he was accustomed to physical discomfort, and he moved more gracefully. In the reflection from the security lights, she saw that his lips were beginning to turn blue. Her fingers had cramped so painfully she lost her grip on the frozen towel and it fell. He stumbled on a patch of frozen ground. "Jesus, Liv . . ."

He said it like a prayer, and for a moment she forgot the cold. But only for a moment. "Don't be a j-j-jerk."

He raised his arms in mock surrender and turned toward the back door. It had glass panes, and while she looked in the snow patches for a rock to break the glass, he tried to see through it. "There's a dead bolt that needs a key. I'm going to have to kick the door in."

The door was metal, and kicking it in didn't seem like it would be all that easy, not even for him.

She stood, shaking so much she could barely speak. "H-h-how about th-th-this?"

She held out a key.

"Where'd you get that?"

"I saw a r-r-rock that looked different. Tell your f-f-friend, if his fake rock didn't fool me, it won't fool a b-b-burg . . ." He had the door open, and she gave up trying to get the word out.

They rushed inside, closing the door behind them. Grabbing her arm, he pulled her through the house and up the stairs. "Of all my life experiences," he muttered, "I never imagined myself wandering around in the Colorado mountains with only a pair of boxer shorts, my old Nikes, and a naked diva."

"L-l-life is strange."

The master bedroom's walk-in shower had slate walls, a river-rock floor, and a stone boulder to sit on.

Moments later, they were both inside. He adjusted the water, running it cool until their frozen bodies adjusted to the temperature, then gradually making it warmer. Finally, he flipped on the overhead rain fixture.

The water cocooned them. He was naked except for those silky boxers molding to his skin. How could a healthy woman be standing next to him and not look? She was hogging most of the spray, and she moved aside to let him in. As steam filled the room, the water painted his dark hair to his forehead and turned his eyes into green sea glass. She wanted to touch. To have him touch her. She wanted to slide her hands down that incredible chest, to kiss him. She wanted everything his body offered.

"I'm trying to be a gentleman and keep my eyes straight ahead, but can I look now?"

She yearned to have him look. To have him see the same beauty in her body that she saw in his. But she was more vulnerable than she'd ever been, and throwing herself into an ill-fated affair with a man she was growing increasingly fond of—no matter how tempting—would take her into a whole new universe of self-destruction. "You really should model for a body-wash commercial."

"Already done it." He kept his gaze fixed on her face, beads of water clinging to his lashes. "Now can I look?"

He made her knees weak, and the heat that had crept back into her body turned to flame. Calling on every ounce of her legendary self-control, she forced herself to reach for one of the towels hanging at the end of the shower. "Sorry, soldier. I'm not into self-destruction these days."

"Self-destruction? What are you talking about? How about two people having a good time?"

As she tucked the towel between her breasts, she grew even more aware of the way the silky fabric of his boxers detailed his body, showing her exactly what she was turning down. She gripped the towel as if it were a life vest. "I'm on a long-term sabbatical from men, and I know you understand why. For the foreseeable future, all my good times are going to be onstage."

He groaned. "That's the most depressing thing I've ever heard you say."

She smiled despite the bone-deep sadness that had become part of her. "You think it's depressing for you? What about me?"

"So you admit you want to."

She let her eyes enjoy every bit of what she couldn't let herself have. "Oh, yes . . . You're a female fantasy."

His brows drew together. "I'm not sure I like being reduced to a stereotype."

"Own it." She shuddered, this time not from the cold. "Stay away, Thad Owens. This is a terrible time for me, and you're almost too tempting for a mortal female to resist."

"Why am I not flattered?"

"Because you're not used to being rejected." She gave him a deliberately insincere smile, determined to keep things light. "It's not you, it's me."

"Damned right it's you!" He whipped off his boxers and turned back into the water, giving her a fine view of his very firm, very untouchable ass.

He was still grouchy the next morning. "You can make your own damned breakfast."

She reached for the box of Wheaties he'd left on the counter and spilled it into a bowl. She suspected she wasn't the only one who'd practiced a little self-gratification last night before she'd gone to sleep. Not that it had helped.

The only way to deal with her attraction to Thad Owens was to give him a hard time. She splashed milk on her cereal and regarded him with fake concern. "Rejection is hard for you, isn't it? Do you want to talk about it?"

"No, I don't want to talk about it. If we can't f— If we can't get naked, I don't want anything to do with you."

She plopped down across from him. "You're cute when you're petulant."

"And you're sexy as hell, and I've seen you naked, and I want to see more."

"No one could ever accuse you of being indirect."

He abandoned his petulant act, which she'd suspected he'd specifically adopted to annoy her, and kicked back in his chair. "I don't get it. We like each other. We have a great time together. You look at me like I'm an ice cream sundae, and I look at you the same way. So what's the big deal?"

The big deal was she'd never again let anything—especially not the temporary temptation of Thad Owens—derail her. Her career was her life, and unless a man like Dennis Cullen came along—a man with no personal ego who devoted himself to his wife's career—she was keeping her focus where it needed to be, on her work.

She knew the perfect way to deal with Thad. "I have a rule. No hookups, no flings, no affairs. Not without a commitment."

"Commitment!" Those green eyes shot open. "We've only known each other a little over a week!"

She arranged her face in her most earnest expression. "Is commitment a problem for you?"

"Damn right, it's a problem. I can barely commit to what I want to eat for dinner, let alone to a woman."

A long, theatrical sigh. "Sorry. Unless you're thinking about the possibility of marriage, we're a nonstarter."

He dropped his spoon, splashing milk on the tabletop. "Did you say 'marriage'?"

She was an actress, and she had no trouble keeping a straight face. "If you want it, put a ring on it."

She couldn't have come up with a more efficient way of defusing the geomagnetic storm of sexual heat that sizzled around them. He shot up from the table. "I'm going out."

"I thought you might want to."

It wouldn't take him long to realize she was baiting him, but for now, she'd enjoy the solitude. Or at least try to.

The piano in the great room was out of tune, but she played it anyway. Tested her voice. Bent her arms over the keyboard and tried not to cry.

Light snow fell on the windshield early the next morning as they drove back toward Denver. They'd taken a hike yesterday and listened to good jazz over dinner. Thad had grilled steaks and sidestepped her questions about his secretive computer habits. Her attempt at making mashed potatoes had ended up in the trash, but she'd made a killer salad. She wished they could have stayed longer.

He eased up on the accelerator. "That was some bullshit you were dishing out yesterday morning. Congratulations."

She cradled her cup of the coffee they'd brought along. "I do like to take my entertainment where I can find it."

He turned the wipers to slow speed. "Fair enough. But there's something between us, and we both know it." He glanced over at her. "So what's the real reason you don't want to take the next logical step?"

She tore her vision away from his profile and shimmied around the truth. "Amazingly, we like each other. We even sort of understand each other. Agree?"

"Agree. And . . . ?"

"I think we need to honor that. Wouldn't you like having a female friend who's not jumping you? Somebody you could confide your woman problems to and who could tell you when you're being a jerk?"

"I already have one of those. Her name's Piper. Cooper Graham's wife."

"But she's part of your professional world. You need someone outside football you can trust."

"Considering that I can't wipe the image of you naked out of my brain, I don't think it's realistic to expect we could have that kind of friendship." He glanced at the driver's side mirror and pulled into the left lane. "What's really holding you back? Tell your good buddy, Thad."

She returned her coffee to the car's cup holder. "I've already told you a lot more about my personal life than you've told me about yours. Why is that? Why is it that you want me to spill my secrets when you haven't revealed anything personal to me?"

"And just like that, you change the subject."

"Well?"

"I like women. Always have. And before you get offended, I'm not only talking about sex. I spend most of my life with men, and that means lots of sweat, blood, broken bones, and trash talk. Being with a smart woman who smells good and looks good and wants to do something other than play video games and talk about sports is important to me." He glanced at the speedometer. "I've never jumped from woman to woman, if that's what you're thinking. I've probably got a lower number than ninety percent of the men in the NFL."

"Admirable. I guess."

He swung back into the right lane. He drove too fast, but he wasn't a road hog. "I'd describe myself as a serial monogamist. I've had some great women in my life, and I only regret a couple of them. Your turn."

She didn't have to be honest with him, but she wanted to be. "I've learned the hard way. No singers, actors, frustrated artists, or anyone who needs a mother instead of a lover."

"So far, I'm in the clear."

She regarded him pointedly. "Also, no ambitious, successful men with well-deserved egos who are as dedicated to their careers as I am to mine and who, as it turns out, have only limited tolerance for a woman who's their mirror image." There. She'd said it.

He regarded her warily. "Adam burned you in more ways than one."

She shrugged. "I don't do well with needy men or with successful men, either."

He started to ask her how she defined "successful" and then thought better of it. "It kind of narrows your dating pool."

"Women like me: our careers come first. We can't accommodate a romantic partner's schedule. We're not always available when a man wants to talk or have sex or needs a shoulder to cry on. We have our own money, and we don't need theirs."

"I think you're underestimating a lot of men."

"Am I? Men like you are attracted to women like me because we understand you. We understand what drives you. But, ultimately, our lives are as big or bigger than yours, and once the newness wears off, that starts to grate."

"I'm not buying it."

She might as well go all the way. "Before the disaster with Adam, I was involved with a prominent architect. A good man. Decent. He thinks of himself as a feminist."

"And then he turned into a creep."

"Not at all. He respected my career, but things came up, and I was smitten with him. I skipped a class because his old college friends were in town. Then I was late for a rehearsal because he was getting an award. He had an open slot in his schedule, and we'd talked about taking a vacation together. I was about to turn down a concert when I finally woke up and realized I was losing myself. I made a vow never again to get involved with another alpha type."

"Which explains Adam."

"Pathetic, aren't I? I can't have a relationship with someone successful because it hurts my career, and I can't have a relationship with someone who's struggling because it hurts my career." She slumped into the seat. "I need a Dennis. Unfortunately, I gave him away to Rachel."

He ignored that piece of self-pity. "You're making something simple too complicated. Sometimes a relationship can just be fun. Casual."

"At what point have I ever struck you as a casual person?"

"Fair point."

It felt good to be honest. "I've learned a hard lesson. Relationships compromise my work, and it's my work that gives my life meaning."

He kept his gaze fixed on the highway. "Since you're so clear-eyed, it wouldn't have to be that way with us."

She took her time replying. "I like being with you, Thad, and you like being with me, and before long, I might end up turning down *Carmen* at the Mariinsky to sit on the sidelines and watch you not play."

He shifted in his seat as if he weren't entirely comfortable. "That could work two ways, you know."

"Oh, really? I can see it now. 'Sorry, Coach, I can't show up for the game today because my lover is singing Despina in *Così fan tutte*, and I need to be there to support her.'"

"Okay, maybe not that."

"You're the anti-Dennis, and we're not going to happen, no matter how much I might be lusting after you. I'm not saying I am, but I'm not saying I'm not, either."

"Flattering," he said dryly.

She needed to make sure there was no misunderstanding, but that meant revealing something she'd never confessed to another person. She steadied herself. "I want to be one of the immortals, Thad," she said quietly. "I want to do great work. Not just good. Great. I want to do work so monumental people will still be listening to my recordings long after I'm gone."

Her openness took him aback, and he responded in the only way he knew how, by launching an offensive. "You're making something as simple and natural as sex way too complicated."

"Says the man who wants to get laid."

"You do, too."

"And I hope it'll happen one of these days. But not with you." She gripped her hands in her lap. "I can't go to bed with you, Thad Owens, no matter how much I might want to. Because, whether you admit it or not, who I am is more than a man like you can handle."

His mouth set in a grim line. "That's what you think."

They rode the rest of the way to Denver in silence.

They arrived at the hotel at nine in the morning. Henri had kept his word. Thad and Olivia had adjoining suites. Hers had a kitchen and dining area. His didn't. But they were back in civilization again, and as long as the door stayed open between them, he didn't care about having the smaller space.

She went off to unpack. He hung up his jacket. Their conversation in the car had rattled him—not because he didn't understand what she'd said but because he did, and it had tilted his perspective in a way he didn't like. She was right. No matter how intelligent or successful the women in his life had been, they had accommodated themselves to him more than he'd ever accommodated himself to them. He'd come first. Always.

An eerie sound emerged from the next suite, breaking his train of thought. It wasn't exactly a scream, but something close enough to make him rush into the other room.

She stood in the center of the living area, a brown envelope at her feet, a crumpled white T-shirt in her hand. He took in her ashen face and the rust-colored stains that covered the shirt.

"Jesus . . ."

She dropped the T-shirt. Beneath the bloody stains, he made out the T-shirt's inscription. *Tenors do it better.*

He hurried to her side and picked up the envelope. It was postmarked San Francisco with no return address. Had whoever mailed this been in San Francisco when they were there? Had they been watching her?

She pressed her fingers to her lips and stared down at the T-shirt. "Adam . . . He . . . must have been wearing this when he shot himself. I—I gave it to him."

Thad knelt down and examined the T-shirt. "When?"

"What do you mean?"

"How long ago was it? When did you give it to him?"

Her fingers balled into a fist. "I—I don't remember exactly. Not long after we started dating." She turned away.

"Did he wear it much?"

She gave a jerky nod.

He picked up the T-shirt and came to his feet. She recoiled as he held out the shirt. "Look at the tag, Liv."

She recoiled. "Get it away from me."

"Look at it."

Her shoulders heaved, but she finally did as he demanded. "I don't see—" She broke off as she saw what he saw. The T-shirt's tag was stiff and crisp. It had never been washed.

"This isn't his shirt," she said as the realization struck her. "It's never been washed, and the size is wrong. It looks like the shirt I gave him, but this isn't it."

"Somebody is playing a nasty mind game with you."

They both jumped as a knock sounded on the door. A bellman stood on the other side with a gift basket so large he'd brought it up on a cart. Emerging from the cellophane were two bottles of champagne, a pair of crystal glasses, and an assortment of gourmet cheeses, nuts, crackers, and designer chocolates.

The bellman wheeled in the cart. "Compliments of Mr. Rupert Glass."

8

The next night, Thad propped himself against the pillows in his bed with the doors open between their suites and his mind switching between insights he didn't want to examine too closely, the fake bloody T-shirt, and the gutter. Olivia had appeared at tonight's client dinner in full diva regalia—shiny, dark hair worn loose, dramatic eye makeup, and crimson lipstick. She'd worn a long, white gown with an Egyptian collar necklace, probably a gift from Rupert. He didn't ask. With her stilettos, she'd been taller than all the men there but him.

He'd stuffed the T-shirt back into its envelope and tucked the whole thing in the bottom of his suitcase. Out of sight, but not out of mind.

Olivia hadn't yet turned the light out in her suite. Maybe she was having a hard time falling asleep, too. He slipped on his headphones and pulled up YouTube on his computer. It wasn't long before he'd found a video of her singing Carmen.

Even people who didn't know opera knew the melody of its famous song, but now he also knew its name: "Habanera." And there she was. Commanding the stage. Smoldering in a tatty red dress with her breasts spilling over its low, square neckline like offerings poured from a cornucopia. Dirty bare feet, skin tanned and glistening with sweat, she taunted the men, her skirt swirling around her strong, spread legs, her arms as sinuous as snakes, her tumble of hair roiling and seething around her head. And that voice. That magnificent voice.

He watched one clip and then another. No wonder she was being hailed as the opera world's premier Carmen. Like Carmen, Liv wouldn't let any man stand between her and the freedom to live life on her own terms. In the final clip, he saw Don José stab her, watched her die, and wanted to kill the son of a bitch, wanted to rip off his head with his own bare hands.

He shoved his computer aside. He was way too emotional for opera.

"You're ridiculous," she told him the next afternoon as he sat in the chair by her side, one foot in the water, getting a fucking pedicure. Some of his pals submitted to this affront to all that was masculine, but never him. And yet here he was because he didn't want her going off alone, not while she was fair game to whoever was out there trying to spook her.

"No reason my toenails shouldn't be as pretty as the rest of me," he said.

She attempted to give him the stink eye but spoiled it with a smile. "If your looks matched your personality, you'd be one of those WWE fighters with no neck and a cauliflower nose."

He ignored the compliment. "I'm surprised you even know what the WWE is."

"I get around. This isn't necessary, you know."

He pretended to misunderstand. "Who wants ugly toes?"

"I appreciate your concern, but nothing is going to happen to me in a Denver nail salon in broad daylight."

"Rupert could show up with a diamond necklace and a damned machete."

She laughed. "If only you knew him."

He didn't care to. Maybe he was being overcautious, but between the threatening messages, tossed suitcases, the T-shirt with the phony blood, and those over-the-top gifts, he didn't like the idea of her roaming around alone. Since he couldn't be with her all the time, he'd pulled Henri aside, told him something vague about Olivia having an overly aggressive fan, and asked him to keep an extra eye on her.

"Please don't schedule one of those waxing things," he said. "I have to draw the line somewhere."

"I'll be merciful." Olivia grinned. "Or not."

When they arrived in New Orleans, the final proofs from their photo shoots at the Seahawks' stadium and the Seattle Opera were waiting for them at their French Quarter hotel overlooking Royal Street. Mariel Marchand was there, too. They hadn't seen her since last week in San Francisco, and Henri was clearly unhappy that she'd managed to get hold of the proofs before him. Still, as Henri spread them across the coffee table in their suite, her reappearance couldn't diminish his excitement. "These are *extraordinaire*. Even more impressive than I hoped."

The photographer knew what she was doing. The rich, muted colors gave the photos the look of old master oil paintings—an eye-catching contrast with the crazy poses he and Olivia had adopted.

Their watches were perfectly displayed, and they'd nailed it with their expressions—his nonchalance and her regal dignity as they stood by the goalposts—he, in a tuxedo, holding the football as if it were a cocktail shaker; Olivia nearby, her queenlike audaciousness daring the viewer to mock the patches of eye black on her cheekbones.

The photos at the Seattle Opera were even more striking. Olivia crouched fiercely over him in a billowing scarlet dress, hair eddying in a torrent around her head, pale white arms outstretched, fingers clawed, while he lounged on his side, shirt falling open, football on end, prepared to meet his demise.

Olivia frowned at him. "I look like a witch next to you."

So wrong. She looked like a goddess. He patted her on the head. "I can't help it if I'm photogenic."

She sighed. "I hate you."

"Enough!" Mariel pointed her finger at Paisley, who was taking photos of Thad studying his photos. Paisley looked like she wanted to swallow her phone. Instead, she fled from the suite.

Mariel gave a sigh of disgust and told them what they already knew. "Her grandfather and Uncle Lucien went to school together."

Later, Mariel pulled Henri aside and bombarded him in furious French, either forgetting that Olivia was fluent or not caring. Thad got the gist without a translation, but later, Olivia filled him in on the details.

"Mariel thinks the photos are frivolous and vulgar, an affront to Marchand's heritage. She says Uncle Lucien didn't like Henri's idea for this campaign in the first place—meaning that I passed muster as a brand ambassador, but that Henri should have chosen someone like Neil Armstrong instead of a football player."

"He's dead. And the Stars are a Marchand sponsor."

"Not sure Mariel cares. Despite her personal response to your studly allure, she believes the campaign needs gravitas, and that Uncle Lucien will never approve the photos. After that, there were a bunch of 'I told you so's.' Then she said their uncle might be old, but he wasn't senile, and this would finish Henri off."

"Bloodthirsty, isn't she?"

"The company's always had a Marchand heading it," Olivia pointed out, "so it'll be either Mariel or Henri."

"Henri doesn't stand a chance against her."

"You're right. She's all about tradition, and a company as stodgy as Marchand isn't going to change easily. Poor Henri. She'll eat him alive."

"Hey, aren't you supposed to be on the woman's side? Glass ceiling and all that?"

"Those photos are great, and we both know it."

"Despite you looking like a— What was it? Witch?"

She gave him a deliberately smug smile. "A powerful witch. And don't you forget it."

He nodded sagely. "I wouldn't think of it."

They'd finished their morning interviews. Henri had slipped away to the men's room when Paisley approached Olivia and Thad. "I don't think Henri or Mariel has seen this yet—maybe they won't—but I thought you should be prepared . . ." She could barely conceal her excitement as she scrolled to the Ratchet Up gossip site on her phone and pointed out an item at the bottom of the page.

> Has a little mountain madness struck the newest celeb couple? Sources tell us that the Chicago Stars' dreamy quarterback Thad Owens and opera megastar Olivia Shore were seen picking up groceries outside Breckenridge, Colorado. They call her the "beautiful typhoon." Will T-Bo be able to tame the storm?

Olivia swore under her breath. "It's 'tornado,' not 'typhoon,' and since when did I get to be part of a 'celeb couple'?" She turned an accusing eye on Thad. "Nobody outside the opera community cares about singers' private lives, but apparently everyone is interested in gossip about athletes."

"Hey, they called you a 'megastar' and me 'dreamy.' It could have been worse." He studied the screen. "It could have been better, too. We're the last item, and the print's so small it's barely readable."

Olivia rubbed her temples. Paisley offered up a sly cat's smile. "I feel sorry for you guys if Mariel sees it."

Mariel might be old-fashioned in her views about brand image, but she was up to date on technology, and Olivia suspected Google Alerts would be chiming away on all her devices.

They took a break at the hotel so Olivia could change before their afternoon television interviews, and, sure enough, Mariel was waiting for them. "A romance is fine," she said, all cold politeness, "but this feels . . . Not tawdry, of course. But there's something a bit . . . common about it."

Olivia watched Thad's eyebrow hitch, a sure sign he'd lost patience with her. "What would you suggest we do about it, Mariel?"

"We're not having a romance," Olivia declared.

Mariel ignored Olivia and gave Thad her most charming smile. "Please be more aware of the heritage of the brand you're representing. Henri, could I speak with you privately?"

She drew her unhappy cousin into the hallway where she no doubt lambasted him for not being smart enough to hire Gandhi and Florence Nightingale to represent the hallowed Marchand brand.

After Olivia had changed her dress and jewelry, they went off to their television appearances. When they were done, she had a few hours' break before a meet-and-greet with clients, but Thad had to stay behind to tape a segment with the station's sports reporter. Henri insisted on delivering her to the door of her hotel suite, even though she told him she could get there on her own. Thad's doing, she felt certain.

Thad's protectiveness was touching, but unnecessary. Someone was playing mind games with her. She wasn't in physical peril, only mental, and her mind was already such a mess, she could surely cope with a bit more chaos.

Ironically, the only time she seemed able to stop the mental tape that insisted on replaying in her head was when she was with Thad. Only then could she begin to relax. She touched her throat. Was it too much to hope that his self-confidence would transfer to her? That it would ease the painful grip of guilt she couldn't shake off?

As she traded her stilettos for a pair of flats, she wondered how he'd react if he knew all her secrets. She prayed he'd never find out because the idea of him losing respect for her was too painful to contemplate.

She stepped from the hotel into the heart of the French Quarter. It was early April and Mardi Gras was over, but the streets still bustled with tourists, street performers, and fortune-tellers. She passed vendors selling postcard views of Bourbon Street and oil paintings of Jackson Square. The late-afternoon sunshine was warm, but she had to meet client buyers in less than two hours, so she hadn't changed from her black sheath into something more casual.

Samorian Antiquarian Books sat tucked away in an alley not far from Rampart Street. The faded ocher exterior with its weather-beaten green shutters and dusty front window hadn't changed since she'd last visited two years earlier. Even the pot of geraniums in desperate need of watering seemed the same.

The overhead bell rang as she entered the shop, which smelled exactly as a store that specialized in rare books, manuscripts, and other fine arts ephemera should—old and musty with a faint overlay of chicory coffee.

Arman Samorian still refused to wear hearing aids, and hadn't heard the bell or noticed she'd entered until she stood directly in front of him.

"Madame Shore!" He rushed from behind the scarred wooden counter, grabbed her hand, and kissed it, his shrub of gray, Albert Einstein hair sprouting around his head like a mushroom cloud. "Such an honor to see you again."

"You, too, Arman," she shouted, patting his age-spotted hand.

"Are you performing? But why did I not know this?"

"Just visiting." No need for a long, loud explanation of an advertising campaign that would undoubtedly bewilder him.

"Whistling? When did you start whistling?"

"Visiting!"

"Ah. Of course."

She dutifully asked about his son, who lived in Biloxi, and petted his elderly cat Caruso, before she ventured into the dusty stacks. She found a long-out-of-print biography of the Russian soprano Oda Slobodskaya, then ventured up the creaky wooden steps to the store's second floor. The last time she'd been in this cramped attic space, she'd discovered an autographed photograph of Josephine Baker costumed as La Créole in Offenbach's operetta of the same name. Freshly framed, it was now one of her favorite possessions.

The attic was hot and windowless, the only light provided by three flyspecked bulbs hanging from the water-stained ceiling. She sneezed from the dust as she browsed the shelves, but unearthing a manuscript copy of Domenico Scarlatti's *Narcisso* more than made up for her discomfort. Samorian's store and its ancient proprietor might be relics of the past, but the store was a treasure house for serious musicians.

A slim volume entitled *George Kirbye and the English Madrigal* caught her attention, but just as she began to leaf through it, the overhead light bulbs went out.

Without even a window, it might as well have been midnight. She held on to the Scarlatti manuscript with one hand and used the other to grope her way along the bookcases in the general direction of where she thought the stairs were.

A board creaked from across the attic. And then another. Her heart jumped, as she realized she wasn't alone. She told herself not to be so skittish. This was an old wooden building. Of course it creaked. Besides, it was broad daylight outside and she was in a bookstore, not a dark alley. "Arman?" she called out.

A figure rounded the bookcases, barely fifteen feet in front of her. "Arm—?"

The figure lunged at her, and she fell back against the shelves. A shower of books hit the floor. She cried out as the demon figure grabbed her and caught her by the arms.

Male or female, she couldn't tell, but strong. She heard the rasp of their breathing, felt the bite of fingers digging into her flesh. It had to be a man.

He shoved her against the shelves as more books hit the floor. Her reflexes finally fired. All the classes she'd taken over the years—everything she'd learned in dance and yoga, fencing and weight lifting, trapeze, tai chi—all of it kicked in at once. She pushed hard against the demon's bulk. Her strength took him by surprise, and he let her go, but only for a moment before he lunged at her again and wrenched her arm. As she tried to twist free, she jabbed her elbow into his gut. He gave a guttural exclamation and tried to capture her free arm, but she curled her hand into a fist and punched him in the chest.

The strength of her defense took him by surprise, and the pressure on her arm eased for a few seconds, but still, he didn't let her go. Her shoulders hit the shelves as she torqued her body and kicked out, only to have her tight skirt imprison her. He released her arms to grab her around the chest, which gave her the seconds she needed to yank up her skirt and lash out again with her leg.

The blow from her knee landed with lucky precision. He yowled and buckled. She kicked again, aiming for his groin. This time she didn't connect, but she got close enough that he began backing away. She targeted his knees. Connected with one of them.

The struggle must finally have penetrated Arman's impaired eardrums because he called upstairs. "Madame Shore? Did you find the Scarlatti?"

Whether it was from the old man's interruption or the struggle she'd put up, her assailant backed off. She went after him, following the thud of his footsteps until a shard of light from the stairs illuminated his shadowy silhouette.

Only then did she realize the old bookseller might still be standing at the bottom. "Arman!" she cried. "Get out of the way!"

"What did you say?" the old man shouted.

She got to the top of the stairs just in time to see the dark figure of the intruder hit the bottom steps and shove the old man aside. As Arman crumpled to the floor, the intruder ran for the bookstore door.

"Arman!" She flew down the stairs and knelt beside him. "Arman, are you all right?" If anything had happened to him because of her . . .

He sat up slowly. "Madame . . . ?"

Her cell was in the purse she'd dropped upstairs, along with the Scarlatti manuscript. She made a dash for the landline phone on the wooden counter and called the police.

Miraculously, Arman seemed to have been unhurt, but an ambulance took him to the hospital to be checked. Thad was waiting for her at the police station after she'd made her report. As soon as they were outside, he lit into her as if she were a wayward teenager who'd violated curfew. "We had an agreement! You weren't supposed to go anywhere without either Henri or me. How could you do something so idiotic?"

Her hand hurt from the punch she'd delivered. She'd ripped her dress, bruised her shoulder. She was drained and too shaken by what had happened to remind him they had no such agreement, and he should shut the hell up. He finally seemed to realize she was in no shape for a lecture because he draped his arm around her and said no more.

Henri canceled the evening events, and Olivia slipped away to her room. After she'd reassured herself that Arman wasn't harmed, she took a long soak in the tub and slipped into her yoga pants and a loose top.

When she emerged from her bedroom, she found Thad sitting on the couch talking on the phone with a baseball game muted on the television. However annoying his lecturing might be, she knew his concern was genuine.

He quickly ended the call. "This is a hell of a way to avoid another of those client dinners."

"No more lectures, okay?" She sat on the couch, leaving one seat cushion between them.

"No more lectures. As long as you promise not to take off again until this is settled."

"I'm not irresponsible." She held up her hand before he could argue the point. "That store is a treasure trove." She told him about the autographed Josephine Baker photograph she'd bought and the Scarlatti manuscript. "I've been thinking . . . What if there was something in the store the thief wanted? Maybe even the Scarlatti? Maybe I was just in the wrong place at the wrong time."

"You're suggesting this was coincidence? A thief decided to burglarize the store at the exact moment you were there instead of walking in like a normal customer, finding what he wanted, and bargaining for it? Are the old man's prices that high?"

She knew her explanation was far-fetched, but she tried to defend it with a shrug.

Thad bore down. "How much was he charging for that Scarlatti manuscript?"

"I don't know . . . A couple of hundred," she muttered.

"Well, there you go. A big prize in the rare manuscript black market." He plowed his hand through his hair, barely disturbing a single strand. "I know you don't want to believe you're a target, Liv, but look at the evidence. Threatening letters, an eerie phone call, the T-shirt, and now this."

"The only people who hold a grudge against me are Adam's sisters, and they live in New Jersey. Besides, that wasn't a woman who attacked me."

"They could have hired someone, and even you can't deny that you're somebody's target."

He was right, but she slouched deeper into the couch cushions. "Don't you have some football buddies in town to go drinking with?"

"I'm not going anywhere tonight."

She started to tell him she had no need of a bodyguard, but that didn't exactly seem to be true, so she told him to turn up the volume on the baseball game instead.

"You know anything about baseball?" he asked.

"I've watched *A League of Their Own* at least a dozen times."

"An authority, then."

"I'll explain anything you don't understand."

As he came out of his room the next morning, The Diva was doing her daily vocalizing. The night before, she'd escaped to her bedroom after the sixth inning, leaving him alone with the remote control, a baseball game he didn't care about, and his thoughts. When this tour had started two weeks ago, he'd anticipated doing nothing more than what he'd signed up for. Now, here he was, enmeshed in a situation he couldn't control.

Yesterday had scared the hell out of him. They were leaving for Dallas today. From there they'd travel to Atlanta, Nashville, New York, and Las Vegas, before they ended up in Chicago, where they'd started. A couple of days of events there, followed by a two-week break before his final obligation, attending the Marchand-sponsored Chicago Municipal Opera gala. During that two-week break, Liv would be in rehearsals for *Aida*, and he'd probably head to Kentucky to visit his parents. No more interviewers asking the same questions, no more packing and unpacking a suitcase. And no more diva.

That didn't sit well with him. He and The Diva were . . . pals. More than pals. Potential lovers if he had anything to say about it. She was funny and fascinating, stubborn and thoughtful. She knew as much about hard work and career dedication as he did. All he had to do was overcome her entirely rational objections to having an affair.

She'd hit the midpoint in her morning exercises, past the tongue trills and lip rolls, through the eeees and *ues*. She was on to the *nings*, and *nays*, her voice running up and down the scale with ease and brilliance. He'd miss hearing those full, rich sounds first thing in the morning. How was any mortal capable of producing such otherworldly tones? Just once, he wanted her to sing for him. Only for him. "Habanera."

He wandered across the suite. Her bedroom door was slightly ajar. He lifted his hand and knocked. The door edged open a few inches, enough for him to see her reflection in the mirror above the bureau.

She was brushing her hair. It glided through her fingers like a midnight waterfall. The *nays* became *yahs*, every tone round and plush. Soon she'd hit the *lahs*, his favorite part. He waited, hearing each perfect *lah*. Except—

Her lips weren't moving.

The brush swept in a glissade through her hair. Her voice traveled up the scale and down. But her lips didn't move. Only the hairbrush.

She spotted him in the mirror. A smile flickered across her face for a fraction of a second before it froze. She dropped the hairbrush, made a dash for the door, and pushed it shut, leaving him out in the cold on the other side.

9

Thad took a step back. The closed door told him everything. He pushed it back open.

She stood in the center of the room, hairbrush stalled in midair, her vocalizations playing in the background. "I'm on vocal rest," she declared. "You wouldn't understand."

"Oh, I understand, all right, and I'm calling bullshit."

Her head came up. She looked snooty as all hell. At the same time, vulnerable. "Which is meaningless since you don't know anything about the human voice."

"Maybe not, but I know when somebody's pulling a scam."

Her chin stayed high. "It's not a scam!"

Her arrogance was an act. He could feel it, but he didn't care. "Is that even you singing?"

"Of course it's me singing!" Her chest heaved as she drew in one of her long breaths. "Even on vocal rest, it's helpful keeping to a regular routine."

"That's crap. And I should have figured it out days ago. Serious singers like you who are on vocal rest aren't supposed to talk much, isn't that right? Hardly the case with you."

She turned her back to him and moved away from the mirror. "I'm not discussing this."

He was furious. They were friends. Good friends, despite the short time they'd known each other. They'd shared things about themselves. They'd laughed together, insulted each other, nearly frozen to death. The fact that she would mislead him like this felt like the worst kind of betrayal.

"Suit yourself," he retorted.

Her shoulders sagged.

He turned on his heel and left the room. He was done with her.

Heartsick, Olivia sank onto her bed. She'd lost her voice. Not from laryngitis, allergies, polyps, or nodules—nothing was physically wrong—she'd lost it from guilt. And now Thad knew the truth about her.

You let me believe we were forever. You meant everything to me and I meant nothing to you. Why should I keep on living?

The email Adam had sent before he'd killed himself had laid it out, and despite what Rachel said and what the psychologist she'd visited had told her, despite Thad's opinion on the subject, Olivia knew she was responsible.

Rachel had witnessed the scene at the funeral. She knew Olivia's singing was suffering, but she didn't know how badly. Only the doctor she'd seen and Thad knew the truth.

Technically speaking, she had a psychogenic voice disorder. She couldn't get a full breath when she tried to sing. Her heart would begin to race, and an unnatural, gritty quality distorted the full, rich tones that were her hallmark. Her reliable vibrato had grown unsteady. Without her customary breath support, her tongue fell back, and she strangled her high notes. Worst of all, she sometimes went flat.

She was Olivia Shore. She never went flat. But now she did, and in exactly twenty-five days, she was scheduled to sing Amneris in *Aida* at the Chicago Municipal Opera.

She jumped up from the side of the bed, the thought of the looming deadline filling her with panic. She was doing breathing exercises and yoga, trying to meditate, and drinking copious amounts of water. After the disastrous drunken night when she'd attacked Thad, she'd restricted herself to a single glass of wine each evening. She'd never smoked, she avoided carbonated beverages, and she drank so much lemon and honey in warm water that she'd forgotten what plain cold water tasted like. She'd hoped this tour would be the distraction she needed to break the cycle she was trapped in, but it only seemed to be making things worse.

Everyone in the opera world understood medical issues could cause a singer to temporarily lose her voice, but her career would be impacted in all the wrong ways if word got out that she'd lost her voice for psychological reasons.

Each morning since the funeral, she'd played a recording of her daily vocalizing, hoping the familiarity would ease her breathing enough so she'd naturally begin to sing, but it wasn't working. Her guilt was literally choking her.

As Thad ignored her on the flight to Dallas, she tried unsuccessfully to convince herself she hadn't been deliberately deceiving him. But the truth was, she'd been afraid he'd discover the secret she hadn't been able to reveal to Rachel. By purposefully bumping up the volume on the recording whenever she knew he was nearby, she'd knowingly misled him.

They landed, and while Paisley stayed behind to gather the luggage, she and Thad, along with Henri and Mariel, took a stretch limo to the hotel. Olivia couldn't escape the sinking feeling she'd destroyed a friendship that had become invaluable to her. She had to talk to him, but he was seated as far away from her as he could get. Finally, she pulled out her phone and texted him.

I'm sorry.

He glanced at his screen. She half expected him to ignore her, but he didn't. **Don't care.**

It's complicated.

This time he did ignore her. She recalled the little she knew about professional athletes and tried again. **Haven't u ever hidden an injury?**

He studied the screen. His thumbs moved. **Not from my friends.**

What about all ur mysterious phone calls and that computer screen u keep hiding.

His jaw set. **Business.**

She tugged on her bottom lip with her teeth and typed. **Forgive me and I'll have sex with u.**

His head shot up. He looked down the length of the limo at her. His thumbs raced over the keypad. **Ur trying to bribe me with sex?**

I guess. But only once.

You lie to me and now u want to REWARD yourself by having sex with me?

Those capital letters were a clear insult, which deserved a response in kind. **It should be obvious by now that I'm emotionally unstable. Which is why I LOST MY VOICE!**

As an afterthought, she added a hashtag. **#compassion**

His reply was brief. **#bullshit**

She sighed and tucked her phone away.

He glanced over at her. His thumbs started to move and then stalled. He tucked his own phone away.

Thad was in a foul mood, and the construction holding up Dallas traffic didn't help. He was used to Chicago's incessant road work, but Dallas seemed worse, or maybe his mood had more to do with what had happened this morning. He remembered the sprained ankle he'd once hidden for fear the Dolphins' defense would capitalize on his weaker side, and the fractured rib he'd made sure no one knew about. But that was different. He had his teammates to think about.

But The Diva had her reputation at stake. She had to deal with audiences who would boo her, with opera companies that wouldn't hire her, and with music critics who'd rip her to shreds if she wasn't on her game.

Still, she should have told him because—

Because she should have.

Olivia had been doing most of the talking during their interviews all day to cover up his own muted responses. They ended the afternoon in a city garden being photographed for *D Magazine.* The garden shoot had been Mariel's idea. Henri had wanted them photographed at a retro pinball arcade. Henri's idea would have produced more memorable photographs, but in the end, Mariel was clearly the power play in the battle between them, and she'd won.

They hadn't been back to the hotel for a full hour when he discovered Olivia had run off to the hotel's indoor swimming pool. By herself. After what had happened in New Orleans, he grabbed his room key and raced to the pool in his gym shorts and a T-shirt.

She was alone swimming the length of the pool. *Alone!* No couples reclined on the white-cushioned loungers. No kids called out "Marco . . ." "Polo . . ." He stripped off his T-shirt and dove in.

As he came up next to her, her stroke faltered, and her eyes widened under her swim goggles.

"Good move," he said sarcastically. "Coming down here by yourself."

The Diva regained her rhythm. "You're not speaking to me, remember?" She pulled away from him, the threads of dark hair that had escaped from her swim cap clinging to her neck.

It occurred to him that he might be sulking. He'd called bullshit on her. Maybe it was time to call it on himself.

But she was already half a pool length away. She had a strong kick, a long reach, and a smooth stroke—better form than he did. But he was stronger, and he set out to prove it, although being in waterlogged gym shorts instead of swim trunks handicapped him.

As he finally drew even with her, he spotted an ugly bruise on her arm from where she'd been attacked. That mark felt like failure on his part for not keeping a closer watch, but if he mentioned that, she'd only insist she wasn't his responsibility.

He stayed even with her for a few strokes, the smell of chlorine strong in his nose. When she reached the deep end, she did one of those underwater flip turns he'd never quite mastered and took off again, showing no intention of stopping to talk to him. He pushed awkwardly off the end of the pool. He couldn't match her style, but he damn well could beat her on endurance. He checked out the clock on the wall.

6:32

It was on. One highbrow opera diva versus one superbly trained NFL quarterback.

6:39

He didn't try to stay even with her and let her swim at her own graceful pace.

6:45

He chugged along—all strength, no style. One end of the pool to the other.

7:06

Her stroke had grown choppy. She was tiring, but she refused to stop before he did.

7:14

The fading light outside the windows had developed an orange tint. He'd only been swimming for forty-two minutes. She'd been swimming longer.

7:18

It belatedly occurred to him that her bruised shoulder had to be bothering her, yet she refused to give up. He was an ass.

He blocked her as she approached. “Uncle.” He set his feet down. “Damn, but you’re strong.” He took some deep, unnecessary breaths so she wouldn’t feel bad.

She didn’t seem to. They stood in a little less than five feet of water, so he could only see part of what looked like a modest black bikini. Her face was flushed, right along with the tops of her breasts. It was time to get this over with, and he tried not to look at the bruise on her shoulder. “I wish you’d been honest with me,” he said.

She pulled off her goggles and moved to the side of the pool. “It’s not exactly something I wanted to talk about.”

“You push me to talk about things I don’t want to talk about.”

“Like . . . ?” She climbed the ladder, giving him an unrestricted view of her very fine butt. When he didn’t respond, she looked down at him from the pool deck. “Like talking about how being a backup makes you feel? Or what’s going to happen to you when you age out of the game? Or those mystery phone calls you’re always making? Or how about your track record as a serial dater?”

"Serial monogamist. There's a difference." She stood above him, water sluicing down her long, strong legs, goggles dangling from her fingertips. "You should have told me the truth instead of playing that recording every morning."

"I'm telling you now." She dropped her goggles on one of the white-cushioned loungers, pulled off her swim cap, and tossed her hair. As she wrapped herself in one of the pool towels, he drew his gaze away from her legs and climbed the ladder. She turned toward the long windows that looked out on a garden. He fetched a towel for himself, giving her time.

"In less than a month," she said, "I'm scheduled to sing Amneris in *Aida* at Chicago Municipal Opera."

"I know that. And the big gala at the Muni is the next night." He hooked the towel around his shoulders. "I'm going to take a wild stab and guess that performing has become a problem."

Her head wobbled in a jerky nod as she turned back to him. He'd never seen her look so defenseless. "When I try to sing—really sing, as opposed to warbling Garth Brooks with a karaoke machine—nothing comes out the way it should."

"How long has this been going on?"

She collapsed at the end of one of the loungers. "It started the day I opened that email. I had a concert that night, and I noticed a constriction in my chest. The more I sang, the thinner my voice grew, until, by the end, I barely sounded like myself." She plucked at a loose thread on the towel. "Since then, it's only gotten worse. I've seen a doctor." She seemed to be forcing herself to look at him. "I have what's called a psychogenic voice disorder, a polite way of saying I'm crazy."

"I doubt that." He could either loom over her or sit down, too. He chose the end of the adjoining lounger. "You've lost your voice because you believe you're responsible for your ex killing himself, is that right?"

"It's abundantly clear that's the case." She pushed her feet into the flip-flops she'd left nearby. As serious as this conversation was, he wished she'd drop the towel. He was a dick.

"I told you. He was sweet, handsome. He loved me. We were part of the same world. We loved the same composers, the same singers. It seemed natural for us to get married, even though I knew how sensitive he was. But instead of ending it when I should have, I let it drag on." She tugged on the strap of her bikini top. "I'll never forget the way he looked at me when I told him. Like I'd shot him. Ironic, right?"

"You didn't shoot him. You broke up with him. It happens all the time."

"Adam was a better person than I'll ever be." She pulled the towel tighter. "Thoughtful. Kind."

"Kids and dogs. Yeah, you already told me."

She tucked a lock of wet hair behind her ear. "I did love him. Just not the same way he loved me."

"Who doesn't screw up when it comes to relationships? You made a mistake. It happens."

"This mistake cost Adam his life."

Thad didn't like that. "Adam cost Adam his life."

She gazed at him, looking both raw and mystified. "He thought we were forever."

"People break up. Afterward, you get drunk, cry, whatever. You move on."

She finally dropped the towel. It settled in a damp fold at her waist. "How do *you* break up with someone? What do you say? I assume you've had a lot of practice."

"Sometimes they break up with me."

He'd sounded defensive, and of course she picked up on it. "But it's usually the other way around, isn't it? Do you give them that old line, 'It's not you, it's me'?"

"Never say that when you're breaking up with someone."

"Now you tell me." She gave him a wobbly smile. "So how do you do it?"

"I'm upfront from the start. I don't have anything against marriage for other people, but I enjoy my life the way it is. I don't like committing to the kind of beer I drink, let alone to marriage. I'm selfish like that."

"I can't believe in your long, serial monogamy journey, you don't run into women who think they can change your mind."

"They're easy to identify. Also, not every woman is in a race to the altar, as you know. Plus, I have good taste, and most of the women I date are smart enough to see right through me."

"You're not that bad."

He leaned toward her. "I'm too self-centered for marriage. And even thinking about taking on the responsibility of having kids makes me break out in a cold sweat."

"So you've never had one of those dramatic breakups? Tears and screaming matches?"

"There've been some hurt feelings, but nobody sure as hell ever killed herself!"

"Lucky you."

An older couple came through the door and headed for the whirlpool. The man had a furry gray chest, and unlike Olivia's sleek swim cap, the woman wore one of those old-fashioned bathing caps with rubber flowers all over it.

The noisy bubble of the whirlpool kept them from being overheard, but he still lowered his voice. "Maybe you should have been upfront with him earlier, but waiting too long to break up with someone isn't a crime. This is on him, not on you." He could see she didn't believe him. "You know what your trouble is?"

"No. Be sure to tell me."

"You're a perfectionist. You want to be the best at everything you do. Singing, acting, dancing, promoting watches, and relationships. In your mind, there's no room for error. No room for mistakes. But whether you want to accept it or not, you're human." He realized she could shoot those same words back to him. But she didn't.

"So am I forgiven for deceiving you?"

"I guess that depends."

"On?"

He cocked his head at her. "On how serious you are about that night of sex you offered me if I forgave you for your grievous betrayal of our friendship."

"I don't think I was serious."

"You're not sure?"

She shrugged, looking more like an insecure teenager than a seasoned opera singer.

"So just to make certain everything's out in the open . . . You want to get down and dirty with me, but you're worried that could lead to a relationship. Which you don't want."

"Definitely not."

"Hardly an insurmountable problem since neither do I." He tugged on one end of the towel draping his neck as he briefly debated how far to push her. "Here's my suggestion. Las Vegas. The last night of the tour before Chicago. You, me, and a bedroom. We have all the sex we can pack in before morning. And then . . ."

"Then?"

"We fly to Chicago. Hang out together for two weeks until the gala. After that, I dump you forever."

She smiled. "Go on."

"This gives us something to look forward to—Las Vegas—and it also solves the relationship problem you're worried about." It didn't solve the problem of the danger she was in, a complication he still wanted resolved.

She thought it over. "Just to clarify . . . You'll look past my small deception, but only if I have sex with you?"

"Your brutal, *hurtful* deception. And, as a gentleman, I'm deeply offended that you believe I'd bargain with sex. Unlike you."

She tilted her head so her hair fell over one shoulder. "I'm forgiven, right?"

"As long as you promise to be straight with me from now on."

"I promise." She made a cross over her heart that was such a little girl move, he wanted to kiss her. "We have three days of interviews in Chicago, then a two-week break while you laze around and I work hard in rehearsals. Assuming I have the voice to show up at rehearsals." The distress he'd hoped never again to witness clouded her eyes. She combed her fingers through her hair. "But as soon as those rehearsals start, we're done."

"Hold on. Once the gala is over, we're done. It's our last obligation to Marchand, and no way are you depriving us of those two weeks of sexual bliss."

"Wrong." She pushed her hair away from her face. "We have sex the last night in Las Vegas. Sex for those three nights we're in Chicago before rehearsals start. And then you dump me on Sunday night, right before my rehearsals start on Monday morning."

"Fine. I'll compromise. We have the last night in Las Vegas. Three nights in Chicago. *And* the two weeks while you're in rehearsal. I'll have dinner and a back rub waiting for you when you come home. The night of the gala, I dump you."

"Exactly how is that a compromise?"

Because he wanted it to be.

She pointed a long, elegant finger at him. "There's no compromise. As soon as rehearsals start, I'm on the job, completely focused, and we're over."

"Now, Liv, be reasonable."

"The only time we'll see each other again is at the gala. We'll greet each other like old friends, pose for photos, and go our separate ways. That's it. We're history. No dates. No cozy dinners. No lakefront walks. Nothing."

"You really are afraid of me, aren't you?"

She shifted her knees. "Do you agree or not?"

"This is like a bad labor negotiation, but I agree." For now, anyway. Once things unfolded, he intended to revisit the situation.

"Great." She gave him a bright smile. A smile he had to spoil because he couldn't stand the knots that had formed in her shoulders, the tension in her neck.

"Liv, you need to get your head together."

"How do you suggest I do that?"

"Ease up on yourself about Adam. Accept your many imperfections—which I'll be happy to keep pointing out, starting with your tendency to run off by yourself." A thread of an idea formed in the back of his mind. "You also have to start singing for me."

She jumped from the chaise, leaving the towel behind. "I told you. I can't sing!"

The elderly couple in the hot tub looked over at them. He rose and blocked their view of Olivia. "I didn't say you had to sing opera. Maybe some blues. Rock. 'The Wheels on the Bus.' I don't care. I'm only a football player, remember? I won't know if what I'm hearing is good or bad."

"We've listened to jazz together, remember? You know music. And that's the worst idea ever."

"Is it? I have to deal with Clint Garrett, remember? A guy with all the talent in the world who still manages to choke under pressure. The two of you have strong similarities."

"Such as?"

"You're both a hell of a lot of work."

What had only been the glimmer of an idea began to take shape.

When Thad pounded on her bedroom door an hour before they were scheduled to leave for Atlanta the next day, she politely suggested he go to hell. Unfortunately, that didn't discourage him, and the next thing she knew he'd barged inside her room, grabbed her hairbrush from the dresser, and held it out. "Sing!"

"No."

"Don't mess with me on this, Olivia. We're going to try a little of my kind of therapy."

She pushed his arm away and tried withering him with her most condescending look. "Opera singers don't use microphones."

He was un-witherable. "Right now, you're not an opera singer. You're an ordinary singer. And they use mikes." Once again, he extended the stupid hairbrush. "I was thinking I'd enjoy some Ella or Nina Simone."

"Try Spotify."

His lip curled, but not in a good way. "And you brag about your work ethic. What I see is a woman who's given up. Instead of fighting the good fight and doing the work to fix what's wrong, all you want to do is whine." As if that weren't scathing enough, he added, "I'm disappointed in you."

Nobody was ever disappointed in Olivia Shore. She snatched the hairbrush from his hand and gave him Billie Holiday. A few stanzas of "God Bless the Child" sung so badly it was a good thing Billie was already dead, because if she'd heard Olivia's choppy phrasing, she would have killed herself.

Thad smiled. "You could take that to Carnegie Hall right now."

She threw the hairbrush at him. She targeted his chest instead of his head—unnecessary, as it turned out, because he plucked the hairbrush right out of the air before it could land.

"I'm that good," he said at her expression of astonishment.

If only she were.

"And you're not as bad as you think." He patted her cheek. "I ordered us breakfast. Strawberry cheesecake French toast."

She regarded him glumly. "Only for me, I'm sure. While you have an arugula-kale smoothie with a side order of garden grubs."

"Now don't you worry about it."

As it turned out, she never got to enjoy that French toast because she made the mistake of checking her phone before she sat down to eat.

10

Her New Orleans attack had gone public. The mainstream newspapers restricted the item to a few factual sentences, but the Internet gossip sites were all over it.

> Police are giving few details about a bizarre attack on opera star Olivia Shore. The assault occurred in a New Orleans alley. Shore was apparently unharmed, but what was she doing in a back alley? And what part did Thad Owens, the Chicago Stars' backup quarterback, who is rumored to be involved with the opera diva, play in the incident? So many questions.

It couldn't have looked sleazier.

Thad was still upset as they rode the elevator to the lobby where they'd meet the limo taking them to the airfield for their flight to Atlanta. "They're insinuating that I beat you up!" he exclaimed.

They were doing exactly that, but she tried to minimalize it. "Not really," she said weakly.

"Close enough."

"I don't understand why we're getting all this attention."

"Because I'm a dumb jock and you're a high-class diva, and it's too good a story to pass up."

"The only thing dumb about you is your taste in T-shirts." His, she happened to know, was a two-hundred-and-fifty-dollar Valentino.

He gazed down at the navy-and-red graphic of astronauts floating in space. "Might have been a mistake."

"You think?"

Only Henri and Paisley were waiting by the limo. Fortunately, Mariel had left the tour, but Olivia suspected she'd turn up again, like a head cold that wouldn't go away. She'd probably run off to Uncle Lucien so she could complain about the rubes Henri had hired to represent the company.

"We'll look on the bright side," a less-than-cheerful Henri said as they arrived at the airfield, "two new radio outlets called to schedule an interview."

"For all the wrong reasons," Thad said.

Once they were on board, Thad received a phone call of his own. Since he'd taken a seat across from Olivia, she could hear his side of the conversation, which mainly consisted of unhappy grunts. When he pocketed his phone, she regarded him with concern. "Everything okay?"

"The Stars press office. Phoebe Calebow isn't happy."

Even Olivia knew about the legendary Phoebe Calebow, the owner of the Chicago Stars and the most powerful woman in the NFL.

He extended his legs as far as the space would allow. "Phoebe has a low tolerance for anything that even hints at one of her players abusing a woman."

"I can talk to her, if you'd like."

He curled his lip. "No thanks, Mom. I'll take care of it."

"I'm only trying to be helpful."

"Nobody just 'talks' to Phoebe Calebow, not unless they're royalty. Or a member of the Calebow family. She's the most intimidating hot woman you've ever met."

"I've seen the photos. She could have been a *Playboy* centerfold in the old days when she was younger. Or even now, if they still had centerfolds."

"People used to underestimate her because of her looks, but only an idiot makes that mistake now. Trust me when I say nobody wants to get on her bad side."

She could see he was worried, which meant she was worried for him.

As the next few days unfolded, Marchand Timepieces received more press coverage than they could have expected, but not entirely the right kind. Too many of the country's X-rated morning radio show hosts suddenly wanted interviews, all of which Henri refused in favor of the more respectable media.

Olivia quickly perfected her responses to questions about New Orleans. Instead of disclosing that the attack had happened in a bookstore, which only made it seem more bizarre, she referred to a small shop in the French Quarter and a case of being in the wrong place at the wrong time. "It was so random. Obviously, someone who's mentally disturbed was behind it. I'm so thankful Thad rushed over to meet me at the police station. He's a good friend."

That ended the questions from all but the most persistent.

They moved from Atlanta to Nashville, and Thad kept trying to make her sing. She appreciated what he was attempting to do for her, but singing a few bars of Billie Holiday wouldn't overcome the kind of block she was dealing with. Still, he was persistent and she was desperate. Whenever they were alone and had a break between interviews, he shoved his phone at her with song lyrics displayed. Today it was "Georgia on My Mind."

"Let's hear it," he said.

"This isn't going to fix me," she retorted.

"Stop being so negative. You sounded better this morning than you did yesterday, and you like singing jazz."

She glanced at the lyrics to "Georgia on My Mind." "There's a big difference between singing Ray Charles and launching into an F-natural for Amneris's "Quale insolita gioia nel tuo sguardo." At his quizzical expression, she translated. "'What rare joy shines on your face.'"

"Thanks."

"Not your face. Radamès's face. And he's thinking about his love for Aida, not any passion he holds for Amneris, worse luck for her."

"Shows what happens when a woman gets too serious about someone, even in ancient Egypt."

"Exactly." She thought of Adam. Of *Aida.* Of the way Amneris sends Radamès to his death. She snatched the phone from him and began to sing. "Georgia . . . Georgia . . ."

Thad closed his eyes and listened.

This was jazz, not opera, and her chest constriction eased. Not enough to produce the sounds she needed to perform. Far from it. But as he'd said, better than yesterday.

Thad had promised to take some of his Nashville buddies out that night, but he'd committed before he'd gotten tangled up with keeping The Diva safe. He couldn't see himself dragging her along into another noisy bar. She'd have to strain her voice to talk, and she was under enough stress. Besides, it was guys only, and he was supposed to meet them in an hour.

As he pondered his options, he wandered into her adjoining suite where she was doing some yoga sun salutations by the windows. He sprawled on the couch and pretended to look at his phone when, in fact, he was admiring her strength right along with the stretch of her yoga pants over her butt.

He considered his dilemma. He owed these guys, and he didn't want to cancel, but Henri was busy and Paisley was useless.

The suite's doorbell rang. Thad blocked her from answering and opened the door himself.

Clint Garrett stood on the other side. "I was visiting a girlfriend in Memphis, and I thought I'd drop in."

"Memphis is a couple of hundred miles away," Thad pointed out.

Clint shrugged. "Whatever."

For once, Garrett's timing was exactly right. "Come on in."

"Hey, Clint." The Diva waved at him and returned to her sun salutations.

"Sorry I couldn't get here earlier," Clint said. "I saw that crap in the papers, and I heard Phoebe's all stirred up about it. I want you to know I'm here for you, T-Bo."

Thad slapped him on the back. "Appreciate it. As a matter of fact, I'm glad you're here."

Clint regarded him suspiciously. "Why's that?"

"I have to go out, and I need you to stay with Liv."

Olivia came out of her down dog. "I don't need anybody to stay with me."

"Yeah, she does." He gave Clint more details of the New Orleans attack and mentioned the threatening letters. "There's been some other nastiness. A phone call, a couple of packages. She also has a stalker named Rupert."

Olivia reared up. "Rupert is not a—"

Thad continued, ignoring her. "I don't trust hotel security. Point of fact—you didn't have any trouble getting up here. Plus, she has a habit of running off."

"I do not—"

"I need to slip out for a couple of hours." He gave Clint another tap on the back. "Can you keep an eye on her?"

"Sure."

"I don't need a babysitter," the yogi huffed from the window.

"She's slippery," Thad said. "Don't let her get away from you."

"I am not slip—"

"Got it," Clint said. "Can I make out with her?"

Bastard. "You can try. Doubt you'll succeed." On the other hand, Clint was a good-looking guy, and he met The Diva's most important requirement in a lover: no possibility of a relationship.

Thad eyeballed The Diva. "Clint's not the brightest guy in the world, and sex is the only way he knows how to relate to women. I don't *think* you'll fall for his routine, but if you do . . . make sure he's got that herpes outbreak under control."

Clint laughed and pounded Thad extra hard on the back. "You're one of a kind, dude."

The Diva smiled. "I don't need a babysitter, but it would be lovely to be with someone who's not bossing me around."

"I know what you mean," Clint said. "Boy, do I ever know what you mean."

Thad glared at him. "Do *not* let her out of your sight."

"Roger that."

Thad met his pals that night, but he didn't have a good time. He was too busy thinking about what might be going on back at the hotel.

"That part always gets me." Clint's voice was suspiciously woolly with emotion. "'You complete me.' Everybody talks about that other thing. That 'had me at hello' thing, but when he says, 'You complete me.' What kind of dude says something like that? But still . . . It gets me."

Olivia wiped her eyes as the credits rolled on *Jerry Maguire*. "Why have I never seen this movie? I know why. Because I thought it was about football."

"Not enough action." Recovering from his brief emotional display, he draped his arm over the back of the couch. "If T-Bo asks, tell him we watched *The Waterboy*."

The leg she'd been sitting on had gone to sleep, and she pulled it out from under her. "Isn't that one of those Adam Sandler movies?"

He nodded. "It's most players' favorite."

"Because *Jerry Maguire* is too girlie, right?"

"I wouldn't exactly say that."

"Then what would you say?"

"It's too girlie."

She laughed and rose from the couch, wriggling her numb leg to get the blood moving again. "I'm going to bed, and you don't have to stay. Really. Thad's being ridiculous."

"S'okay. I'll just hang out here for a while."

"Don't be such a wimp. You're not his bitch."

"Says you."

"You shouldn't let him talk to you like he does." She sat back down. "I did a little research, and you have a higher quarterback rating after your second season than Dean Robillard did, and I know he's supposed to have been this big shot Stars player. But Thad treats you like you're a high school kid."

Clint nodded. "In football, you have to earn respect."

"And you haven't done that?"

"Not the kind of respect I want from him."

"But you're a better player than he is. That's what I don't understand. You're the starter. Not him."

"It's not that simple. I'm faster than he is, and my arm's stronger. But T-Bo . . . He's this wizard. Even with his vision thing, he can find a receiver where nobody else can, and the way he reads a defense . . . It's like he's got ESP. I have to learn how to do what he does."

"Even if it means putting up with his abuse?"

"Me and T-Bo . . . We have an understanding. I love the guy." He regarded her more sharply. "Now when it comes to T-Bo and women . . . you might want to be careful."

"You don't have to warn me. I've never been more clearheaded about anyone. No man is going to derail me." She could see he didn't believe her, and she tried to explain. "The three of us . . . You, Thad, me . . . We're not like most other people. Our work comes first."

He nodded and then grinned. "Do you want to mess with him?"

She tilted her head. "What do you have in mind?"

Where the *hell was she?* When he'd returned to the hotel and found the suite empty, he'd texted her and gotten no response. Then he'd texted the idiot he'd stupidly left to watch her.

Crickets.

He stalked to the lobby and talked to a bellman who'd seen Garrett drive off with The Diva in his Maserati GT convertible.

Thad told himself she'd be fine. The idiot wasn't an idiot. He'd keep her safe. But . . .

She should have been sound asleep here in the suite with Garrett standing guard outside her bedroom door.

He paced the floor like a parent waiting for a kid who'd violated curfew.

Half an hour passed. An hour. Finally, he heard them laughing in the hallway. Fucking *laughing*!

The door opened. She was all rumpled. Her dress had a swirly skirt, her hair was down and tangled, and she was barefoot, carrying her heels. What mainly struck him about Garrett was how young the kid looked. The epitome of youthful manliness. No fine lines webbed his eyes, no brackets ridged his mouth, and he'd bet anything that Garrett's knees didn't creak when he got out of bed in the morning.

Thad kept his voice in control, but he still sounded like a reprimanding parent. "Where have you been?"

"At a club," Olivia said brightly.

"A club?" He lost it, venting his anger on Garrett. "You took her to a club?"

The kid shrugged. "She's a wild one."

Thad turned on Olivia. "What about your voice? What kind of opera singer goes to a nightclub where the noise level is off the fucking decibel chart?"

Her smile was maddeningly serene. "I didn't talk."

"She's a great dancer," Garrett said quickly.

"You are, too." She gave the kid all kinds of smiles.

Garrett glanced uneasily at Thad. "I guess it's time I go."

"Good guess," Thad snarled.

One of Garrett's eyebrows lifted ever so slightly, and then, out of nowhere, he called an audible. In the sneak play of the century, he kissed The Diva with pinpoint accuracy, right on the lips—a full-on, wide open, All Pro, forward pass . . .

. . . with an eligible receiver kissing him right back.

Thad leaped forward.

The Diva shot out her arm—toward *him,* not toward the quarterback sneak—keeping Thad at a distance while she also kept her lips glued to Garrett's. Finally, she unglued and patted the asshole on the chest. "Good night, lover."

Garrett smiled and headed into the hallway only to turn back and make a small, quick movement—so small and quick Thad doubted The Diva even noticed. The kid lifted his arms and pointed toward Thad, the gesture over almost as soon as it had begun.

Son of a bitch. Garrett had tossed Thad a game signal. The same signal referees used to indicate that the offense had just earned a first down.

The clueless Diva shut the door and smiled at Thad. "That was fun."

He took a deep breath. Then another. He barely recognized himself. He was Thad Walker Bowman Owens! He'd never been jealous of another man in his life, yet here he was, fuming over a wet-behind-the-ears kid barely out of college. A kid who could run faster than Thad, throw farther . . .

The Diva smiled and gave him this soft, melty-eye, non-Diva look. "I adore you. I really do."

And that was it. Before he could conjure up even a semblance of a response, she'd sauntered into her bedroom, that swirly black skirt spanking her thighs.

Olivia smiled around her electric toothbrush. She was crazy about Clint Garrett. He was the mischievous little brother she'd always wanted—although she definitely wouldn't have kissed her little brother the same way she'd kissed Clint. But tonight, with Thad looking on, it had been too much fun to resist.

Fun. Something that hadn't played a big part in her life until Thad Owens had appeared.

Being with Clint tonight—trying to follow his steps in the country line dances—had been a reprieve from the overwhelming sexual sizzle she experienced when she was with Thad. The sizzle, mixed in with foreboding—an ominous sense she was inching too close to the rim of an active volcano.

She rinsed her mouth and stowed her toothbrush in the charger. Even though Thad's jealousy had only been a manifestation of his professional rivalry with Garrett, she'd enjoyed tweaking it.

As she slathered her face with her almond-scented cleanser, dabbed on her toner, then her retinol, she decided Thad Owens might be the most decent man she'd ever met. He'd assumed the role of her caretaker, whether she wanted him to or not. It was so odd. She'd been the caretaker in her relationship with Adam. The guardian of his career, the custodian of his feelings, the one who always accommodated. Having someone watch out for her was a new experience.

She hesitated, then turned the water on full force to mask the noise of her voice as she began singing her scales. Finally, she reached for a high C.

She didn't make it.

11

Thad played it cool for the next two days, acting as if the incident with Clint hadn't happened, but her attitude still bugged the hell out of him. Thad had been leading the offense since he was a kid. He was the play-caller, not The Diva. What kind of game was she running?

She gazed at him across the room service cart. They'd gotten in the habit of eating an early breakfast together in one suite or the other, and today she was deep into an egg white omelet.

He looked up from his phone. "I've got this urge to hear you do Cassandra Wilson's version of 'Time After Time.'"

Her nose went up. "Then call Cassandra Wilson. I'm sure she'd be more than happy to sing it for you."

"Come on, Liv. Give a guy a break."

"I can't even do Cindy Lauper's 'Time After Time.' And I don't know what Cassandra's version sounds like."

"I'll play it."

And he did. She sat back in her chair, breakfast abandoned, and listened to Wilson's wrenching, soulful version of the ancient Lauper hit. When it ended, she turned her head away and gazed out the window at the Manhattan skyline.

She began to sing. It wasn't Lauper or Wilson; it was some beautiful hybrid only she could produce. But even he knew it wasn't opera, and as her voice faded away, she looked so wistful that he couldn't bear it.

He pushed back from his own breakfast. "We've got a couple of hours before we have to be at Tiffany, and I have an idea . . ."

The eleven crystal chandeliers in the lobby of the Metropolitan Opera House were still a spectacular sight in the morning light. This place couldn't be more different from the basement jazz clubs where Thad usually hung out.

"There are twenty-one more chandeliers in the auditorium." Liv looked her normal superstar self in one of those black pencil dresses she'd changed into for the day, along with some gold Spanish earrings, her wide Egyptian cuff, and the Cavatina3. A pair of nude stilettos made her thoroughbred legs look ready for the runway.

She rested her hand on the curved railing. “Right before the performance begins, twelve of the big chandeliers in the auditorium ascend above the audience. It’s a spectacular sight.”

“I’ll bet.” Outside the Metropolitan’s soaring windows, a swarm of tourists clustered by the Lincoln Center fountain for photos, and in the distance, traffic jostled for position on Columbus Avenue. Manhattan was crazy. The noise. The traffic. The city’s chaos bothered him in a way Chicago’s midwestern bustle never did. Or maybe his sour mood had more to do with the memory of Clint Garrett’s lips on The Diva’s mouth.

“The Met’s chandeliers were a gift to the United States from the Austrian government in the 1960s,” she said. “A very nice thank-you present for the Marshall Plan.”

She shot him a sideways look that suggested she doubted he knew what the Marshall Plan was. He hadn’t taken only finance classes in college, so he suspected he knew more about the billions of dollars the US had earmarked for Western Europe’s World War II recovery efforts than she did.

He decided to deadpan it. "Not all jocks are ignorant, Liv. If it hadn't been for the Marshall Plan, small towns all across America wouldn't have a sheriff."

She blinked and laughed, but whatever retort she intended to make was cut off by the appearance of a short, rotund man with steel-wool hair and an elastic smile. "Olivia! My dear! Does Peter know you're here? And Thomas? It's been forever since we've seen you."

"Four months," she replied, after they'd done one of those double-cheek kisses Thad considered anti-American. "And this isn't an official visit. Charles, this is my . . . friend Thad Owens. Thad, Charles is one of the administrators who keeps this place running."

Charles shook hands politely, but he was far more focused on The Diva. "I was thinking about *Elektra* this morning and your Klytaemnestra. 'Ich habe keine guten Nächte.' I still get shivers. You were incandescent."

"Elektra," she said. "Our operatic version of a slasher movie."

"So deliciously bloody." He rubbed his hands. "And you're doing Amneris at the Muni in Chicago. Everyone's thrilled." The Diva's smile momentarily froze, but Charles didn't notice.

They exchanged more opera talk, with Charles treating Liv as if she were a goddess who'd descended into his midst. A few more staff members appeared, and one of them actually kissed her hand. Thad had to admit it was interesting watching someone other than himself being fawned over. It was also enlightening. He knew Liv was a big deal in the opera world, but seeing the reality drove the point home.

And made his mission even more urgent.

The expression on her face over breakfast as she'd listened to Cassandra Wilson had been too much for him. He'd told her he wanted a backstage tour of the Met because he was curious about the place, which was true, but more important, he hoped being back in these familiar surroundings might somehow unlock her voice.

Helping The Diva get her voice back had become almost as much of an obsession for him as picturing the two of them in bed on their last night in Las Vegas. It still seemed months away even though it was only a few days. As he knew from experience, great athletes didn't choke under pressure—except when they did. He'd done some research into psychogenic voice disorders, and he wondered if the lessons he'd learned from athletics through the years could carry over into music.

Unlocking the potential of others was something he'd become good at. The Diva was a head case, but so was every athlete at one time or another. Maybe it was his ego talking, but he liked the idea of being the person who freed her.

Eventually, Liv extricated herself from her admirers and took him up some stairs to the parterre level, where the box seats were located, and where they could look down on a rehearsal for an upcoming production of something in Russian, the name of which he didn't catch. Seeing what had to be a hundred singers moving around was impressive. "There are three additional big stages," she told him. "They come out on motorized platforms."

And he thought putting on an NFL game was complicated.

Liv took him to the maze that made up the various rooms of the costume department: areas packed with bolts of fabric, sewing machines, long tables where garments were being cut and hand-stitched, and rows of headless mannequins wearing parts of costumes.

"Madame Shore!" An older woman with cropped, pumpkin-colored hair bustled toward them, a pair of reading glasses jiggling on a long chain at her chest.

"Luella! It's good to see you."

Liv performed the introductions, and Luella took over the tour, showing him vast racks where thousands of garments were stored. "We had fourteen hundred costumes for *War and Peace* alone," Luella told him.

He met a cobbler resoling a pair of boots and watched a wig being made. The meticulous process of adding only two hairs at a time required a patience he couldn't imagine.

Everywhere they went, he witnessed the staff's affection and admiration for Olivia, an affection she returned. She remembered the names of husbands, wives, children, and boyfriends. She asked about ailments and work commutes. She advanced through her world the same way he did through his, paying attention to everyone, from the top administrators to the most junior employee.

A few people recognized him—the guy in charge of pressing the wrinkles out of bolts of fabric, a middle-aged woman doing intricate embroidery work, a couple of millennials, but this was clearly Olivia's show.

Luella disappeared around the corner and returned with the gown he recognized from YouTube videos of *Carmen*: a deliberately tatty, low-cut dress with a purposely grimy white bodice, a corseted middle, and a full scarlet skirt. Olivia tensed next to him as Luella spread it out on the table and opened the back.

"L'amour est un oiseau rebelle," the woman said. "Love is a rebellious bird."

He knew that one by now; it was the official title of "Habanera." As he took in the neckline, he remembered the way Liv's oiled breasts had spilled over the top. The way the skirt had swirled around her bare, splayed legs. Sexier than porn.

Luella opened the back of the gown. "Look at this, Mr. Owens."

Three white labels had been sewn in, each one printed in black marker with the name of the performer who'd worn the gown, the act number, and the opera in which the costume had been worn.

Elīna Garanča, Act 1, *Carmen*
Clémentine Margaine, Act 1, *Carmen*
Olivia Shore, Act 1, *Carmen*

Olivia touched the label. "The history of each costume."

"I hope it won't be long before you wear it again," Luella said.

Olivia nodded, even as her lips tightened at the corners.

Luella's comment stayed with Olivia for the rest of the day. What if she never again wore Carmen's costume? Or, more pressing, Amneris's elaborate Egyptian headdress and jeweled collar? The last time she'd sung the

Judgment scene as Amneris, the audience had come to its feet. Now, she'd be booed.

Henri accompanied her as she spoke to high school students at an Upper East Side music conservatory the next morning, while Thad visited a group of student athletes with Paisley. The conservatory teens were a dynamic mixture of scholarship kids and kids from wealthy families. Their enthusiasm for music, honest questions, and uncensored opinions reminded her of the way she'd been in that innocent time years earlier when she could never have imagined she'd let her voice be stolen.

Henri had insisted on a limo, although they could have made the trip faster on the subway. As he spoke on the phone, her thoughts took an unpleasant turn to Adam, the threats she'd been receiving, and her upcoming performance at the Muni. They stopped at a light on Fifth Avenue. She glanced over at the Metropolitan Museum of Art, and what had been only the faintest notion grew in urgency. She checked the time on her Cavatina3. It was 9:56 a.m. on the dot. Perfect.

"Henri, the museum is opening in four minutes, and I'm going to make a quick stop. I'll meet you at the hotel."

"*Non, non!* Thad has insisted—"

"It's the Metropolitan. I'll be fine." She jumped out of the car before he could stop her, crossed through a break in traffic to the curb, and waved him on. An impulsive visit to the Metropolitan Museum of Art just as the doors were opening hardly counted as high risk.

"We will wait for you!" Henri shouted, sticking his head out the open window, his brown hair streaming straight back from his face. "Text me when you're ready."

She waved in acknowledgment and climbed the front steps.

It didn't take long to clear security and pay her entrance fee. She knew exactly where she wanted to be—where she needed to be—and she took a quick turn to her right. She moved through the Tomb of Perneb without stopping. He was only a Fifth Dynasty court official, and she needed more power than he offered. She wove past the mummies and funerary equipment of the Ptolemies and the chapel reliefs of Ramses I until she reached the Temple of Dendur.

The hordes of visitors hadn't yet descended, and the spacious light-filled gallery with its sweep of angled windows was quiet. This might be the Met's most popular exhibit, but popularity hadn't brought her here, nor had nostalgia for the times she'd performed in this same spot at cultural events and black-tie galas. She'd come here because the Temple of Dendur was dedicated to Isis, and Isis was one of the Egyptians' most powerful gods of both healing and magic, two things she sorely needed.

The reflecting pool representing the waters of the Nile glistened in the morning light. She bypassed the temple's gate and went directly into the temple itself, passing through its twin columns with their papyrus plant capitals. Two other visitors had beaten her here. Maybe they, too, felt the sacredness of this space because neither was speaking.

She'd once visited the temple with an Egyptologist who'd been able to read each of the ancient hieroglyphics covering the sandstone walls, but she'd been more interested in imagining the lives of the Nubian people who'd gathered here.

She touched the wall. *Isis, if you have any mojo left, would you fix me? Would you ease my chest, open my throat? Give me back my confidence. Let me—*

"Olivia?"

She spun around to see a small woman entering the temple. Her hope for solitude vanished.

"My dear." The woman took Olivia's hands. "I was just thinking about you!"

"Kathryn, how are you?"

"So busy! With the *Aida* gala only three weeks away, my head is spinning with ideas. We're building a re-creation of Dendur at the front entrance for the guests to pass through."

"I'm sure that'll be amazing."

Eugene Swift's widow looked like the stereotype of a seventy-year-old art patron. Slim and trim, with a black velvet headband holding her gray bob away from her face, she wore what was surely vintage Chanel, along with the low, square-heeled black pumps—probably Ferragamo—that women of her age and social status favored. As her husband's replacement on the board of the Chicago Municipal Opera, as well as one of its most generous donors, she was the last person Olivia wanted to know about her voice. "What are you doing in New York?" she asked.

Kathryn gave a dismissive wave. "We have a place here. Only myself and my son now that Eugene is gone."

"He was a wonderful man," Olivia said truthfully. "We all miss him."

At Kathryn's request, Olivia had sung at his funeral. Eugene Swift had been a true opera scholar with a deep appreciation of all its forms. He'd also been Olivia's friend.

"He would have loved the *Aida* gala," Kathryn said. "I'm suggesting costumes, but only for the women.

Frankly, the idea of potbellied men draping themselves in white linen would put me off my dinner. I'm having a robe made for the event. I can give you the name of my dressmaker if you'd like."

"I'm sure I can borrow something from the costume shop."

"You're a dear. Everyone will look forward to seeing what you wear." Kathryn gazed up at the temple walls. Olivia knew her real passion lay with art museums, not opera, and Olivia appreciated her continued involvement with the Chicago Muni Opera to honor Eugene's memory. "I adore this temple," she said. "Since it's not looted like the Elgin Marbles, one can admire it without feeling guilty."

Olivia was well acquainted with the history of the temple, a gift from the Egyptian government for the part the United States had played in saving it, along with other artifacts, from the bottom of Lake Nasser when the Aswan Dam was constructed.

Unlike other socialites' brows, Kathryn's still had the ability to wrinkle. "It's such a dilemma. One has to believe museums should return stolen artifacts to their rightful country, but what if it's a country like Syria or Iraq where ISIS has destroyed so much? I don't want to be accused of cultural insensitivity, but until those countries stabilize, our museums should hold on to what we have." She set her hand on one of the temple's oval cartouches. "I'll never forgive LBJ for giving Dendur to the Metropolitan instead of to Chicago. It would have been such a magnificent addition to the Art Institute. Still, one has to admit that the Metropolitan's done well by it."

Olivia didn't hear the rest of Kathryn's monologue as a familiar, unwelcome figure made his way through the gate. He headed directly toward them, all athletic grace and frosty glare. As he stopped at Olivia's side, she offered up her brightest smile. "Kathryn, this is Thad Owens. Thad, Mrs. Swift is our honorary hostess for the Muni gala."

Kathryn extended a wrinkled hand displaying, among other things, an impressive jade ring. "Yes. The football player. I've met your delightful owner, Mrs. Calebow, several times."

Before Olivia could point out that Phoebe Calebow owned the team, not Thad personally, he'd taken the older woman's hand. "A pleasure to meet you, Mrs. Swift." The look he shot Olivia was anything but pleasurable.

She appreciated his concern, but she didn't enjoy having a full-time watchdog. "We have to run, Kathryn."

As soon as they cleared the temple gates, Thad started lecturing her. She barely listened. Instead, she was distracted by his Victory780—not the watch itself, but the way his wrist displayed it, with masculine perfection.

No matter what Mariel Marchand might think, she couldn't have found a better man to represent that watch. He was a natural leader, protective of others and demanding of himself. He was self-confident, but didn't take himself too seriously. He was intelligent, charismatic, and sexier than any man should be.

Desire thrummed through her body. *Las Vegas.* Why had she struck that crazy deal with him? Why wait for Las Vegas? Why not now? This morning? Tonight?

Never?

The world was spinning out of her control.

"When are you going to get a handle on your porn addiction?" she said, as they stepped out onto Fifth Avenue.

"My what?"

"Don't think I haven't noticed how much you're on your laptop, and the way you make sure no one can see what's on the screen. You're clearly addicted to porn."

He smiled. "When you can't have the real thing . . ."

He was messing with her again. He wasn't watching porn. Something else had his attention, and she wondered what it was.

Four-star hotels excelled at fulfilling their guests' last-minute requests—in this case, supplying Thad with a pair of rain jackets. Liv's was too big, his too small, but at least the top half of them was staying dry.

The weather, in typical April fashion, was cold and drizzly, which gave Thad the opportunity he'd been looking for. They had a few hours before tonight's dinner, and after this morning's visit to the Metropolitan Opera and Olivia's reckless side trip to the museum, Thad's determination to do something to help her had strengthened. But he needed a special place for what he had in mind.

Liv peered at him from under the hood of her rain jacket, a few drops slithering down her nose. "Where are you taking me?"

"Never you mind where I'm taking you. You keep forgetting I'm the man in this relationship, and what I say goes."

That cracked her up, as he'd known it would, and she emitted a trio of unladylike snorts.

They were in his favorite part of Central Park, the North Woods. During his days with the Giants, he'd often come here to run. Because of its location in the park's far northwest corner, the North Woods wasn't as heavily visited as the central and southern sections, and today's inclement weather had left it virtually deserted.

Which was exactly what he needed. Hotel suites, no matter how luxurious, weren't soundproofed, leaving him to wonder where, in this busy, crowded city, he might take a woman who could potentially break glass with her voice. The answer had come to him as they were leaving the museum. The North Woods on a rainy day when no one would be around.

He'd been surprised how easily he'd gotten her to agree to go out with him in this less-than-ideal weather until he remembered she liked being outdoors nearly as much as he did, although in typical diva fashion she'd wrapped her neck in a couple hundred wool scarves.

"It's raining," she pointed out unnecessarily.

"It's drizzling. There's a difference. And I thought humidity was good for your voice."

"Not if I'm freezing to death."

"Are you?"

"No. But I might be."

"If that happens, we'll head right back to the hotel, lock all the doors, and settle into whichever one of our beds we get to first."

Apparently, he looked exactly as lecherous as he felt because she gave him another of her snorts. "This is Manhattan. Not Las Vegas."

"We could pretend."

She laughed, but she sounded nervous. He wasn't exactly calm himself. They'd made too big a deal out of the last-night-in-Las-Vegas thing. They should have been getting it on from the beginning. This was what came of lusting after a high-strung diva.

He steered her off the paved pathway onto a side trail leading in the general direction of the part of the North Woods known as the Ravine. A woodpecker drummed on a dead tree, and ferns pushed their way through the winter leaf debris bordering the stream that ran through this section of the park. He could hear water rushing down one of the cascades. Frederick Law Olmsted had wanted to re-create the Adirondacks here, and he'd designed the woodlands with a stream, waterfalls, and outcrops of boulders.

They hadn't seen anyone for a while, and as they reached a thick grove of ironwoods where the distant sound of traffic was barely audible, he decided now was as good a time as any. "I need a rest. It's been a busy day and after this morning, I'm in the mood for one of those arias you're so famous for."

She looked so hurt he wanted to snatch the words back, but that wouldn't help her. "You mean one of those arias I can't sing well?"

"I've got a theory about that."

"You don't know anything about opera, so how can you have a theory?"

"I'm that smart."

"Seriously?" She managed a skeptical smile.

"Face it, Liv. You don't have anything to lose and everything to gain. Start with those warm-ups. There's nobody around to hear except me, and I'll stick my fingers in my ears."

Her forehead knit in frustration. "I can't do my warm-ups, not the way I used to. You know that. My chest feels like it has a boa constrictor around it."

"That's why you have to stand on one leg."

"What are you talking about?"

"What I said."

"That's crazy. I can't sing on one leg."

"You can't sing on two legs, so what difference does it make?"

Her face fell. She looked as if he'd betrayed her, and his gut twisted. He fought against it. "It's starting to rain harder, and we're not leaving until you try. So do us both a favor and stop procrastinating. Warm up on one leg. And stick the other out in front of you. I dare you."

"I'll do it just to show you what an *ass* you are!" She shot one leg out in front of her, wobbled, regained her equilibrium, and balanced on the other leg, pulling her scarf up to her chin. She started with her *ees*. *Ees* to *ewws*, then some *mahs*.

They sounded okay to him, but they didn't to her, and he could feel her getting ready to clamp her jaw shut. "Louder!" He grabbed the ankle of her extended leg with one hand and her rain jacket with the other to keep her from falling.

She shot him a murderous glower, but she kept going. A red-tailed hawk circled above them The *ees* transitioned into *ewws* into *mahs*, and son of a bitch, her voice was gaining strength. He knew it wasn't his imagination because he could see it in her face.

He kept his grip on her extended leg and moved it ever so slightly to the side. She wobbled, shot him another death ray, but kept on vocalizing.

It continued that way as she flew through her exercises. Whenever he suspected she was starting to overfocus, he did something to unbalance her. He'd move her leg. Bend her outstretched knee. He made sure she didn't fall, but he also made sure she had to focus on keeping her balance instead of judging her singing, because one of the biggest reasons athletes choked was from overconcentrating in crunch situations. Tension disrupted rhythm. An experienced player going through a bad streak only made it worse by focusing so much on the outcome he lost touch with his natural instincts. It was exactly the kind of mental disconnect he suspected had happened to her.

She wasn't quite done when he cut her off. "That's enough." He released her leg. She ducked her head and shook out the leg she'd been standing on without making eye contact. "I'm not done vocalizing."

"Yes, you are."

She raised her head, regarding him with fake condescension. "You know nothing about opera singers."

"But I know a lot about athletes, and I want to hear one of those arias you're so famous for. You get to choose which one."

"There's a big difference between warming up and singing a complicated aria in the freezing cold while—"

"No excuses." He pushed his hands under the bottom of her jacket and set them on her waist, just under the hem of her top so he could feel a few inches of bare skin.

"What are you—?"

"Sing!"

She did. Launching into something that sounded like really, really pissed-off German. Her voice began to strain. He gave the bare skin under his right hand a tiny pinch.

"Stop that!"

Son of a bitch. She sang the words at him instead of speaking them.

She looked as shocked as he felt. But she kept going. Launching herself into the dark, foreboding aria.

The music began pouring from her, the notes big and furious enough to make his ears ring.

Her skin was warm under his palms, but he somehow kept his focus. If he sensed her struggling for a note, he slid his hands higher along the bumps of her spine. He forced himself to stay below her bra line, not getting nearly as personal as he wanted to because this wasn't about his goddamn lust. It was about her.

The aria went on, and she sang and she sang and she sang. The wind picked up, the rain turned to sleet, and that glorious voice challenged the oncoming storm.

As they walked toward the 103rd Street subway stop, he kept quiet, giving her the time she needed to process what had happened, but the longer the silence stretched between them, the more he wanted to know what she was thinking.

"That was from *Götterdämmerung*," she finally said. "The last of Wagner's *Ring* cycle. It was Waltraute's 'Höre mit Sinn was ich dir sage.'"

"And you chose it because . . . ?"

"Waltraute is one of the Valkyries. I'm not a Wagnerian singer, but I figured I needed supernatural help."

"It seems like you got it."

"My vibrato still has a wobble, my lower passaggio isn't close to where it should be, and I'm strangling my high notes."

"You're the expert."

"But at least I was singing." She gave a choked half laugh, half something else. "All I need to do now is perform on one leg with somebody feeling me up."

"Happy to oblige."

She squeezed his wrist through the sleeve of the rain jacket. Only for a moment before she withdrew. "Thanks."

"You can pay me back in Las Vegas."

Her hair was tangled, and she needed a shower before their client dinner. As she adjusted the water temperature, she saw that her hands were shaking. She understood the psychology of what Thad had done for her. Focusing on keeping her balance instead of thinking so much about the sound she was producing had helped her over one psychological hurdle. But she was still a mess.

She slicked the shampoo through her hair. Amneris's aria in *Aida*, "Già i sacerdoti adunansi," swelled in her head, but even in the protective womb of the shower, she was afraid to try singing it.

Eight more days until she started rehearsals. Two more days until they reached Las Vegas. One event filled her with panic, the other with a mixture of lust and panic.

Thad had left his sport coat in Olivia's suite. She didn't answer the door, so he let himself in with the duplicate copy of the key he made sure he had in every hotel.

The shower was running in the bathroom. His sport coat lay on the couch, right where he'd left it. On his way to retrieve it, he spotted an unopened brown manila envelope on the table by the door. It was addressed to her. He picked it up without a qualm and opened it.

Inside was a glossy photograph of a .38 pistol with the Smith & Wesson logo stamped on its grip.

12

Thad wasn't an indecisive person. His job required instant decision-making, yet all through their client dinner in the hotel dining room, he wrestled with whether to tell Olivia about the photo. She knew someone had it in for her, and nothing good would come of showing it to her. The aria she'd sung this afternoon might not have been up to her standards, but it had given him goose bumps. One look at that photo could completely derail her. It would be like showing a horror movie to a kid who was already spooked.

But Olivia wasn't a kid.

As Henri escorted the last of their guests from the hotel dining room, Thad and Liv headed for the elevator. He inserted his room card and pushed the button for the top floor. "Something came for you in the mail."

"I didn't see anything."

"I grabbed it before you could open it."

She cocked her head, waiting. He hesitated. "It's from whoever's playing mind games with you."

"What is it?"

"A photo. You don't need to see it. There's no new information, and nothing will be gained from looking at it."

"Don't you think that's for me to decide?"

"That's why I'm telling you."

The bell dinged for their floor. She nodded slowly, considering.

The door opened. He blocked it with his body to keep it from closing but didn't get out. "You sang again today, and you can't let something this stupid derail you. That's why I'm asking you to let it go."

She touched his arm. "I understand you're looking out for me, but I have to see it."

He'd known she'd say this. They stepped into the empty hallway with its plush carpet and softly glowing wall sconces. "I'm going to tell you what it is first," he said.

She stopped walking. "Okay."

"It's a photograph of a gun." He kept his voice calm and level. "A Smith & Wesson pistol."

She sucked in her breath.

"My guess is that's the kind of gun Adam used."

She gave a short, tense nod.

"I suspect whoever is behind this wants you to think it's a photo of the real thing, but it's been copied from a site on the Internet."

"I want to see it."

"Leave it alone, Liv. There's no point."

"I have to see it." She set off toward their rooms, her stilettos sinking stubbornly into the carpet.

He came up next to her. "If you even think about freaking out, I'll never let you forget it."

"Fair enough." She passed the door to her suite and stopped in front of his, waiting for him to unlock the door. He needed to prepare her as best he could. "One more thing . . . There's a bullshit message written across it." He hated what he was about to tell her. "It says, 'You made me pull the trigger.' Now go ahead. Do your big freak-out just like whoever's behind this wants you to do."

Maybe he'd said the right thing because he liked the way she set her jaw. "Open that door."

His suite was identical to hers, and she saw the opened envelope lying on the table. She marched toward it and pulled out the photo. He prepared himself for the worst, but instead of looking stricken, she looked mad as hell.

Thad hated sitting in the passenger seat with Olivia driving, but she'd insisted, and he'd only look like a sexist troll if he'd pressed her.

"You didn't have to come with me," she said, as they sped along I-78 toward Plainfield, New Jersey. "As a matter of fact, the way you keep twitching around and scowling makes me wish you hadn't."

"I like to drive, that's all."

"So do I. And I'm a better driver than you are."

"You're deluded."

"I haven't forgotten our Breckenridge trip. You speed."

"Says the lady going six miles over the limit."

"Six is reasonable. Twelve isn't."

She had a point.

Adam's hometown of Plainfield, New Jersey, lay about an hour west of the city. It was late afternoon, the day after Thad had shown her the photo. Tomorrow night, they'd be flying to Vegas, and they couldn't get there fast enough, although it bothered him that she hadn't once brought up their agreement since they'd made it.

"You could at least have rented a decent car." He sounded sulky.

"Excuse me, Mr. Big Shot, but I don't need to rent a Rolls. I'm perfectly fine with a Mazda."

"Because you're not six foot three," he retorted.

"I'm also not a whiny baby."

If he kept complaining, he'd only prove her point. Until today, he hadn't thought twice about riding with a woman driving, so sexism wasn't his problem. What specifically bothered him was being Olivia's passenger.

He'd never regarded himself as controlling. He respected women. Appreciated them. Hell, he worked for Phoebe Calebow. But when he was with Olivia Shore, all of a sudden, he wanted to call the shots, something she clearly wouldn't allow to happen.

He tapped his foot against the floor mat. "I don't know what you hope to accomplish on this trip."

"I don't, either. But I'm tired of feeling like a victim, and I need to do something."

"What exactly?"

"I'm still thinking about it."

Meaning she had no clue. As she pulled onto the freeway exit ramp, he stretched out his legs as far as the Mazda would allow. "I've got a better idea. Let's find a nice Holiday Inn and do what we've been wanting to do ever since we met."

She stared straight ahead, but he saw her blink. "This isn't Las Vegas."

"Almost. We're leaving tomorrow night, remember? And neither of us signed anything. We can change our minds any time we want."

The troubled crease that formed between her brows made him regret bringing it up. "As soon as we cross that line," she said, "everything will change between us."

"It'll change anyway," he pointed out, trying to regain lost ground. "You're the one who set the ground rules. Once the gala is over, we finish our commitment to Marchand, and we never see each other again, remember?"

She turned onto a four-lane road with modest houses set on large, wooded lots and tightened her grip on the steering wheel. "There are so many people we can have sex with, but how many of them can we rely on? Can we trust? How many understand each other the way we do?"

It sounded as if Olivia Shore was trying to move him into the friend zone, something he wouldn't let happen. "Our agreement stands," he declared, as if he were the only one who had a say. "Our last night in Las Vegas. You. Me. A bed. And a long night of sin."

***A long** night of sin . . .* She had a good imagination, and all the erotic images that had been plaguing her for weeks played in her head like a film on fast-forward. How could she help that with Thad sitting right next to her? As the Plainfield, New Jersey, sign slipped into view, she imagined what it would be like to be in bed with him. Explore his body. Hold him naked against her. Feel him inside her.

"Watch it!" he exclaimed.

She slammed on the brakes. After all her bragging about being a better driver, she'd nearly rear-ended a Chevy Malibu.

He seemed to believe that continuing their relationship after the tour ended was a simple matter. It probably was to him, but she knew better. Sex changed everything. As unlikely as it would have seemed three weeks ago, The Diva and the quarterback were weirdly compatible. He was a special man—his humor, his loyalty, his decency—and he was as driven as she. He didn't see the complication of extending their relationship, but he wouldn't be the one handing over pieces of himself—little pieces at first, and then bigger ones, until she was once again lost.

She checked the GPS. They were nearly there. As she passed a plumbing truck doddering along in the right lane, she promised herself she'd enjoy every moment of their short, sex-fueled affair, and then she'd let him go. Since they'd never really been together, it wouldn't even be an official breakup, and it would be easy to get through. She could only have one focus. Getting her voice back. Her goal from the beginning of her career was set in stone. To be the best, the stuff of legends, one of the immortals. She wouldn't let anything derail her.

The bakery occupied the end of a strip mall that also included a tile store and a dog groomer. She pulled into a spot close enough to see the window, but not directly in front. Thad checked out the vintage sign hanging from a bracket over the front door. "My Lady's Bakery?"

"Adam's grandfather named it. He thought it sounded genteel." A mess of plastic pennants were draped at the top of the window, and the artificial wedding cake at the center of the display looked particularly unappetizing, even from a distance. "It didn't used to be this bad," she said. "It was never exactly cutting-edge, but . . ."

"You're not going to take responsibility for their bad window display, are you?"

"It seems symbolic. As if his sisters have given up now that Adam's gone." She saw the concern written on his too-handsome face. "I have to do this alone." His jaw set in that stubborn line she was coming to know so well. She set her hand on his thigh. "I'll be fine."

He wasn't happy, but he didn't argue.

She approached the bakery's door. The plaster roses on the wedding cake had lost some petals and the groom was missing a hand.

She'd learned a lot about Adam's family during the time they were together. Neither of his older sisters had married or even dated much. They, along with their mother, were too busy focusing on the unexpected baby brother who'd arrived ten years after Brenda was born and nine years after her sister Colleen.

Their father was largely absent during Adam's early years. He'd arrive at the bakery at four in the morning, work all day, and fall asleep after dinner, a schedule that resulted in a fatal heart attack when Adam was five. His mother and sisters took over the bakery, but Adam, with his magical voice, was always exempt from duties. Boys needed their sleep, so he was never required to get up early to tend a hot oven. His piano and voice lessons were more important than scrubbing heavy baking sheets or waiting on customers behind the counter. He was their crown prince, and they gave him everything they denied themselves.

Instead of resenting him, his teenage sisters set aside every dollar they could spare to help send him to Eastman, one of the best music colleges in the country. Even after their mother's death, they still continued to dote on him. He was their life purpose. The only way their lives could have meaning was if he became successful, and they expected Olivia to make sacrifices just as they had. Now they wanted her to pay for failing him.

She took a deep breath and turned the knob.

The late afternoon's unsold baked goods sat on paper doilies in the glass display case: a few black-and-white cookies, muffins, some cupcakes decorated to look like Cookie Monster. Everything palatable; nothing imaginative.

Both sisters were working behind the counter. Brenda glanced up as Olivia came in, and her welcoming shopkeeper's expression vanished. Colleen was taking a cake from the case. As she spotted Olivia, she shoved it back inside so hard it slipped off its doily. "What do you want?"

What, indeed? Now that Olivia was here, she couldn't think of anything to say.

They resembled Adam in different ways. His more sculptured features had become blurred in Brenda—as if someone had run an eraser over her face, leaving her with lost cheekbones, a short, unfinished nose, and small eyes turned down at the corners. Colleen had Adam's dark brown eyes, but everything else was more angular: sharply pointed chin and nose, inclined eyebrows, rigid mouth. They both seemed to have used the same drugstore hair dye, a shade of red that stripped their short hair of any sheen.

Olivia stuffed her hands in the pockets of her trench coat. Her fingers brushed a crumpled tissue and the edge of her cell phone. "Adam used to talk about how hard both of you worked to keep him in voice lessons," she said. "He felt guilty about it."

Brenda's insignificant chin came up. "We didn't regret a moment of it."

A pot banged in the back of the bakery. Colleen splayed her hands against her apron. "He was always good to us. Always."

Olivia knew Adam frequently sent them money, although if he was short of cash, the money had come from Olivia. When he'd died, Olivia had made a private arrangement with the funeral home to take care of the expenses. The sisters believed Adam's last opera company had paid for it.

She stepped closer to the counter and pointed stupidly toward the bakery case. "I'll take whatever you have left." She had no money on her. She'd left her purse in the car.

"We're not selling to you," Colleen said.

Olivia's chest tightened. Even if she'd been standing on one foot with Thad holding her other foot, she wouldn't have been able to get a note out. "I couldn't make Adam happy," she finally said.

"You broke his heart!" Brenda cried.

"I didn't mean to." Only in retrospect did Olivia see that Adam was suffering from depression. She remembered how difficult it had become for him to memorize a new libretto. The way his periods of insomnia had alternated with nights he'd sleep for twelve or thirteen hours. If only she'd gotten him to a doctor.

Colleen whipped around from behind the counter, her sharp features vicious. "You always had to come first. It was always Olivia this, Olivia that. It was never about *him*."

"That's not true. I did everything I could for him."

"All you did was rub your success in his face," Brenda retorted.

That wasn't true, either. Olivia had made herself smaller for him, giving up her own practice time, downplaying her achievements, but there was no point in arguing with them. No point to this visit. "I've been getting some ugly letters," she said. "I want them to stop."

"What kind of letters?" The raw hatred in Colleen's eyes, so like Adam's, made Olivia feel sick.

Brenda seemed almost smug. "Whatever's happening, you've brought it on yourself."

This was hopeless. Olivia understood their pain and grief, but that didn't give them the right to torment her. "I don't want to go to the police," she said as calmly as she could, "but if this keeps on, I'll be forced to."

Colleen crossed her arms over her chest. "You do whatever you have to."

"I will."

The visit had been a waste of time. She found Thad pacing in front of the tile store, hands shoved in the pockets of his three-thousand-dollar—she'd checked—Tom Ford leather jacket. He stopped walking. "That didn't take long. How did it go?"

"Great. They fell on their knees begging me to forgive them."

"I like it better when I'm the sarcastic one." He reached out as if he intended to hug her then let his arm fall back to his side. "Let's get going. I'm driving."

This time she didn't fight him.

"Sing for me," he said, as they passed the sign for Scotch Plains on their way back to Midtown.

"I can't sing now."

"No better time. You're mad, but it won't take long before your overworked guilt engine kicks in, and you'll be right back where you were. Let me hear you sing before that happens."

"I know you want to help, but this isn't as simple to get over as an interception or an incomplete pass."

"Just as I suspected. You know more about football than you pretend. And there's nothing simple about an interception. Now stop stalling and sing."

She emitted a pained sigh and then, to his surprise, began to sing. A piece so mournful he wished it weren't in English.

"When I am laid . . . am laid in earth . . ."

Despite its maudlin subject, the notes she produced were so round and rich they could only have come from the throat of the best in the world.

"Passable," he said over the constriction in his own throat when she finished.

"It's 'Dido's Lament' from *Dido and Aeneas*."

"That's what I thought." He smiled at her and she gave him a wobbly smile in return. "It was beautiful, but kind of depressing," he said. "How about you slay me? Right now. One of your big numbers."

"Trust me when I tell you that you don't want me singing full voice inside a car."

"You don't think I'm man enough to handle it?"

"I know you're not." She dug in her purse, pulled out a tissue, ripped off a couple of pieces, and wadded them into balls. She leaned over, a breast pressed to his upper arm, and stuffed them in his ears. It was a wonder he didn't drive off the road. "You asked for it."

And she let it rip. Even with his makeshift earplugs, her lavish, crystal-shattering Bugatti of a voice raised the hair on the back of his neck.

When she was done, all he could do was breathe a prayer. "Jesus, Liv . . ."

"I was holding back," she said, almost defiantly. "It's called marking. It's what we do sometimes to save our voices during rehearsals."

"Got it. Like a no-contact football practice." He tried to figure out how he could say what he couldn't get off his mind. "Do you feel like taking requests?"

"I'm not doing 'Love Shack.'"

He smiled. "I was thinking more like . . ." He hesitated, but he couldn't make himself say it. Couldn't reveal how much he'd been thinking about it. "Forget it. I changed my mind."

"Forget what?"

He played dumb. "What do you mean?"

"What do you want me to sing?"

"Whatever you want. I'm easy."

"But you said . . ."

He couldn't do it. Couldn't ask her to sing Carmen's sensuous, rebellious "Habanera" just for him. Wouldn't admit how much he wanted to be her private audience. He shot into the left lane. "Who am I to dictate anything to the Beautiful Turnip?"

"Tornado. And you're speeding again."

He backed off on the accelerator, and she began to sing, first something in French, then German, then Italian—none of them "Habanera." She sang all the way to the Lincoln Tunnel, and the next evening, as they boarded the plane to fly to Las Vegas, his ears still buzzed. She wasn't happy with her sound, but for him . . . it was glorious.

She was due at the Muni in a week. Olivia gazed out the window of the plane on their flight to Las Vegas, her feelings in turmoil. She could mark for the first few rehearsals to buy herself time. She'd sung Amneris enough that no one would think twice about it. But sooner or later, that time would run out.

She told herself she was making progress. When they were in the car, she'd had to sing down an octave on the highs, but at least she was singing. At least? When had delivering anything but her best become her career goal?

Las Vegas loomed ahead, enticing and terrifying. Every day her physical need for him grew more urgent, her sleep more restless, her dreams more erotic. If she didn't see this through to its logical conclusion, she'd always regret it. And if she did? Their relationship would never be the same.

She closed her eyes and tried not to think.

The panoramic windows of their connecting suites at the Bellagio looked out over the flamboyant sprawl of Las Vegas. It was midnight, and Rupert's latest offering had already arrived, a woman's Louis Vuitton duffel packed with exotic cheeses, imported caviar, and ludicrously expensive chocolates. "He's going to go broke," Liv said.

"Yeah, I'd feel real bad about that." Thad whipped his phone from his pocket. "Give me his number. I'm sure you have it."

The thought of what he might say to Rupert alarmed her. "I'm not giving you his phone number."

"Never mind. I already have it."

"How did you get his number?"

He looked down his nose at her, deliberately condescending. "I'm a spoiled professional athlete, remember? I can get whatever I want."

As he tapped at his phone, she tried to grab it from him. "It's the middle of the night. You'll scare him!"

"That's the general idea." He'd fended off opponents for years, and using both his height and the barrier of his elbow, he kept her at a distance as he moved over to the windows. "Mr. Glass, dis is Bruno Kowalski. Sorry to wake you up." His fake tough-guy accent suggested he might have seen too many Scorsese movies. "I'm Miz Shore's bodyguard."

She rolled her eyes, torn between pity for poor Rupert and a curiosity about what Thad was going to say.

"The thing is . . . all these presents is upsettin' her lawyer." Thad winked at her. "Dude says she's gonna be in trouble with the IRS. Somethin' about exceeding fed'ral tax limits. She's real stressed out about it. Maybe thinkin' about givin' up opera and goin' on the road with a rock band."

What? she mouthed at him.

He shrugged at her. "So all I'm sayin' is . . . if you don't want her to keep bein' upset, you better cut it out." Long, menacing pause. "If you know what I mean."

She could faintly hear Rupert's high, squeaky response.

"Yeah, I thought you'd understand. Now you have a real good day, Mr. Glass, okay?"

She planted her hands on her hips as he disconnected. "'Exceeding federal tax limits'? Who comes up with something like that?"

"Somebody with a degree in finance from the University of Kentucky and an unhealthy interest in the IRS." He slipped his phone back in his pocket. "Better than threatening to shoot out his kneecaps, right?"

"You're all heart."

The International Jewelers Convention in Las Vegas was the busiest stop on their tour, and they spent two days meeting with jewelers and buyers. Several of them felt duty bound to point out what she already knew about her own jewelry. Her pigeon's egg necklace didn't hold a real ruby, her Egyptian cuff was a fake, her poison rings not real antiques, and her dangling Spanish earrings souvenir quality. When they offered to give her a good deal on the real thing, she told them she lost jewelry too easily instead of telling the truth, that she had genuine pieces she seldom wore locked up in her apartment.

She and Thad posed for photos, sat for interviews, and chatted with bloggers. Through it all, the air between them crackled with erotic anticipation. Every gesture, every glance carried extra meaning.

I can't wait to see . . . To touch . . . To taste . . . To feel . . .

Even in the air-conditioned exhibition hall, her cheeks felt flushed, her skin hot. She forgot names, lost track of conversations, and he was doing even worse. At one point, he addressed a clearly pregnant woman as "sir."

As they walked through the crowded aisles, his hand stroked the small of her back. She brushed against his hip. When they posed for photos, their fingers touched behind the person standing between them. It was foreplay shot into the stratosphere.

Their last night arrived. She dressed with extra care for the private client dinner at José Andrés's newest restaurant. Hair down. Barely there underpants. She debated between two black cocktail dresses. Under the more modest one, she could wear a deliciously sexy lacy black bra. But a bra would show beneath the other, a simple black sheath with a severely plunging V that required a set of silicone gel lift pads and a little fashion tape to hold everything together. Not nearly as alluring as the sexy lace bra. But the neckline of that more modest dress didn't come to a point well below her breasts and wouldn't drive him crazy all through dinner.

She imagined herself toying with the edge of that enticing V and trailing her fingers along her exposed skin. Definitely worth sacrificing the lacy bra, she decided.

She set aside her customary statement jewelry for understatement—a simple pair of earrings and an extra-long delicate silver chain dangling a tiny silver star charm. Rachel had bought that for her when they were both flat broke. As Olivia fastened it around her neck, the little star nestled between her breasts, right where she imagined the Stars quarterback would put his lips.

She shivered. First, they had to endure a long, boring dinner.

Las Vegas venues were brutally air-conditioned, and she dug out a vintage flamenco shawl that had been a gift from a *Carmen* fan. Bringing the ghost of Sevilla's sultry Romani cigar maker along for the evening felt like the perfect good-luck charm.

A knock sounded on their connecting door. She draped the shawl over her shoulders and picked up her small evening purse.

At first, he didn't say a thing. He simply stood there taking her in. Then he breathed a soft, flattering obscenity.

She tilted her head so her hair fell over one shoulder and breathed just deeply enough to swell the exposed inner slopes of her breasts.

He groaned. "You're diabolical."

Exactly what she wanted to hear.

The front desk called up to tell them their limo had arrived. It was early, but she and Thad were both ready, and they headed down to the lobby. As they settled into the car's back seat, they were so focused on each other she barely heard the driver tell them that Henri had already left and would meet them at the restaurant.

"Just what we don't need." Olivia slipped the flamenco shawl higher around her shoulders. "More time alone together."

Thad gazed at her legs. "The next three hours can't go by fast enough."

Olivia slid onto the bench seat that ran the length of the limo, putting a little distance between them. He gave her a lazy smile. "Don't expect me to go easy on you tonight."

She swallowed hard, let the shawl slip down over one shoulder, and relied on her acting skills for false bravado. "You worry about yourself, cowboy, because I'm in the mood for a long, hard ride."

"That's it! There's only so much a man can take." He grabbed for his phone and plunged in a set of earbuds. "You entertain yourself with some Candy Crush and ignore me. Dizzy Gillespie and I have a date."

She smiled as he closed his eyes. This was going to be a night to remember.

But as she gazed at the limo's blue and purple ceiling lights, her amusement faded. She'd dictated the terms. They would have tonight along with three additional days in Chicago before she went into rehearsals. In four more days, it would be over between them. There'd be no more hotel suites with connecting doors, no more late-night chats and early-morning breakfasts. Their relationship would end.

The thought of never seeing him again was a knife through her heart. She closed her eyes. Tried to shut herself off from the truth that had been nagging at her for days like a bad toothache.

She'd fallen in love with him.

Stupid! Once again, she'd fallen for the wrong man, but how could she not? He was exciting, perceptive, and rock-bottom decent. His intellect upended every stereotype about professional athletes. Whenever she saw him, her senses went on high alert, and denying the depth of her feelings for him wouldn't change them. Besides, when it came to Thad Owens—denial was dangerous.

Thad was a powerful, ambitious man with a big life. His career had made him a second stringer, existing on the edge of Clint Garrett's spotlight, but unlike Dennis Cullen, Thad would never be happy taking a back seat in his private life, and she could never be happy with a man unable to do exactly that. A man who'd be willing to follow her from Johannesburg to Sydney and on to Hong Kong. Who'd put up with her rehearsal schedule, her crazy hours.

Opera was her life's blood. Its drama and grandeur fueled her. The euphoria of hitting impossible notes, of digging so deeply inside herself that she became the character. The exhilaration of having an entire audience stop breathing as they waited to hear what she'd do next. That was where her heart and soul lived, and she couldn't give that up, not even for love.

His eyes were still closed, absorbed in Dizzy's riffs. Thad represented everything she couldn't have without giving up on herself. Without abandoning her destiny.

She had to use these next few days to build memories she could tuck away for the rest of her life. Memories she could unearth when she was alone in some distant hotel room or when she gave a bad performance or a critic was brutal. She would savor the memories and know she'd made the right choice.

Thad shifted on the back seat and punched a button on the limo's overhead control panel. "Driver?"

She'd been so engrossed in her thoughts that she'd lost track of time. Now, as she looked out through the darkened limousine windows, she could only see desert. They'd left the lights of Las Vegas behind.

13

"Driver!" Thad shouted into the ceiling intercom.

The limo picked up speed—going much too fast—and the smoked-glass partition separating them from the driver stayed shut. Thad scrambled past her and banged on it. "Stop the car!"

The car swerved off the highway. She clutched the bar for support as they lurched onto a bumpy road. Thad regained his balance first. "Let me have that." He grabbed Olivia's silky flamenco shawl and began twisting it around his hand.

Olivia snatched up her phone and hit the emergency SOS button.

Nothing happened.

"Get back!" Thad pushed her behind him and slammed his wrapped arm into the partition window, shattering the tempered glass between them and the driver into pebbles.

The limo careened, throwing them both to the floor. As Thad scrambled to his feet, she tried again to use her phone. “I can’t get a signal!”

“Cell jammer.”

The car lurched to a stop.

Thad dove toward the broken place where the partition had been, but the driver threw open the door, killed the headlights, and jumped out before Thad could touch him. She leaped for one of the passenger doors, while Thad went for the other. They were both locked. He glanced toward the limo’s bar, looking for something to make into a weapon—a wine bottle or glass—but the compartments were empty.

“Whatever happens, stay behind me,” he ordered.

“This is because of me,” she cried. “You know it is.”

“Do what I say.”

A click. The rear passenger door flew open, and the dome light went on. “Get out,” a gruff voice said.

Thad pushed in front of her and stepped from the limo. Her flamenco scarf dropped to the ground as he blocked the door with his body to shield her inside.

This was all wrong. She should be the one protecting him. She made another desperate visual search of the interior. Nothing in the bar. Nothing in her purse except a room key and tissues. She dropped her cell and scooped up two handfuls of the security glass pebbles that had fallen onto the seat from the broken partition. Even though it was tempered glass, the edges bit into her palms.

"Move over," that same gruff voice shouted outside. She could see nothing through the windows except the dark.

Thad stayed where he was, blocking the rear door. "What do you want?"

"Move over or I'll shoot. Both of you! Out here!"

"Stay inside," Thad ordered her.

She wasn't having it. Keeping her fists clenched, glass inside, she pushed against him and wedged herself out of the limo into the emptiness of the Mojave Desert.

At first, she could see nothing beyond the ooze of dim yellow light from the limo's interior. A jet flew overhead, maybe from Nellis Air Force Base, maybe from McCarran. As her eyes adjusted, she took in the hulking shape of the man standing outside the light. He wore a dark suit, but the brim of his chauffeur's hat concealed most of his face. Was he the man who'd accosted her at the bookstore? They seemed to be roughly the same size, but so were millions of other men.

"Step away from the car!" he shouted into the darkness.

Instead of fear, a hot rush of fury took over. "We're not going anywhere!"

The earth erupted in front of them. She gasped. He hadn't been bluffing about the gun.

Thad grabbed her and pushed her into the darkness. "Do what he says."

"Why?" She was furious. Possessed by a raging wildfire. Furious with their kidnapper. With herself for involving Thad in her mess. With this cretin who was terrorizing them. "Big man with a gun!" She gripped the glass pebbles tighter in her fists. "What do you want, big man?"

"Shut up, Liv," Thad ordered.

"Shut up!" their kidnapper shouted at exactly the same time. He spun on Thad. "Give me your wallet. Toss it over there."

Thad did as he demanded.

"Now your phone," the man said.

"Don't do it!" Olivia exclaimed.

Thad ignored her. The man kept the gun leveled as he bent down to snatch them both up.

"Now that watch."

Thad unclipped the Victory780 and tossed it toward his feet.

The man turned in her direction. "Give me your purse."

She couldn't get past her fury. "It's in the limo, you moron."

"Liv . . ." Thad's voice sounded a sharp, warning note.

But she'd sucked Thad into what should have been her crisis alone, and she was beyond reason. "Big man wants to do drama! I do drama better than anyone!"

The man lunged for her. She let both hands fly, hurling the glass at his face.

He gave a howl of shock, and that was all Thad needed to charge him. The gun fired and flew into the air. She screamed, lost her balance, and fell.

"Liv!" Thad spun toward her.

With no weapon, the driver lurched for the limo.

The car door slammed, and Thad went to his knees beside her. His hands frantically moved over her body, and in the adrenaline rush flooding her, she couldn't comprehend why he was feeling her up at a time like this.

"Liv! Where did you get hit?"

He wasn't feeling her up. He was . . . "I didn't." She rolled to the side. "I fell."

Thad spotted the gun and rushed with it toward the limo, but by the time he fired, the car was peeling onto the road, gravel spraying like shrapnel.

For a long moment, neither of them spoke. In the distance, the lights on a transmission tower blinked, and she heard the faraway sound of a freight train. They were alone in the thick desert dark.

As she breathed in the dusty cloud from the car tires, all her fury evaporated, leaving her with a racing heart and wobbly legs as she pushed herself to her knees. "I'm sorry," she whispered.

"For what?"

"For dragging you into my problems."

"Shut up, Liv, okay?" It was the second time he'd said that to her, but now his gentle tone made her want to weep. "Maybe he was after the watches."

As she started to argue with him, she felt something by her hand. She closed her fingers around his watch and held it out. "A lot of effort for nothing."

"Bastard." He clicked on the safety and shoved the gun in his waistband. As he took the watch from her, he helped her to her feet. "Let's go."

One of the gel breast lifts she'd worn instead of a bra had fallen from the V of her dress. She fumbled for it, but layers of sandy grit adhered to the sticky surface, so she retrieved her flamenco shawl instead. He helped her to her feet. "Let's go."

Having lopsided breasts, she decided, was only a minor complication compared to the bigger challenge of trekking down a dark, rutted gravel road wearing five-inch stilettos.

Thad was thinking the same thing. "You'll never make it to the highway in those shoes. I'll carry you piggyback."

"Never." Olivia Shore, the toast of the Metropolitan, the jewel of La Scala, the pride of the Royal Opera, did not piggyback on anyone, no matter how broad and strong they were. She tossed the dusty shawl around her shoulders. "I'll be fine."

"You'll kill yourself."

"But I'll keep my dignity."

"You're a stubborn fool."

She sighed and looped a knot in the front of the shawl. "I know."

Her refusal made the awkward trip last twice as long, but Thad's tight grip kept her from twisting an ankle, and at least she held on to a shred of pride—or as much as her cockeyed breasts would allow.

With both their phones gone—hers abandoned in the limo's back seat and his stuck in the asshole's pocket—they had to rely on the kindness of strangers for a ride back to the city. Unfortunately, the strangers turned out to be a trio of drunken frat boys. Fortunately, Thad let them know right away that he was the one and only Thaddeus Walker Bowman Owens, so they let him drive. Unfortunately, he introduced her as a Chicago Stars cheerleader. It shocked her that she still remembered how to laugh. A pathetic laugh, for sure, but at least she wasn't crying.

She borrowed one of the frat boys' phones and called Henri. He was frantic. He'd been waiting for them in the hotel lobby when the real limo driver had shown up, and the doorman had informed him that she and Thad had already left. Henri had assumed they'd decided to get to the restaurant early to have a drink, but when he'd arrived and discovered they weren't there, he'd grown increasingly worried. It took much of the rest of the trip to convince him she and Thad were unhurt. Physically, anyway.

"I can sense a middle linebacker twitching his left eye!" Thad exclaimed, as they took the elevator up to their suite sometime around four in the morning. "But I have no idea what our limo driver looked like. And do you know why?"

She knew exactly why because she'd already listened to his rant twice.

"Because I was too busy staring at your ass! That's why!"

Their grilling by the Las Vegas police hadn't gone well. The officer who'd interviewed them found it hard to believe that neither of them could describe the driver, and by the second hour of their stint at the police station, he'd stopped trying to hide his skepticism. "You didn't see the driver when you approached the car? You didn't speak to him before you got in?"

"Yes, but . . ." Olivia took over this round. "Thad and I were having a . . . a conversation, and neither of us was paying attention."

Their interviewer had an egg-shaped head, dark-rimmed glasses, a brush mustache, and a mistrustful nature. "So let me get this straight. You think he was white, but maybe not. He wasn't short, but he wasn't tall. And his voice sounded maybe middle-aged but maybe younger."

"He had a hat on," Olivia said defensively, "and it was pulled low. I remember that." She tugged the dirty flamenco shawl more tightly around her to conceal her unfettered breasts and briefly wondered how the frat boy would feel about the single silicone lift pad he'd find in his car when he sobered up.

"He was wearing a dark suit," Thad added. "We told you that."

"Are you even sure it was a man? Could it have been a woman?"

"Thad and I weren't really having a conversation,"

she said desperately. "It was more of an argument, and you know how that is."

The officer—his name tag read *L. Burris*—looked up from his computer screen. "You've been getting a lot of publicity lately." Olivia should have seen what was coming next, but she hadn't. Burris pulled off his glasses. "Ms. Shore, this isn't the first incident you've been involved in since this tour of yours started."

"It's not my tour. Marchand Timepieces is sponsoring—"

"That assault in New Orleans . . . They never found the man responsible." His chair squeaked as he leaned back into it. "You're aware, aren't you, of the penalties involved in filing a false report?"

That had brought Thad right out of his chair. "If you're implying that we made this up for publicity, you couldn't be more wrong."

"Sit down, Mr. Owens. I'm not implying anything. Just pointing out a few facts." He brushed the corner of his mustache with his thumb. "You say you were kidnapped, but you have no description of the perpetrator. It's possible he was after your watches—worth over twenty grand, as you pointed out—but all he got was your phone and wallet."

"Explain that gun we handed over," Thad countered. "Instead of doubting us, why don't you see if any limo companies reported having one of their cars stolen?"

"We're doing that right now."

Not long after, Burris had left them alone, which was when Thad had launched into his initial "staring at your ass" rant.

The officer had kept them waiting nearly an hour, during which time they agreed it was highly unlikely Adam's sisters would have had the resources to pull something like this off. "Then who?" Olivia said, thinking out loud.

Thad shook his head. "That's the question."

Officer Burris returned with the news that the Nevada Highway Patrol had found an abandoned limousine northwest of the city that had been stolen from a local transport service.

"We'll look at security tapes from the hotel," Burris said before he showed them out. "Unless they give us more information than you have, it'll be hard to find this guy."

"What about the gun?" Thad asked.

"We'll put a trace on it. Don't get your hopes up."

Burris wasn't happy that they were scheduled to leave for Chicago the next day, but Olivia couldn't wait to leave Las Vegas behind.

It was nearly dawn when they got back to the hotel. Thad had finally stopped berating himself for not paying attention to the driver's appearance, but as they got off the elevator on their floor, something else was bothering him. "Liv, promise me you won't ever again mouth off to somebody who's holding a gun on you."

"I can't help it. I hate being pushed around."

"I get it. You're a soprano." He gazed down at her. "But let's agree that men like him aren't as enlightened about the artistic temperament as I am."

She smiled. "One of the best things about you."

He opened the door of their suite with the new key card they'd gotten at the desk. As she stepped inside, her flamenco shawl fell to her elbows, and she caught her image in the mirror across the room. Tangled hair, dirty face and arms, gown filthy from where she'd fallen. The thin silver chain must have broken when she'd fallen because her necklace and its silver star charm were gone.

"Liv, I don't mean to be insensitive, but did something happen to your breasts tonight? They're still sexy as hell, don't get me wrong. But they seem to look a little—I don't know—different than they looked at the start of the evening."

She jerked the shawl back over her shoulders, but not before a quick glance showed that, without support, her breasts were spilling from the V of the gown, and they'd also lost some of the perk. "No idea what you're talking about."

"Forget I said anything."

"I will."

He eyed her bedroom door. "Maybe after a quick shower . . . ?" But even he knew their window of opportunity had passed.

She pushed a strand of hair from her face with a grubby hand. "We're dirty, exhausted, and we have to leave for the airport in three hours. So much for our night of passion." *And maybe that was for the best.*

"Tomorrow," he said. "Chicago."

She fingered the fringe on her shawl, not quite looking at him. "What if this is a colossal sign from the universe that we've gone as far together as we should?"

"That's defeatist thinking. Knock it off."

"But you have to admit—"

"I admit nothing. If you want to be a champion, Olivia Shore, you have to stay in the game."

And that's what this was to him. A game.

In the morning, the police returned Olivia's phone and purse, which they'd retrieved from the limo, the twenty dollars still folded neatly inside. Thad had spent what was left of the night canceling his credit cards, ordering a new phone, and reliving what had happened. He didn't sleep until their flight back to Chicago, and when he awoke, he saw Olivia sound asleep herself, lips slightly parted, purple headphones cockeyed on her head. She looked young and defenseless, far different from the furious woman who'd gone after their kidnapper last night.

Henri had booked them into the Peninsula Chicago on Superior Street. Thad's condo and Olivia's rental apartment weren't far away, but they'd agreed it would be inconvenient to shuffle back and forth for their engagements, so the hotel would be their home for their last three nights.

The three nights Olivia insisted were all they would have together.

For the first time in his life, Thad had lost control of a relationship. He had to turn that around.

Their suite at the Peninsula had a baby grand piano and a wraparound terrace that looked out over Lake Michigan. While Henri waited for his room to be ready, he camped out with his laptop, and Paisley took off for Sephora.

Liv gave Thad her Queen of Sheba look. "I want to walk."

He wanted to do more than walk, but not with Henri temporarily working in their suite. "Fine with me."

She changed from flats into sneakers and traded her trench for a fleece jacket he'd never seen—one more item she'd stuck away in those 799 suitcases she traveled with. On their way out the door, she stole the Chicago Stars ball cap he was wearing and stuck it on her own head. "It makes me feel young," she said, as she pulled her ponytail through the hole in the back.

"You are young," he pointed out. "Relatively."

"I don't feel that way."

"Thirty-five is only old in football years."

"You're almost forty, so that makes you ancient."

"I'm not almost forty. I'm thirty-six."

"Going on thirty-seven."

"Not yet."

"Je m'excuse."

They turned onto Michigan Avenue. The day was sunny, but cold and crisp, thanks to the spring chill coming off the lake. The chill hadn't discouraged the pedestrians bustling along the wide sidewalks with their shopping bags from Nike, Bloomingdale's, Chanel, and the Apple Store.

"What are you going to do with yourself when your football career is over?" she asked.

"Not sure."

"Give me a hint."

"I don't know. I've been doing some work with a friend." Work he wasn't ready to talk to anybody about. "I've got an idea. The Omni's close. Let's check in for a couple of hours. Just you and me."

"It's too pretty to go inside."

"It's cold, and you're nervous. Afraid you can't keep up with me, aren't you? Afraid you'll be a dud."

"I'm not afraid I'll be a dud." She stuffed her hands in her jacket pockets. "Okay, I might be a dud."

He laughed. "You're adorable when you're insane."

"Dude! It's Thad Owens!" Three guys in hoodies and backward baseball caps strutted toward them. Early twenties. One wore jeans, two were in cargo shorts even though the temperature was in the forties.

"We're big Stars fans." The tallest bro, ablaze in neon-green sunglasses, stopped in front of them.

"Glad to hear it," Thad replied, as he usually did.

His companion, whose hoodie advertised his preference for Miller Lite, poked the guy next to him. "Except Chad. Bears all the way."

"Bears suck," Neon sunglasses declared. "So does Clint Garrett. You should be playing."

"If I was better than Clint, I would be," Thad said mildly.

Neon sunglasses snorted. "What about those interceptions he threw against the Patriots?"

"It's easy to be a quarterback when you're home on your couch."

Sunglasses missed the dig. "And that pick six in St. Louis? What about that?"

Thad set his jaw. "Happens to the best of us. Nobody in the League has a stronger arm than Clint or quicker feet. The Stars are lucky to have him."

"I still say—"

"He's fast, he's aggressive, and he's smart. I'm proud to be on his team. Nice talking to you." Thad took Olivia's arm and made his escape.

Behind him, one of them groused, "We didn't even get a picture."

Liv slipped her hand through his elbow. "Pick six?"

"The idiot threw the ball right into traffic," Thad grumbled. "Their safety picked it off and ran it in for a touchdown. Six points."

"Pick six, I get it." She grinned and shook her head. "Idiot."

"It's not funny."

"Oh, it's funny, all right. Some singers I know could learn a few lessons about team loyalty from football players." She stopped without warning, backed him into the window of the Burberry store, and kissed him, right there in the middle of Michigan Avenue.

He didn't know what had brought this on, but he wasn't going to argue about it. It was a long, deep kiss. Her hands looped around his neck. Her lips parted, and so did his. Their tongues met in an intimate romp. His hands went to her waist. Her breasts pressed against his chest. This was the prelude to everything he'd been waiting for.

"Ew!" A teenage girl's shrill giggle dumped cold water all over that kiss. "Get a room!"

He released their kiss and gazed into a pair of dewy, diva-dark eyes that made Liv look as young as those teenagers snickering behind her.

"Omni?" he whispered.

She nodded. A short, barely there nod, but a nod nonetheless.

He took her hand. They jaywalked . . . *jaywalked!* . . . across six lanes of Michigan Avenue traffic with horns blaring and drivers cursing.

Still holding hands, they stormed through the doors of the Omni. He had just enough sense left to steer her away from the registration desk. "Wait here." No need to have both of them standing at the desk without a single piece of luggage.

He made quick work of registering, paying with the emergency cash he'd borrowed from Henri until he got to his bank. He didn't care about the Wi-Fi code or the hypoallergenic pillows they offered. All he wanted was a room. And a bed.

14

It wasn't like in the movies. Thad didn't crush her against the wall the instant the hotel door banged shut. They didn't rip off each other's clothes, mouths welded, or pull at each other's hair, or drag each other to the floor, so overcome with lust they couldn't make it to the bed. It wasn't like that at all.

First . . .

They didn't have condoms. Which wasn't really a problem. They'd had a talk about this earlier. Neither of them had any STDs, and she was on the pill. The real issues were . . .

They'd let this go on too long, built it up too much, put too much pressure on themselves.

She said she had to pee, locked herself in the bathroom, and breathed the long, deep inhalations and slow exhalations of an opera singer with magnificent breath control . . . except when she was singing.

He knocked on the door. "I'm coming in."

"No! I'm throwing up."

"You are not," he said from the other side.

"I think I have a stomach virus."

"I think you have a chickenshit virus."

"That, too."

"I'll wait."

She turned on the faucet and washed her hands. She was used to seeing herself in wigs and tiaras. She was not used to seeing herself in a Stars ball cap, but she liked the way it looked on her head. Sporty. Carefree. Everything she wasn't. "Can I have this hat?"

"No." From the next room.

"You must have dozens of them. And you won't let me have one?"

"I'm not feeling generous right now."

"I understand."

She reluctantly took off her fleece jacket and slipped out of her sneakers, but kept the cap on. "I'm getting undressed."

"You do that." He didn't sound happy about it.

She pictured the beautiful underwear tucked away in her suitcase and the plain pair of sporty briefs she'd pulled on instead, along with an ugly, flesh-colored sports bra. What had she been thinking? That she'd pop into a gym for a quick pickup game?

Since she'd barely had three hours of sleep last night, she was lucky to be wearing underwear at all.

"Confess," he said from the other side of the door. "You're a virgin, right? That's your deep, dark secret and why you're running scared."

"I'm not a virgin, and I'm not running scared. I'm just not good at transitions, and you know this is going to ruin everything. Next to Rachel, you're sort of my best friend."

"Exactly what a sex-starved man does not want to hear."

"You're right. I'm being stupid." She slipped off her Cavatina3 and set it on the bathroom counter, followed by her poison ring, her Egyptian cuff, and, finally, her Stars ball cap.

She shook her hair out of its ponytail and took another deep breath. She was going to do this. She was going to forget that she'd fallen in love with him and simply enjoy it. This was about her body, not about her heart. She turned the knob.

He was sitting on the floor outside the door, his back against the wall, looking bored. "Sorry to tell you this," he said, "but I've lost interest."

"Regrettable." She sat cross-legged on the floor next to him.

He bent one knee and propped his elbow on top. "Here are all the reasons you and I can never have a serious long-term relationship."

"Keep talking dirty to me."

"You're completely dedicated to your career."

"True."

"In the world of opera, the sun pretty much rises and sets on you."

"A slight exaggeration, but go on."

"You're a first stringer. A superstar."

"Thank you."

"And I'm a man who's tired of playing backup."

"Understandable."

"I'm not designed to hold your purse while you sign autographs."

"Hard to envision."

"Or hand you a water bottle when you come off-stage."

"Environmentally unsound, those plastic water bottles, but I get your point."

"In conclusion . . ."

"There's a conclusion?"

"In conclusion, you're a first stringer, Liv. And I could never be happy running around after you playing your backup."

"So, you're saying . . . ?"

"It's not possible for me to have a serious relationship with you."

She cocked her head. "You agree? We're doomed?"

"Completely."

"Fantastic!" She swung herself over him, braced her knees on each side of his hips, and kissed him all over. Long, deep kisses. Kisses that had nothing to do with love, only with need. The kiss changed shape, grew hungrier. He plowed his hands under her sweater and fumbled for the clasp of her bra.

Which didn't exist. Because . . . sports bra.

He tugged at it.

She hopped off him. "Just for you." She stretched out her arms and pulled him up. With her hands against his chest, she drew him to the bed, pushed him down on it, and tossed aside his shoes. Stepping back, she gave him her most seductive Delilah smile and tugged her sweater over her head. It was time to play. Not to think. Not to let her feelings surface. Only to enjoy.

She might be self-conscious about her utilitarian underwear, but it didn't seem to bother him—this gorgeous man with his kryptonite green eyes and hell-raising body.

He leaned against the bed's many pillows to watch her. She took forever unzipping her slacks and sliding them past her hips. She bent over slowly, offering up a prime view of her cleavage, as she stepped out of them.

Utilitarian bra. Serviceable underpants. She looped her hands behind her head, tunneled her fingers through her hair, and lifted it, letting it slither over her hands and wrists, all the time smoldering him with her eyes.

"You . . . are . . . killing . . . me," he said in a rough rasp.

Her voice was liquid smoke. "Enjoy your death."

Playing the seductress. This was what she did onstage. Carmen. Delilah. Crazy, sexy Lady Macbeth. Her body was performing as it had been trained to perform, but performing only for him—this strongman she had under her power just as Delilah had bewitched Samson.

She moved her hips, toyed with her hair, and contemplated how to most gracefully, most seductively, get a sports bra over her head without breaking the mood.

A dilemma for any woman, but she was not any woman.

She turned away from him and surreptitiously slipped the bottom band above her breasts so it wouldn't catch. She gracefully crossed her arms. A twist, a tug with her thumbs, a determined pull without any visible sign of effort . . . Just like that, she had the ugly thing over her head. She dangled it from her fingertips and dropped it to the floor.

She let him take in the expanse of her back, the long ridge of her spine. She tucked her thumbs in the rear band of her briefs. Toyed there for a bit, teasing him as if she were about to take them off, only to remove her thumbs and leave them in place.

A soft groan came from the bed. Slowly, still in her briefs, she turned to face him, her breasts bare to his gaze. His eyes were half lidded, lips parted, the portrait of a fully clad, fully aroused man.

She smiled. *You, my love, might be the king of the gridiron, but I, I am* La Belle Tornade.

Once again, she reached for her hair, lengthening her torso, emphasizing her breasts. Reveling in her power. Until he said the most extraordinary thing.

"Sing for me. 'Habanera.' "

For an instant she thought this was one of his desensitizing exercises, except horrifically ill timed. But those half-lidded eyes, his husky voice, told her otherwise. This was the seduction he wanted, a seduction no woman from his past, from his future, could offer. Only her.

And so she sang, leashing the power of her voice but making each note a smoky, pitch-perfect seduction.

The French lyrics, the Spanish temptress. She warned him of her impermanence.

"L'amour est un oiseau rebelle . . ." Love is a rebellious bird no one can tame . . .

She spread her legs. Breasts bare. Moved her arms in subtle, liquid arcs. *I can't be tamed. I am my own woman.*

Her hair cascaded over her wrists. She arched her back, her waist supple, voice molten. *I love your perfect face. I adore your beautiful body. But I'm fickle. True only to myself.*

She bathed him with her silken glissando. She was in control. Never again would she lose herself for a man. Make herself smaller. She was a wild, untamed bird taking what she wanted. *If I love you, be afraid, because I will never be any man's slave. Instead, I will fly away.*

As the last note faded, he came up on his knees, and with a groan, pulled her onto the bed. "That . . . ," he whispered, "was perfect."

Her briefs quickly disappeared. Together, they struggled with his clothes until he was as naked as she, and she could take in the powerful body that had made his career. Strong and sculpted, lean and aerodynamic. She touched. Enjoyed. Toyed. She would have frolicked in his playground forever if he hadn't taken her down, deliciously trapping her under his weight.

Now her hair was spilling over his big hands. His thumbs nested on her temples as they kissed again. A fierce, carnal kiss that was a graphic overture of what was to come.

Her thighs were open. His mouth trailed down her body, finding every pleasure point—nipples, waist, belly—going lower, lingering there but never quite long enough. She moaned, begging him.

He pinned her wrists to the bed on each side of her head, capturing the wild bird as he entered her. She laughed at the impossibility of it. Sank her teeth into his shoulder. He nipped at her ear. She wrapped her calves around his, her laughter turning into a throaty moan.

He drew back and smiled, the possessive, wicked-eyed smile of a man who'd buried himself thick and heavy inside her. The smile of a conqueror. She dug her nails into his back in retaliation. He moaned and thrust deeper. This was sex as grand opera—outrageously over the top, a cast of thousands playing with her body.

He crushed his mouth to hers and they moved together. Long, hard invasions and exquisite ripostes. Missionary sex blessed by the devil. Their bodies glistened with sweat. Their breathing rasped hot and jagged. They were endurance athletes. He knew how to wait for the perfect receiver. She knew how to hold a note until it pierced the sky. Neither would give up.

Until . . .

Even the finest of athletes reached a breaking point. He drove his hips, coming down hard. She met his aggression with her own.

They broke.

She fought against the tsunami of unwelcome emotion threatening to drown her. This was play. Only play. Delicious, sexy play that had nothing to do with the overwhelming rush of love she felt for this impossible man. "That was too perfect." She curled into his shoulder. "From now on, whatever happens is going to be one big disappointment."

He kissed the top of her head. "We set the bar high."

"I lasted longer," she said mischievously.

"You did not."

"Did, too."

His hand curved around her hip. "You are so asking for it."

"Please."

"Give me a couple of minutes."

"That long?"

He gave her butt a light slap. "For weeks, you've been holding me off, and now you want it all at once?"

"I'm a prima donna. We're allowed to be unreasonable."

"You're telling me." He came up on his elbow and toyed with a lock of her hair, mayhem lurking in his eyes. "I don't want to be insulting—you being a prima donna and all—but I think you need a little more practice."

"Really?"

"I'm sure of it." He trailed his fingers from her collarbone between her breasts to her stomach and lower. She gazed along the length of his body and fell back on the bed. He grinned, covered her, and they were kissing all over again.

She made him lie still while she explored, taking in everything she'd been yearning to see. Testing what pleased him. What pleased her. Marveling that a man who'd devoted his life to such a violent sport could have such a perfect body.

Then it was his turn. At first, she gave his curiosity free rein, but enough was enough. She settled on top and used him in the most exquisite way until they were bound together in a tumultuous, heart-stopping free-for-all. Not love. Only play.

Afterward, they napped.

He bent her over the arm of the easy chair.

They dawdled in the shower.

Held each other.

"Shit!" He shot up in bed.

She followed the direction of his gaze to the bedside clock. *"Merde!"*

It was nearly seven thirty. Their first Chicago client dinner began in half an hour. They scrambled for their clothes. She didn't bother with her bra. He stuffed his bare feet into his sneakers and shoved his socks in his jacket pockets. They dashed from the hotel and out into the cold Illinois night.

Thad beat her to the dinner, but by less than ten minutes, and considering she'd had hair to untangle and makeup to apply, he was impressed with how quickly she'd pulled herself together. She'd arranged her hair in some kind of low, twisty bun that nested at the nape of her neck, and put on one of those pencil dresses she wore better than anyone. He hoped he was the only one who could see the faint red marks she'd tried to hide. By tomorrow, the marks she'd left on him would show up, but they'd be under his clothes. He'd have to be more careful with her next time.

And there definitely would be a next time.

It was the best sex of his life, like being in bed with a dozen different women. Her quicksilver changes of mood, of character—virgin to vixen—her sensuous movements and beautiful body, the laughter in her dark eyes, the danger. She'd sung for him just as he'd fantasized. "Habanera." He had the uneasy feeling that she'd spoiled him for other women. Which was unfair. How could any woman compete with a trained actress of Olivia's stature? But Olivia hadn't seemed to be performing. Instead, he had the distinct feeling she'd shown him exactly who she was.

"Who's your favorite player, Thad? Other than yourself?"

It took supreme effort to bring his attention back to the effusive, overly cologned male owner of a chain of Illinois jewelry stores sitting next to him and chomping on filet mignon.

Thad had several prepared answers to this question, but since this was Chicago, only one would do. "Gotta be Walter Payton." Depending on where he was, he sometimes went with Jerry Rice or Reggie White. Maybe Dick Butkus. He tended to stay away from quarterbacks. How would he compare the great Stars QBs—Bonner, Tucker, Robillard, and Coop—against guys like Montana, Brady, Young, and Manning?

Maybe—one day—Clint Garrett. Those kinds of comparisons messed with his head.

His dinner companion nodded approvingly. "Walter 'Sweetness' Payton. Greatest running back of all time."

Jim Brown might have argued with that, but Thad nodded.

At the other end of the table, Liv was enduring her own interrogation from the bearded husband of a department-store buyer. "So how's come you never went on *American Idol*?"

He could sense her trying hard not to grit her teeth. "*American Idol* isn't really an opera competition."

His own dinner companion had launched into a monologue about Peyton Manning, and Thad nodded without paying attention. His conscience was giving him trouble.

"You and I can never have a serious, long-term relationship." That's what he'd told Liv, and he remembered how happy it had made her. But he and Liv had different ideas about what "long-term" meant. In his mind, they'd sail on the lake this summer and maybe even head to the Caribbean after the football season was over when she had a break between her gigs.

In her mind, she was dumping him in two days.

After what had transpired between them, that was unacceptable.

Unthinkable.

There they were . . . plastered all over the Internet. An enlarged photo of Liv and him.

THE DIVA AND THE QUARTERBACK
LOCK LIPS ON CHICAGO'S MAG MILE

Only the *Chicago Tribune*, his hometown newspaper, put his name first.

> Popular Stars backup quarterback Thad Owens is in a surprise relationship with opera megastar Olivia Shore, who'll soon be performing in *Aida* at the Chicago Municipal Opera. . . .

He set his laptop aside in the rumpled bedsheets. It was the morning of their third day. In her mind, their last day. Olivia jammed her hands in the pockets of the hotel's white terry-cloth robe, her hair pulled on top of her head with a scrunchie, looking not at all like the sex kitten he'd been enjoying less than a half hour ago. "How can they keep doing this?"

He crooked his elbow behind his head. "We're an item right now, Liv." He knew how skittish she was, and he was careful to emphasize "right now."

She planted one hand on her hip and renewed her protest. "Everybody doesn't need to know about it."

He swung his legs over the side of the bed. "You have to admit that a hookup between the Queen of High Culture and a lowbrow jock like myself is something people might find interesting."

She leveled him with her regal glare. "You are not, in any way, a lowbrow jock. And I hate the term 'hookup.' It makes me feel like a salmon." She reached for a towel. "I'm taking a shower. Alone this time because we have to meet Henri soon, and if you get in with me, you know what'll happen."

He gave her a lazy smile. "Tell me."

She momentarily forgot how pissed she was about the photo and gave him her own sexy smile in return, a smile that made him hard all over again. "You're incorrigible." She disappeared into the bathroom.

He sank back into the pillows. He, Thaddeus Walker Bowman Owens, had one of the greatest voices in opera singing just for him. Naked. All he had to do was ask. True, she couldn't completely unleash that powerful voice in their hotel suite without security showing up. Also true, she wasn't happy with the sound she was producing. But at least she was singing—Whitney Houston when they were in the shower together, Nina Simone after breakfast, and this morning in bed, rising up on her knees gloriously naked, she consecrated him with Mozart.

He begrudged every minute they had to spend on this, their last official day of the tour, doing interviews and meet-and-greets. He wanted it to be just the two of them.

He'd never been with a woman who was so generous, so free, so unexpected. They tangled, they experimented, they laughed. They played the best kind of mind games with each other, and neither of them could possibly be ready to throw that away for some ridiculous deadline that only one of them felt was necessary. Liv was stubborn, but she wasn't stupid. She knew as well as he they had something special. Now all he had to do was get her to admit it. That photo couldn't have come at a worse time.

For all her professional outrage, Olivia wasn't entirely unhappy with that photograph. Her ego had taken a battering these last few months, and being publicly linked with a man like Thad Owens made her feel better, which was depressing because it signaled that she might be measuring her self-worth in terms of a man, which was absolutely not true, but it was still satisfying to know that people might now see her in a different light—not as an elitist opera singer, but as a woman who could attract a man like Thad Owens, which—

She slapped her hands over her ears. Everything about Thad had sent her into a tailspin even before they'd had sex. And now that they'd had sex, it was a thousand times worse. Maybe this wasn't love. Maybe it was simply a crush. Could a woman her age have a crush? Maybe she could convince herself that's exactly what it was because she couldn't have found a worse man to have fallen in love with. Thad Owens, the anti-Dennis.

She reminded herself to stay focused on the present—today—not on the future, because wiping him out of her life would be horrible, and if she thought too hard about it, she'd ruin the little time they had left together.

Henri and Paisley met them in the suite for their last day before the tour ended. Instead of being upset by the photo, Henri was pleased. "Very romantic, yes? *Windy City Live* has already called. They want you both on tomorrow morning's program. I hope you don't mind adding it to your schedule." His cell rang, and his smile became a frown. “Excuse me.” He stepped outside into the hallway.

Olivia and Thad were still at the table finishing their coffee. She scrunched her nose at him. “What do you bet that’s Mariel calling to ream Henri out for the way we’re dragging the Marchand name through the mud.”

Paisley, who’d been working on her eye makeup in the hotel suite’s mirror, shoved her mascara wand back in her bag. “Mariel doesn’t understand anything about publicity. She’s, like, all caught up in the 1950s or something. She’s not even on LinkedIn. At least Henri is starting to get it.” She reached back into her bag—maybe for a lipstick, maybe for her phone—but her hand stalled. “I was thinking . . .” She withdrew her hand. “Maybe you guys could, like, recommend me as a PA to some of your celebrity friends? Or as a publicist. Not you, Olivia, no offense—unless you know some pop stars or, like, even B-listers who want a personal assistant?”

“Gosh, I can’t think of anyone,” Olivia said innocently. “But I bet Thad has contacts.”

He stared into his coffee cup, taking the coward’s way out. “I’ll keep it in mind.”

Paisley twisted the strap of her bag between her fingers and stared at them both. “Neither of you wants to help me, do you? You don’t respect me.”

"It's not about respect," Thad said tactfully.

"You don't think I do a good job," Paisley muttered.

Olivia regarded her with some sympathy. Paisley had been raised in privilege, and it was as much her parents' fault she was so clueless as her own. "Paisley," she said as kindly as she could, "you haven't gone out of your way to be helpful on this tour."

Paisley abandoned her purse. "That's only because of how can I get excited about passing out sandwiches to reporters and, like, making sure your suitcases get to the right room?"

A task Paisley hadn't exactly performed well.

Thad stepped in. "I understand promoting watches isn't what you want to do, but once you take a job, you give it your best. That includes the parts you don't like. And every job has those. You need to do them as diligently as you do everything else."

Olivia had a strong suspicion he might be talking about himself and the work he was doing with Clint Garrett.

Paisley looked ready to cry. "That's so not fair! I work hard! And I've gotten you twice as much publicity as you'd have gotten if you'd left it up to Henri or Mariel! I—" She stopped abruptly. Grabbing her bag, she headed for the door.

Olivia shot up from the table and blocked her. "Maybe you'd better explain that."

"Forget it." Paisley tossed her hair, looking as defiant as a teen who'd been caught out after curfew.

It all fell into place. Olivia looked at Thad and could see he was thinking exactly the same thing. "You took those photos," she said. "You're the one who's been feeding them to the gossip sites."

15

Olivia stared at Paisley as the pieces came together. If she hadn't been so distracted, she'd have figured it out days ago. Those four photos: Phoenix, LA, New Orleans, and yesterday's kiss on Michigan Avenue. "You've been following us," she said, stating what was now so obvious.

Thad rose from the table, and Paisley took a step back, as if she were afraid he'd hit her. "So what if I did? You got twice as many interviews as you'd have gotten if all you had to talk about was your lame watches."

"That's not the point," Olivia said.

Paisley looked down at her hands. "I told you I know how to work hard. Like, I got up really early to take that shot of you and Thad coming back from your hike. And I know how to get publicity. *Obviously.*"

Thad's expression was as stern as Olivia had ever seen it. "You didn't have any right to expose our private lives."

"I was doing my job! Exactly what you said, Thad. If you sign up to do a job, do the work. And that's what I did."

"What you did was unprofessional and unethical," Olivia said.

"I'm sorry, okay!"

She wasn't sorry, and Olivia dug in. "Becoming successful means working hard, but it also means working with integrity. You won't go far with any celebrity if you're not discreet and trustworthy."

Paisley began picking at a cuticle. "I guess I shouldn't have done it. But seeing how lame their feeds are made me crazy. I knew I could do better."

"Then be straightforward about it," Thad said, "and do some photo mock-ups for Henri. Images that feel fresh but also work for the Marchand brand."

"Images that don't involve Thad's butt," Olivia added.

Paisley looked only momentarily disappointed. "I can do that." She tugged on her hair. "So are you guys still pissed? Because if you're not, maybe you could, like, write a recommendation for me?" She hurried on. "And maybe you could ask Clint if he'd show me around Chicago or something."

"You're pushing it," Thad said. "Let us see those mock-ups before you show them to Henri, and then we'll talk."

The Logan Square jazz club sat half a flight of stairs below street level. It was tiny and dark, with mismatched chairs, sticky tabletops, and an eclectic crowd of hipsters, boomers, and suburbanites. This was mellow, introspective jazz. Restrained and melodic, played behind the beat, a perfect counterpoint to the roiling emotional mess she'd become.

Tonight was their last night in a hotel. Tomorrow, she'd move back into the apartment she'd rented not long before the tour had started and Thad would return to his condo. Tomorrow, she'd go to her first rehearsal. Tomorrow, their relationship would be over.

She gazed at Thad's hand curled around the tumbler of scotch. Those strong, capable fingers were as beautiful as the rest of him. He'd restrained his wardrobe for tonight: jeans, a long-sleeved black T-shirt, and his Victory780. No bright colors or fashion-forward cuts—his sockless ankles visible above a pair of designer loafers the only concession he'd made to his status as a male fashionista. As much as she loved giving him grief over his clothing choices, he wore everything beautifully.

They should be in bed now, but they weren't, and Thad seemed as reluctant as she to bring this last night to its natural conclusion. She focused on the music. If she let her mind stray, she'd lose the beauty of this last night, a night she wanted to hold on to forever.

He sipped scotch. With her unsettled stomach, she avoided her single glass of wine. The combo slid into "Come Rain or Come Shine." She wanted to take the stage in this seedy jazz club, close her eyes, and let those dusky notes pour from her. She could become a jazz singer. She could rewrite her career, travel from one jazz club to another singing all the old standards. She loved jazz, and she sang it well.

But jazz wasn't in her bloodstream. It wasn't opera. Thad might not be able to tell the problems with her voice, but the moment Sergio heard her sing—the moment anyone at the Muni heard her sing—they would know something was wrong. Her voice was good enough for a small-town opera company, but not for the Muni. Not for the Royal Opera House or La Scala or Buenos Aires. Not for the Lyric or Munich or the Palais Garnier. Most of all, not for herself.

He gave her a lover's smile, affectionate and full of promise. But the only promise between them was one more night of sex, and that suddenly felt tawdry, which was all wrong. There was nothing tawdry about what they'd shared these past few nights. She returned her gaze to the stage, determined to push the blues away and enjoy every last moment.

They didn't leave the jazz club until after midnight, which was technically their fourth day, but she wasn't that much of a stickler. Back at the hotel, they made long, slow love, hardly speaking. She'd never been so conscious of the rawness, the vulnerability, of seeing a person she loved stripped of his public face, her skin pressed to his.

It wasn't quite dawn when she opened her eyes. She slipped out of bed, careful not to wake him. Even in sleep, he was perfect.

Blinking hard, she turned away and crept from the room.

She sneaked out of his bed like a thief in the night, although technically, it was five in the morning. He heard her, but he needed to be clearheaded for the conversation they had to have, and he pretended to be asleep. She was due at the Muni at ten this morning, but first, they needed to have a reckoning.

Three hours later, after a shower, a few phone calls, and two cups of coffee, he banged on her apartment door. Their personal reckoning was no longer the first item on his agenda.

She answered, perfectly coiffed—dark slacks and white blouse open at the throat, with that pigeon egg–sized fake ruby necklace on display. Her expression softened, but only for a moment before she looked at him as though he'd noisily unwrapped a piece of candy in the middle of her aria. "How did you get in?"

"All I had to do was hop into the elevator with one of your neighbors. Now tell me this: Why would a diva like you live in an apartment without security?"

She didn't shift to the side to let him in. "I only moved here a few months ago. I told you that. It's temporary until I find a permanent place."

He slipped his sunglasses into his shirt pocket and pushed past her into her two-bedroom apartment in the River North area of Chicago. Polished hardwood floors, a postage-stamp balcony, beige carpet, and expensive, but generic, modern furniture that had probably come with the rental because it wasn't her style. The place would have been boring if she hadn't personalized it with career mementos: framed photos, posters, some cut-glass trophies. Various props and bits of costumes sat on tables and chests: Venetian carnival masks, a collection of Cherubino cherubs, the crown he'd seen in photos of her as Lady Macbeth, along with a wicked-looking dagger.

His Heisman, on the other hand, was shoved away on the top shelf of his guest room closet, along with a bunch of plaques, game balls, and a couple of his own cut-glass trophies. He didn't display any of it. Instead of making him feel good, those mementos only reminded him of unfulfilled potential.

He stepped around one of the seven thousand pieces of luggage the limo driver must have hauled up to her apartment. He hoped to God she'd made sure the driver was legit before she'd climbed in. "For somebody who spends so much time on the road, you'd think you'd have figured out by now how to downsize."

"I have an image to maintain." She shoved a makeup bag into her tote. "When I go on vacation, I only take a carry-on."

"Hard to believe." A poster from *The Marriage of Figaro* hung next to a framed, autographed photo of her with a guy who looked like a young Andrea Bocelli. The message at the bottom was written in Italian, but he didn't have any trouble translating the word "*amo.*" "Liv . . . you know this isn't going to work." He picked up a needlework pillow that read, *When Basses Go Low, I Go High.*

She regarded him warily.

"You can't stay in a building without security."

"There's an intercom system," she said defensively. "Which you could have used."

"No need. All I had to do was step into the elevator, remember?" He set the pillow back down. "Bottom line—any moron carrying a pizza box could get in this place."

She knew exactly what he was talking about, but she still protested. "I'm being careful, and I'll find a permanent place as soon as I have time. I like Chicago."

"I remember. Middle of the country and all." He bumped into one of her wheeled garment bags. "The point is, you were attacked in New Orleans, kidnapped in Vegas. Do you really think this is over?"

"I'm home now," she said carefully. "I can't spend the rest of my life hiding."

"We're not talking about the rest of your life. We're talking about now." He hadn't planned on this, but he couldn't see another way around it. "I want you to move in with me for a while."

Her head shot up. "That's ridiculous. We're over, remember?"

"I'm not talking about us living together."

"That's exactly what you're talking about."

"No, this is about security. Your personal safety. And this place can't provide it."

"So I'm supposed to pack up, and—"

"You're already packed up."

"—move in with you?"

Her skittishness wasn't surprising, and he tried to make this more palatable. "Full disclosure—I've never invited a woman to move in with me, and I wouldn't be doing it now if you weren't living here. My God, you have a broom handle stuck in your sliding doors."

"I'm on the tenth floor!"

"With other people's balconies on each side of you."

He picked up the deadly-looking dagger and pointed it in her general direction. "My building is secure. There's a doorman, cameras, alarms, a concierge. You don't have any of that."

"I don't need it."

"Yes, you do." He couldn't avoid this any longer. He set the dagger next to an inkpot with a feathered plume and withdrew the folded, letter-sized envelope he'd already opened from his back pocket. She hesitated before she took it from him. She extracted what was inside as carefully as if she were handling a snake. Not far off.

It was the newspaper photo of the two of them kissing on Michigan Avenue. Except someone had ripped a hole in the paper where her head had been and written a note in red ink across the bottom.

> You destroyed me and now I'm destroying you, my love. Think of me with every note you try to sing.

"This was delivered to your room at the hotel an hour ago," he said gently.

She snatched the paper from his hand, ripped it, and shoved the pieces into the wastebasket by the couch. "I'm not letting this get to me. I'm absolutely not."

"You already have, and ripping it up won't make the threat go away."

She sank into the couch, dropped her head, and rubbed her temples. "I hate this."

He sat next to her and took one of her silver rings between his fingers. "The message says, 'Think of me with every note you try to sing.' What does that mean to you?"

"It doesn't mean anything. It means—" Her head came up. "I don't know."

"Whoever is sending you these messages knows you're having trouble with your voice and is capitalizing on it. Someone wants you to stop singing."

"That's impossible. No one knows about my voice except you."

"And Rachel, right? The best friend you tell everything to."

"I'd trust Rachel!" she exclaimed. "Besides, I haven't told her all of it. She has no idea how bad it's gotten."

He knew she didn't want to hear this, but he had to say it anyway. "The two of you are in competition for the same roles. You told me she also sings Amneris, right?"

"So do dozens of other performers!" she exclaimed. "Rachel and I are on different career paths."

"But maybe Rachel wants to be on the same path."

She jumped up. "I won't hear another word. I mean it, Thad. I'd trust Rachel with my life."

Which might be exactly what she was doing, but he knew better than to say that. "Regardless of who's behind this, someone is threatening you, and you can't stay here." He rose and cupped her shoulders. "We've been traveling together for almost a month. We know how to share space. This doesn't have to be complicated. You can go your way. I'll go mine."

She looked away. "You know it won't be that easy."

"It'll be as easy as we make it."

She turned from him. "I don't want to do this."

"I understand."

"I'll . . . rent another apartment."

"That'll take some time."

Her shoulders slumped in defeat. "This isn't the way it was supposed to be."

"I know," he said. "We'll figure it out as we go along."

If the Lyric Opera's baronial, throne-shaped, art deco building was the grand dame of Chicago opera, the Chicago Municipal Opera was its stylish, sassy granddaughter. In the chilly, midmorning sunshine, the Muni's flowing, contemporary glass-and-concrete curves were perfectly reflected in the Chicago River.

"I went here once," Clint said, as they pulled into the parking lot.

"Your audition for *The Bachelor*?" Thad chimed in from the back seat where Clint and Olivia had exiled him.

Clint grinned. "Dude, I haven't been to one of those since you made me hold your hand when you auditioned. Remember how hard you cried when they said you were too old?"

Thad snorted, and Olivia smiled, her first of the morning. Watching the two of them spar was her brightest moment since she'd gotten out of Thad's bed that morning.

Thad had insisted on driving her to the Muni, even though her beloved old red BMW M2 waited patiently in the garage. He'd shrugged off her reminder that his license had been stolen, along with his wallet. "When you're playing for a Chicago sports team, the cops tend to overlook crap like driver's licenses."

"Not all of them, I'm sure," she'd said. "And the last thing you need is to be picked up for driving without a license."

So he'd put in a phone call to Clint, and now here she was—with an unsteady voice and the ominous mental image of her headless body in the newspaper photo—being driven to her first day back at work with two of the city's most famous jocks. Her life had shot so far from its orbit she'd entered a different universe.

Clint parked by the rear entrance, close to the spot that had been reserved for her. Her costume fitting came first, then the meeting she dreaded with the maestro, Sergio Tinari, and then a full afternoon of blocking rehearsals. Her stomach had already been in knots before Thad had shown up with that ugly photo, and now it was ten times worse.

Thad was right about the poor security in her apartment. It wasn't as if she hadn't thought about it, but she'd convinced herself she'd be spending so much time at rehearsals she could make it work. A perfect example of delusional thinking.

Clint stepped out to open the door for her, something Thad couldn't do since he was trapped in the tiny back seat, his knees accordioned to his chest. Not that she needed anybody to open a car door for her. What she needed was someone to give her back her voice, her breath control, and her confidence. "Make sure he gets to the DMV today," she told Clint as she got out of the car.

"Aw, Livia, there's not a cop in this town who'd give T-Bo a traffic ticket."

"Exactly what I told you," Thad declared triumphantly.

She eyeballed Clint. "Just do it."

Thad extracted himself from the back seat, a process that would have been entertaining if she weren't so concerned with what lay ahead. "I'll go to the DMV," he said, "but only if you promise to let me know when you're done so I can come pick you up."

"I don't need a chauffeur," she declared.

"You really do." All of a sudden, Clint, her loyal ally, had shifted allegiance. "Thad filled me in, and you've got some crazy sh— stuff going on. You shouldn't be wandering around by yourself."

"I'm going to talk to a friend on the Chicago police force." Thad took a firm grip on her arm, walking her toward the building.

She nodded begrudgingly. As much as she hated the idea of involving the police, this had gone too far.

"You're going to be great," he whispered, when they reached the rear door. *"Toi, toi, toi."*

"Toi, toi, toi" was the traditional good-luck wish opera singers exchanged, their version of the theater world's "break a leg." The expression was well known among classical singers, but not to the general population, and she was touched that he'd taken the trouble to discover this.

He smiled and opened the door. She stepped back into her world.

She'd sung at the Muni multiple times, but nothing felt the same. Yes, the costume department smelled as it always did of steam irons, fabric, and must. The Egyptian headpieces fit well, and her costumes needed only a little alteration. She chatted with the wardrobe mistress as she always had and exchanged pleasantries with the technical director. She passed a rehearsal room where singers were at work on an upcoming concert. But she was more aware of new faces when they passed her in the hallway, more alert as she walked from one room to the next.

On her way to meet with the maestro, she mentally reviewed the master schedule. She wouldn't have to sing today for the blocking rehearsal, and she could easily mark at piano tech, which was for the benefit of the production team, but she'd have to sing in full voice for *sitzprobe*, their first rehearsal with the orchestra.

And, of course, she needed to bring her best to next Thursday's dress rehearsal, not to mention Saturday's opening night.

She braced herself at the door of the maestro's office and knocked.

"Avanti!"

Sergio Tinari, the Muni's great conductor, was short in stature but giant in presence. With his lion's mane of gray hair, bushy eyebrows, and long Tuscan nose, he was a caricaturist's dream subject. "Olivia, *mia cara.*" He kissed her hand with Old World graciousness.

She switched to Italian, telling him how happy she was to see him, how much she was looking forward to working with him again, and that she was recovering from a head cold and would need a few days before she could sing.

Sergio replied in his beautifully accented English. "But of course. You must protect your voice. Tomorrow, if you are able to mark, we can rehearse the phrasing in 'A lui vivo, la tomba!'"

Alive in the tomb . . . She twisted her lips into a smile. "Of course."

The note she'd just received . . . *You destroyed me and now I'm destroying you, my love. Think of me with every note you try to sing.*

Her fake ruby pendant felt as if it were choking her.

As she left the maestro's studio, she knew she couldn't offer up the excuse of having a cold for very long.

A striking woman about Olivia's age emerged from the last rehearsal room. Olivia's spirits immediately brightened. "Sarah!" She hurried down the corridor to greet the gifted South African soprano who would be singing Aida.

She was no longer comfortable singing Amneris opposite a white Aida. Having a black artist singing the enslaved Ethiopian princess added complexity and dimension to the production for modern audiences, and Sarah Mabunda was one of the best. But as Olivia reached out to hug her, Sarah drew away, and her tight smile had an off-putting brittleness to it.

Olivia was taken aback. She and Sarah were friends. They'd performed *Aida* together before, once in Sydney and once at the Staatsoper in Vienna, where they'd spent free afternoons exploring the city's museums and where Sarah had told her about her life growing up in Soweto before she'd made her way first to Cape Town Opera School and then on to the Royal Academy of Arts in London. They'd established an immediate connection, and the only part of today she'd been looking forward to was seeing Sarah again.

Olivia searched her mind for what she could have done to offend her but couldn't think of anything.

Maybe Sarah was simply having a bad day? "How have you been?" she asked uncertainly.

"Very well." With a formal nod, Sarah swept past Olivia.

Olivia stared after her. Stunned, she entered the rehearsal stage. Lena Hodiak, the Polish mezzo who had been covering for her during the early rehearsals, greeted her enthusiastically. "Ms. Shore!" She rushed forward with a wide smile. "It's such a privilege to be working with you."

Lena, a statuesque blonde with lush features, regarded Olivia with the adoring eyes of a young singer meeting her idol. Olivia thought how excited Lena would be if she knew she had a real chance of performing in Olivia's place. But she couldn't think that way. "Please. Call me Olivia. Rachel Cullen speaks highly of you."

Olivia remembered her own days covering for bigger artists. The work had given her a steady paycheck when she'd badly needed it, and since covers had to attend every rehearsal, she'd learned from watching the best. But the frustration of perfecting a role, yet not having the chance to perform it, had been real. Still, although stories abounded of a young understudy stepping in at the last minute for the incapacitated star and soaring to instant fame, that seldom happened. In reality, covers spent most of their time stuck in a room offstage playing games on their phones.

"Let me know if I can help in any way," Lena said.

"Thanks. I will."

"Someone wants you to stop singing."

That was Thad's opinion, and Olivia rejected it. Lena was immensely talented or she couldn't be here, and taking over a role as important as Amneris—especially on opening night when critics would be present—could advance her career immeasurably. But her welcoming manner hardly marked her as an understudy planning to sabotage the leading lady.

"Olivia, I'm so glad you're here." Gary Vallin, the director, came over to greet her. Opera directors, unlike musical conductors, generally weren't musicians, but the best of them brought a fresh perspective to a piece, seeing it as a work of theater and not just a musical score. Gary was one of those.

As he familiarized Olivia with the staging, Lena sat off to the side keeping a close eye on the rehearsal and making notes exactly as she was supposed to.

By the time the day ended, Olivia was exhausted from the strain of pretending everything was normal. She needed to hear a friendly voice, and as soon as she got to her dressing room, she called Rachel.

It didn't take her friend long to get to the point. "How are you really doing?"

Olivia hedged. "Okay. I'm not where I want to be, but . . ."

"You'll get there. You will!"

"Sure, I will." But Olivia wasn't sure of anything right now.

When their conversation ended, she stowed her phone in her tote and gathered up the rest of her things. As she came out of her dressing room, she glimpsed a figure ducking around the corner. The shadowy light at the end of the corridor made it impossible to see whether it was a man or a woman, but something about the way the person moved seemed furtive. Still, too many things seemed furtive these days, and she no longer trusted herself to judge what was real and what wasn't.

She passed Sarah Mabunda on her way out of the building. The Muni's current Aida walked by without a word.

"Let me see your driver's license," she told Thad as she slipped into the front seat of a very expensive snow-white Chevy Corvette ZR1 that looked as if it belonged on a NASA launchpad. She'd wanted to call an Uber, but she wasn't up to the confrontation that would surely follow.

He flipped open his wallet to show her his temporary license. "For future reference, sending two of the town's most recognized jocks to the DMV together wasn't your best idea. We nearly caused a riot."

"Sorry. I didn't think of that."

As he pulled out onto West Kinzie, she began to unwind. His presence didn't exactly relax her. How could she relax with memories of all their creative sex acts ping-ponging in her brain? Instead, being with him, absorbing his self-confidence and energy, made her feel as though she might be able to regain control of her own life.

"I'm guessing you want to stop by your place first to pick up some of your things," he said.

"I phoned my real estate agent this afternoon. He's going to find me a safer furnished rental in the next few days. Moving in with you is only temporary. Very temporary."

"It better be. I'm not sure how long I can handle having a high-strung roommate. And if you get into any of my beauty products, I'm kicking you out."

She smiled. As far as she knew, his only beauty products were a bar of soap and a tube of sunblock.

He parked in the garage next to her beloved old BMW, and they rode the elevator up to her apartment. She unlocked the door and gazed at the mess she'd left.

Unfortunately, no magic elves had appeared to unpack all her suitcases.

Except . . . the dagger Thad had been toying with . . . She distinctly remembered watching him set it next to the inkpot instead of by the Lady Macbeth crown where it belonged. Now, it was lying on an end table next to the couch.

Someone had been in here.

16

The small suitcase that held her toiletries lay on its side. Two more suitcases didn't seem to be where she'd left them. There were other small things. The bedroom door had been closed when she'd left, and now it was open. She hadn't used the master bathroom this morning, but the drawer next to the sink was ajar.

Not surprisingly, Mr. Chill lost his cool, erupting with an astonishing string of locker room obscenities that concluded with his insistence that they immediately go to the police. This would be her third visit inside a police station in a little over two weeks—a record she'd never counted on achieving.

All she wanted to do was curl up in her pajamas with a glass of wine and some good jazz. But she knew he was right.

His "friend" in the Chicago Police Department turned out to be a leggy brunette about her age, and, if her suspicions were correct, a former girlfriend. Olivia confirmed the details he'd already given Lieutenant Barbie in a telephone conversation they'd apparently had earlier in the day. And calling her "Lieutenant Barbie" was totally unfair. Lieutenant Brittany Cooke was efficient, competent, sympathetic, and Olivia was a jealous disgrace to the sisterhood.

"I've talked to the police in New Orleans and Las Vegas," the lieutenant told her. "And I'm making some inquiries about your ex-fiancé's sisters and one of your superfans."

Olivia glared at Thad. "Rupert is not part of this!"

"Just following protocol," the lieutenant said with a soothing smile. "For now, be smart about what you do and where you go."

Thad looked as if he had something to say about that but kept his mouth shut.

Thad's condo was exactly what she would have expected a multimillionaire bachelor with excellent taste to own. Modern and spacious with sweeping windows showcasing both city and lake views. The decor was contemporary, mostly tones of gray, steel, and blue with unexpected hits of color here and there. But with the exception of a full bookcase and a great vinyl collection, Thad himself was missing. No personal photos sat on display. Nothing that reflected the people he'd met over the years, the places he'd traveled. And not one object that testified to his many accomplishments on the field.

"I'm putting your things in the guest room," he said, "but I'm requesting that not include your actual body."

She tugged on her necklace. "We need to talk." But Thad had already disappeared with the two suitcases she'd brought along, and he either couldn't hear her or chose not to.

She took in an abstract painting she recognized as a work by the famous American street artist Ian Hamilton North—a vast, multicolored kaleidoscope that took up most of a wall.

She had to find a new place quickly. Definitely by the time the show opened. She'd talked to her real estate agent twice already today, and he'd assured her it shouldn't take long to locate a more secure apartment. Definitely by the time the show opened. Maybe she could find a temporary rental. Or maybe . . .

Maybe this was a sign from the universe that she was allowed to relax her vigilance for a few more days—a week. Maybe a little more.

They ate turkey sandwiches and potato chips for dinner. She learned Thad had planned to use part of the next two weeks until the *Aida* gala to visit his parents in Kentucky. "You should definitely go," she told him.

"Maybe." He reached into the potato chip bag. "I have a couple of business deals I want to look into."

Meaning he wasn't budging from Chicago, and she doubted it had anything to do with business deals. His sense of responsibility toward her was a weight he shouldn't have to bear. "As you've pointed out ad nauseam," she said, "your building is secure. I'll be in rehearsal most of the day, and when I'm not, I'll babysit this hovel for you, so there's no need to change your plans." She set down the remains of her turkey sandwich. "Just to get any awkwardness out of the way, I'm sleeping in the guest bedroom tonight."

"Fine with me." He couldn't have looked less interested.

She was sleeping in the damned guest room! What kind of crap was that? As much as he wanted to argue with her, she was tired and on edge, so he let it go. For now.

Her vocalizing awakened him the next morning. It was her real voice, not the tape-recorded version, and she sounded amazing. But he knew her well enough by now not to compliment her because she'd only say her voice was too fat or too skinny or coming from her elbow instead of her butt or some crap like that.

She walked in on him as he was shaving. She'd dressed casually for rehearsal. Slip-on sneakers, a pair of perfectly fitted black joggers, and a long, black knit sweater. A purple woven scarf looped her neck to protect her from the drafts that were the archenemy of serious singers. Her makeup was flawless—bold eyeliner, dark brows, and crimson lips. She looked as formidable as The Diva she was. But he knew she didn't feel that way.

"*Sitzprobe* is next Monday," she said. "Counting today, I have five more rehearsal days until then."

"Siltz probe?" Thad lifted his head to shave under his chin.

"*Sitzprobe.* It's the first time the singers and orchestra really come together. There are no costumes, no props. Everything gets stripped away except the music. You sit and you sing." She gazed at a spot above the mirror, no longer seeing him, lost in her thoughts. "*Sitzprobe* is pure. The instruments, the voices. There are these magical moments when the music becomes transcendent."

He thought of those moments when he no longer heard the roar of the crowd. It was just him and the field and the ball.

"It's my favorite rehearsal." She gazed down at her hands. "You can't fake it in *sitzprobe*. There's no marking. You either have it or you don't." She gazed at his reflection. "I lied," she said.

He waited.

"I lied to the maestro. I told him I had a cold." She turned away and disappeared into the hallway. "I'm driving myself to rehearsal."

Olivia had loaded up her tote with everything she'd need for the day: an extra sweater, her reusable water bottle, a pencil, a highlighted copy of the score so she could note any new blocking. She'd packed Throat Coat tea, cough drops, saline spray, a couple of packs of almonds, an apple, hand sanitizer, makeup, tissues, her wallet and phone, her Carmex lip balm. Now all she needed was a big box of nerve. *Sitzprobe.* A week from yesterday.

She'd left her own car in one of Thad's two parking slots. He'd surprised her by not putting up an argument about her driving herself until she looked in her rearview mirror and saw a sleek, snow-white Corvette following her to the Muni. And parking right behind her.

He got out of his car and came toward her, the lenses of his sunglasses flashing in the cold morning sunshine.

Even as she felt a stab of trepidation, she thought how much she loved this man. What if—?

No what-ifs. She grabbed her tote and got out of the car. Drawing herself to her full height, she offered up her haughtiest, "Yes?" as if he were her vassal instead of the man she so desperately loved.

He slammed her car door shut, grabbed her arm, and marched her around the side of the building with her tote banging against her leg. In warmer weather, the singers gathered in the small, enclosed green space for fresh air. Now, the wooden benches were unoccupied, the big flower urns waiting for spring planting.

She found herself wedged between him and the side of the building. She lifted her chin and gazed down the length of her nose at him. "What?"

He knew her tricks, and he wasn't intimidated. "You said you had a cold."

Her distorted reflection looked back at her from the lenses of his sunglasses. "I told you that."

His perfect mouth set in a deadly line. "You lied."

"I told you that, too." She wished she'd kept her mouth shut.

He whipped off his sunglasses and drilled her with those ridiculous green eyes, which now seemed exactly the same color as a particularly virulent patch of poison ivy. "Guess what, babe? You've had a miraculous recovery."

"You don't understand." She tried to get away from him, but he shifted his weight to block her.

"Oh, I do understand." He shoved his sunglasses in his jacket pocket. "You're Olivia fucking Shore. The greatest mezzo in the world!"

"I'm not the greatest—"

"You're at the top of your game. In the starting lineup! A fucking *tornado*, not some twenty-year-old pretender afraid to open her mouth!"

"That's easy for you to say. You're not—"

"Stop being such a pussy." He gripped her by the shoulders. "I heard you loud and clear this morning. *Sitzprobe.* It means everything to you, and you only have five rehearsals to get ready for it. You've worked too damned hard to give in to this crap. Your voice is exactly where you need it to be."

"You have no idea—"

"You're going in there right now, and you're going to sing your ass off." He actually *shook* her! "Do it one-legged, standing on your head, or with your eyes crossed. I don't care. You pull yourself the hell together and show them exactly who they're dealing with. Do you hear me?"

"Yes."

"Louder!"

"Yes!"

"Good."

He stalked away.

She straightened the collar of her trench coat and glared at his back—the ignorant jock. She marched from the abandoned garden. It was easy for him to say. He didn't understand. He knew nothing about the kind of pressure she faced. Nothing about the critics who were waiting to gnaw on her bones, the fans who would desert her, the reputation that would turn to dust. He never had to face—

But he did. He knew exactly how she felt. He'd played hurt. He'd played with the crowd booing him. He'd played in blistering heat waves, frigid snowstorms, and with the clock ticking down to its final ten seconds. He'd played under every kind of pressure, and he understood what she felt as well as she did.

She marched directly to the maestro's office and rapped on the door.

"Avanti."

She stormed in. "Maestro." She dropped her tote by the door. "I know I'm early, but . . . I'm ready to sing."

It wasn't pretty, but it wasn't horrendous. She didn't have the breath support she needed to make her vibrato dependable or keep from falling off some of the notes, but she didn't once go flat.

Sergio still believed she was suffering from the aftereffects of a cold, and he wasn't overly concerned by what he heard. "Most important now is for you to take care of your voice."

Back in her dressing room, she made a phone call. The voice that answered sounded distinctly displeased. "Olivia Shore? I do not recognize this name."

Olivia ignored that. "Can I come in today? I have a long break at one o'clock."

"I suppose. Bring me plums. The purple ones." The connection went dead.

The old woman met Olivia at the door of her musty Randolph Street apartment. She wore her customary black serge dress and pink bedroom slippers run down at the heels. Her coarse, gray-streaked black hair was knotted on top of her head, with wiry strands escaping around her wrinkled face, which bore her customary scarlet lipstick.

She greeted Olivia with a gruff, "You may enter."

Olivia replied with the gracious nod of her head she knew Batista expected.

Batista Neri was one of Olivia's longtime vocal coaches, and someone Olivia had been deliberately ignoring since she'd lost her voice. Batista had once been an accomplished soprano. Now she was one of the best opera coaches in the country. She was maddeningly condescending, but also highly effective.

Olivia set the bag of plums on an ornate mahogany side table near the door. "My voice . . . ," she said. "It's gone."

"Ah, well." Scorn dripped from Batista's every word. "Now you will find a husband to take care of you, and you will make him gnocchi every night for supper." She waved a dismissive hand. "Enough of this bullshit. Let me hear you."

When Olivia reached the rehearsal stage later that afternoon, she found Lena Hodiak moving through Amneris's blocking for the Judgment scene in act 4. Olivia watched as Lena mouthed the lyrics, *"Ohime! Morir mi sento . . ." Alas! I shall die! Oh, who will save him?*

Lena waved as she spotted Olivia and quickly moved into the audience to give Olivia the stage.

It felt like midnight instead of late afternoon. Olivia had sung badly for the maestro and only a little better for Batista. At least Batista had abandoned her crotchety prima donna routine and gotten serious when she heard the state of Olivia's voice.

"Lift your palate, Olivia. Lift it." At the end of the lesson, Batista had prescribed bee propolis throat spray and more abdominal exercises and ordered Olivia to come back the next day.

Arthur Baker, the aging but still handsome tenor playing Radamès, came in, along with Gary, the director. A few hours later it was time to rehearse the second scene of act 1, where Amneris tricks her servant Aida into revealing her true feelings for Radamès with the lie that Radamès is dead. Sarah was meticulously prepared, as always, but the chemistry they'd once shared onstage was gone.

Olivia had never been happier for a day to be over. At five o'clock, as she opened her dressing room door, she saw Thad sprawled on her chaise waiting for her. "How did you get in?" she demanded.

"I'm a famous football player. I can go wherever I want."

Witnessing her lover playing the part of the arrogant asshole lifted her spirits. "I should have known," she said, closing the door behind her.

"Bad news." He idly crossed his ankles. "Someone stole your car."

She regarded him suspiciously. "Any idea who that might have been?"

"Probably Garrett. He's a punk."

"I see." She remembered the spare set of car keys she'd unwisely left on the dresser in his guest bedroom. "And under whose order might he have performed this particular act of felony?"

"I'm fairly sure he thought it up all by himself."

"And I'm fairly sure he didn't."

He tilted his head toward her private bathroom. "Want to get it on in there?"

Her answer was as surprising to him as it was to her. "Yes. Yes, I do."

They locked themselves in the small bathroom, pulling at their clothes and groping each other, exactly what she needed to wipe out her day. They ended up partially naked in the cramped shower, water not running, Olivia against the wall with her pants pooled around one ankle, Thad's jeans at his knees, both of them awkward and frantic—out of their minds. It wasn't the third night. It was the fifth day, and this wasn't supposed to happen because she couldn't keep loving a man who wasn't part of her world, but at that moment, she didn't care.

Afterward, she did. "What's wrong with me? This only makes everything tougher," she said, as she reassembled herself.

"Only if you want it to be." He closed the lid of the toilet and sat on top, watching as she finished pulling herself back together. “Not to criticize, Liv, but you’re way too uptight.”

“Taking care of my career is not being uptight,” she retorted, sounding uptight. She grabbed a hairbrush. “What did you do today? Other than arrange for my car to disappear?”

“I bought a couple of new stocks and nosed around in your portfolio again. You need to dump Calistoga Mutual Fund. It’s been underperforming for years.” His leg brushed the back of hers as he crossed an ankle over his knee. “I also spent some time with Coop and his wife, Piper. That’s Cooper Graham, the Stars’ last great quarterback.”

“Until the idiot came along.”

“The idiot’s not in that category yet.”

“But he could be.”

“I guess,” he said begrudgingly.

“It’s good you have something to do.” She picked up a makeup brush, stalling for time. “I sang for Sergio Tinari this morning,” she told him.

“Did you now?”

She turned on the bathroom faucet. “And I went to see my old voice teacher.”

He ignored the broader significance of that. “How’d you get there?”

“I walked.”

"Not smart."

"It's hard to get abducted in the Loop at midday. And I need my car back. I have to look at apartments."

"I'll do it for you."

"You don't have to—"

"You're working. I'm not. It's only fair."

The offer was enticing. The last thing she wanted to do after a full day of rehearsals was go apartment hunting. On the other hand, the sooner she found her own place, the better it would be for her, especially after what had just happened.

That night, he went to her room, testing the new boundaries she'd set. "I think I'll sleep in here," he said. "But no touching, okay?"

She gave him a soft smile and held out her arms. "No touching."

He laughed, got in next to her, and pulled her body to his. As he kissed her, he thought how much he loved being with this woman. Not love-love. But pure-enjoyment-love. What meant the most, however, was how well someone who wasn't part of his world understood him. If The Diva had been a guy and athletically gifted, she'd have made a hell of a teammate.

He rubbed her earlobes with his thumbs. Kissed her. It wasn't long before she was making those beautiful, throaty sounds. They traveled together, climbing, reaching, falling . . . The world splintered into a million pieces.

Afterward, God help him, she wanted to talk. He snuffled into his pillow and pretended to be asleep, which didn't do anything to discourage her.

"This is only temporary, Thad. Temporary insanity on my part. It all ends on opening night. I'm serious."

He muttered something deliberately unintelligible. Mercifully, she said no more.

He didn't get it. Career or not, even prima donnas needed a private life, and he wasn't high-maintenance like her. Sure, he attracted a lot of attention when he went out, but she wasn't exactly invisible. And yes, now that the tour was over, he had a lot of catching up to do—putting in extra hours with his trainer, digging deeper into his sideline work. There were people he needed to see, meetings he had to take, rookies who wanted to talk to him about managing their money. And maybe he hid more of himself than she did, but all that didn't add up to him being high-maintenance, right?

In the end, she fell asleep long before he did.

Wednesday. Thursday. The rehearsals ticked away. Olivia worked with Batista every day and started feeling a little more like herself. But it was never good enough. Next Monday's *sitzprobe* hung over her head like a guillotine blade. She could mark through Tuesday and Wednesday's technical rehearsal, but not *sitzprobe* and not Thursday's final dress rehearsal, where there would be a selected audience. Friday was a rest day, and then opening night on Saturday.

She sensed members of the company talking about her behind her back. Their highly trained ears noticed the muting of the dark, tonal luster in her low range. They detected the occasional wobble, the awkward phrase. But everyone believed she was recovering from a cold, and only Sergio had begun to look concerned.

Lena, in the meantime, had become Olivia's shadow, watching everything Olivia did during rehearsals, asking the occasional question, but also never being intrusive. Despite her youth, Lena was the consummate professional, yet Olivia had begun to hate the sight of her. She'd never felt this way about any of her other covers, but then she'd never felt so threatened by one. She was ashamed. Lena wasn't a vulture standing on the sidelines waiting to fly off with Olivia's bones. She was hardworking and respectful, doing exactly what she'd been hired to do, and once this was over, Olivia would make up for her unjust thoughts by buying her a great piece of jewelry or treating her to a spa weekend or . . . What if she fixed her up with Clint Garrett?

The last idea seemed genius until she saw Lena kissing a long-haired young man she later identified as her husband. Jewelry, then.

Thad picked her up at the Muni after his first day of apartment hunting. As it turned out, he'd found fault with every place he'd seen. One was too noisy, another too dark, the third had no place for her piano, the fourth had a Jacuzzi, but no decent shower. And the fifth . . .

"Smelled like dead rabbit," he said. "Don't ask me how I know this."

"I won't."

On Friday morning, she had three hours of free time while the company rehearsed *Aida*'s famous Triumphal March—a complex piece of staging that involved over a hundred performers, twenty-six dancers, and two horses, but fortunately, no elephants, not for this production. She used the time to schedule a meeting with her real estate agent and wasn't surprised when Thad decided to tag along.

Refusing to meet Thad's disapproving gaze, her Realtor showed her three of the apartments Thad had rejected. One, as he'd reported, lacked enough natural light. The second was almost perfect, but would be crowded with her piano. As for the third . . . It had a doorman, video camera surveillance, and plenty of room. The location was great, she could move in right away, and it smelled nothing like rabbit.

"I'll take it," she told her Realtor.

"You'll regret it come Easter," Thad said.

17

Of course someone had broken into her dressing room at the Muni while she was gone! Why not, when everything else was so messed up?

She whipped off her coat and tossed it on the chaise. Dressing room thefts happened. A dozen keys floated around. It could have been anyone. Maybe this was simply coincidence.

But she no longer believed in coincidence, and she began what had become an all-too-familiar routine of trying to see if anything was missing.

Unlike all the other times, something was. The thief had made off with her snack pack of almonds.

She sank onto the chaise. What did this person want? The only item of value she had with her was her

Cavatina3, and that had been on her wrist. When was this going to end? If she told Thad, he'd plant himself at the Muni to watch over her, and that would make it look as if she'd turned her famous lover into her lackey. He'd do it, too, because that's who he was.

Unthinkable. She wouldn't let him humiliate himself.

Her Realtor pulled off a miracle, and Olivia used Sunday, her day off, to settle into her new video-surveilled, concierge-secured, furnished apartment. Her piano sat by the front windows, but she'd only begun opening up the boxes of mementos the movers had packed and delivered under Thad's supervision.

He emerged from her kitchen with a banana. "I don't know why you had to do this so fast."

She held up a notepad she'd scribbled with the words, *I'm on vocal rest.*

"Only when it suits you."

She smiled at the softness in his voice. He understood how much was at stake for her tomorrow. He understood everything.

"Grab your coat," he said, after he'd polished off the banana. "This mess isn't going anywhere, and there are some people I want you to meet."

The Cooper Graham and Piper Dove Graham household was a noisy one. Their three-year-old twins, Isabelle and Will, fought over possession of two identical cardboard boxes while their father stood idly by. "Survival of the fittest," Coop declared, as he showed Thad and Olivia into the family's spacious, toy-cluttered great room at the rear of their Lincoln Park home. "Piper and I try not to get too involved unless bloodshed is imminent."

Cooper Graham was the Stars' former quarterback and Thad's best friend. The instant the twins spotted Thad, their tug-of-war over the boxes turned into a race to see who could get to him first. Thad diplomatically scooped them both up at the same time, one under each arm. "Look what I've got. A pair of elephants."

"We not elephants!" Will squealed.

"We monkeys!" Isabelle shrieked.

"Truth," Coop said.

A pretty, dark-haired woman in leggings appeared and gave Thad a hug. Thad introduced them. "Liv, this is Piper, Coop's deluded wife and the owner of Dove Investigations. Piper, this is the great Olivia Shore."

Piper Dove Graham didn't look anything like Olivia's idea of a detective. No cigarette hung from the corner of her mouth, and the leggings she wore instead of a dirty trench coat revealed no sign of a paunch. "I feel like I should curtsy," Piper said.

Her grin was so engaging that Olivia immediately laughed. "From what Thad's told me, it should be the other way around. I've never met a detective, let alone a female one."

"We're pretty great," Piper declared, with an even bigger smile.

"Liv's on vocal rest," Thad said. "And in case you're wondering, that means she talks whenever she wants, but not if I ask her a question she doesn't want to answer."

Olivia nodded agreeably. "That's true."

Isabelle wanted Thad's attention, and she grabbed his face between her hands. "Where do piggies keep all dey money? In a *piggy bank*!"

Both twins found this hysterically funny.

"Good one, Izzy," Thad said, setting them both down. "Although you might work a little on your delivery."

"I got a bettuh one!" Will exclaimed. "Why do a birdie fly? 'Cause it's a *poopy*-face birdie!"

Piper groaned. "That's a clear sign you kids need to run upstairs and find your helicopters so you can show them to Uncle Thad. He loves helicopters."

The kids scrambled from the room, each trying to beat the other to the hallway. Coop raised an eyebrow at his wife. “You hid their helicopters, didn't you?”

“Don't act like you've never hidden them.” Piper turned to Olivia. “I'm down with anything that buys us a few minutes of peace and quiet. Turns out, my husband is only a man of honor when it comes to football. He promised me all I had to do was give birth and he'd take over raising them. I was so besotted I believed him.”

Coop grinned. “By the time she figured out I'd conned her, it was too late. She'd already fallen in love with the little hellions.”

Piper smiled.

“They're both a couple of do-gooders,” Thad told Olivia. “Coop runs the largest urban gardening project in the city along with a training center to help disadvantaged kids get jobs.”

“My wife's a lot more impressive,” Coop said. “She's become an expert on putting child sex traffickers behind bars.”

Piper nodded. “Only because it's illegal for me to kill them.”

Coop draped an arm around his wife's shoulders. “Do you see why I have to sleep with one eye open?”

Olivia had never met a couple like these two, so obviously in love and so respectful of each other's work.

"Thad told me over the phone that you've run into some trouble." Piper gestured toward one of the room's two couches. "He gave me a general idea but I'd like to hear the details from you. Why don't you tell me about it while the men check on the children?"

"I'm staying here," Thad said. "I love those two kids, but Liv tends to minimize the situation."

"No, I don't," Olivia said. "All right, maybe I do. It keeps me sane."

While Coop dealt with his children, Olivia and Thad filled Piper in on everything that had happened on the tour. Only at the end, when Thad finally went off to join Coop in the kitchen, did Olivia tell Piper about the dressing room incident.

"A lot doesn't add up here," Piper said.

"At first, the Las Vegas police thought the whole thing was a publicity stunt. Thankfully, they found the limo."

"But not the driver." Piper glanced at the notes she'd been making. "I'll do some checking around. In the meantime, keep your eyes open, and call me right away if anything else happens."

"I will."

Piper tapped her ballpoint pen on the notepad. "You and Thad . . . Did you hit it off right away?"

"Not exactly."

"What then?"

"Is this relevant?"

"Not a bit." Piper grinned. "I'm nosy, and he's obviously crazy about you."

"Attraction of opposites," Olivia said.

"Maybe, maybe not. He's an interesting guy. Did he tell you that he does a lot of unpaid work for me?"

"What kind of work?"

"Investigative. Thad is a genius when it comes to finance, and human trafficking is a multibillion-dollar industry. Sex traffickers use banks to deposit money and launder it. Thad understands the banking and financial industry in a way I don't, and when he looks at financial reports, he sees things that get past me."

It all came together. This was what was behind his secretiveness when he was on his computer and the whispered phone calls she'd witnessed. "He never said a word to me."

"He downplays his own do-gooder instincts. And, practically speaking, it's better for him to keep a low profile. Jocks have access to people who won't talk to investigators."

As Olivia tried to absorb this new information, the twins charged back in, their helicopters in tow, and demanded their mother's attention.

On their way back to Olivia's new apartment, she confronted Thad with what he hadn't told her. "Don't you think you could have mentioned this to me?"

"It's no big deal. Piper does the hard work."

But it was a big deal and a testament to his character. "I know why you do it. You're secretly one of the Avengers. Finance Man."

He smiled. "It's interesting work, and don't tell your pal Garrett this, but I get as much satisfaction helping put those creeps behind bars as I do on the field."

"Fascinating."

Thad spent Sunday night at her new apartment. Since the final week of rehearsals took place in the evenings, she tried to sleep in on Monday morning, but she was up at seven after a fitful, nightmare-plagued night. In twelve hours, she would have to show up for *sitzprobe.* What was normally her favorite rehearsal was now a writhing snake pit.

When she emerged from the bedroom, she found Thad sitting with his laptop at her new kitchen counter, a mug of coffee in his hand—rumpled white T-shirt, sweatpants, bare feet. Her heart turned over in her chest. This was all she wanted. The two of them forever. She wanted to make his breakfast and have him make hers. She wanted to wash his socks and rub his shoulders when he got home from a long day. He would go into coaching. She'd sit on the sidelines and cheer on his team and maybe make lasagna for the squad. Did they even call it a squad?

She didn't know how to make lasagna, and she didn't want to learn, and he could wash his own socks. *La Belle Tornade* did not sacrifice her quest for immortality, not even for this man who was caressing her with his lazy smile and unending kindness.

She quickly turned away, a beautiful tornado whose heart was breaking with the knowledge that she couldn't have both—the immortality she craved and a personal happily-ever-after.

In the old days, everyone had dressed up for *sitzprobe*, the men in suits, the women in beautiful gowns and their best jewelry. But those days were gone. Now the singers showed up in everything from athleisure to biker jackets. In an effort to boost her self-confidence, Olivia chose slim black trousers, a silky black tunic top, and a cashmere scarf in case the rehearsal hall was cold. She added her Spanish earrings, Egyptian cuff, imitation ruby necklace, poison rings, and a coin Yo-Yo Ma had given her that she tucked in her shoe. She was only missing Rachel's silver star necklace, the one she'd lost in the Mojave Desert.

Thad drove her to rehearsal despite her protest that it could run late. He knew how nervous she was, and he let her brood in peace, without offering up one of his pep talks.

She'd had a new lock installed on her dressing room. As she opened it, she spotted something that had been slid under the door. She picked it up. An eight-by-ten copy of her engagement photo. There she was sitting at the keyboard of a grand piano with Adam standing close by, the two of them staring into each other's eyes. She looked like a woman deeply in love, but she was an actress, and even then, she'd known it was wrong. If only she'd had the courage to send the photographer away and call it off before the shutter had snapped.

No note was scrawled across the photo. Her head hadn't been cut out. Just the photo of the two of them, along with the memory of how Adam had loved her and how incomprehensible his suicide would have been on that day.

She curled the palm of her hand over her diaphragm, willing it to expand. *"You're going to be amazing,"* Thad had whispered that morning.

But she wasn't.

Everyone else in the company brought their best to *sitzprobe.* Sarah sang a "Ritorna vincitor" worthy of Leontyne Price. As the last notes faded away, the orchestra musicians tapped their bows on their music stands in the traditional sign of appreciation.

Pit . . . pit . . . pit . . . pit . . .

Arthur Baker might be an aging Radamès, but his "Celeste Aida" was thrilling.

Pit . . . pit . . . pit . . . pit . . .

After she sang, however, those same bows didn't tap for her. They had expected more from *La Belle Tornade.* Much more.

Lena, in the meantime, sat offstage taking it all in.

Afterward, Olivia saw the maestro huddled with Mitchell Brooks, the Muni's esteemed managing director. A sideways look from Mitchell told her exactly who they were talking about. They both looked so troubled she felt sorry for them. This was on her, not them, and she needed to do the right thing.

She forced herself to approach them. "I know I wasn't at my best." An understatement.

"The critics won't be kind, *mia cara,*" the maestro said bluntly. "It is no longer enough for Olivia Shore to be competent. You must be exquisite."

She knew that as well as he did. She turned to Mitchell Brooks. Ultimately it was up to him, the managing director, to make the final decision. “What do you want to do, Mitchell?”

He was a good man. He set his hand on her shoulder. “No, Olivia. What do *you* want to do?”

She wanted to push back time. To never have met Adam. To never have become so concerned about his needs that she forgot her own and let her voice be lost in a swamp of guilt. To never again forget that work formed the core of her life.

She must have looked as helpless as she felt because Mitchell spoke kindly. “You have two more rehearsals before we have to decide. We’ll reassess before final dress.”

She ticked off the days in her head. Today, Monday, a disastrous *sitzprobe.* Tuesday, piano tech, when she could mark. Wednesday, first dress rehearsal. Under different circumstances, she could have marked, but after what had just happened, she would have to perform at full voice, and if she didn’t deliver, Lena would take over, not just for final dress rehearsal, but for—

She couldn’t let herself think about opening night.

As she began packing up her things, Sarah approached, but at the last minute changed her mind and turned away.

Thad didn't ask any questions as he drove her home. One look at her face seemed to have told him everything he needed to know.

"Drop me off at the front," she said, as he drew close to the parking garage entrance. "Thanks for the transportation, but you don't need to drive me any longer. I've made arrangements with one of the crew. He's an old friend, and I'll be perfectly safe."

With an abrupt nod, he pulled up to the lobby door. She didn't lean over to kiss him as she got out of the car, and that felt as reprehensible as the way she'd sung tonight.

Thad was done with The Diva and her complications. She couldn't have dismissed him more clearly. He was a simple man. Maybe not simple-simple, but simple when it came to enjoying life and friends, sports, good jazz, good clothes, a great book, and great women. He enjoyed the hell out of great women. He enjoyed their smarts, their insights, their talent, and their ambition. He enjoyed their sense of humor, the way they could spar with him, make him laugh. And God knew, he liked looking at them. Then there was sex. Was anything better than sex with a woman who threw herself into every moment? A woman who could laugh and cry out, who could give as well as take. A woman who would sing "Habanera" naked just for him.

Yes, he cared about her. Cared a hell of a lot. She was his friend, his compadre, but she had a vision for her life that didn't include him and too many issues he couldn't help her solve. He was a fixer, a man who took care of problems. But he couldn't do that with her.

He thought about the ultimatums she kept dishing out. From the day he'd stepped on that plane five weeks ago, his life had entangled with hers. It was time to put a stop to it, no matter how much he hated to erase the plans he'd made for the two of them—sailing together on the lake this summer, going to the beach, catching a Cubs game, hiking. Despite all they'd shared, despite the new interests she'd brought into his life, despite the sex—the most amazing sex—and the music—the incredible music . . . Despite the way she looked at him, as if she could see into his soul . . . Despite her caring, not just for him, but for everyone. It was time to break up with her.

He thought about those interminable dinners. Unlike him, she'd been genuinely interested in hearing about the clients' lives, their kids' lives. He'd watched her take their cell phones and FaceTime an elderly parent who loved opera or a student someone knew who was in music school. Despite her drama and her critiques of his wardrobe, she had a moral compass set to true north.

He had to break up with her.

He wouldn't do it now. He'd wait until next week, after she got through opening night and the gala. As for the threats she continued to face . . . He'd hire Piper to watch out for his diva, to do what he no longer could.

The roller-coaster ride had reached its station. This time he was the one who'd set a deadline instead of her. Next week. Six days from now. Breaking up would tear him apart, but he'd move on. He always did.

He had to stop at her apartment the next morning to pick up his laptop. She answered the door. He'd seen her fresh-out-of-bed look—sexy, with tousled hair and a couple of pillow creases on her cheek. This wasn't it. She looked like hell: dark shadows cratered under her eyes, pasty skin, hair hanging loose on one side and clumping on the other. And she was dressed all wrong. A pink T-shirt, pink sweatpants. What the hell? She dressed in black and white. Sometimes classic gray. Maybe a touch of deep purple now and then. He was the one who wore pink.

Her face softened with tenderness, and then the shutters went down. "Come in," she said with a cool formality that made him wary.

Unlike the way the place had looked yesterday, it was now orderly—boxes unpacked, suitcases tucked away. She'd either put it to rights last night when she should have been sleeping or early this morning when she should have been sleeping. He didn't like it. Didn't like the neat apartment or the way she looked. "I need to get my laptop," he said. "What's wrong?"

"Bad night."

"I can see. Got any coffee?"

She tilted her head toward the kitchen, which was as tidy as the rest of the place. He grabbed a souvenir mug of the Sydney Opera House from the shelf, filled it, and took a sip while she stood in the doorway watching him.

The coffee was undrinkable. She'd forgotten something when she made it. Something important like coffee. He leaned his hips against the counter. "I take it *sitzprobe* didn't go well last night. Do you want to talk about it?"

"I can't see you anymore."

It took a moment for her words to register, and when they did, something ripped open inside him. He slammed his mug on the counter, its undrinkable contents splashing over the rim onto his hand. "And here we go again."

"It has to be over, Thad," she pleaded. "It's been wonderful. More than wonderful. But we're breaking up now."

He hardened his heart against the glint of tears in her eyes. "Uh-huh."

"I can't do this any longer. You're too big a threat to me."

That made him furious. "Threat?"

She waved her hand in a jerky, arbitrary motion. "I keep setting these deadlines and rolling right past them because I don't want it to be over."

"Yeah, you do have a thing for deadlines," he said, as coldly as he could.

She tugged on the bottom of her pink T-shirt. "This one has expired."

He'd had enough. "Great. I'll see you around." He stalked out of the kitchen and grabbed his laptop.

"The thing you have to know," she said to his back, "is that I've fallen in love with you."

That stopped him cold. As he turned, he saw a whole universe of emotions smeared all over her face. Helplessness, pain, resolution. "Jesus, Olivia, you're not in love with me. You're— We're . . ." He stammered for the right word. "We're teammates. We don't love each other. We have goals. Ambitions. We think the same. We're teammates, that's all."

She pressed her fingers to her throat as if she were choking. "It won't do, Thad. Some part of me wants to give up everything for you. To refocus my life. Put music in second place. Give up my *song*! I can't do that."

"Nobody's asking you to."

"But I can feel it. Wanting to be in your world—to cut out on a rehearsal early to give us more time together. To trim my schedule so I can watch you play ball. To stop getting on planes. To cook dinner for you!"

"Goddammit, you can't *cook*!"

A tear hung on her bottom lashes but refused to fall. "Don't you see? I want to prioritize you over my career, just like I did with Adam. It's a pattern. And that pattern is going to destroy who I am. What I live for!"

"You and your goddamn drama." The words came spewing out, propelled by fear, by pain. "You create drama. You live for it. And I've had enough of it."

He'd meant to hurt her, but what he'd just said wasn't true. She didn't love the drama that had been foisted on her any more than he did. He tried to think of a way to tell her that. To take it back. But she'd gone cold on him.

"Yes. Of course, you're right. And now you understand why this is for the best."

The words he didn't mean to say spewed out. "Damn straight it is. We're done."

He stalked to the door and left her alone, just as she wanted to be.

None of Thad's friends had ever seen him drunk, and as they looked at each other over their table at Spiral, Coop's old nightclub, they weren't exactly sure what to do about it. Thad wasn't either a mean drunk or a happy drunk. He was a dead-silent drunk. In the end, Clint volunteered to take him home. "But if he throws up in my car, I'm making him buy me a new one," he told Ritchie.

Clint knew Olivia was responsible for Thad's current state because when he'd asked where she was, Thad had snarled, "How the hell would I know?"

Clint drove Thad out to his own house in suburban Burr Ridge and dumped him on one of the brocade couches in the living room. When he was sure he wouldn't roll off, he headed for the kitchen to get a bag of chips. Right from the beginning, he'd liked Olivia, but now he wasn't sure. Thad was his teammate, and no matter how big a pain in the ass he was, Clint loved the guy, and he'd always have his back.

As he ripped open the chips, he considered the possibility of getting T-Bo to watch some game film once he sobered up in the morning. The odds weren't good, and he blamed Olivia for that, too.

Thanks to Thad, Olivia had bodyguards. It was so like him. She'd hurt his pride, but he'd still done what he saw as the right thing. He'd also told Piper he was picking up the tab, something Olivia immediately fixed. He might be a lot wealthier than her, but she'd still pay her own bills.

Either Piper or one of her female employees now drove Olivia to and from rehearsals, but even though someone had gotten in her dressing room, Olivia wouldn't let them come inside the theater. The walls were too thin for anyone to murder her in here. And if they tried? Right now she didn't much care.

She marked through piano rehearsal and sang for first dress rehearsal, giving it her best, which wasn't good enough. She was the star attraction for this production, and the Muni had a big financial stake in her appearance. She was the one responsible for this crisis, not the Muni, and if Mitchell wanted her to perform, she'd do it, regardless of the consequences.

But Mitchell didn't want her to perform, not on opening night. He broke the news as kindly as he could. "Olivia, every great singer has these spells where they aren't able to perform up to their own standards. I'm sure this is only temporary, but for now, it's best for the company and for you if Lena takes over for opening night."

Olivia was heartsick. *You win, Adam. You wanted me to fail, and now I have.*

But Adam wasn't at fault. She was the one who'd handed over her power.

Instead of being in the theater the night of final dress rehearsal, Olivia locked herself in her apartment and got drunk on Negronis. She'd perfected this combination of Campari, sweet vermouth, and gin during her twenties when she'd studied in Italy, but she'd never drunk so many at one time. She'd also never drunk them at midnight, with her tears turning into ugly sobs at the memory of that cold, hard look on Thad's face.

She was an emotional screwup incapable of having a healthy relationship. He'd accused her of loving drama, but he was wrong. She only loved drama on the stage. In real life, she hated it. She was bad at love. The worst. A bad person. A person who needed another drink. She mixed one, going extra heavy on the sweet vermouth. How many of these would it take before she passed out?

She didn't get an answer because the concierge called to tell her she had a visitor.

18

If Olivia hadn't been so drunk, she wouldn't have let anyone in, but apparently her alcohol-soaked brain decided she needed a drinking companion. Once she opened the door, however, and saw Sarah Mabunda on the other side, she changed her mind.

"What do you want?" Olivia had lost her good manners. Sarah, a woman she'd considered her friend, had frozen her out.

Sarah's long Aida wig was gone, but she still wore her stage makeup with darkened brows, matte brown lipstick, and exaggerated eye makeup. Neither she nor Sarah ever left the theater without taking off their makeup, yet now one of them had.

Sarah slipped her finger under the strap of her shoulder bag. "I'm sorry."

Olivia didn't need her pity. It wasn't Sarah's fault Olivia couldn't perform. "Thank you." She proceeded to close the door on her, but Sarah was strong, Olivia was drunk, and Sarah managed to push her way in.

"Lena was fine, but she isn't you," Sarah said.

"I don't care." Olivia looked for her drink, but saw only the pile of cocktail napkins the previous renter had left behind. "Amneris loved Aida." Her tongue wasn't working as it should. "They were friends. Both born princesses. Both in love with the same man. Friends."

"Except one was a captured slave." Sarah dropped her bag on an easy chair near the couch, disregarding the fact that she wasn't welcome.

Olivia needed to blow her nose from her crying jag, but she couldn't find a tissue. "Amneris didn't mean for Aida to die. They were like sisters." Her voice sounded woolly, and she felt like crying again. Where was her drink?

"Jealousy does strange things to a woman," Sarah said.

Olivia picked up a cocktail napkin that said *Save water. Drink gin*, and blew her nose on it. "Jealousy's never been my problem, so I wouldn't know."

"Lucky you." Sarah found Olivia's drink on the fireplace mantel, but instead of handing it over, she took a gulp.

"Alcohol isn't good for your voice." Something Sarah should know for herself.

"I'll risk it."

"It's your funeral." Olivia gave a choked laugh. "That's funny, right? Because of Aida getting entombed and all. Thanks to me."

"Hysterical," Sarah said dryly. She carried Olivia's drink to the windows and gazed out at the view across the street. "I loved him, you know. It happened so fast, but I loved him more than you did."

Olivia's fuzzy brain made it hard for her to sneer. "Nobody could love him the way I do."

Sarah turned. "Still?"

"I'll never stop."

"Then why did you leave him?"

"Because I had to." Olivia picked up another cocktail napkin—*It's five o'clock somewhere*—and blew her nose again. "I'm not like other women. I can't handle a career and a relationship. Look what's happened to me." She gave her nose another honk. "I let my voice get stolen."

Sarah's hair was matted from the wig cap, but she still looked beautiful and defiant, more like the powerful Amneris than like Aida. "If he loved you so much, he wouldn't have fallen for me so fast. We had something special right from the beginning."

"You're crazy." Olivia grabbed her Negroni from Sarah. The ice had long ago melted, but she didn't care. "You don't even know him."

"He asked me out on what was supposed to be your wedding day."

"Wedding day?" Olivia tried to focus because she was clearly missing something.

"You didn't know that, did you? Less than a week after you broke up with him, he asked me out, and by the end of our first date, we knew we had something special. He loved me more than he ever loved you."

Olivia scrambled to put the pieces together. "Are you talking about Adam?"

"Who else would I be talking about?"

"Thad! I love Thad!"

"That football player you've been seeing?"

"He's not just any football player! He's one of the greats. He's—" The Negroni sloshed onto the floor. "He's the greatest second-string quarterback of all time."

"You're drunk."

"Of course I'm drunk! I can't sing, and I've lost my way." She couldn't hold it in any longer. "Adam killed himself because of me!"

Instead of being shocked, Sarah scoffed at her. "Don't flatter yourself."

"What's that supposed to mean? He sent me an email!" she exclaimed. "A suicide email. Technology, right? I mean, what happened to the old-fashioned suicide note? Now everything is electronic."

Sarah cocked her head. "He emailed you, too?"

"'Too'? What do you mean, 'too'?"

"That bastard." Sarah didn't say it angrily. More like she wanted to cry. She sank into the couch. "Now there are three of us." She picked up a cocktail napkin.

"Three?"

"You, me, and Sophia Ricci."

"Sophia Ricci?" Olivia didn't understand. Ricci was the lyric soprano who'd stolen the role of Carmen from a mezzo. Rachel had told her about that when they'd had lunch in LA, and Sophia had dated Adam before Olivia. But an email . . . ?

Sarah blew her nose on a cocktail napkin with a gold embossed, *Drink up, bitches.* "Sophia and I met at the Royal Academy. We've been friends for years, but I hadn't heard from her in a while. A few days ago she called. She's been having panic attacks, and she thought I could help. I don't think she intended to tell me about the suicide email, but it came out."

"I don't understand."

Sarah hugged herself. "It seems he sent all three of us an email. Sophia's and mine were identical. 'You let me believe we were forever. You meant everything to me and I meant nothing to you.'"

Olivia's mushy brain finally absorbed what it was hearing, and she finished what had been in the note. "'Why should I keep on living?' Yes, that's what mine said, too."

Sarah slumped into the couch. "You lost your voice, Sophia's having panic attacks, my eczema's out of control—my legs, back, chest. And I can't stop eating. I've gained twenty pounds."

"You look good." A stupid comment, but that's how Olivia was feeling now. Stunned and stupid.

"I loved him with all my heart." Sarah swiped at her eyes with the napkin, smearing some of her makeup. Even in her drunken state, Olivia could see Sarah's pain, and it made her want to cry right along. "I fell hard and fast," Sarah said, "but I wasn't blind to his faults. He was a wonderful teacher, and he could have been a great coach, but he wanted to be Pavarotti, except he didn't have the voice." She wadded up the napkin, looking at it in her lap. "When he lost out on a part, he blamed the acoustics or his accompanist. The weather. Sometimes, he blamed me. Not directly. More like, if only I hadn't insisted on going to the Turkish restaurant, he would have sung better. Little things like that."

Olivia circled back to the beginning. "But those emails? To all three of us? The Adam I knew was spoiled, but he wasn't cruel."

"He lost out on one too many roles. He fell into a severe depression and refused to see a doctor. He kept saying there was nothing wrong with him."

"It was always other people." Olivia gazed at what was left of her drink. It reminded her of sewer water, and she couldn't imagine taking another sip. "You weren't at his funeral."

"I'd seen him the day he killed himself. We'd had an argument." She stared straight ahead, looking haunted. "He never told his sisters about me, and I couldn't face them. Cowardly, I know."

"But why have you been so cold to me? We were friends."

"Jealousy. That's why I came here, to tell you about Adam and apologize for the way I've been behaving." She tugged on her bottom lip with her teeth. "I always suspected he loved you more. Ironic, isn't it? Aida eaten up with jealousy toward Amneris. I wonder what Verdi would have made of that."

"Adam was no heroic Radamès." Olivia experienced a moment of drunken clarity. "He didn't love me more. He loved what he thought I could do for him."

They both took a moment to ponder that. Olivia rubbed the glass across her forehead. "Adam couldn't ever have been a great tenor, but he could have done other things: taught, been satisfied with smaller roles at smaller companies."

"Instead, he put a gun to his head and blamed us for making him do it." Sarah wiped her eyes. "It's such a waste."

Olivia set aside her glass. "So you and Sophia have been going through the same emotions I have. But neither of you lost your voice."

"It didn't affect my voice, but you've obviously never had eczema so bad you gouge bloody tracks in your skin."

"I'm so sorry." Olivia gazed down at her hands, sticky from her spilled drink. "Blaming other people . . . He wanted us to feel responsible for what he did."

"I'm done with it," Sarah said angrily. "I've had enough of scratching my skin till it bleeds. You and Sophia and I need to schedule a three-way conversation."

Sarah was right. "Let's make it a four-way and include a therapist," Olivia said.

"Good idea. And, Olivia, I really am sorry for the way I froze you out."

"I understand. Truly." She knew too well the damage guilt could cause.

Sarah had started crying again. Olivia moved over to the couch and put her arm around her. "You loved him, and you tried to help him." She rested her cheek against Sarah's head, not sure which one of them she was talking to. "No more guilt. You're going to forgive yourself, and I'm going to forgive myself, and so is Sophia." She thought about what they hadn't discussed. "Then we're going to talk about those threating notes . . ." She shuddered. "That bloody T-shirt."

Sarah lifted her tear-streaked face. "What do you mean? What threatening notes?"

Olivia awakened at noon the next day, her head throbbing. She downed two ibuprofens, swore never to drink again, and stumbled into the shower.

Sarah and Sophia had only gotten the suicide note, none of the other things. They hadn't received any newspaper clippings with their heads cut out or watched a T-shirt covered with fake blood tumble out of an envelope. Neither of them had been assaulted on the second floor of an antiquarian bookstore or kidnapped in the Mojave Desert. She yearned to call Thad. Knowing she couldn't do that was worse than the hangover.

She wrapped herself in her fuzziest bathrobe and staggered into the kitchen for coffee. Three days ago, when she'd broken up with Thad, she'd added twice as much water as she needed to the pot. Since then, she'd lost her apartment key and found it later in the piano bench. She'd added cumin instead of cinnamon to her oatmeal and nearly brushed her teeth with a tube of facial serum.

If only Thad were a man like Dennis, a man with a portable career and no ego. A man who'd never won a Heisman or completed seventy percent of his passes during one shining football season. Thad was her male doppelgänger. They'd taken different career paths, but they had the same internal makeup, the same passion for what they did, the same drive for excellence, and the same refusal to let anyone stand between them and glory.

Cradling a fresh mug of coffee, she called Piper and told her what had happened last night. Afterward, she wandered into the living room and gazed at her piano. What would it be like to sing without the heavy weight of guilt hanging over her? She plucked a few keys with her free hand. What would it be like to sing with nothing but a broken heart?

Thad had become familiar with the Internet's opera news sites, and the story was all over the place. Liv had been benched for opening night. He'd gotten her to sing, but he hadn't gotten her to sing well enough to perform, and he hated failure.

He talked to Piper daily. Sometimes more than once. Sometimes enough to make her tell him to get a life. But he couldn't stop thinking about Liv wandering down some dark alley or jumping into a strange limousine. Even secure apartment buildings weren't always secure. He called Piper again, and this time she had news. "It turns out Olivia's former fiancé liked to spread the guilt around."

"What do you mean?"

She told him about Sarah Mabunda's revelation. "I've done some digging since then," she said, "and it turns out Adam had a fourth target, a French horn player he dated between Sophia Ricci and Olivia."

"He sure didn't have any trouble attracting women."

"He was very good-looking, like a floppy-haired angel."

Thad suppressed the desire to ask which one of them was better looking—himself or Adam—which only went to show how far he'd sunk.

Saturday came, the day of the *Aida* premiere. To distract himself, he biked all eighteen miles of the lakefront trail. Olivia had said she loved him, and he knew her well enough to know she wouldn't toss around those words lightly. But what kind of person announced they loved somebody and broke up with them?

When he got home from his bike ride, he saw that his favorite opera blogger had put up a fresh post.

> Despite stories to the contrary, Olivia Shore will be taking the stage tonight for the Muni's premiere of *Aida*.

Olivia arrived at the Muni early. She'd somehow managed to convince Mitchell to change his mind about her appearance tonight by reminding him how angry the season ticket holders would be if she didn't sing. Eventually, he'd capitulated.

Last week, when she'd still had hope, she'd ordered beautifully boxed mini–opera cakes as opening night gifts for her fellow cast members. Now she traveled dutifully from one dressing room to the next with her gifts and "*Toi, toi, toi . . .*" for the others who'd arrived early.

Everyone treated her carefully, as if she had a terminal illness. Only Sarah gave her a long hug. "*Toi, toi, toi*, my friend. Let's make magic."

Magic was a long way off, but Olivia was done with the burden of responsibility she'd been carrying for too long. It was time to do what she loved, even if she did it badly. She'd honor Amneris, Verdi, and herself in the best way she could. If the critics massacred her, so be it. If she shredded her reputation, it was hers to shred. She'd let her fear of failure rule her for long enough. Tonight, she would be as fearless as Amneris vying for the love of Radamès.

Which ended very badly for everyone.

She shook off that unpleasant reminder.

Good-luck gifts from the others were waiting in her dressing room: a gag key chain from Arthur Baker; an alabaster statue of Isis from Sarah. Lena had left a fragrant package of Egyptian incense sticks and a note saying it was a pleasure watching her work. Jose Alvarez, who was singing the high priest, Ramfis, gifted her with chocolates, and the maestro sent flowers.

After makeup and costume, she closed the door of her dressing room for her solitary preperformance ritual: a few vocal warm-ups, a quick double-check of the notes she'd made, and a teaspoon of Nin Jiom cough syrup in warm water to keep her throat clear.

Yesterday's vocalizations had been promising, but her chest still felt tighter than it should. No more fear, she told herself. Public humiliation was better than private cowardice.

She wished Thad could see her now. In her formfitting amethyst-blue gown with its elaborately jeweled collar piece, she looked every inch a pharaoh's daughter.

Fortunately, the collar piece wasn't as heavy to wear as it looked from the audience. A wide white sash embroidered with gold papyrus hieroglyphs extended to the gown's hem. She had dark, winged eyebrows and a fierce lapis-blue cat's eye outlined in black extending to her temples. The long, intricately braided black wig bore a gold cobra on top, poised to strike. With gold sandals on her feet; big, lotus drop earrings; and her own gold cuff at her wrist, she was a portrait of fierce Egyptian royalty—a woman entitled to have everything she desired, except the man who'd claimed her heart.

Another gift had appeared on her dressing table while she was gone, a small box wrapped in white tissue paper. She glanced at the wall clock—twenty minutes to overture—slid her finger under the tape to pull off the paper, and opened the lid.

With a gasp, she dropped the box.

A dead yellow canary fell at her feet, its single black eye staring up at her.

She shuddered. Who would do something this depraved?

There was a scent. A strong scent she recognized. But not from the dead bird. No. She picked up the box that had contained its corpse. The cardboard held the smell of Egyptian incense.

Rage bubbled up inside her. There was only one explanation, the one she'd been refusing to accept. The wrapping paper was different, but the box held the identical scent as the incense Lena had given her.

She picked up the bird in her bare hands, too furious to grab a tissue, and marched through the hallways, the dead canary extended in front of her. She stormed past the extras on their way to be costumed for the Triumphal March, her gold sandals striking the tile floor, amethyst gown swirling around her calves. They took one look at her and backed away.

She stormed into the stairwell, lifting her gown with her free hand so she didn't trip on the hem. Up one flight, out into the hallway, and down the corridor to the room where the covers were required to stay during a performance so they'd be close at hand if they were needed. If, for example, a famous mezzo-soprano was so traumatized by a dead bird that she lost her ability to sing.

They were gathered in the lounge, a golf tournament muted on the television. The tenor covering for Arthur Baker played a game of solitaire. Sarah's cover was doing a crossword. Others were on their phones, while Lena sat at a table reading a book.

Their heads came up in unison as she stormed into the room—her gown rippling at her ankles, dead canary in her hands, gold cobra on her head. She marched across the floor and dumped the bird in Lena's lap.

Lena shrieked, leaped to her feet, and then fell to her knees in front of the bird. "Florence?"

The rawness of Lena's emotions—the way her expression shifted from horror to shock to grief—gradually penetrated Olivia's fury. She began to realize she might have made a mistake.

Three people she didn't recognize were in the room. Someone's wife or girlfriend, an older woman who might be one of the singers' mothers, and a person she did recognize. A man Lena had introduced as her husband, Christopher.

Instead of showing concern for his wife's distress, his eyes were on Olivia, as if he were assessing her—or wary of her. As if he'd been caught doing something he shouldn't have.

Lena's husband . . .

It all came crashing back to her. Rachel had worked with Lena in Minneapolis. She'd said the couples had hung out together. As much as Olivia adored Dennis, he was a gossip. How many conversations had she had with Rachel where she'd said, "Don't you dare tell Dennis"? Rachel generally kept her word, but occasionally she'd share a piece of news with him before

Olivia was ready to make it public. Olivia had talked to Dennis about it, and he'd apologized. "You're right. I'm sorry. Rachel told me not to say anything, and I didn't mean for it to slip out."

Olivia didn't know exactly how the pieces fit, but she was certain they did. Rachel knew Olivia was guilt-plagued about Adam's suicide, and she'd suspected Olivia's vocal issues were worse than Olivia was letting on. Rachel had put two and two together and mulled it over with Dennis. If Dennis knew, he could very well have told Lena's husband sometime when the couples were together.

Lena hadn't been her saboteur. It was Christopher, Lena's husband, a man who had a sizable stake in his wife's career. A man who wanted his wife onstage instead of Olivia.

Lena lifted her tear-streaked face to her husband. "What happened to Florence?"

"That's not Florence!" he exclaimed.

"It is Florence! Look at the white on her tail feathers, the little dash by her eye."

Christopher addressed the rest of the room with a fake, dismissive laugh. "Florence is Lena's pet canary. The bird stopped eating, and Lena's been worried, but . . ." He returned his attention to his wife. "Florence was alive when I left home. I swear."

His swearing lacked conviction. Lena, looking lost and confused, her dead pet cradled in her hand, gazed up at Olivia. "I don't understand."

From the speaker, the opening notes of the overture began to play. "You and your husband need to have a long talk," Olivia said. "And if I were you, I'd hire a lawyer."

She hurried back to her dressing room. When she got there, she made a quick call to Piper outlining what had happened and then muted her phone.

The stage manager's voice came from the speaker. "Mr. Baker, Mr. Alvarez, please report to the stage." Her call would be next.

She locked the door and turned off her dressing room lights. She had so many questions, but for now she had to set them all aside. Lena's husband's sabotage had stolen enough from her. She wouldn't let it steal any more.

Be fearless. She drew herself to her full height and breathed into the darkness. Long inhales. Slow exhales. Even, deliberate breaths. Trying to trust herself once again.

Inhale . . . Exhale . . .

"Ms. Shore, please report to the stage."

19

Olivia made her entrance to thunderous applause. Thad had a hard time catching his breath. She wasn't alone onstage, but she might as well have been. How could the audience look at anyone else? In her purplish gown with that cobra on her head, she was six feet tall.

He'd read the libretto, and he knew what she'd be singing first. "Quale insolita gioia nel tuo sguardo," "What rare joy shines on your face?"

She'd joked with him about it. *"Not your face,"* she'd teased him. *"Radamès's face."*

Now here she was, throwing herself at the old dude playing Radamès who wasn't going to love her back in a million years. Stupid fool.

He'd sneaked in at the last minute, and so far, he'd attracted only the minimum of attention. He didn't want her to know he was here, but he couldn't imagine staying away, even though he was still mad as hell at her. But not mad enough to want her to fail.

Aida appeared, dressed in white. Sarah Mabunda had a curvier figure and lacked Olivia's height, but she had a luminescence that lit up her face and made her a worthy adversary. Too bad she had to die at the end.

His attention returned to Olivia. As magnificent as she was, he couldn't help wishing she was singing Carmen so he could see her in that red dress.

No. He didn't need to see her in that dress. Better she was covered up.

The scene came to an end, and the audience applauded. She'd sounded incredible to his ears, but nobody was calling out "bravo," and the applause seemed more polite than as if the audience had been swept away.

His phone vibrated in his pocket. He ignored it and kept his attention on the stage.

Curtain call . . . Olivia had survived opening night.

She and Sarah had begun to connect in the first act, and that connection had continued through the bedchamber scene in act 2. As for the all-important final

Judgment scene . . . Olivia's pitch had sagged here and there, and she'd smudged some of her runs, but she'd been good. Acceptable. The audience might not be getting everything they expected from *La Belle Tornade*, but it wasn't the disaster she'd feared. She hadn't sung brilliantly, but she'd sung competently. That's what the critics would say. A competent, if rather lackluster, performance. Competent was fine.

No, it wasn't fine. She wanted greatness, not competence. Something Thad would understand.

Backstage, she greeted her well-wishers, many of them wealthy donors to the Muni. It was easy to separate those who truly knew opera from the others. The pretenders told her she had been magnificent. The true fans merely commented on how glad they were that she'd returned to the Muni.

Kathryn Swift was of the former group. "Olivia, darling, you were superb. Spectacular! I so wish Eugene could have heard you tonight."

Olivia was glad he hadn't, because he would have known right away that she hadn't been spectacular at all.

The person she wanted most to see—the person who would understand how she was feeling more than anyone else—was missing. And why should he be here after she'd thrown him out of her life?

Her guests finally left. The dresser took away her costume and wig. Wrapped in a white robe, Olivia sat in front of the mirror removing her makeup. She was drained. Empty. As she wiped away Amneris's winged eyebrows and elongated lapis eyeliner, she tried to make herself feel better with the reminder that she'd at least had the courage to go onstage tonight. That was something.

But it wasn't enough.

She took off her wig cap and ran her fingers through her hair. She understood Christopher Marsden's twisted motivation for doing what he'd done, but how had he orchestrated it? And what about the bookstore and kidnapping?

A knock sounded at her door. She had this absurd leap of hope that it might be Thad. "Come in."

It was Lena Hodiak. Her tangled blond hair; round, blotchy face; and red eyes told their own story. She dashed across the room and fell to her knees in front of Olivia. "I didn't know what he was doing! You must believe me!"

Olivia imagined how Thad would view this grand, operatic gesture, and she could almost hear him muttering "sopranos" under his breath. "Please get up, Lena."

Lena gripped Olivia's white robe tighter, staying on her knees. "I didn't know. Please believe me. I would never have let him do something like this."

As exhausted as she was, Olivia couldn't dismiss Lena's anguish. "Sit down," she said gently.

Lena stayed where she was. Weepy and beseeching, she gazed up at Olivia. "You're everything I aspire to be. I'd never do anything to hurt you. Please tell me you don't think I did this."

Lena's incredulity as she'd gazed at her husband was all the proof Olivia had needed that Lena wasn't the one who'd tried to sabotage her. She drew Lena to her feet and directed her to the room's single easy chair. "I know you didn't. And I'm sorry about your bird."

Lena dropped her head in her hands and started crying all over again. "Florence was special. She'd trill for me when I left the room. I could cuddle her in my hand, and if she didn't think I was giving her enough attention, she'd sulk." Lena dragged her sleeve across her nose. "She stopped eating a few weeks ago, and she was sleeping all the time, so I knew she was sick, but . . ." She gulped for air. "I think he killed her."

Olivia winced.

The words came pouring out. "After you left, he pulled me into the hall and tried to convince me nothing you said was true. I said I knew he was lying. That made him furious and he told me all of it. Everything he'd done to you. He threw it at me. Like it should make me happy. He said since I wasn't looking out for my own career, he had to."

Olivia sat at her dressing table and rubbed her eyes. "He wanted to get rid of me so you could have your big moment."

"Covering for you *was* my big moment, but he couldn't see that. He kept talking about how this was my chance and that I should see what he'd done to you as a sign of how much he loved me."

"Twisted."

"I should have figured it out. He's been so secretive. I told him I hated him. That I was divorcing him and never wanted to see him again." She bit her bottom lip. "I thought he was going to hit me, but Jeremy came out to check on me and kicked him out of the building."

Jeremy was the big, barrel-chested bass covering for Ramfis.

"You're not safe with your husband," Olivia said.

"I know." Lena plucked at the chair arm. "When I met him, he was so charming. He was interested in everything I did. I'd never had anyone care about me that way." Lena looked up. "A few months after we got married, things started to change. He wanted to know where I was every minute. Nothing I did was good enough. I wasn't working hard enough. I gained a few pounds, and he told me I was fat. He started monitoring everything I ate. He made me feel stupid. He said he had to be tough with me because he loved me so much, and he only wanted the best for me. He said I should feel lucky to be married to a man who cared so much. But I knew it was wrong. As soon as the *Aida* run was over, I was going to tell him I wanted a divorce."

"Where is he now?"

"I don't know."

"You can't go back to your apartment."

"I called a friend. I'm going to stay with her."

"Promise me you'll let me know if I can help."

"How can you say that after what happened?"

Olivia smiled at her. "We sopranos have to stick together, right?"

That made Lena start crying all over again.

Thad banged on the door of Lena Hodiak's apartment, then moved to the side so only Piper could be seen through the peephole.

The door swung open. Thad shouldered Piper away—exactly what she'd warned him not to do—and stepped into the door frame. "Christopher Marsden?"

Marsden wiped the early-morning sleep from his eyes. "Who are you? Wait— Aren't you—"

"Yeah. Thad Owens. A good friend of Olivia Shore."

Christopher tried to slam the door, but Thad wasn't having it. He shoved his way in before Piper could stop him and delivered a perfectly targeted undercut to Marsden's jaw followed up with a punch to the gut that sent the vermin sprawling to the floor.

"Okay, that wasn't helpful," Piper said. "But completely understandable." She shut the door, closing them inside the apartment.

Thad wanted to finish the job, but Piper pushed him away and advanced on Marsden. "I have a few questions for you, Mr. Marsden. And I think it's only fair to inform you that my friend here has a hot temper and short patience when it comes to liars, so I suggest you stick to the truth."

Marsden whimpered. His lip was bleeding, and he looked like he might throw up. Thad had a strong stomach, and he wouldn't mind seeing that.

Piper put one of her small feet, clad in a black leather motorcycle boot, on Marsden's chest. "I think we should start at the beginning, don't you?"

It all came out. Marsden had formed a friendship with Dennis Cullen, Rachel's husband, when their wives were appearing together in Minneapolis. From

Dennis, Marsden had learned that Olivia wasn't handling her ex-fiancé's suicide well. Dennis, who needed to learn how to keep his fucking mouth shut, had repeated Rachel's speculation that Olivia was traumatized with guilt after her ex-fiancé's suicide, and that her vocal problems were worse than she was letting on. That was all Marsden needed to hear, and it didn't take him long to come up with a plan to prey on Olivia's guilt. The possibility of his wife being able to step into Olivia's shoes and have her shot at the big time had been his catnip. He saw playing mind games with Olivia as low risk, with a potentially huge payoff for his wife's career.

"Lena can't do anything for herself!" Marsden whined, clutching his stomach. "She was happy being second rate. I have to do everything."

"Uh-huh." Piper toed him with her motorcycle boot, not enough to hurt him, but enough to establish female solidarity with his wife. "Let's begin with those notes you sent."

Marsden started singing like his wife's canary once had. He'd come up with an idea as an experiment—seeing if he could get into Olivia's head by sending her the anonymous letters. After a couple of chats with Big Mouth Dennis, he'd learned Olivia seemed to be getting worse, and that motivated him to step up his efforts with the photographs, bloody T-shirt, and the phone call Olivia had gotten when they were hiking. He was behind it all, right up to the moment when Piper mentioned the hotel room break-in and the New Orleans incident.

The guy practically peed his pants. "I've never been to New Orleans. I swear. And I didn't break into any hotel room!" He curled into a ball, afraid Thad would go after him again.

Thad and Piper exchanged a look. Marsden was a coward and a bully—not the kind of guy with the guts to pull off a direct attack or a desert kidnapping. Olivia was still at risk.

Olivia slept in late the next day. Tonight was the *Aida* gala, her final obligation to Marchand and the last place she wanted to be after her lackluster performance. Holding her head high and pretending not to overhear any of the whispered conversations about her singing last night would be exhausting. Except . . . she'd be able to see Thad again.

She'd kill him if he brought a date.

He'd bring a date. She knew it. He wasn't a man who'd ignore any kind of rejection without fighting back.

She needed a date, too. She mentally sorted through possible candidates but couldn't bear the idea of spending the evening with anyone who was part of the opera world. She could ask Clint, but if she brought him, Thad would think she was trying to rub his face in their breakup when all she wanted was to throw her arms around him and tell him once more she was sorry. He deserved his retribution. She'd choke down her resentment, go alone, and make herself be extra nice to the woman he'd almost certainly bring with him. Even though it would devastate her.

She tried to focus on the positive. It would be good to see Henri again. Paisley had somehow landed her dream job as a personal assistant to one of the Real Housewives, so she wouldn't be there, but Mariel would. Mariel's blind ambition to best Henri had grated on Olivia from the beginning. The advertising campaign had been expensive, and if it wasn't paying off, she'd be gloating over Henri's remains.

Olivia had to talk to Dennis. He needed to know what his loose lips had cost her. She intended to keep this between the two of them because Rachel would be crushed if she found out the part her husband had played in what had happened.

She texted him.

Call me.

Less than a minute later, her phone rang. It was Rachel. “Now you’re sending secret messages to my husband?”

Olivia thought quickly. “Somebody with a birthday coming up shouldn’t be asking questions.”

“My birthday isn’t for two months.”

“So?”

Rachel laughed. “All right. Here he is.”

He answered quickly. “Hey, pal. What’s up?”

She couldn’t do this with Rachel standing next to him. “Call me when big ears isn’t around. We need to talk.”

Dennis turned his head away from the phone. “She needs to talk to me in private. We have a thing going on.”

Olivia heard Rachel laugh. “If you’re planning a surprise party, I’ll kill you both.”

“Hold on. I’m going into another room.” A few moments later, he’d returned to their conversation. “What’s up? Rachel’s birthday isn’t for two months.”

“This isn’t about her birthday.” She steeled herself. “I’m afraid you and I have a problem . . .”

She laid it out. Everything that had happened and Dennis’s part in it. As the story unfolded, he began stammering apologies. "God, Olivia . . . God, I'm sorry . . . I hate myself . . . Rachel keeps telling me I have a big mouth . . . Jesus, Olivia . . . I never meant . . . Shit . . . I'm sorry . . ."

"No more apologies." Olivia had heard enough. "You're a gossip, and your blabbering has threatened my relationship with Rachel. I know wives confide in their husbands, but they expect their husbands to keep their mouths shut. How can I ever again talk openly with her if I know she'll tell you, and you'll broadcast it to the world?"

"You're right. I've learned my lesson. God, have I ever. Don't tell Rachel about this. Please. She already has enough issues with the way I butt into her life."

That was news to Olivia. "Dennis, I swear, if you ever again pass on anything that I've told Rachel, I'll tell her every detail about what happened with Christopher Marsden." She hung up on him before he could issue any more apologies.

Afterward, she moved over to the piano and began her vocalization. Only a few more hours before the gala when she'd see Thad again.

The Muni's Grand Foyer had been transformed into a facsimile of ancient Egypt. Guests entered through a reproduction of the Temple of Dendur as projections of ancient temple columns and statues of Ramses II, interspersed with the Marchand logo, played on the walls. An array of artificial palm trees decked out with fronds made of twinkle lights added to the glamorous setting.

Her late entrance caused a stir. Heads swiveled, and a brief lull fell over the crowd. The *Chicago Tribune*'s review of last night's performance hadn't yet appeared in the paper, but the online reviews were posted on all the big opera sites, and nearly every one of them used the word "disappointing." She forced her head higher, even as she wished she were anywhere but here.

Kathryn Swift, the chair of the gala committee, rushed over all in a flutter. "Olivia! My dear, you look incredible!"

Olivia wore her own floor-length gown for the evening—slender, white, and sleeveless, with a narrow gold belt. She'd left her hair long and borrowed an Egyptian-style circlet from the costume department to wear across her forehead. Her fan-shaped gold earrings, like the wings of Isis, were studded with coral and turquoise.

The majority of the men wore tuxedos, with only a handful disregarding the suggested male dress code. One had confused a Greek toga with an Egyptian robe. A few had adopted the more modern djellaba. Fortunately, no one had shown up in a loincloth. Almost all of the women were in some form of costume, many dressed in embellished robes, some with collar pieces. A number of women had donned long, black wigs. Kathryn Swift had chosen a gown with accordion-pleated wing-shaped sleeves in a silver fabric that set off her gray society matron bob. She snatched up Olivia's hands and examined her rings. "Is that a poison ring? Eugene gave me one from the Victorian period, but I can't remember what I've done with it."

"It's a poison ring, but not an antique." Olivia had paid thirty dollars for it on Etsy, one of her favorite sources for costume jewelry. Of the five rings she was wearing, only the cushion-cut sapphire she'd bought as a gift to herself after winning the Belvedere Singing Competition had any value.

She couldn't win the Belvedere Competition now. She would barely make it through the qualification round.

Most of the guests had taken their places at the tables, which were draped in white linen with the Marchand logo embossed in gold. Over Kathryn's shoulder, Olivia spotted a place waiting for her at the center table, where Henri sat with a good-looking younger man she assumed was his husband, Jules. Mitchell Brooks, the Muni's manager, and his wife were also at the table, along with the chairman of the Muni's board of directors and a man she recognized from photos as Lucien Marchand. Then there was Thad.

A man appeared at Kathryn's side. He was around forty, stocky, with a ruddy complexion and an Ivy League haircut. Olivia recognized him from a family photo Eugene had shown her as his stepson. "Excuse me for interrupting, but Wallis and her husband want to talk to you about the hospital ball," he said.

Kathryn brushed him off impatiently. "I'll get to them. My son Norman Gillis," she said, as he retreated. "He's more interested in basketball than opera."

Kathryn squeezed Olivia's hand. "I suppose I do need to go. Have a wonderful time tonight, my dear."

"I'm sure I will," Olivia said, even more sure she wouldn't. Excusing herself, she approached the table. Time to get this over with.

Centerpieces of flowers and pomegranates, along with pyramid-shaped place cards, brightened each table. Paper masks hung from the gilt chair backs—Tutankhamen for the men and Nefertiti for the women. Some of the guests had put them on for photos. A few others wore them on top of their heads.

Henri greeted her with an embrace and introduced her to Jules, then to Lucien Marchand. "And this is my uncle."

Olivia inclined her head. *"Enchanté, monsieur."*

The president and CEO of Marchand Timepieces had a stately beaked nose, a carefully groomed mane of silver hair, and an elegant manner. "Madame Shore. I'm delighted to finally meet you."

Mitchell rose to greet her. She suspected he'd rather be sitting at the adjoining table with Sergio, Sarah Mabunda, and Mariel Marchand, instead of near his disappointing diva.

She couldn't postpone the inevitable any longer, and she nodded at Thad's date for the evening. "Lieutenant Cooke."

"Please. Call me Brittany."

Liv and Brittany were hitting it off as if they'd been girlfriends forever, something he didn't appreciate. He hadn't exactly invited Brittany to make Liv jealous, but he'd at least hoped seeing him with another woman would give her a taste of what she'd thrown away. Namely, him.

Plus, he wanted to make her jealous.

But *La Belle Tornade* was above such petty human emotions.

Olivia wasn't as elaborately dressed as some of the other women, but she outshone them all like the empress she was. She had to know by now what the opera cognoscenti were saying about last night's performance, but you couldn't tell by looking at her. She was every inch a queen, graciously allowing the ordinary people around her to breathe her rarified air. She couldn't have been more different from the soft, giving, everyday woman he'd once held in his arms.

At the next table, Mariel Marchand looked as if she'd swallowed a bowl of bad mushrooms. Mitchell Brooks took him over to make introductions. Thad seemed to be developing a fondness for sopranos, because he immediately liked Sarah Mabunda.

He returned to his own table as the speeches began. There were lots of thank-yous, a speech about the afterschool music program that was receiving the proceeds from the evening, and still more thank-yous. Mitchell Brooks introduced Lucien Marchand as the evening's sponsor, even though Henri should be taking credit. But Uncle Lucien, with his French accent and diplomat's mien, did cut an impressive figure. He called up Thad and Olivia to draw the winning tickets for tonight's grand prizes: a Victory780 and a Cavatina3. Thad was glad he didn't have to give a speech because he wasn't up to it.

On their way back to the table, he took Liv's arm. The gesture was automatic, and for just a moment, he could have sworn she leaned against him.

The moment passed. She drew away. "Rupert! How lovely to see you."

Rupert?

She introduced him to a small man sitting at a table off to the side. "Rupert, this is Thad Owens. Thad, Rupert Glass." She shot Thad a telling look he immediately understood. Rupert resembled one of the Seven Dwarfs, the one who wouldn't look at anybody. Bashful? The top of his head came just to Olivia's shoulder. He had a tuft of hair at the crown, a couple more tufts near his ears, and he looked about as dangerous as a plastic spoon.

"My dear," he whispered, turning several different shades of red. "My deepest apologies if I did anything to distress you with my meager gifts."

"You could never distress me, Rupert." Olivia patted his hand. "But there are so many young singers who would bloom under the kind of support you've given me."

Thad couldn't help himself. "Plus the IRS won't bother them like they do her."

Olivia quickly excused them both. "You didn't have to say that," she hissed, as she hustled him away.

"It's those quiet ones who turn out to be serial killers."

Just for a moment they exchanged one of their quick smiles, but then he remembered he was furious with her and wiped his away.

"I'm sorry," she whispered. "I wouldn't hurt you for the world."

"You didn't," he snapped back.

She squeezed his arm. That was it. Just squeezed it.

Back at the table, she chatted with Brittany in English and with Lucien *en français.* The Muni's conductor came over to the table, and they spoke in Italian. Then—son of a bitch—didn't she switch to German when an old dude with a silver-topped walking cane appeared.

Damn, but he missed her. He'd never been so in sync with another person. None of his ex-girlfriends. No buddy or teammate. No one.

He told himself to snap out of it. She said she was in love with him, but it wasn't like he'd marry her. That would be a nightmare and a half—living his life as Mr. Olivia Shore. All he wanted was for them to be together for a while. Simple. Uncomplicated. Why couldn't she see that?

He barely tasted his food, a filet topped with some kind of shrimp thing. As Liv and Brittany chatted away, he mainly talked to Henri's husband, Jules, an interesting guy who was a big soccer fan. Still, he wanted Liv's attention for himself.

Between dinner and dessert, the room darkened to show a video of the student music program. Olivia whispered something to Brittany about the ladies' room and excused herself.

He didn't realize he was staring after her until he caught Brittany's sympathetic smile. "You shouldn't have let that one get away," she whispered.

He wouldn't tell her it was the other way around.

Olivia hadn't intended to duck out on the after-school music program video, but her drunken binge two nights ago had temporarily soured her on alcohol, and she'd drunk one too many glasses of water. She entered the ladies' room to find Mariel Marchand washing her hands at the sink. Mariel gave her a cool nod in the mirror. "You look lovely tonight, Olivia."

Mariel didn't. Although she wore her black gown and glittering jewelry with all the elegance of a true Frenchwoman, her skin looked sallow, and she seemed tired.

"Thank you. And your gown is beautiful," Olivia replied honestly.

"Chanel." The word was sad, almost bitter, as if she were reciting her state of mind instead of the luxury designer's name. "I suppose you've heard by now that Henri's campaign was a rousing success. Hideously expensive, of course, but sales of Marchand products doubled. A triumph for him."

"I hadn't heard."

"Henri did not say anything to you?" She snatched up a towel. "He has always been so much a better person than I am."

Olivia refrained from agreeing.

"Lucien raised us both on the Marchand tradition, but it seems Henri was smarter than me."

Olivia sidestepped. "I'm happy the campaign is doing so well, but I know this must be a challenging time for you."

"I am an ambitious woman, something you understand." She dried her hands on the towel as if she were scrubbing them. "The press release goes out tomorrow. Lucien Marchand is retiring in September, and Henri is taking over as president and CEO while I continue my role as chief financial officer."

"I see."

"My career is everything to me. You understand. You're just like me. Our careers are our lives. Women with *husbands* and *children*"—she spoke the words as if they were frivolities—"allow themselves to be distracted from their goals, but not us. We do not lose sight of what we want."

Olivia didn't like being put in the same category as Mariel. "You're a bright woman, Mariel. I'm sure you'll adapt."

"I don't want to adapt!" She balled her towel and threw it in the trash. "I want to lead!" The door closed behind her.

Successful people had to be able to adapt, Olivia thought. Throughout her career, she'd learned to be flexible—to new directors, different staging, a variety of teachers. She was good at adapting, something she hadn't thought much about until this very moment.

She finished in the restroom and stepped into the empty hallway. Music from the video played in the background, and the lights seemed dimmer than when she'd entered.

As she turned into the corridor leading back to the Grand Foyer, she wished she didn't have to return to the table. If only she could go home now. If only—

Something seized her from behind. Before she could scream, a rough hand clamped over her mouth.

20

It happened so quickly. An arm dragged her from behind around one corner and another into a deserted corridor that led to the building's maintenance area and from there into a storage closet. He was big and strong, and his hand across her mouth muffled her screams. The closet door slammed shut, closing them both inside with the scent of chemical fumes and rubber.

Her gown hobbled her legs as she attempted to kick out. He pinned her face-forward to the wall with his body, her neck pulled back at an awkward angle as he kept his hand clasped over her mouth.

His knee jabbed into her back to hold her in place, turned away from him. The sound of his breathing rasped in her ears. He grabbed for her fingers. Pulled at her rings. She struggled to breathe as she heard them hit the floor. The poison ring fit more tightly and wouldn't come off. He moved to her Egyptian cuff, scraping her wrist as he yanked it free. He reached for a necklace, but she wasn't wearing one.

Her pierced earrings would be next. Knowing that he would rip them through her earlobes sent a fresh flood of adrenaline surging through her. She stabbed him as hard as she could with the point of her elbow. With a grunt, he edged back just enough so she could twist around.

She stared into the face of Tutankhamen.

He was hiding behind a mask. The cowardice of his anonymity, the threat to her earlobes . . . It was all too much. With her free arm, she clawed at his face. Her dress ripped as she kicked him. She fought—fingernails, arms, legs, and feet. Her shoulder hit something sharp, and light flooded the closet.

She'd triggered the overhead light switch. She tore at his paper mask.

The elastic band snapped.

Kathryn's son Norman stared back at her.

"That was a mistake." He slammed her against the wall again. Something hard pressed into her ribs. It could have been a finger, but she knew it wasn't. He had a gun. He twisted her arm behind her back. Her shoulder screamed with pain, and her cheek smashed into the closet's cement-block surface. Out of the corner of her eye, next to her face, she saw the gun—black with a short barrel. Ugly. Awful.

"You scream and I shoot." His voice was a hiss, his breath hot in her ear. "Now I've got nothing to lose."

Because she'd seen his face.

His forearm snaked across her neck and pressed against her windpipe. She clawed at his arm, trying to free herself. He dug the gun into her temple and maneuvered her out of the closet into the dark hallway. She heard faint music from the video that was still playing in the Grand Foyer. Only a few minutes had elapsed since he'd attacked her. A lifetime.

His arm pressed harder against her throat. She made herself deadweight as he dragged her toward the service door at the end of the corridor. If he was going to kill her, she'd make him work for it.

He kicked her hard in the side of her leg. "Walk!"

Thad was going to be furious about this. That random thought kicked through her brain as she struggled to breathe.

They'd reached the door. He hit the bar with his hip. As he dragged her outside, she tried to gulp in the fresh, rain-drenched air.

Through the downpour, she saw that he'd dragged her to the Muni's loading dock area on the far side of the building, away from the front windows where the guests were gathered. Away from everything except Dumpsters, cargo vans, and the dark coil of the Chicago River.

"A lot of thugs around here." He dug the gun into her temple, his arm still pressing against her windpipe. "You came out for air. Too bad you got robbed and shot."

He was going to kill her. No one would stop him. She dropped her head and bit him hard in the arm. He jerked and eased his grip just enough for her to twist free.

She began to run.

Something whizzed past her head. A bullet. The river was just ahead.

He fired again. And again.

She was in the water.

Olivia had been gone too long. As the video played, he pushed back in his chair and wended his way through the tables out into the hallway. No sign of anyone. He headed for the ladies' room and barged in without knocking. Empty. He checked his watch. It read 9:48 p.m. He hurried down a second hallway. Around a corner.

Her purse lay abandoned ahead of him on the tile floor. His heart kicked into overdrive. There was a service door at the end of the hall. He ran toward it on an adrenaline rush.

He burst outside into a rain-pounded scene from a horror movie. A big man with a gun. The crack of three bullets firing. And Olivia.

Going into the river.

The goon heard the door slam and spun around, gun pointed.

Quarterbacks didn't usually tackle, but Thad sure as hell knew how. As the goon raised his arm to fire, Thad went low, powering with his legs, targeting the bastard's chest with a drive from his shoulder.

The goon was big, heavy, and solid. Thad took him down.

The gun flew. *Loose ball!* A scramble for possession. Even quarterbacks could end up in the scrum, and Thad had been here many times. Grab the ball at any cost. Go for the eyes, the nuts. Gouge. Choke. No gentleman's code in the pileup, only raw, bleeding violence. Survival of the fittest.

The goon hadn't been schooled in the NFL's killing fields and Thad came up with the gun.

The bastard lay curled on the ground, the wind knocked out of him, but Thad couldn't trust him to stay that way. Olivia was in the river. Drowning? Shot? Fair play wasn't an option, not with her life in jeopardy. Was she still alive? Thad reared back, aimed for the bastard's kneecap, and fired.

The goon cried out in agony. Thad raced for the river. Stripping off his jacket as he ran, he launched the gun into the water, kicked off his shoes, and dove.

The shock of the water—still frigid in early May—hit him like a tsunami. He opened his eyes underwater but couldn't even see his hand in front of him, let alone the glimmer of a white gown. He surfaced, grabbed air, and went under again, fighting the icy temperature and the awful knowledge that she could be dead.

Again and again, he dove and came up, the water shooting needles into him.

The luminous dial of his Victory780 showed 9:52 p.m. Four minutes had elapsed since he'd left the Grand Foyer. At least three minutes had passed since he'd seen her go in. She'd been underwater too long to survive.

Desperate, he swam farther out and went under again. Came up.

Four minutes.

Five.

One of those bullets had hit its target. She was gone. He'd lost her.

He threw his head back and howled at the sky.

The water erupted.

Olivia shot to the top, sucking precious oxygen into her starved lungs. Where had that primitive, animal howl come from? Was Norman Gillis still there?

Numb with cold, she looked toward the riverbank but could see nothing through the heavy rain. Her hands and feet had lost all feeling, and her teeth were chattering. That howl . . . It had echoed underwater like the devil's own cry. She glanced frantically around for the source.

A man was in the water, maybe fifteen feet away. Not Norman Gillis. She cried out, *"Thad!"*

He twisted frantically in the water. *"Olivia?"*

His wet white shirt made a dim beacon in the rainy darkness. She tried to swim toward him, but her limbs were so clumsy from creeping hypothermia she could barely move.

He reached her side and crushed her to him. Strands of dark hair plastered his forehead as he took her head in his hands, his breath ragged. "I thought you were dead. I thought . . ."

Her teeth were chattering so hard she couldn't speak. Couldn't do anything but cling to him. Love him.

"Liv . . . My Liv . . ." He had her in his arms, keeping their heads above water. "Where were you? I couldn't find you. I thought . . ."

Her mouth wouldn't form the words to tell him she'd been underwater the whole time, afraid if she resurfaced, she'd be shot. She had no breath left to explain the enormous lung capacity of an opera singer or tell him about the contests she and Rachel used to have to see who could stay underwater the longest. The last time, Rachel had won, but only by a few seconds.

"Liv . . ." He kept saying her name as if couldn't get enough of it. Even in the darkness, she could see his expression. Stark. Stricken. "Hold on to me." Looping his arm around her, he swam toward the riverbank, providing the power the cold had stolen from her.

They reached the cement wall that edged the riverbank, a place where, in warmer weather, people sat to enjoy the sun. The numbness had spread, disconnecting her from her body. With the arm strength that had served him so well over his career, he hoisted her onto the walkway and pulled himself up next to her.

They collapsed together, him holding her shivering body. She'd never been so cold.

"Don't ever . . . do that again," he said nonsensically.

She clung to him. The diadem she'd worn around her forehead was gone, along with her shoes. She heard someone groaning. Not Thad.

He came to his knees. Willing her arms to work, she pushed herself up far enough to see the hulking shadow of Norman Gillis curled on the grass beyond the walkway. He lay there moaning, as if he were coming out of unconsciousness. He wasn't alone.

"You incompetent fool!" Kathryn Swift bent over the body of her son, grabbing at his clothes. "You're just like your father. You can't do anything right."

Somehow Olivia made it to her knees, but Thad was already on his feet, his wet tuxedo shirt and dark trousers clinging to his body. "Step away from him, Mrs. Swift," Thad said, in a voice accustomed to commanding obedience.

Kathryn ignored him and continued searching through her son's clothes.

"I said get back!" Thad barked out the order.

Kathryn straightened. In one hand, she held Olivia's Egyptian cuff. In the other, a purse-sized pistol.

"R-really?" The word, barely audible, crept through Olivia's chattering teeth. Why did Kathryn have a gun and Olivia's bracelet?

"Quiet, Liv," Thad said softly, undoubtedly remembering how she'd lost her temper with their mysterious limo driver—a man he now suspected was Norman Gillis.

Norman staggered to his feet, whimpering in pain, but instead of standing by his mother, he hobbled toward the loading dock area. Kathryn ignored his desertion, as if he were no more than an irritant. Instead, she kept the gun trained on Thad. "This was a gift to myself when I turned seventy. I had Swarovski crystals embedded in the grip."

"You're a real trendsetter," Thad said.

If Olivia's tongue had been working, she'd have suggested a nice pair of diamond earrings instead. Out of the corner of her eye, she saw Norman staggering into a car he must have stashed there ahead of time.

Thad, with his wet clothes and the frigid breeze, had to be just as cold as she was, but he stood steady. "Your son is going to survive."

"Probably," Kathryn said bitterly. Behind her, Norman's car peeled from the building. "He's always been a disappointment to me."

Thad moved ever so slightly to the left, working to put his body between Kathryn and Olivia, but no way would Olivia let him take a bullet for her. Willing her legs to support her, she came to her feet. With her sandals gone, it was like standing on blocks of ice, and her skin prickled with gooseflesh under her drenched white gown.

She'd drawn Kathryn's attention, just as she'd intended. "Men make messes," Kathryn said to her, "and I have to clean them up. First Eugene and his carelessness. And now Norman."

"What kind of messes, Mrs. Swift?" Thad deliberately drew her focus back to himself.

"This bracelet!" She gripped it tightly in one hand and turned the gun on Olivia. "He was so ridiculously infatuated with you."

"What's so special about the bracelet?" Thad said quickly.

"Enough questions!" She made a sharp gesture toward Olivia with her gun. "Into the river with you both."

"Stay right where you are, Liv," Thad ordered. "Mrs. Swift, neither of us is going into the river. Now drop that gun."

She gave a harsh bark of laughter. "You think because I'm old, I don't know how to use this? My daddy took me hunting before I was six years old."

"A tender memory, I'm sure, but let me point out that putting bullet holes in the bodies of two of the city's more famous people—because that's the only way we're going in—is a very bad idea. The police will be relentless."

"Chicago can be a dangerous city."

"The police aren't stupid."

"No one would ever suspect me. Now move!"

Olivia could read Thad's mind. As surely as she knew anything, she knew he intended to go after Kathryn and take the bullet himself.

The riverbank was deserted. No one inside the Muni would hear if she screamed, and her strength was sapped. She could sense Thad getting ready to spring, and Kathryn could, too, because she pointed the gun directly at his chest, right at his beautiful heart. If Olivia could make Kathryn drop her guard for a few seconds, he might have a chance of disarming her. But Olivia had nothing to distract her with. No pebbles of glass from a broken limousine partition. No shoe to throw. All she had was her voice.

The idea was ludicrous.

But it was the only idea she had.

Thad tensed his muscles, waiting for his moment. Garnering her strength, Olivia pulled in every molecule of air she could collect—opened her chest, her throat, her soul—and sent Brünnhilde's Valkyrie battle cry out into the wild night.

"Ho-jo-to-ho!"

A punch of furious, ear-shattering sound. The roar of the earth cracking open. The scream of the universe exploding.

"Ho-jo-to-ho!"

The high was strident, the middle broke. She was a mezzo. She didn't have the voice for Brünnhilde, but the Valkyrie's battle cry did its job, startling Kathryn Swift into jerking her head around and lowering her pistol just for a moment.

Just long enough for Olivia to rush at her with every bit of strength she had left.

Thad, of course, got to her first. He grabbed the old lady's arm, forcing her to drop the pistol.

"Everybody freeze!"

Brittany stood thirty feet away, her service revolver at the ready.

Is everybody in this city armed?

Kathryn let out a pitiful shriek, puny compared to Olivia's battle cry, and collapsed to the ground.

The Muni's docking area filled with flashing red lights and emergency vehicles. The EMTs wrapped Olivia and Thad in Mylar blankets and checked their vital signs while Brittany phoned in the information about Norman Gillis. The Egyptian bracelet was already tucked away in an evidence bag.

Some of the crowd exiting from the gala grew aware of the commotion. With umbrellas over their heads, they huddled in the parking area and watched Kathryn Swift being hauled away in a squad car.

Thad gazed at Olivia from his Mylar cocoon as if he expected her to disappear at any moment, but he said nothing, and she had a shocking glimpse of how he would look as an old man. Still handsome, but tired, the cares of a lifetime etched in his face.

She wanted to rest her head against his shoulder, but he'd erected an invisible barricade she had no right to cross.

The EMTs urged them to go to the hospital, but they both refused. Thad watched Olivia being helped into a squad car that would deliver her home. He couldn't go with her. He couldn't be with her now.

He drove himself home and took the longest, hottest shower of his life. As the remnants of the Chicago River eddied down the drain, he wished he could send the images swirling in his brain along for the trip. That moment when he believed he'd lost her would be seared in his memory forever . . . Believing that this brave, smart, funny, ambitious heartache of a woman was lost to him forever had been the worst moment of his life, worse than sitting on the bench, worse than playing backup, far worse than knowing he'd never be number one.

Piper sat with Olivia at the police station the next morning as she gave her statement to Brittany. Olivia appreciated having Piper with her today, but it should have been Thad by her side, both of them giving their statements together.

And whose fault was that?

She'd barely slept last night. Even after she was warm, clean, and awash in Throat Coat tea, she couldn't fall asleep. It was ironic. Like every opera singer on the planet, she was paranoid about catching a cold. She guarded against drafts, stayed away from cigarette smoke, slept with at least one vaporizer running, and didn't drink water that was too chilled—only to end up underwater in the Chicago River in early May. She was lucky to be alive, but that wasn't what kept jerking her awake. It was the image of Thad's face when she'd come up for breath.

Olivia and Piper had barely settled into the chairs across from her desk before Brittany told them they'd caught Gillis. "He was apprehended on Sheridan Road a little before midnight."

Brittany looked as if she'd spent the rest of the night interrogating him instead of sleeping. She'd abandoned her ice-blue gown and high, strappy sandals for dark pants, a wrinkled white blouse, and sensible loafers.

Leaning against the side of her desk was the same big purse she'd been carrying last night. Olivia had wondered why she hadn't brought a more fashionable evening bag to the gala, and now she knew. A pretty evening bag wouldn't have held her service revolver, and like most cops, she liked having it with her.

Brittany looked up from her notepad. "Tell me about the bracelet."

Tell me about Thad, Olivia thought. *Is he all right? Have you talked to him? Did he ask about me? Do you love him?*

Olivia didn't say any of that. "Kathryn's husband Eugene loved *Aida*, and not long before he died, he sent me the bracelet. He told me one of his buyers had picked it up at a souvenir market in Luxor. I remember that. He called it a costume piece and said it was unworthy of my talent." She rubbed her temple. "I think we can safely assume it's not a costume piece."

"How long have you known the Swifts?" Brittany asked.

"I knew Eugene for almost ten years. He was a fixture on the Muni's board of directors. Our friendship was never inappropriate, if that's what you're wondering. He enjoyed reminiscing about singers he remembered from his boyhood or talking to me about obscure operas—*La finta giardiniera*, *Medea in*

Corinto, *Tolomeo*—that sort of thing. I loved listening to his insights. I adored him."

Piper forgot she wasn't the one leading the interrogation. "What about his wife?"

"I never met his first wife. As for Kathryn . . . She was always cordial to me, but she didn't share Eugene's enthusiasm for opera. Eugene told me she used to sneak out of performances at intermission. Art museums are Kathryn's passion. That and maintaining her status with Chicago's social elite."

Brittany clicked her ballpoint pen. "She doesn't like opera, but she's on the Municipal Opera's board of directors? That seems odd."

"She took over Eugene's seat after he died. It added to her social currency. She's also a good fundraiser, so the Muni was more than happy to have her."

"What about Norman?" Piper asked.

"Eugene never said much about his stepson. They weren't close."

Piper pulled out her own notepad. "I've done some research on Swift Auction House. It's a high-end operation dealing in fine arts: paintings, sculpture, jewelry—a smaller version of Sotheby's." She raised her head from the notepad. "It specializes in antiquities."

"Not all of them legal," Brittany informed them. "Norman was chatty, at least for a while last night. He said Eugene Swift was running a side business dealing in illegal artifacts—pieces smuggled from their home countries and sold to wealthy, and very discreet, private collectors in Asia, the Middle East, Russia, some in the US."

"Never!" Olivia exclaimed. "Eugene would never have done anything like that. If the auction house was involved with illegal antiquities, Kathryn was behind it."

"Not according to Norman."

"He's a snake. Dig deeper, and you'll find if anything illegal was going on, it happened after Kathryn took over the business."

Piper stepped in. "Dozens of museums have pieces of ancient Egyptian jewelry in their collections. That's what I don't understand. What makes this bracelet valuable enough to kill for it?"

Brittany shook her head. "Norman clammed up before we got that far, and right now, Mrs. Swift isn't talking."

Piper closed her notebook. "Let's hope that changes."

Thad had gone for a five-mile run after he gave Brittany his statement, but the exercise hadn't lightened his misery. He needed someone he could take out his ugly mood on, so he called Clint, but when the kid arrived, Thad couldn't summon the energy to watch film with him, or even tell him he was an idiot, so he kicked him out again.

On his way to the door, Clint dead-eyed him like the leader he already was. "You'd better get your shit together, old man, because right now you're useless."

Thad mumbled something under his breath and closed the door on him.

He spent the next few hours on the Internet learning everything he could about ancient Egyptian jewelry. All the time, he was thinking about what had happened in Las Vegas. Olivia had been wearing her bracelet the night Gillis had abducted them, just as she had the whole time they'd been in Las Vegas, but Gillis had initially gone after Thad's wallet and watch. That had obviously been a diversion, a way to make it look like a robbery and keep anyone from suspecting Gillis had only been after the bracelet.

Last night, when the police had interviewed Olivia, she'd said that Gillis had pulled off her rings before he'd taken her bracelet. One more attempt at a diversion. It seemed obvious that Kathryn wanted to keep anyone from linking the bracelet to the auction house, but once Olivia had seen Norman's face, that was no longer possible.

Toward midafternoon, he couldn't endure the knot in his stomach any longer. He had one last thing to do.

21

Olivia handed Rachel a tissue. "Are you done crying yet?"

Rachel blew her nose. "I'm never going to be done. Dennis and I are responsible for all the crap that's happened to you."

"You had nothing to do with Norman Gillis trying to kill me."

Rachel wasn't listening. "All the problems with your voice. I hate myself. You should hate me, too."

"I do."

Another honk of her very red nose. "No, you don't, but you should. Every time I think about poor Lena and that dead canary . . . About what he did to you . . ." She shuddered. "I'm sorry. I've never been so sorry about anything in my whole life."

"I believe you've mentioned that," Olivia said. "About a dozen times. Forgiving you is getting boring."

It was early Monday afternoon. Rachel had shown up at her door two hours ago after driving in from Indianapolis, where she was doing *Hansel and Gretel.* She'd been crying and apologizing ever since.

"I love you," Rachel said. "You're the best friend a person could ever have, and I violated our trust." She started crying all over again.

Olivia handed her one more tissue and rose from the couch. "I'm making us something to eat, and you're going to stop crying long enough to eat it."

"Okay . . ." She sniffed. Blew her nose. "Let me help."

Olivia lifted an eyebrow at the wadded tissues in her lap. "Wash your hands first."

That elicited a watery smile. Rachel headed for the bathroom, and Olivia went to the kitchen. She'd had groceries delivered that morning, although she wasn't sure why since she was too miserable to eat.

Thinking about Thad led her into a painful, fruitless spiral, so she thought about Eugene instead. She'd spoken to Brittany again this morning. Kathryn still wasn't cooperating, but the details Norman had provided about Swift Auctions were checking out. In addition to its legitimate operation, the company had been smuggling artifacts, only a few at a time, but each one highly profitable.

The investigators didn't have a timeline yet, but as Olivia had predicted, it looked as though the illegal activities had begun several years before Eugene died, after he'd turned the operation over to his wife and her son. Only when Norman was questioned about Olivia and the bracelet had he clammed up out of self-protection. Smuggling was one thing. Attempted murder another.

She reminded herself she was safe now. Norman and Kathryn were in jail without bond. Marsden faced federal charges of interstate stalking and harassment. No one was threatening her.

But she'd lost Thad, and what would happen when she took the stage again tomorrow night? Her body had survived its icy plunge. She had no sniffles, no sore throat. But her heart wasn't in nearly as good a shape.

She wanted to see Thad. Talk to him. See how he was doing. To understand why they couldn't be together again. Why they couldn't take their relationship day by day. Why they couldn't stop worrying about the future.

Which was exactly what he'd asked of her and she'd rejected him. She was the one who'd put a stop to their relationship because her work always had to come first. Even before love.

She opened the refrigerator. Nothing appealed to her except the tub of raspberry sorbet in the freezer. As she dished it up, Rachel reappeared and sat on one of the counter stools. Olivia stayed on the other side of the counter, holding her glass dish and a spoon. Rachel gazed at the sorbet. "You got any chocolate syrup?"

"No. Would ketchup do?"

"Never mind." Rachel poked the end of her spoon into the dish without taking a bite. "I think Dennis and I need to separate for a while."

Olivia's head shot up. "You're not separating from Dennis over this! He should never have told you."

"It's not only this." She impaled her spoon. "My life isn't my own anymore." Rachel regarded her with stricken eyes. "He's suffocating me!"

Olivia set down her bowl, the sorbet untouched. "Rach . . ."

"I hate feeling this way. He does everything for me. I never have to pay a bill or make a plane reservation. He plans our meals, keeps the apartment clean. He buys birthday presents for my family. Calls my father every week. I don't have to do a thing. He takes care of it all." Her eyes started leaking again, although this time without the noisy sobs. "I feel like it's his career instead of mine."

"Rachel, you need to talk to him."

"I've tried to, but he gets so hurt. He wants to know what he can do so I feel better, and I want to scream at him to start having his own life and stop living mine!"

A wave of vertigo made Olivia grab the edge of the sink. Her world had flipped over. A man like Dennis was everything Olivia had dreamed of in a life partner, everything she'd believed would make her happy. But Rachel was miserable. Olivia took in her friend's blotchy face and red eyes. "I never suspected . . . I thought . . . You love each other so much."

"I need space!" Rachel stuffed a spoonful of sorbet into her mouth followed by another, and then pushed her bowl away. "Don't ever get married, Olivia. Look at what happened to Lena."

"Dennis is not Christopher Marsden. Not even close. Marsden was threatening and abusive. Dennis is a good man."

"But maybe not good for me. Don't ever marry a man who doesn't have a life of his own unless you want him to take over yours."

Olivia sank onto a stool. "You've never told me any of this. You and Dennis are what I've always wanted for myself."

"I know and telling you this makes me feel like a complaining, entitled, ungrateful bitch." She grabbed her spoon and pointed it in Olivia's face. "You're going to sing the hell out of Amneris tomorrow night. Do you hear me? You're going to own that stage. You're not going to let anybody—not Marsden, not Dennis, not me—steal your voice for one second longer. You'll sing like you've never sung before or I won't ever speak to you again."

Rachel wasn't exactly in a position to make threats, but Olivia understood and gave her a weak smile. "I'd love nothing better, but—"

"Then do it! Don't you dare let the assholes win."

Rachel drove back to Indianapolis, and Olivia alternated between absorbing the bombshell news about Rachel and Dennis's marriage, agonizing over tomorrow night's performance, and obsessing about Thad. When she couldn't stand the tumult in her head any longer, she settled in front of her computer, something she'd been doing periodically when she should have been sleeping.

Her bracelet obviously wasn't the costume piece Eugene had assumed or the copy that the Las Vegas jewelers had declared it to be. But stolen artifacts did occasionally show up at an auction house. All the management had to do was plead ignorance and attempt to return it to its owner. Why hadn't Kathryn done that? What was so special about her bracelet?

Although she wasn't a trained Egyptologist, she'd studied Egyptian history the same way she studied the historical background of every character she sang. She'd already googled Egyptian jewelry, ancient Egyptian jewelry, Old Kingdom, Middle Kingdom, New Kingdom jewelry. She'd checked out Pinterest boards and followed links to the Egyptian Book of the Dead, but she'd found nothing.

Both men and women in ancient Egypt wore jewelry, and before Rachel's arrival, she'd begun a search of pharaohs. Now, she took a detour into the pharaohs' wives, looking for images of any pieces that might be connected to the most obvious queens: Hatshepsut, Nefertari, and Nefertiti. She found nothing. Cleopatra was more Greek than Egyptian, but she also searched for her and found nothing.

And then . . . Olivia sucked in her breath. "Oh my God . . ."

Brittany wasn't on duty that evening, but she wanted to hear what Olivia had uncovered, so instead of making the drive to the station house, they met at a local coffeehouse with brick walls, lots of dark wood, and wing chairs upholstered in worn green and gold velvet.

"Your bracelet was looted?" Brittany said, after they'd ordered their drinks and settled in a quiet corner.

Olivia nodded. "Yes. It was looted on January 28, 2011."

Brittany regarded her quizzically. "How do you know the exact date?"

"Because it was the day looters broke into the Egyptian Museum of Cairo during the uprising against Mubarak's regime, the so-called Arab Spring. Among other objects, they took a gilded wooden statue of Tutankhamen, a couple of wooden sarcophagi, and the bracelet of Queen Hetepheres." Olivia paused. "The sarcophagi and statue were both located and returned."

"But not the bracelet."

"Not the bracelet." She passed Brittany her phone. "This photo is from the museum's archives."

Brittany studied the photo. "It's your bracelet. Either that, or an exact copy."

"Considering what's happened, I think we can assume it's the real thing. I've been wearing Queen Hetepheres's bracelet."

"You said Mr. Swift gave you the bracelet over a year ago, right before he died. Why would Kathryn and her son wait so long to try to get it back?"

"They probably didn't know until recently that I had it." Olivia leaned into the chair's worn cushions. "One of the stones fell out right after he gave it to me. I slipped the bracelet in a drawer and forgot about it until just before the tour when I was packing my costume jewelry. I superglued the stone back in and added the bracelet to the pile." She frowned. "I dread telling the Egyptian Museum about the superglue."

"I'm guessing they'll forgive you."

Olivia leaned forward. "A couple of days into the tour, a photograph of me wearing it showed up in the newspaper. That was the first time I was photographed with it. Right after was when the trouble started, so Kathryn must have seen that photo." Olivia considered the carefully timed arrival of the limo driver at their Las Vegas hotel. Because of Kathryn's position on the Muni's board, she had easy access to every detail of the Marchand tour schedule.

"She finally knew where the bracelet was," Brittany said, "and she was afraid people would recognize it."

"Once that happened, it would be simple to trace it from me to Eugene Swift and from there to his company."

"Establishing a direct link between a stolen Egyptian artifact and Swift Auction House would have ruined them."

"Not necessarily. It isn't easy to trace the provenance—the chain of custody—of ancient artifacts. If one that turns out to have been stolen or looted shows up in a catalog, the auction house acknowledges the mistake, tries to make it right, and all's well."

"Why couldn't the Swifts do that?"

"Because my bracelet was stolen from a museum that issued a well-publicized list of every object that had been looted."

"Meaning that Swift Auctions couldn't plead ignorance."

"Exactly. Every dealer in the country knew what was on that list, and if Kathryn couldn't get the bracelet back, her entire illegal operation would be exposed." Olivia ran her thumb over her wrist. "Eugene loved *Aida.* It felt right to wear his bracelet onstage opening night. I can only imagine how panicked she must have been when she saw it."

"She must have been even more panicked when you walked into the gala wearing it."

"I think she expected that. I ran into her about three weeks ago when I was in Manhattan, and she specifically asked me to come to the gala in costume. She didn't know for sure I'd wear the bracelet, but it would be a logical accessory for me to choose, and she must have seen it as her fail-safe opportunity to get it back if her son couldn't retrieve it before then. I'm guessing she didn't have a lot of faith in Norman."

"He did turn out to be a bit of a bumbler."

"Fortunately for me." *And for Thad.*

Brittany took more notes and promised to follow up with Olivia as soon as she knew more. After she left, Olivia ordered another herbal tea and called Piper.

"Amazing work," Piper said, when she'd heard Olivia's story. "I'd hire you for myself if you didn't have that other silly career going on."

Olivia smiled, and then hesitated. "Thad should know about this. Would you tell him?"

"Why don't you tell him yourself?"

Piper would never know how much Olivia wanted to do exactly that. "It . . . would be better if you told him."

There was a long pause at the other end. "All right."

She couldn't keep from asking. "How is he?"

"He's not in great shape," Piper said bluntly.

"Did he get sick? He was in the water so long, and the Chicago River isn't exactly clean. He shouldn't have jumped in. He— Is he all right?"

"He's not sick. He's quiet. I've never seen him quiet. Earlier today, Coop went to check on him. He said Thad looked like hell. Also, he was wearing something like bike shorts with a plaid dress shirt and black tuxedo shoes. You know that's not right. Coop almost took him to the emergency room."

Olivia gripped her phone tighter. "Would you . . . Maybe you could . . . I don't know. Invite him to dinner or something?"

"It'll take more than a dinner to fix what's wrong with him." Olivia heard papers rustling in the background. "Olivia, I like you, but Thad has been my friend for a long time, and I owe him my first loyalty. You've hurt him badly."

But not as badly as she'd hurt herself.

She walked home from the coffee shop with her head down, eyes on the sidewalk, wishing she were invisible.

She warmed up her voice in the humidity of her shower the next morning. She tested her low range, her high, not pressing too hard, merely exploring. Unlike her heart, her gut and diaphragm felt strong and steady. She searched for the constriction that had stolen her breath. She found sadness, despair, but none of the tightness that had strangled her voice.

She got to the theater early, unable to shake the feeling that the gains she'd made would be stolen from her at any moment. She went to the piano and assessed her voice. Still steady. Maybe . . .

She finished hair and makeup. By the time she was done and on her way back to her dressing room, she was resolved. Tonight, she would give the performance she should have given on opening night. Tonight, she would reclaim herself.

And then she turned the corner.

Unlike Piper's description, Thad looked perfectly put together—blazer, dress shirt, pants, shoes—all coordinated.

He wasn't alone.

Sarah Mabunda, striking in her white gown as Aida, stood with him. Or rather in front of him. Or rather, between him and the wall.

Both of them turned to look at Olivia, their glances smug and dismissive. They returned their attention to each other. Sarah snaked her arms around Thad's neck. Thad snaked his arms around Sarah's waist. And the two of them kissed.

Not a little peck on the cheek. This was a full-on, mouth-to-mouth, grind-it-out, passionate kiss. Sarah Mabunda and Thad Walker Bowman Owens.

They made a beautiful couple.

Too beautiful.

Of all the—

The orchestra concluded the overture. Radamès and Ramfis sang about the aggression of their enemy Ethiopia. Ramfis exited, leaving Radamès alone dreaming of leadership, victory, and his beloved Aida. His beloved "Celeste Aida."

Olivia stood in the wings, heart pounding, waiting for her entrance. Unlike Amneris, she understood exactly who Radamès loved.

He hit the high B-flat that finished his aria, and she swept onstage, a royal princess accustomed to having whatever she wanted. She sang of her love, her passion, for this beautiful warrior. She sang from the bottom of her heart.

But all he wanted to talk about was war.

She stomped her foot. *Amneris stomped her foot!* She'd never stomped her foot at this particular moment before, but now she did. She was giving him her heart, and all he wanted to talk about was leading his team to victory.

Her toes curled in her sandals. Something in his expression, the way he carried himself, the way he wouldn't quite look at her. Something was very wrong.

An ugly thought needled its way inside her. What if he loved another?

He dodged her questioning.

Her beloved Aida appeared. Yes, her slave, but also her closest friend. The sister of her heart. So why the hell was Radamès looking at Aida that way?

And why was Sarah starting to cry? Thad loved beautiful, talented women. He'd taken one look at Sarah, and every other woman he'd known had ceased to exist.

Aida might as well have plunged a knife into Amneris's ribs.

Something was happening onstage. Thad could feel it. He saw it in the way the audience sat straighter in their seats. The way they leaned forward. One woman covered her mouth with her hand. Another caught the back of the seat in front of her. A man in the next row tilted his head to the ceiling as if he couldn't bear to see what was about to unfold.

Olivia loomed above everyone. Fierce. Tortured. Vicious. She had all the power while her slave had none, which made her manipulations even more unforgivable. He wanted to tell her not to use the power she'd been born with. Not to betray her friend. Friends should stand together. That guy wasn't worth either one of them. Thad understood exactly what extreme jealousy felt like. Everyone sitting around him understood. But she was too trapped to see how this would play out.

He could see it.

The hair on the back of his neck stood up.

Betrayal and vengeance. Olivia fumed. Fuck the consequences! No one else in Egypt cared about consequences, and Amneris didn't, either.

She seethed. She raged. She begged and pleaded. Radamès was to marry her, love only her!

Finally! Egypt's victory over Ethiopia and Radamès's victory parade. He'd been given the hand of the princess of the land in marriage for his service. Amneris's hand. Not his beloved's.

But Radamès wasn't having it. And Olivia wasn't having him not have it.

Radamès made his fatal mistake. Treason.

Pigheaded, stubborn bastard only wants what he wants.

So be it.

The Judgment scene . . . The famous Judgment scene. *La Belle Tornade*'s colossal tour de force. She begs him to defend himself. He won't. She cajoles. Threatens.

Give up Aida, my beloved, and marry me. In return, you'll live! And trust me on this. Nobody in the kingdom will make you a better offer. Marry me, and we'll rule all of Africa together, right along with ESPN and the NFL. All you have to do is renounce her, and I'll save you!

But he would rather die.

The knife twisted. Amneris's love turned to destruction. She would have her revenge, and in the fire of her hatred, she watches him being condemned to die.

Wait! Hold on! I take it all back. She cries out. Her cry shakes the stage, blisters the audience, echoes right down Michigan Avenue, and shoots across the lake into eternity.

Too late, cupcake. He's doomed.

No! You can't do this! He doesn't deserve to die! She curses her father, curses the priests. She caused this, and she curses her own jealousy as she watches her beloved being led alive into the vault where he will be entombed forever.

With his love.

Although she doesn't know that.

She collapses on his tomb, pleading for peace. But she's too late. There's no peace for her without him.

Curtain.

Brava! Brava! *Brava!*

It was a triumph.

Later the critics would write:

> "The luminous varnish of Shore's legendary voice swept effortlessly from honeyed, pianissimo hushes to fortissimo screams of blistering rage."

"Shore was incandescent, capturing the astonishingly brilliant high C-flats that only a handful of mezzos have been brave enough to attempt."

"'A lui vivo, la tomba!' was crystalline perfection."

"Shore claimed the role of Amneris as few have ever done. Decades from now, an old man will tell a young opera fan, 'Ah, but if only you could have heard the great Olivia Shore sing Amneris.'"

La Belle Tornade was at the top of her game. Doing what she lived for.

And it wasn't enough.

22

Olivia went through the motions of greeting her guests backstage, all the while hoping Thad would appear. She'd delivered the performance of a lifetime and longed to share that with him.

Flowers arrived, more well-wishers poured into her dressing room. Mitchell Brooks had tears in his eyes. Sergio held her so tightly he nearly crushed her ribs. It wasn't until the last guest had left and she'd removed her makeup that she accepted the fact Thad wasn't coming backstage to see her.

Sarah appeared, dressed in street clothes with her face scrubbed. She'd dodged Olivia after the final curtain, and now she regarded her warily. "Don't be mad at me. It was his idea."

"I know it was. His latest version of making me sing on one leg."

"What?"

"Never mind." She saw no reason to go into Thad's theory about elite athletes choking under pressure from various mental blocks. That kiss had given her something else to focus on besides waiting for her voice to fail her. She was fairly certain she could have delivered a strong performance without their shenanigans, but she couldn't deny that the sight of the two of them locked together had been the perfect image to plant in her brain and carry with her onstage.

She smiled at Sarah. "I hope you enjoyed every second."

"You're not upset?"

She pulled on the purple hoodie she'd worn to the theater. "I know you both too well to have bought your act for even a second, but it did seem to go on longer than necessary."

Sarah's grin was pure mischief. "He really is a good kisser."

"And I'm sure you are, too. Don't try it again."

Sarah leaned against the doorjamb. "You killed it tonight."

"I'm not the only one." Sarah had sung her heart out. Never had their onstage chemistry been so electric.

Sarah ran a hand through her hair. "He didn't come backstage, did he? He's probably afraid you'll kill him."

"I doubt that." Thad would surely have known she'd see through his performance, and it wasn't fear of retribution that had kept him away.

"You're a strange person, Olivia," Sarah said. "Any other woman would be clawing my eyes out right now."

Olivia smiled. "I know who my friends are."

Sarah shoved her hands in her jacket pockets. "I called Adam's sisters and told them everything."

"I can't imagine that was an easy conversation."

"They needed to know the truth. Maybe now they can start living their own lives."

Olivia hugged her. "You're a good woman, Sarah Mabunda."

"Likewise, Olivia Shore."

After Sarah left, Olivia gathered up her things. Thad was furious with her, and yet he'd cared enough to do this. She hesitated, and then texted him.

I didn't buy it for a second.

Figured you wouldn't but it was worth a try.

And Sarah's hot.

Duly noted. And thank u.

You're welcome.

I'm on my way home. Meet me there?

No.

As she left the theater, she waited for more from him, but it didn't come. When she got back to her apartment, she tried again.

Are u asleep?

I was.

Can we talk?

No. And I'm turning off my phone.

She had another horrible night's sleep. When she got up the next morning, she didn't bother reading the reviews. She knew exactly how good she and Sarah had been. No one else's opinion mattered. She had to see Thad.

I need to talk to you.

I'm not up for it.

I won't beg.

No need to. I'm blocking you.

He was blocking her?

No!

She got dressed—all in black to show him she meant business—and set off for his condo, only to come up against one more person intent on ignoring her.

The concierge reminded her of a snotty Ralph Fiennes. "He isn't in, Ms. Shore."

"Did he say where he was going?"

The concierge regarded her from behind the curve of his reception desk. "He didn't."

"Do you know when he'll be back?"

"I don't."

"When did he leave?"

He glanced at his watch as if he were late for an appointment. "We're not permitted to give out information about our residents."

"I understand. But Mr. Owens and I are dear friends. I'm sure he wouldn't mind."

"I'm sorry. That's our policy."

He didn't look sorry. He looked happy—a small man wielding his sliver of personal power over someone he regarded as more privileged than himself. She hated him.

She gave him her most withering look and strode from the lobby. Once she was on the street, she pulled out her phone.

Where are u? Call me.

She waited. Traffic flew by. She waited some more, but he was ghosting her. She hailed a cab and called Piper from the back seat. "I'm looking for Thad. Do you know where he is?"

"I don't."

"Have you talked to him?"

"I haven't."

"Would you check with your husband?"

"Hold on." She could hear Piper turning away from the phone. "Coop, have you talked to Thad?"

Olivia heard him in the background. "Yeah, why?"

"Olivia is trying to find him," his wife said. "Do you know where he is?"

"Nope."

"Sorry." Piper was back on the phone. "Maybe Clint knows."

"Could you give me his address? I've lost it." Olivia had never actually had it.

It turned out Clint lived in Chicago's western suburbs instead of in the city like any other normal guy in his twenties.

Olivia texted him.

Can I come over?

It's not the best time.

I'm coming anyway.

The taxi dropped her off at her apartment where she got her car and headed west to the wealthy DuPage County suburb of Burr Ridge.

Clint's massive French chateau-style home stood ready for the reincarnation of Louis XVI. The house had steeply sloping slate roofs, five tall chimneys, numerous second-story balconies with elaborately curled wrought-iron railings, and—capping it off—a tower. The only thing missing was Marie Antoinette prancing through the topiaries. Clearly Clint had more money than he knew what to do with.

Before she got out of her car, she tried Thad once again.

Stop messing with me and call.

She waited.

A midnight-blue Alfa Romeo whipped around the side of the house and sped down the drive onto the street. She caught a glimpse of not one but two gorgeous young women.

The pervert looked rumpled when he answered the door.

She stomped past him into the marbled entryway. "Really? Two?"

He shoved a hand through his rumpled hair. "No idea what you're talking about."

An unwelcome thought intruded. "Is Thad here?"

"You think I'd tell you if he was?"

Which meant he wasn't. A relief. "I need to talk to him."

Clint yawned and stretched, revealing one hairy armpit through the sleeve of his baggy white T-shirt. "Not my problem."

"Don't you dare cop an attitude with me, young man!"

That cracked him up. "Come on. I need coffee."

"And an STD test," she muttered.

"I heard that. Things aren't always like they seem."

She favored him with the disapproving humph of a septuagenarian dowager.

His kitchen was as over-the-top as the rest of house. White marble, white tile, and not one but two crystal chandeliers. "Just out of curiosity. How much did this place cost you?"

"You'd have to ask T-Bo."

"I would if I could get hold of him!" She took in a bevy of cherubs painted on the ceiling. "And why would he know how much your house cost?"

"He's kind of my financial adviser. He negotiated the deal. He keeps tabs on some of us younger guys to make sure we don't blow all our money."

She studied the chandeliers, gazed more closely at the frolicking cherubs. "He failed you."

"Not really." He grinned. "You have no idea how big my contract is."

"Big enough to give raises to a lot of schoolteachers, I'm sure."

"Now you're playing dirty." He pulled out one of the counter stools.

"I'll play dirtier if you don't tell me where Thad is."

"You think it's my job to keep tabs on him?"

"You've been doing a good job of it so far, so yes, I do."

He leaned back on the stool. "Let's put it this way. If he wanted you to know where he was, he'd tell you."

"You seriously intend to withhold this information from me?"

"Yeah. 'Fraid I do."

"Fine. Then call him for me."

"Sure. Give me your phone."

Damn it. He was so much smarter than he looked. "Call him from your phone."

"That's a definite no."

She stated the obvious. "Because he'll pick up for you but he won't pick up for me."

"You want to make me some pancakes?"

"I do not."

"Want to go out for pancakes?"

"What I want is to talk to him." She sounded whiny and pitiful, exactly the way she felt.

Clint cocked an eyebrow at her. "The last time you did that, things didn't go well."

"He told you about it?"

"Let's just say I had to pick up the pieces you left behind."

She winced. "I need to fix this."

"I'm afraid your idea of fixing it might be different from his."

"I won't know that until I talk to him. Please. Call him on your phone."

"Exactly how self-destructive do you think I am? I need him."

The stubborn set of his jaw told her no amount of pressure would make him agree. Who else would know where he was? Maybe his friend Ritchie Collins, the Stars' wide receiver she'd met that night in Phoenix? "Ritchie! How do I find him?"

"Ritchie's on a mission trip to Haiti with his church."

"Shit. Who are his other friends on the team?"

"Most everybody, but if you think I'm handing over a roster, you're wrong."

"His agent, then. He has to talk to his agent, right?"

Clint gave her an oily smile. "A guy named Heath Champion. The top sports agent in the business. And a word of advice: they don't call him 'the Python' for nothing."

Superagent Heath Champion's office was all intimidation with lacquered walls, luxury leather, and a set of silver-framed family photos to give it a human touch—a pretty auburn-haired woman and some children. The man himself—rugged, hard-edged, handsome in an intimidating way—regarded her with cool politeness. "That would be a violation of agent-client privilege."

"I'm not going to kill him!" she exclaimed. "I just want to talk to him."

He gazed at her over his desk. "So you've said. But Thad's had some stalking incidents in the past."

"Do I look like a stalker?"

"You do seem a little unhinged."

And that was why they called him the Python.

She was getting nowhere, although she did contemplate the possibility of trading her own easygoing agent for this hard-edged browbeater. She planted her hands on his desk and leaned forward. "Throw me a bone, Mr. Champion. Who can I talk to who won't care so much about your precious agent-client privilege?"

Six hours later, she was in Louisville, Kentucky.

Thad's mother was the coldest, most hostile woman Olivia had ever met. Understandably so, Olivia reluctantly admitted, since Dawn Owens also believed Olivia was stalking her son.

She appeared to be in her fifties, but Olivia calculated she was older. She could have been a model for senior fashions with her slender body, light brown bob, good skin, and Thad's perfect nose.

"I'm not a stalker. I swear," Olivia said, which only made her seem more like a stalker. She tried to peer past Mrs. Owens's tall silhouette into the front hallway of the Owenses' colonial-style home: brass wall sconces, a grandfather clock, no Thad. She tried again. "I'm Olivia Shore. Google me. I'm completely respectable. Thad and I traveled together for a month promoting Marchand Timepieces. We're friends. And I—" She knew she was looking crazier by the second, but she couldn't help herself. "And I love him. With all my heart."

Mrs. Owens pointed toward the street. "Leave before I call the police."

Olivia gave it one more try. "I've driven all the way from Chicago. Is he here?"

Thad's mother turned her head toward the foyer. "Greg, call the police."

A deep, male voice—but not the one she wanted to hear—rumbled from inside the house. "Thad's on the phone, Dawn. He says to let her in and feed her, but that's all. Hold on. Uh-huh . . . Uh-huh . . . He says if she seems like she's drunk, put her up in his room for the night and don't let her drive, but kick her out first thing in the morning."

Totally defeated, Olivia rubbed her cheek and turned away toward the front sidewalk. "I'm sorry I bothered you."

"Wait," Dawn Owens said from behind her. "Come in."

Thad's old bedroom was disappointingly stripped of his childhood mementos. The ivory walls displayed a series of floral watercolors instead of sports posters. There were no shelves full of Little League trophies, no abandoned Trapper Keepers, or boxes of old mix tapes. It wasn't as though his parents had forgotten him, however. The downstairs was filled with photographs of Thad at every stage of his life.

His father, Greg, was an accountant, a good-looking one—tall and lean like his son, but with salt-and-pepper hair. Over dinner last night, he'd confessed to Olivia he had little interest in football unless his son was in the game. "I'd rather read. Dawn's the athletic one."

"I played division three varsity basketball all through college," Dawn said.

Despite Thad's directive, his parents had not kicked her out first thing this morning, but since it was already ten o'clock and she had another performance the following night, she needed to get on the road. As she packed up the toiletries she'd tossed in her overnight bag before she'd left Chicago, Dawn spoke up from her perch on the side of the guest bed. "I wish you could stay longer."

"Me, too. You really didn't need to put me up, you know. I could have found a hotel."

"But then I'd have missed the opportunity to entertain a world-famous opera singer."

Olivia smiled. "At least now you know I'm not a stalker."

Dawn laughed, not at all embarrassed. "Or a big drinker, despite what Thad said. That boy . . ."

"Is a menace." Last night, Olivia had told Dawn far more than she'd intended about her relationship with Thad, including an account of her drunken tussle with him on the terrace that first night in Phoenix.

Thad's mother had proven to be the perfect listener—nonjudgmental, sympathetic, and unshockable.

Olivia had to ask. "Do you have any advice for me?"

"I'd love nothing more than for things to work out between the two of you."

Olivia heard the hesitation in her voice. "But?"

"But . . . I'm not saying this to hurt you." She busied herself rubbing her hands along the thighs of her khaki slacks. "I've never known Thad not to go after something he really wants."

The truth of those words cut right through her. If Thad wanted her, he would have talked to her by now.

On Friday, the day of the next performance, she took a late-morning yoga class, picked at her lunch, and nursed her pain. She wanted to cry, but she stomped around her apartment instead—livid with herself for falling for such an insensitive, arrogant jerk.

Her anger took her through another spectacular performance.

Only as she lay on Radamès's tomb, mourning the part she'd played in his death, did the fog clear from her brain. She'd learned a lot about herself recently, things she wanted to share with him. Things he did not want her to share.

As Aida and Radamès died behind the tomb walls, she saw herself years from now, padding to her apartment door just like Batista Neri, her hair lusterless from the black dye she'd use to conceal her gray. Maybe wearing a similar pair of run-down bedroom slippers. She'd let her students in one by one, doing her best to train them, even as she couldn't quite suppress the bitterness that she no longer possessed the voice or the stamina to sing Amneris or Azucena. That she didn't have the agility to play Cherubino. That she'd be laughed off the stage if she attempted the sultry Carmen.

That was her future. Unless . . .

"What's behind your sudden desire to cook for me?" Clint asked from his perch on one of the counter stools in his over-the-top kitchen.

"Guilt for dumping my problems with Thad on you." She made killer salads and decent omelets, so how hard could it be to whip up a tasty pasta sauce? She gazed at the mess she'd made chopping a giant yellow onion. It didn't look like the ones on cooking shows.

"You're not too good with a knife," Clint said.

"I'm very good with a knife. It's just that I mainly use it to stab people. Or, depending on the role, myself."

"You do know how to make pasta, right? You said your special sauce was a recipe handed down from your Italian great-grandmother."

Her great-grandmother was actually German. "Something like that."

He eyed the package of ground turkey she'd bought, along with the rest of the ingredients. "I didn't know Italians use turkey in their meat sauce."

"I'm eastern Italian. And instead of standing there making cracks about my cooking, would you check my car windows? I think I left them down, and it's supposed to rain."

"Who knew you'd be such a bad date?"

"A reminder not to pursue older women."

"Hey! You called me!"

"Windows, please."

He threw up his hands and headed out the back. The second the door closed behind him, she dashed for the end of the counter where he'd unwisely left his phone.

The pasta was underdone, the sauce too sweet from all the sugar she'd dumped in to counteract an overabundance of thyme and oregano. After a couple of bites, Clint set aside his fork. "What part of Italy did you say your great-grandmother was from, and did they happen to have a lot of famine there?"

She poked at the mess on her own plate. "I'm new to cooking."

"Next time, practice on somebody else."

The doorbell rang. She curled her bare toes around the rungs of the stool she was sitting on.

"If that's one of my girlfriends," Clint said as he rose, "you're out of here."

"Ingrate."

The moment he left the kitchen, she hurried to the doorway, but the house was the size of an aircraft carrier, and she couldn't eavesdrop. Why did a single guy have to live in such a monstrosity?

She wasn't able to make out anything they were saying, not even a rumble, until she could. *"Olivia!"*

It was Clint.

She was suddenly more nervous than before she walked onstage. She wanted to run out the back door, get in her car, and make this all go away. Instead, she forced herself from the kitchen, turned three corners, and walked down the long stretch of hallway toward the two towering figures waiting for her. One of them stood quietly, but the other was irate. "You took my phone!" Clint exclaimed. "What the fuck, Livia?"

The text she'd sent had been right to the point.

T-Bo, I broke my wrist. Can you come to my house right away?

"I only borrowed your phone," she muttered, which, she knew, missed the point.

Clint threw up both of his big hands. "You got his hopes up that he'd start for the Stars this fall!"

She hadn't thought about that part.

Clint stormed upstairs. "She's all yours."

23

She saw herself as he was seeing her, with wild eyes, bare feet, and tomato sauce smearing her white top. The steam from the boiling pasta water had unleashed a frizzy tangle around her face. She was a mess—a lunatic—and ambushing him like this was a terrible mistake.

He'd made his intention more than clear, but she'd ignored the direct message he'd sent by ghosting her. She'd shown up at his friends' homes, his agent's office, and—God forgive her—his parents' front door. Now, with him standing stone-faced in front of her, his fists hard curls at his sides, she realized too late that she was no better than the stalker who'd once hounded him.

Her hand flew to her mouth, horrified with herself. She fled down the hallway into the kitchen and out the back of the house.

The security lights came on. She looked at the keys she'd snatched from the counter on her way out. Not hers. This was the key to Clint's black Cadillac Escalade parked in the drive. She threw herself in and peeled out of the driveway.

Thad had pushed her too far. He hadn't intended to ghost her forever, just long enough to build up his reserves before he had to listen to another of her apologies—time enough to be able to put on his game face and convince her that she hadn't meant that much to him in the first place. Time to pull himself together just enough so he could tell her she didn't need to feel guilty about dumping him. Now he realized he'd made a horrible mistake.

That stricken expression on her face . . . It didn't look anything like guilt. It looked like—

He raced after her toward the back of the house. One of the rear doors stood open. The security lights shone on the swimming pool and beds of spring-blooming plants. He followed the twisting paths around the garden fountain, past the pool, and through the shrubbery calling for her, hearing nothing in return.

He hurried to the front of the house. Her car was still here. He wasn't leaving until he found her.

Half an hour later, Garrett pointed out that his Escalade was missing, and Thad realized she'd gotten away.

Olivia waited in the dark shadows of the adjoining street with the Escalade's headlights turned off until she saw Thad drive away. She rested her cheek against the window. The raindrops splattering on the windshield seemed like tears from the gods. The only way she could make up the distress she'd caused him was never to contact him again.

Thad drove to her apartment and parked on the street near her building's parking garage. He jumped out of his car into the rain. The orange barrier gate arm was down, but he could see inside. Garrett's black Cadillac Escalade was missing. She hadn't come home.

The wind whipped through his hair. Rain pelted his face. He'd screwed up big-time. Something was very wrong. He'd seen it in her face. He headed for the Starbucks across the street to keep watch.

Thunder boomed outside the sliding doors that led to the balcony patio of her apartment. She sat at her piano picking at the keys. Her clothes were still damp from the soaking she'd gotten when she'd returned Clint's car and sneaked inside his house to get her own keys. Fortunately, she hadn't seen Clint. She couldn't bear facing another person she'd inflicted her insanity on.

It was too late for a courteous apartment dweller to play the piano, but she played anyway. Something soft, Bach's Prelude in C Major. But the music did nothing to soothe her.

It was ironic. She had her voice back, and with Thad out of her life, no more messy personal entanglements stood between her and her ambition. She tried to swallow the lump in her throat. Nothing held her back from greatness except hard work and dedication.

A tear trickled down her cheek. The concierge had rung half an hour ago to tell her Thad Owens was in the lobby. She wouldn't let him up. She needed him to understand he was free of her. No more texts. No more visits to his friends and his family. She would give him the gift of knowing he was free of her harassment.

A sob tried to escape. She squeezed her lips tight to keep it inside. If she started crying now, she might never stop.

A boom of thunder vibrated the piano bench, followed by a bang against her balcony doors. She spun around and gasped.

A man, silhouetted in a flash of lightning, stood on the balcony of her twenty-second-floor apartment. Tall. Lean. Arms pressed to the glass.

She raced for the door and fought with the latch. When it finally gave, she was hit with a blast of rainwater and the smell of ozone.

"What are you doing?" Terror made her push past him to the balcony rail. She looked down, expecting to see—a ladder? Ladders didn't extend this high, and a fifteen-foot gap stretched between her balcony and her closest neighbor's. The street lay far below. How had he—?

She looked up into the rain. The elderly, white-haired woman she'd once seen in the elevator leaned out the window directly above, oblivious to the rain, gaily waving. Thad pulled Olivia inside and shut the sliding door.

Everything went quiet.

They stared at each other. His wet, dark hair lay perfectly against his head. Rainwater dripped from the tip of his nose, and his shirt stuck to his chest. Her terror at the risk he'd taken—what could have happened to him—blocked out everything else. "You didn't!" The words were hoarse. "You didn't jump down here from my upstairs neighbor's window."

"She's a nice lady. I met her in the lobby." His Adam's apple bobbed in his neck as he swallowed. "She's eighty-four, a widow. She invited me up."

He was here, in her apartment. She couldn't take it in. "She let you jump out her window? You could have killed yourself."

"She gave me the cord from her bedroom drapes." He sounded both nervous and apologetic. "I rappelled part of the way."

"An eighty-four-year-old woman let a man she didn't know into her apartment and helped him rappel out her bedroom window? Is that what you're telling me?"

"I might have told her it was your birthday surprise," he said. "And in her defense, she thought I was her dead brother."

"Dear God." She suddenly noticed the trickle of red running down his arm. "Your arm is bleeding!"

"It's only a scratch."

She dug her fingers into her eye sockets. "You didn't have to do this. You're free of me. No more text messages or phone calls or showing up at your parents' house. No more setting deadlines and then breaking them. I'm sorry! I don't know what I was thinking." She couldn't stop herself. "Well, I do know what I was thinking. I thought if I could finally talk to you, maybe we'd have this big reconciliation. You'd realize you were in love with me after all, the same way I'm in love with you. We'd fall into each other's arms, and everything would work out, and the curtain would come down on happily-ever-after." She wrung her hands. "But that's not reality. You're a more casual person than I am. My life is too big and too complicated for a man like you to put up with. That's what you've been trying to tell me, but instead of listening, I harassed you. And now, I'm going to apologize for the last time, swallow my humiliation, promise never to bother you again, and let you out."

He looked so sorry for her. She couldn't take his pity. She blinked hard and headed for the door. "I understand. Really, I do. You care about me, but you don't love me, and you especially don't love my drama and my career. Just the idea of you being seen as Mr. Olivia Shore would be a humiliation for both of us."

"So that's it?" he said from behind her. "You're bailing?"

She reached for the doorknob. She wouldn't cry. Would. Not. Cry. "What else am I supposed to do?" she whispered. "Keep torturing both of us?"

His hand settled over hers on the knob. "Amneris fought for what she wanted."

"And ended up killing him!"

"That's opera for you." His face was soft, inquisitive, achingly tender. "The night I pulled you out of the river—the night I thought you'd drowned. It was the worst moment of my life. It took you almost drowning for me to realize how important you are to me. How much more important you are than winning a ball game or being a starter. How much I love you."

"You love me?" Her own words sounded as if they were coming from the far reaches of the orchestra hall.

"How could I not love you?" He searched her face as if he couldn't get enough of it. "You're everything. Smart and beautiful and funny and gifted. Sexy. God, are you sexy. When I couldn't find you in the water, I wanted to die myself." She'd worked so hard not to cry, and now he was the one with tears in his eyes. "I love you, Liv. I love you in more ways than I can count."

She'd always known he had a sensitive heart, no matter how hard he tried to hide it. She lifted her hand and gently brushed her thumb along his cheekbone, catching a tear, not saying anything, listening.

He searched her face, taking in every detail. "I need to know I'll always come first. And you need to know I'd never make you choose between me and your career."

Anyone else might have been confused by this statement, but she understood, and it made her dizzy with love.

He took her hand and gently kissed the pulse point on the inside of her wrist. "No more deadlines, Liv, okay?"

"No more deadlines," she whispered. "Ever."

They kissed. A kiss she would remember forever. Deep and sweet and yearning. Everything a woman could want. The kind of kiss dreams were built on, that lives were built on. A kiss that was a forever pledge.

The sweetness of that kiss changed its timbre, becoming hot and fierce. They dragged each other into the bedroom, pulling at their clothes, at the bedcovers, desperate to seal the words they'd spoken with their bodies.

They came together ferociously—two athletes, champions in their own worlds, their bodies moving together, soaring together, hitting that perfect crescendo, that perfect rush. The perfect joining of body and soul.

Later, sated in each other's arms, he brushed his lips across her hair. "We have a busy couple of years ahead of us."

She ran her fingers across the delicious cording of his abdomen. "Yes, we do."

"You've already signed contracts for the next two years, and I have two more years left on my own contract." He stroked the curve of her hip. "I know what I'm going to do after that. I never thought I'd say this, but I can't wait. Still, nothing is for sure. These next couple of years are going to be important ones for us. They'll be our training camp."

It was a perfect analogy. "The time when we work out the logistics. Find out how to make our lives fit together," she said.

"We'll make mistakes." He took her hand and kissed her earlobe. "It'll be trial and error."

"It'll be a mess." She gave him a watery smile, not caring if he saw her tears, because they were happy ones. "We'll need lots of open communication."

"Something we've been good at up until these last few days." He rose onto one elbow, gazing down at her. "Fortunately, we're both disciplined. We know how to set goals and work toward meeting them."

"We do," she agreed, nuzzling his shoulder.

"You have Wednesday and Thursday off between performances next week. Does Thursday work for you?"

She lost herself admiring the dark arch of his eyebrows. "Thursday?"

"Or Wednesday if you'd rather. For us to get married."

His words finally registered, and she shot up in bed, clutching the sheet to her chest. "You want to get married next week?"

He tugged the sheet from her hands. "Isn't that what I said?"

"No, it's not what you said! We were just talking about taking the next two years to figure things out."

"Right." He kissed the top of her breast. "After we get married, we'll definitely need to figure things out."

She grabbed for the sheet, launching into their first postcoital argument. "We're not reckless people! We don't just jump into something this big. We're systematic. We take our time. Prepare."

He laughed and pulled her back down beside him. "Liv, sweetheart, we're already prepared. We know exactly what kind of mess we're jumping into, and we also know that—with our work ethic and big egos—we'll have to make it work because neither of us can handle failure."

That was true, but . . .

He stroked her temple. "You're slippery, honey, and I'm not taking any more chances of losing you. I need a commitment. A real commitment. Enough of a commitment so I know you won't go crazy again and tell me that you've decided you can't sing Figaro or whoever else you've taken a fancy to sing while I'm in your life."

Figaro was a man, but she understood his point. She tunneled her hands through his hair. "I'd never do that to you. I promise."

"Good. Next week then."

And next week it was. On a Thursday night when the Muni had no performances scheduled, the two of them stood onstage with their friends and family seated around them. The bride was deliriously beautiful in a long, Egyptian-style gown that was an updated copy of Aida's costume. The groom was resplendent in a perfectly cut tuxedo with a square pocket handkerchief made from his beloved's favorite flamenco shawl.

Thad's parents had raced up from Kentucky. Coop was best man. Clint walked the bride down the makeshift aisle as Rachel sang, and neither the bride nor groom—both of whom were used to working under pressure—could make it through their vows without choking up.

It was a beautiful ceremony. The flowers, the guests, the music. As Thad and Olivia exchanged the kiss that sealed their union, Cooper Graham leaned over to the man sitting next to him and whispered, "One marriage. Two divas. This is going to work out just fine."

Clint Garrett couldn't have agreed more.

Epilogue

Thad stood in the wings of the Lyric Opera of Chicago, his arms crossed over his chest to keep his heart from spilling out as he watched Liv deliver the best "Habanera" of her life. Her Carmen was a headstrong rebel—sultry, sexy, foolhardy, and answerable only to herself—everything Liv wasn't, except for the sultry, sexy part.

After three years, she still took his breath away.

He liked helping people be their best, whether it was motivating Liv to reach new heights in her career or cheering on the idiot through every game. Damn, but he loved that guy.

Onstage, Carmen had caught ol' Don José's eye. Liv did way too great a job of dying, and Thad made it a policy never to watch the last act. Plus, he'd been forbidden to stick around backstage that long because he made the tenor singing Don José nervous.

Their first year of marriage had been just as messy and hectic as they'd anticipated. He'd started training camp on the exact day Liv had to be in Munich. When the Stars played their first game, she was in Tokyo and after that Moscow. They talked all the time and competed with each other to come up with the most innovative way of keeping their sex life interesting, although it meant installing lots of extra software to guard against hackers.

After Moscow, Liv was back in Chicago sitting in Phoebe Calebow's skybox watching Thad win two games back to back when Clint was out with an ankle sprain. One of the Calebow kids had sneaked photos of Liv screaming her head off every time Thad completed a pass. Embarrassing, but Mrs. Calebow was a big opera fan, and she didn't seem to mind.

The second year of marriage grew more complicated as he finished his contract and moved ahead with his retirement plan. He'd become a certified financial planner so he could play a more active role in keeping stupid, young rookies from blowing all their money, satisfying work but a sideline to his real job. He was Piper's full-time partner in her volunteer crusade to put an end to child sex trafficking. *Follow the money.*

He'd gotten very good at exactly that, and whenever he helped put another of those bastards behind bars, he felt better than he'd ever felt winning a football game.

He was a little busier than he wanted to be, but as a bonus, his work was portable so he could travel with Olivia as much as either of them wanted, which was most of the time.

"I entertain people," The Diva was fond of saying. "You save lives."

Then, just when things were running smoothly, The Diva decided she wanted a baby.

The ovation rolled over her in an endless wave. She'd killed as Carmen tonight, and everyone in the audience knew it. She was ecstatic, triumphant, gratified, and drained—more than ready to go home to her child and the man she loved with all her heart.

This would be her last Carmen for a couple of years. With her family growing, she was cutting down on the number of time-consuming operas she performed and stepping up her concert appearances instead. She loved the concerts. She could spend much less time on the road, reach even more audiences, and also experiment with a broader repertoire. She planned to ramp up her time in the recording studio, beginning with recording a selection of lullabies, all of which she was auditioning in front of Theodosia Shore Owens, her squirmy, cuddly, dark-haired devil-angel. "She's going to be a soprano for sure," Thad had said after Sia had thrown a particularly dramatic temper tantrum because her father wouldn't let her eat the kitchen sponge.

Olivia had never sung better than when she'd been pregnant with Sia. The baby had provided additional support to her abdomen and diaphragm, which—right up until the last month—made singing even the most taxing passages easier.

Unlike Dennis, Rachel's ex-husband, Thad had no interest in micromanaging Liv's career. Thad had more than enough to do staying on top of his own work. She didn't keep her nose out of his career nearly as well as he did hers. She was as passionate as he about his work with Piper, and she liked staying up to date. She'd also developed a fondness for some of the rookies he was coaching. He said he was only helping them manage their money, but since when did money management involve watching hours of game film with them?

Sometimes when she performed, Olivia stole glances into the wings or out into the audience looking for him. The sight of that beautiful face, the knowledge of what they'd created together, gave her singing extra meaning.

They talked, they planned, they adjusted and re-adjusted their lives together. No soprano could hope for a more perfect husband. And he still loved when she sang naked for him.

As Thad headed home, he remembered the serious doubts he'd had about Liv's competence as the mother of his future child. How could he not have doubts after he'd watched her sing Azucena in *Il trovatore*? Crazy Azucena, who throws her own fricking baby in the fire! Witnessing The Diva's glee as she prepared for the role, then watching her onstage as she sang that wacko woman with way too much enthusiasm, made him consider a vasectomy. When he'd expressed his doubts about leaving her alone with an infant, she'd gone off into whoops of laughter, jumped in his lap, and started kissing him.

Nine months later, Sia was born.

The light of his life, Theodosia Shore Owens, should be asleep by now, and it was time for him to get home and relieve their nanny.

Now they had another baby on the way, which meant they'd be facing more of the chaos they'd gotten so good at untangling. He couldn't wait.

He turned the volume up on his favorite classical radio station. Tonight they were playing a recording of Olivia singing bel canto, and his wife hit a Rossini passage that covered him with goose bumps. "I wouldn't be able to sing the way I do without you," she'd told him more than once.

He didn't believe it, but what he did know was this: At the end of the day, when her makeup and costumes came off, Liv loved being Mrs. Thad Owens. Almost as much as he loved being Mr. Olivia Shore.

Author's Note

I am especially indebted to the three women who helped me on my journey through the world of sopranos and opera. Dr. Ramona Wis was there with me as I started my journey. Marianna Moroz, public relations manager at the world-renowned Lyric Opera of Chicago, graciously answered my questions. And the brilliant author Megan Chance, who knows exactly what another writer needs, helped bring this story home. Thank you all and forgive any liberties I might have taken with this cherished art form and with those who keep it alive.

As always, I am more grateful than I can say for my team at HarperCollins, William Morrow, and Avon Books, led by my dear friend and longtime editor Carrie Feron.

I hope readers who aren't familiar with Cooper Graham and Piper's story will enjoy reading it in *First Star I See Tonight.* A list of all my Chicago Stars books is available on my website, susanelizabethphillips.com. Thank you for being the best readers any author could hope to have!